HARRY BLACK

HARRY BLACK

a novel by

DAVID WALKER

THE REPRINT SOCIETY LONDON

FIRST PUBLISHED 1956
THIS EDITION PUBLISHED BY THE REPRINT SOCIETY LTD.
BY ARRANGEMENT WITH WM. COLLINS, SONS & CO. LTD.
1958

PRINTED IN GREAT BRITAIN
BY R. & R. CLARK, LTD., EDINBURGH

To
Colin Mackenzie

Author's Note

There are no real people in this book. The prison escape in Chapter Nine resembles an actual escape made from another camp in another year with different people. Harry Black bears no resemblance to the gallant leader of that escape.

The author expresses his grateful thanks for permission to quote from a poem by Sidney Keyes published by Messrs. Routledge & Kegan Paul in *The Collected Poems of Sidney Keyes*.

Contents

BOOK ONE

CHAPTER ONE

THE PASS cut through the head and shoulders of the highest ridge. The walls were vertical. The red rock floor was flat and smooth. The air was still that afternoon. There was a resonance of his breathing in the place.

He faced north-east at the far end of the pass, looking down to a plain and across to mountains. The plain was wooded, with a few patches of cleared land where mustard was yellow and wheat was green, and mixtures of the two were pretty. The jungle itself was not pretty.

The sun cast shadows of the jagged foothills. He was the king of this small castle, dwarfed by the first Himalayan castles, and they in turn, and so on to the battlements of the world. High snows pleased him ; but there were none to-day, for cloud hung down at six thousand feet. Rain ? he wondered. It was late for winter rains.

He searched back the other way, tacking from wall to wall. His boots had left rubber patterns at one dusty place. There were no other tracks. He did not think that any animal had come through last night. He paused to consider a nook in the right wall—the only pit or pockmark in this curiously smooth-complexioned cleft. It was a place where a man might sit, or a rifle be wedged and aligned and trigger-tripped. I could set a wire, he thought. He could ; but he would not.

He reached the south-west end, whence he had come. He sat on a rock. The drop was greater here. The ridges swung forward to right and left ahead, a precipitous half-circle, thrusting from the backbone of the foothills.

He sat above one end of an oblong or oval of forest, six miles long and three miles wide. He could see all of it from this high place. The oval was in two halves—cut across the shorter way— and the halves were very different. This steep upper half of jungle was framed by a horseshoe of red rock ridges that petered out three miles ahead. The flat lower half of jungle jutted into the open plains of India.

This was Rimli, the forest of the story.

The sun was pleasant on a cool afternoon, and not yet low enough to dazzle him. He felt all right. He put two fingers in his mouth and blew a spittle-whetted whistle, which added to his well-being.

Soon Bapu came, a rubbery small man along a goat-track.

"No tiger has gone that way," said Bapu. He meant by a lesser ravine, forking from the one which they had climbed.

"And no tiger has come through the Pass."

"I heard the janwar," Bapu said again. "I heard the wild things speak this morning early, calling from hither and down to yonder. It might have been a leopard." He cleared his throat and hummed a blandly tuneless tune. "Who knows what it might have been?"

"Go, disbelieving one. Go, famous tracker of tigers, and see for thyself that no tiger has come."

Bapu cackled and went.

He watched the country from aloft. He heard parakeets and saw them in hurtling flight, green into green of forest, green against brown and white, a graceful discordance of parakeets. Nothing else moved or called below him.

He looked south-west to the far end of the oval of the Rimli jungle, to the plains beyond. He looked half-right to the bend of the River Garda. It flowed south-east along below the hills, taking the efflux of the hills. But at Rimli, the Garda turned a full right angle, down and away beside the lower forest and out across the plains. It was a muddy river, bright now against the sun.

Beyond all this was the flat rim of the horizon, broken by one thing only, and that over to the south, on the far side of the forest from the River Garda. It was broken by a sugar factory chimney, a tall metal shaft, two miles from the forest edge. He had passed it by night on his way to Rimli. He wondered who ran the place. He did not want to meet him.

Bapu returned and sat upon his heels.

" Well ? "

" A tiger has come. There is one pug only in one dusty place.
But a tiger has come." He hawked mournfully and spat.

Bapu did not lie about tracks. " This tiger ? "

" It is a big tiger, sahib. I think it is the Bad One. But the pug
is not that scarred pug of the Bad One."

" When ? "

" Since the fall of the night wind."

That meant after three or four a.m. " If thou art right, two
sups of whisky in place of one. If wrong, not any whisky."

" All day my stomach has been sick for lack of whisky-wine."

He smiled. He had known Bapu for a week. He liked him.
Things would be stirring now in the forest. He saw only parakeets
above the forest.

" I am not a man of this country," said Bapu of the jungle tribe.
" My people live yonder." He cocked a finger back south-east,
which was the run of the mountains'-edge. He had said this before,
and in time he would enlarge upon it. " There was bad trouble,"
he explained. He wore the relics of some employer's grey tweed
jacket. " I have been at Rimli many seasons. But now there is
wickedness in this place, and now I have dreams that I will die, and
now I would go back to my own people. But I cannot go back to
my own people. The sahib has the hard way of the soldier, knowing
death and having understanding. Therefore I say that I will die
here."

" There is a song in my country. It is the song or saying of a
stream : *Men may come and men may go, but I go on for ever.*"

" That is a wise saying," Bapu said. He glanced round and
away again. " Doubtless Your Honour has been in many wars ? "

Fair exchange. " In one war only for a short time. I was a
captive in that war, a captive of a people who are called Germans.
I escaped from them and fled to another country, hiding by day
and walking in the night."

" Were you alone, sahib ? "

" Yes, I was alone."

" Is that a land of jungles ? "

" Of jungles and open fields and hills. There is much jungle."
He remembered the German jungle.

" Then a tiger wounded Your Honour, perhaps."

" There are no tigers in that country. But a bomb was hidden
in the ground, a small thing on which I stood. This was at the
very crossing place from Germany into the safe country. Thus I
was wounded, Bapu, and thus I became free." Free from what ?
he thought.

" It explains many things about the sahib," said Bapu.

The sun was an hour from setting now at five o'clock. " Cut
me a stick." He shaded his eyes with his right hand. The Rimli
jungle was a broken country, seamed and scoured by watercourses,
raos, sparsely puddled at this season. The jungle was like many
others in and below these foothills—with one difference. The
enclave lay open to the plains. But from the hills side, from the
precipitous half circle of the horseshoe, Rimli could be approached
only by this pass.

" Listen ! "

He had not heard ; he heard the second time. " KYAA ! " The
alarm call of the cheetal, the spotted deer. It came clearly and
crisply from a long way down. A killer was here. And if Bapu
had been right about a single pugmark, that killer could be the
Rimli tiger.

" Come ! " he said. He slung the double rifle on his left
shoulder, took the bamboo staff in his right hand, and led the way.
Bapu followed with the single rifle. It was tricky going for a
distance down the steep ravine. Then the slope eased, and they
were into jungle—or between jungle, for the watercourse was
already thirty yards in width. He gave the stick to Bapu. He
unslung the heavy rifle and carried it in his left hand. He walked
down the centre, picking a way round white boulders. A party
of brown monkeys loped across, and swung up trees, and the
branches swayed and were still. They crouched thoughtfully
monkey-fashion, watching him and Bapu. There was no tiger
here.

The hard light of day had softened. He sniffed. Yes, rain, he thought. But the sky was clear behind him above the foothills. He felt a spiced contentment here with this tiger perhaps in the forest. It was long since he had felt contentment.

Bapu touched him. They had reached a place where the water-course divided. The two arms swung out and joined below, enclosing an eminence of grass and thorn trees. It was not a verit-able island now, but the flotsam piled at this upper end told of the violence of another season.

Bapu made signs that they separate to inspect two buffaloes which they had tied out earlier that afternoon.

He nodded. He walked by the left fork. He did not have a feeling of tiger here, but he did not trust such intuitions or the absence of them. Nothing moved in the afternoon shadows. He heard jungle fowl clocking like domestic hens.

He swung right at the first crack of sound. Right was his slow direction, but he was quick enough. His heart beat up. The noise moved across the island, a commotion of grass, a drumming scuffle, a deer. Christ, I'm windy, he thought as his heart dropped back. He was not so much windy as out of practice. He was getting better every day.

Here was the male water buffalo, tied beside a pool under an acacia tree. Sometimes they lay down as if safe at home. This buff was propped at rope length, staring downstream. It was shaggily young, and he felt a mild hypocritical compassion when it saw him and relaxed. He had seven tied at various places against the coming of the tiger. They were poor bait for a maneater, but he had nothing better. He inspected damp sand between pools across the *rao*. A barking deer had recently passed this way. No tiger had passed this way. Yet he thought from the buffalo's nostriled stance that danger might be about.

He swung back to the bottom of the island where Bapu waited. He had not seen Bapu shoot, and he did not want to see him shoot ; but Bapu held the three-eighteen as a workman holds his particular tool. This was unusual. He was a man of fifty or thereabouts, with the dignity of a grey tweed jacket. The skin showed firm and smooth through sleeve tatters, and his bare diaphragm bulged solid. This also was unusual in a man of age. Bapu shook his head.

He led the way again. They were half a mile from the Forest Resthouse, which was home for him. The sun was a beneficent saffron ball balanced over treetops down the dry river. Time was short.

He saw the sliver of the new moon. The new moon dipped also, but to a left-hand hill. It was the infant February moon. Being a sound believer in such things, he bowed seven times to the crescent of the February moon. He turned some annas over in his pocket. I wish to kill the maneater of Rimli, he wished with formality. He did not say in himself and to the moon that he wished to kill this tiger by the end of the waning of this February moon, because he did not want calendars at all. He would have liked to make a second wish—for firm sobriety with a quiet mind. But two wishes were against the rules.

Bapu watched him, smiling. They were in harmony at this time.

They went on. The light was kindly. The first peafowl were lumbering up trees. If the tiger came last night, is the tiger hungry? Old Bapu thinks it crosses the pass soon after killing. Well, I wonder. No alarms at all. No jungle gaffuffle. If it did come, it could be miles away from here.

He reached the entrance to the nullah, which was a short-cut home, swinging right, then down to the forest road. He looked once along the main river-bed where the sun was setting beyond the trees. The glow of the sky showed also in a pool. It was the good time of the Indian winter day.

He turned into the nullah, a ravine with earth walls taller than a man, grass to either side, trees closing overhead. There was a dim religious light in here, an adequate light still.

He saw the tracks and heard a peacock scream : " May-awe." He saw and heard these things together. He faced the scream while Bapu inspected. The peacock screamed again, say a hundred yards away beyond dry grass, and beyond the sal trees. He remembered a thick patch over there beside the forest road.

Then a langoor monkey hooted, and the first peacock, and a second peacock farther over. He was right about the place and he was sure about the tiger before he saw Bapu's forefinger pointing, prodding to say unequivocally : *The maneater of Rimli has just moved there*.

He looked for the rib of scar-gouge running diagonally across the main pad of the left forepaw. It was there, and it was unmistakable, as Bapu had told him.

The tiger had climbed the bank at any easy place. The tiger was not jumping twenty-foot ravines. It was on the prowl.

He followed—up the bank, and between high grass. His leg had been sore after much walking, but it was all right now. He went along the animal path. He had ten minutes or less to play with. He was coming now to the graceful sal trees, beyond them that tangle of grass and scrub. He could be quiet as far as here. He heard Bapu breathing short and fast. He wondered if he should have let Bapu come in. He saw the langoor's silhouette against an umber sky. It sat perfectly still at the drooped end of a branch. It was looking in the right direction.

He knew where the tiger was. He knew because the main watercourse lay beyond it to the left, and the forest road on the fireline was ahead. Both these were open flanks, and he did not think the tiger would cross bare ground before dark. For the next few minutes it might stay where it was ; or it might move this way by sparse forest ; or it might go back through grass the way it had come.

He did not intend to commit suicide in the gloaming. He required shooting distance. He therefore decided to skirt that patch. He knew that the sal leaves would be noisy underfoot. He would try a little provocation and enticement. He would make his celebrated imitation of a garrulous hag picking up sticks.

But he delayed with his celebrated imitation because a car was approaching on the forest road. It came fast from the left, changed down at the watercourse, whined over that, and speeded up. It was a Landrover, by the sound. Could Cheddi Khan have been out ? Whatever car this was, it spanked and clanked past the tiger's place and went on at a brisk clip in the direction of the resthouse.

Had the tiger moved ? He did not think so. " Aii ! " he began in a cracked ancient falsetto. " Aii ! " to placate the forest shaitans. " *Aii ! Jangal men bare bare budmashe sher hain.*"

Good hag-sounding imitation. Wrong in this way—— Oh, never annoy the terrible beast by saying *Sher*, the beast's own name. Once he had enticed a man-eating tiger thus ; and he had shot it.

This tiger moved. He thought that it was coming for him. He was ready in the aim. But it crashed at great speed through cover back the way it had come. There was fractional silence and resumption as it jumped the nullah. It was a wary and experienced performer. The close passage of a car and the wailing of a crone might have been a little too much too close together.

The tiger's commotion lingered, as sounds do. Then there was shocked quiet in the jungle.

He had lost a first dim chance with the Maneater of Rimli. He had gained knowledge of the dimension of his problem. He had not made a mistake. There was nothing else, in failing light, that he could have done.

They turned right at the forest road. They were nearly home. His leg was sore. He felt washed-out and needing five drinks.

" I told the *bara sahib bahadur*," Bapu said remotely. " I told the great brave master that a wicked spirit guards the Bad One. How else would Tunna Sahib pass in his motor machine at such a time ? "

He looked round at the little man. He refrained from sarcasm about evil spirits. Who had been bowing lately to the moon ? " What wicked sahib is this ? " he asked, more lightly than his mood.

Bapu smiled without mirth. " I did not say that Tunna Sahib was wicked. I said that a wicked spirit brought Tunna Sahib at such a time."

" Tunna Sahib ? "

" Yes, Your Honour. Tunna Sahib from the sugar factory."

Tunna ? For Tunna read Tanna. " And the appearance of this Tunna Sahib ? "

" A long fellow, Your Honour, a *bilati* sahib who is at Bondha since the ending of the last monsoon."

Oh God, he thought. Not Desmond Tanner from a sugar factory ? But he knew the irrational authentic tap of fate.

CHAPTER TWO

THEY CROSSED the loose-boarded bridge and walked up the rest-house drive. The mauve after-flush had faded. It was not quite dark. He saw the man coming down to meet them. All his memories of those prison times were clear, but he would hardly forget Desmond Tanner's lanky lope.

"Hallo, Desmond," he called from a distance.

Tanner stopped. "Who's that?"

"Harry Black," he said. "How are you, Desmond?" Very good.

The last time had been after nightfall ten years or more ago. Could it be? How could it?

> And they will find who linger in the garden
> The way of time is not a river but
> A pilferer who will not ask their pardon.

If he knew human beings, and Desmond Tanner in particular, he knew Desmond would be suffering the recollection that he suffered. "I'm damned glad to see you," he said, which he was not; but in a way he was dizzy with gladness to see the man he had liked, disliked, tolerated, bullied, and sometimes loved in that adversity when time had never been a pilferer for Harry Black. Desmond was caressing his moustache. He would now make a triteness.

"How fantastic," he said. "I mean what a small world it is."

Harry smiled, and they walked together, and the night wind was beginning from the hills. "You used to be in Bihar," he said.

"They transferred me last October. It's amazing seeing you, Harry. It's absolutely wizard. But isn't your tea garden near Darjeeling? Have you come after the maneater?"

"It was," Harry said. "And I have. Been here a week. I saw

you pass just now." He would not mention the bitching of the
tiger issue.

"We heard there was a chap at Rimli, so we came to make
our number. Also to say, in case you don't know already, that the
tiger killed a woman beyond the foothills yesterday, which means
no chance here, I suppose. Christian heard it on the wireless. You
remember Christian, don't you ? Your bearer asked her and young
Michael in." His voice tailed off.

Christian, Desmond's wife. "The maneater came across last
night," he said, "thus bearing out Bapu's pet theory." He told
Bapu the news of a kill yonder.

"Salaam, sahib," said Bapu, stepping up from anonymity.
"The Bad One is again at Rimli."

"Oh," said Desmond in English vaguely. He did not look over
his shoulder for tigers in the shadows, nor ask more questions.

"I must drive down to the Range Office to warn them. Go in
and get a drink, Desmond, and make my apologies to your wife.
I won't be long." But he needed time.

"Let me go, Harry. Yes, I'll go and tell them. My God, how
extraordinary it is. Back in a jiffy." He babbled all that out. He
got into his Landrover.

"All right," Harry said. "Tell them to batten down. And
tell Tara Singh I'll be along early in the morning."

"Wait," he said on the veranda to Bapu, with whom he had
felt the coming of contentment. He took out the two heavy shells
and snapped the breech shut, and pulled back the side of the unrolled
screen.

The door was ajar, and the woman was saying : "Please leave
it, Michael. You know Daddy doesn't like you touching guns."

Harry went in. The oil lamp was on the table ; the small boy
stood beside the rack, looking at Harry's shotgun ; Christian Tanner
was sitting with her hands out to the fire.

Then she put her hands on the ends of the long wooden arms
or leg-rests of the Roorkee chair.

He nearly said : *Do you remember me?* But he said : "It's ages
since we met."

"Yes," she said soon. "Yes, Harry. Yes, it's ages, isn't it? How are you?"

The wood was too long, as usual, falling out backwards to the hearth. Dryness was the only good thing to be said for that wood. *It takes three logs to make a fire*, he considered wisely, pushing the three farther in, criss-cross fashion. They flared up and lent some colour to Christian's face. Harry stood the big rifle in the rack and closed the hinged wooden bar across to hold it safely. There were the same racks in every forest resthouse. "You're Michael, are you? My name's Harry Black."

"Shake hands properly with Mr. . . . with Colonel Black, darling."

"Mister," he said. "D'you want to have a look at my rifle?" So he opened the bar and took it out and showed it to Michael. Boys and Bapus Harry understood and liked until they annoyed him.

"Gosh, it's heavy. It's heavier than Daddy's. Have you shot a tiger with it?"

"Yes, I have."

"Lots and lots?"

"Some," he said.

"How many?"

He put it back. He did not feel like saying. "How old are you?" he asked.

"I'm eight next birthday. In two weeks. How old are you?"

"Michael, it isn't clever to ask cocky questions back that way." She wore a cotton dress, not woman's trousers like most European women. "You saw Desmond? He must be thrilled. Where did he go? I heard the car drive off."

"He's gone to give a message to the Ranger. Which reminds me." It was indeed time to remember. "I won't be a minute." He went into the bedroom where Cheddi Khan was lurking. He shut the door. "The maneater has come," he said quietly. "Bring thy bedding and sleep here. I do not want a bath to-night. I will eat dinner cooked with the Primus stove. Tell Mihtan to bar his house." Mihtan was the caretaker.

" Sahib, I will sleep in the go-down. I do not fear the tiger."

" Christ, man ! " he said less quietly in English. " Do as I tell you."

" Very good, Your Honour." Cheddi Khan remained impassive through all storms. " The Memsahib did not wish drink-things, but drink-things are there. Also glasses."

Harry went back. He poured out Bapu's double tot and took it to the veranda. Bapu swigged it in quick time, neat. Bapu's tribe were topers. " Hast thou heard the wild things speak ? " he asked him.

" No, Sahib. My ears heard the wind, and my thoughts were of whisky-wine."

" Keep the small rifle, and stand guard while Cheddi Khan moves sundry things to this house. Sleep early, Bapu, and be ready at the dawn. There will be work for us to-morrow."

" Who knows ? " said Bapu. " Who knows what will chance to-morrow ? "

Harry went in. " Sorry about all that," he said. " Now won't you have a drink ? There's whisky, or gin and lime."

" Yes, please," she said. " Yes, perhaps I will. Not much whisky and lots of water."

" What about you, Michael ? *Nimbu pani?* "

" Could I have the limejuice cordial stuff ? I like it better than that old fresh kind."

Harry took some also. " I'm a cordial man myself," he said. " When I'm not a whisky man." He sat down in the other Roorkee chair.

" Don't you drink at all now ? "

" Limited basis for the moment." He drank half of the nice-tasting vapid concoction. " Tell me," he said dim-wittedly. " Do you often go back to Canada ? "

" Michael and I were there last summer."

" I always remember how kind your parents were."

" My mother is well. Daddy died in 1948."

" I'm sorry to hear that," he said, although not. " What a coincidence meeting the Tanners here. Except of course that people have to meet somewhere, so it might as well be here." He wished to God it wasn't here. "How's old Desmond?"

"Just as wonderful and kind as ever," she said with gentleness. She had only a trace of an accent now. "He's terribly overworked at present because of the sugar-crush being on."

"I've heard about it," Harry said. "Tea is less hectic and lasts longer."

"Are you a planter still?"

"I was," he said. "I'm on leave pending retirement, or pending the polite push. I've had tea, and tea's had me, to sum the matter up."

"Oh, I see," she said. "You know I've often thought how dispiriting it must be for the forestry people, I mean however madly they may love them, to have these sad pictures of Gandhi and Nehru in every resthouse. Couldn't they find better ones? I'm sure Mahatmaji would turn over in his ashes, and Panditji would blow his top again. Don't be so fidgety, Michael darling."

"Look at that magazine if you want to." He watched her drink, and he wanted whisky. The portraits she mentioned were certainly dim.

"I can't see," said Michael, bored and alone. "Not even magazine-pictures prop'ly."

"Cheddi Khan!"

"Huzoor?" Cheddi was back again. He always contrived mysteriously to be back again. Which was annoying too.

"Bring the Petromax."

"I remember your wedding photo in the *Tatler*. Your wife looked charming."

"Divorced," he said.

Hiatus in the conversation. Pending the Petromax, he turned the oil lamp higher. He put on more crumbling apology for wood.

"How is your leg, Harry?"

"No trouble at all," he said. "It's a red-hot leg." Strictly the truth. "Dust makes it kick up," he said, "sometimes." He wished they would go so that he could take it off.

"What's wrong with your leg?" Michael was a good-looking

child, as he might well be. Bleached and brown from the winter
sun. But petulant.

" It's a tin one. Want to see ? " Harry undid the dust-excluding
buttons, loosened his jungle boot, and rolled down the sock. " It's
aluminium," he said, " not tin. How's that for a beauty of a
tin leg ? "

Michael was enchanted. " Does it go far up, I mean ? I mean,
is it all tin ? "

" Only half-way to my knee."

" Have you always had it ? "

" He hasn't always had it," Christian said. " He lost his leg by
being brave."

" I lost it by running away like a dose of salts." But he was
pleased.

" You say very funny things," said Michael in a minute. " Shall
I call you Harry ? "

" Michael ! "

" Do," he said. " Call me anything you like, excepting Uncle,
which I do not tolerate."

" I could call you Long John Silver. Mummy and I were
reading that."

" Plain Harry is best, perhaps. A drink, Christian ? "

" No, thank you." She stared at the fire. " Desmond is being
such ages. What did he go to tell them ? "

" He went to say that the maneater is back in its pristine haunts."

" *Here*, you mean ? "

" Yes, here."

" But the Landrover may have broken down. Why didn't you
say ? " Her eyes flickered to Michael and round the room.

" It's quite safe in a car," he said irritably. He went out.

The wind was loud now in the trees, and the rain-smell was
stronger. He loved to listen to that wind at night. The stars were
dusted on black velvet. He had come here for various reasons ;
and a maneating tiger was but pleasurable spice. His heart did not
bleed for his Indian brother. I'll do the job quick, he thought now
in the wind. I'll do it and get out.

He saw headlights in the forest. "Desmond's coming," he called to placate her. But he waited outside while the lights swung away and back. He heard the Landrover's practical whine coming up the drive. They were genuine creatures you could become attached to and revile, unlike piddling limousines. The window beside him showed a petromax whiteness. A nice small boy, he thought.

"Tara Singh went to ground the moment I told him," Desmond said. "So I had to warn them all myself."

"He's a useless bugger and poltroon."

Desmond laughed, and Harry felt better, and they went in.

"Darling, I thought you were never coming." She smiled up at him.

Harry took half his daily ration.

Desmond ranged about the room with a glass, and his toes turned out. He sat on the edge of the table and swung a leg. He sucked air like a bird's alarm *tseep* through that tooth. He had the same true-blue godly sahib's face, but a quieter face. "You're thinner, Harry," he said with love. "How are you?"

Harry smiled. He was happy because Desmond felt all right about it; he was happy mostly because of the years vanished between now and then. He did not understand that or anything worth understanding. "I'm okay, cock," he said.

"What about the tiger?"

Nobody answered Michael. He was drawn to the rifle rack again.

"Leave it," Harry said, thinking of other things.

Michael continued to fiddle.

"Look, boy, when I say leave it, I mean leave it."

Michael left it. Christian frowned. Desmond laughed. "Same deadly Harry Black," he said.

He was not the same. He was an irascible decadence getting better and better for a week until his old pal and his pal's wife came along.

"Fancy seeing you here. Isn't it marvellous, Christian?"

"It's lovely," she said. "So few people come up. Now tell

us about the tiger, sparing the gore. Desmond has sat up for it
twice, and I have the worst heart attacks each time. I do wish you'd
shoot it quickly."

"I will," he said. He was now fully determined in the matter.

"I wouldn't be too confident, old boy. Forty-seven in nine
months, and nobody's fired anything but a muzzle loader at it yet.
But what's this theory of Bapu's?"

"I'll go back to the beginning," Harry said. In his good days
he used to go back to beginnings; and here was a straight beginning
to go back to. He forgot about the Tanners while he talked it.
"Some bania-sportsman came shooting last April. He sat up a
tree and wounded a tiger. Bapu says he hit it in the left foreleg.
There was no elephant available for a safe pursuit. So what did
he do? He sweetened Tara Singh—fifty or a hundred chips, I
suppose—to keep his mouth shut. Nobody followed up. Nobody
even reported the wounding. That is Bapu's story, and it may not
be true, because he hates the guts of Tara Singh. But I think it's
true. Two weeks later a lame tiger started on the human beings.

"The first kill was a mistake, as they usually are—a man
blundered on to it. One swipe, and a lick. But it had discovered
that sacred humans are easy meat. It was starving. What else
would it do from then on?

"One month and seven kills later—just before the monsoon—
things were getting chaotic." Harry paused. "But you know
all this."

"I haven't heard it put together properly. Go on, Harry."

"Things were so chaotic that they called in the Army. The
Army appreciated the situation in the inimitable military manner
and decided to drive the tiger up into the head of the Rimli Horseshoe, where they could corner it. So they put a whole battalion
from Dehra on the job as a hot-weather exercise with a whiff
of danger. It was a sound enough plan, the jungle being bare at
that time, and the steep ridges open. The only snag was that
they omitted to man the pass of Rimli which hardly shows on the
one-inch map. All the locals wanted was to get rid of the animal,
so they weren't recommending plugs for loopholes. The beat was

a crashing success with tommy-guns and everybody trigger-happy. The bag was one Lance-Corporal and numerous deer and a porker or two. But, I need hardly mention, no tiger. It had slipped over early in the proceedings. Furthermore, it had found a shuttle-road.

" That's the beginning," Harry said. " And that's about all. The country beyond the foothills gives a maneater far more scope —three hundred square miles or more, as opposed to about twenty square miles at Rimli. Which is why the great majority of the kills have been over there."

He stood up to pump the Petromax. It was a nasty, useful light, reminding him of prison. Desmond watched him. Christian did not. He wondered if Desmond would like to reminisce. He himself was not a reminiscer. The lines of the years do strengthen faces, he thought, whether people get stronger or not. He pumped till it roared white and naked, and he sat down.

" There hasn't been a kill here for six weeks," Desmond said. " But we know it switches—an occasional one at Rimli, several a month beyond. That's been the form since we came in October. So what is Bapu's special idea ? "

" His idea is that it always crosses soon after a kill. First thing he said this morning was that he heard the *Janwar* speaking in the night, and that the Bad One had come. Sure enough it has, and sure enough it killed a woman yesterday. Chance perhaps, but they're creatures of habit, even maneaters. The next item on Bapu's programme is an animal kill in a day or two, then do its stuff and off again. That's what I'm here to see about."

" Why at Rimli ? " Christian asked. " If most of the people are killed beyond ? "

" Because this is a limited area, and the other isn't. Here you can get quick news and get to the spot and just possibly pin the animal down. There you can't. When I decided to come, I took a look at the map, and thought Rimli was the best hope. With a tracker like Bapu, and a bit of luck, I can make a job of it." He would make a quick job of it now if it did not make a quick job of him. " Have a fill-up, Desmond."

He got more for himself too. He would have an extra one

to-night. The longer they stayed, the more extras he would have. He felt quite good and cheerful ; the Tanner complications did not greatly matter.

"I can think of a million things to ask you," Desmond said. He did not ask them. He was a sensitive chap, with a kindness for other people's troubles ; and he lived quietly with his own troubles. That was what he used to be like under a mantle of good looks and bonhomie and mundane remarks. He was not at all clever. He laughed at witticisms but never made them. *Sympathetic* was the word for Desmond. "Do you remember the night you threw a wine bottle at that sentry on the catwalk ? "

"My recollection is hazy," Harry said. "But I remember talk about it."

Christian laughed. "Once you two start remembering, I know you'll never stop. We *must* go, darling. It's long after Michael's bedtime, and I don't relish nocturnal excursions." She smiled at her son. She was more beautiful and less pretty.

"I was thinking," Michael said. "I was thinking you're a bit lame and the tiger's lame. That's sort of funny."

"The tiger is hardly lame at all now, Michael. Which means it can kill wild animals as well as people, and that makes it a very bad and difficult kind of maneater for anyone to shoot." Lame man hunts lame tiger was the kind of thing small boys thought sort of funny, and grown-up fools made symbols of, but at their peril.

"Can you come over to-morrow evening ? Bondha's only five miles or so."

"Depends on what develops," he said carefully. "May I just blow in the first chance I get ? "

"As long as you do." There was no strain at all between them. "He always was a hermit type at heart, Christian."

"Was he ? Well, do come."

They were leaving at last. Not quite. "By the way, Harry, I'd like to be in on the tiger if you want me. We're pretty busy, but I can always sneak a few hours off. I know my experience is nil compared with yours. Still, if I could be the slightest help as a rear-guard or any other understrapping job . . ." He said it in a hurry and left it in the air. But it hung about the air. His wife sighed.

"Many thanks," Harry said. "I shall probably take you up on that. I detect feminine objections, but that's your affair." Well and lightly said. He intended to do the job alone.

He took his rifle from the rack. "I'll follow part of the way."

"You needn't, Harry. I've got a rifle."

"It's not you, you fool. It's your household possessions."

Desmond guffawed. "So wizard," he said.

So awfully, frightfully, absolutely wizard. "Just a moment," he said to Christian and the boy. He loaded. "Come on, Desmond." They went out. "Shine it round."

Desmond shone the torch. The wind blustered now, and dry leaves flew with it, and green leaves tumbled on lower branches. It was cold. Lighten our darkness from here to yonder. Wait, tiger. Wait for me.

"Start up," he said. "I'll tell them." He smiled to himself at this trivial, necessary melodrama. "All aboard," he said to Michael round the door. "All aboard the lugger, mate."

Harry dipped his lights and followed their scud of dust—down the drive, over the rumbling bridge, along the fire-line, across a watercourse, through forest. No animals moved. Three heads in the car in front. Two lives and the life they made between them. One here. Two squat petrol-eating lives also. These and the wind's life loud about the forest. Who knows what is life and what is not?

Now jungle; now, abruptly, open land. The road ran straight for the lights of Bondha. He gave a double toot, and would have turned without ado. But they stopped. So he got out and went to Desmond's window.

"Thanks, chum," said Desmond. "It's only two miles. Why not come on?"

"No," he said. "I'm for home. Good night, all you Tanners."

"Good night," she said. "Take care."

"Good night, Plain Harry. Please come soon."

He laughed at Plain Harry. Everyone laughed. "'Out of the mouth of babes and sucklings,'" Desmond said inevitably.

Harry Black drove home. Of all people. Of all the people I should have to meet. Oh, my God ! But his God was not a standby, being a suitable expletive. And yet he was very pleased to meet them.

He speeded up. Eyes glowed redly along the road. They were much like a pair of feline eyes. " Fly away, Nightjar," he said, and hooted, and the nightjar flew away.

He drove at fifty, which was a splendid velocity in the forest. Hurry ! Hurry through the swaying tunnel. Hurry back !

CHAPTER THREE

CLOUDS GATHERED, but rain did not come. Seven buffaloes were led to sacrifice each afternoon; seven jogged youthfully home each morning. The humans of the forest might die at work; they would starve if they did not work. They worked, and none died yet.

Shooting maneaters was not the conventional way of finding peace, but for Harry it was a possibility. He had thought that in quiet waiting, and in the learning of the forest, and in some danger when that came, he might make Rimli his retreat.

But now he set about his job in a different fashion. He spent ten hours a day quartering the jungle. He found no tiger and he found no tracks.

" Sahib, it is always thus," said Bapu on the third day. " We must wait."

Bapu was cursed and left behind. He went with his rifle and one companion, which was a single consuming purpose such as he had known in his prison days. He would have liked to wish, at the wishing time of the February moon, for sobriety with a quiet mind. The sobriety was now easy; the quiet mind he did not want. Yet at night, after drinking his drink and eating Cheddi's indifferent hash, he fell into deep dream-sailing sleep.

On the third day, sun and cloud had ruled by turn. It had been uncertain weather, with dull clouds of the shade and black clouds of the sun, heavy with rain that never came, light with the beauty of caprice.

But this was a grey morning, drab as any in the Scottish hills, a rarity in the harsh land. There was gentleness about. Now, surely, the intimate rain would come.

The main forest road bisected Rimli. It ran south-east and north-west, parallel to the massif of the foothills, cutting close below the ends of the horseshoe ridges. To the left now a flat

31

salient of forest, trifling incursion on an eternity of open plain ;
to the right a jumble of hills and dales, petty components of the
enclave. But the heights of Rimli were invisible this morning.

He turned on the windscreen wiper. He was used to cloud-
misted weather in Darjeeling ; he could not remember it down
here before. Down here at the pimples of the plains ; up here
in the U.P., Uttar Pradesh, Independence for United Provinces.
With a flannel shirt and cardigan and bush jacket, he still felt the
nip.

On the lower side, there were many negotiable tracks. On the
upper side, there were a few. He turned up now and put the old
bitch in low ratio four-wheel drive. She was his temporary old
bitch on loan from the Government of India. They lurched and
scratched through scrub-jungle, ugly country. Rimli was many
small places in one place.

I really ought to go, he thought. Desmond had been over alone
last evening and had left a note : *Come to-morrow you bloody man ;*
which he found when he came in at nine o'clock.

Walk and sit and walk all day. Listen in the forest in the early
night. Burn himself and other people up. There was just a chance
this way, a slim chance of an encounter ; knowing that patience
was the sober hope, patience to wait until the tiger killed. Or had
the tiger gone ?

Come to-morrow you bloody man. Harry recognised the jocularity
of hurt feelings. He did not think that he would pay a call this
evening.

" Perhaps the Bad One has gone again," he offered to Bapu,
holding rifles in the other seat, " back to the jungle below the
mountains."

" No, sahib."

" Or to the jungles beside Rimli." He meant to the foothill
forests that lay on either flank.

" Other tigers may come thence ; but thither the Bad One
does not go."

" Thou knowest the Bad One's goings as a man knows the
goings of his friend."

" The Bad One waits for me," said Bapu. He mentioned this often as a matter of sure fact ; yet he was not fearful.

They left the car. They were going to the Elephants' Pool. For all places there were Bapu names, which Harry adopted.

They crossed the *rao*—white stones dampened to grey—and climbed. The horseshoe ridge rose farther on, but the precipice tops were cut off by cloud. It was drizzling now. There was a curious closeness of earth and sky.

The pool lay in a clearing flanked by bamboo. It was a sizeable pool, and the green slope to the banks gave indication of its depth. Wild elephant bathed here and could feed nearby. It was a drinking place for all jungle dwellers.

Harry and Bapu sat under a silk-cotton tree in flower. Birds squabbled high above at the sweet red pods. And red pods were scattered on the ground, like blowsy tulips of the forest.

Listen and watch a while and then go on. Bapu faced the other way. There were two points of view in this pursuit, or in any pursuit, or in all the pursuits of Brahma.

> If the red slayer think he slays,
> Or if the slain think he is slain,
> They know not well the subtle ways
> I keep, and pass, and turn again.

The altercation continued overhead. A Bulbul sang cheerfully elsewhere. The drizzle was just audible on leaves, and clouded the mirror of the pool. And now a cheetal and her fawn were in the clearing. She did not sniff the air, nor twitch ears. She nuzzled her child. They moved sedately to the water's edge. They drank without apprehension, skirted the pool, walked up the bank, dappled deer into dappled cover.

The timorous cheetal would never have moved thus boldly on an ordinary day. She was caught in the filaments of a web, which was the web of intimate weather. All animals would be captive and feel free in the tranquil drizzle. The tigers and the leopards would wake to stroll abroad by muted day, but they would kill.

Harry was an impatient man who could sit patiently with

B

intent.   Now, on the dim fourth morning, he sat against a flowering
tree, and would have been content to sit.   The weather touched
him also.

A sambar belled.   The loud alarm " POOK " came from above
the pool.   Once, and no more.

That might mean a man ; but he did not think so, for there
were no men working in this part.   Or it might mean a predator.
On this unwary day, he was almost sure that the alarm meant
business.   Bapu thought so too.

They circled the water's edge where deer tracks were in pro-
fusion, and the mighty dents of elephant.   They climbed by the
spring-fed stream.

It started from the hillside farther up, and dwindled a brief
furlong course to feed the pool.   Bapu said that it dried up altogether at the end of April.   Now it was a rivulet at the source, and
spent itself meandering to finish as a trickle.   But in the spending
it made a green and charming glade.

Harry reached the foot of that.   He paused.   He saw thirty or
forty yards to a bend.   It was open grass, with rock rising at the
sides.   Safe passage up the middle.   His intuition muttered now.
It was often wrong.   No sound, no animals.   A golden oriole
flashed across, less bright a gold than its sunlit gold.   He liked the
liquid whistle, but it did not whistle.

He went fast again.   The ankle-joint clicked faintly.   Maintenance required.   He gave some time to maintenance.   Old Peg-Legs
used to spend half his waking hours on maintenance, legless upon a
bed in prison.   Stout Cortez. . . .

Now the bend, to be taken wide.   He stepped across the stream.
Bapu came close behind.   Each time he stopped, a whiff of Bapu
wafted on.   Bapu had a reasonable, unwashed, goaty whiff.   Bapu
hissed.   There was no need of warning ; scouts were already out
ahead.

The cheetal were ranged in a ragged line across the glade—two
hinds, three fawns, a yearling with antler spikes.   They faced the
other way—up to the tall grass and the small trees at the next left-
hand bend.   They were quite clearly in a stew, turning to flee and

turning back, making short aimless dashes. But all the ears centred always to one place. Something threatened there, or something had happened there at the corner below rising ground.

Harry went on till deer milled about him. A fawn ran up to stand within arm's length. He had known this before. It pleased him to be taken for a friend against a greater fear. It gratified his ego, possibly, in psychiatric twaddle.

The big sambar were creatures of the forest. The spotted cheetal were creatures of shade and clearing. This was not sambar country ; but this was a special day when glades wore the mantle of deep forest. A sambar must have wandered. His cheetal body-guard still weaved in skittery indecision. They gave no vocal warnings. Had the sambar fled or had it died there ?

A vulture arrived as evidence. It lumbered in level flight to land upon a tree, flap for balance, settle to hunched red-wattled hideosity. There were no vaults of open sky for scavengers to wheel. The vulture must have come from an opportune perch nearby. It waited.

Harry knew what he could not do. He could not investigate uphill in head-high grass, not for the particular animal that might lurk at the corner where this glade ended. He was doubtful if he could approach downhill from beyond. He knew the picture of that ravine. It was recorded, as was anything once deliberately seen.

He moved another twenty yards. The drizzle was stronger. He felt a following dissent of Bapu. He was not leading Bapu into foolishness. He was covering him up a tree. He took the light rifle from him and laid it down. He had not yet tested Bapu in emergency, but he thought Bapu was the best jungle better half that he had known.

He moved down-glade again. The cheetal had gone. He turned and climbed from grass through thorny wild-plum bushes to bare rock. It was slippery. He had to watch his step along above the left side of the glade. He passed under the vulture's tree. He stopped to listen. He looked over to Bapu, who nodded once slowly down and up, but noncommittal. Nothing moved below in the long grass and trees. Nothing sounded but an immanent hiss of drizzle, a tranquil gurgle of the stream, so pretty to-day in the modest weather.

Harry had climbed to cut the corner. He had moved above the base of a triangle, with the stream forming the two other sides, running down to the apex and turning back. If something was in the flat body of the triangle, how would it break? The obvious escape line was beyond the apex where scrub merged into forest. He had thought of approaching that way, but the cover was too thick.

He was going to approach downhill, with his right flank protected by the wall of the ravine. An ordinary tiger might grumble or might demonstrate; but it would go. The maneater of Rimli would wait quietly, or would leave quietly. Such was its reputation, not entirely borne out the other evening. If a grown sambar had been killed, a tiger, not a panther, would have killed it. Whatever tiger might be there, one thing was sure—it had heard him come. If they were awake, they always heard you.

Thunder rumbled many miles away. It was a tremble, not a rumble, as a rumour of guns from distant battle. It heightened the illusion of the cosy rain.

Now he was in the ravine, which widened below him. The rill swung left, the wall swung right. He could see Bapu, simian up his tree. Harry edged along the wall. He noticed what he needed—some egg-sized pebbles. He put them in his left jacket pocket. Then he had gravel on his hand for a better grip on the wet fore-end of the double-barrelled four-six-five by Purdey, by appointment to his late Majesty King George the Sixth.

The likely place was just ahead. A smaller isolated patch of grass was on his left. First clear that. Harry lobbed his stones methodically, swish and thud. Nothing whatsoever. He could not be sure. He could only decide to accept a vulnerable left flank, or to refuse it. He accepted it and went on down.

The affair might be a false alarm. The vulture, cheated of its telescopic sight, might have arrived here on a mere speculative jaunt. Or the tiger might have left already. What tiger?

But Harry did not feel it was a false alarm. His heart beat fast and steady. He bombed the main place where Khair trees, fine-traced acacias, stood over lush grass. He groped for more ammunition, of which there was a too plentiful supply—his stealthy prowl was noisy. He continued to throw stones, swish and thud ; and one loud smack on rock. No movement. He was observing all the rules. Now, in a moment, he would have to decide to break a rule or not to break it.

Bapu whistled a mellow note. Harry looked up, ready to be annoyed by signs for caution. But Bapu waved his hand from this direction to the apex-corner of the stream and to the wooded rise beyond. The gesture of the little man was gracefully explicit. He meant that something had gone that way. If he said so by sign, then it must have happened.

Harry went in. The light rain had not penetrated, but wet grass soaked him through at once. He found the sambar stag, a very large animal, heavier than any tiger. It had been taken from below, for the fang punctures were on the upper neck. It had bled little, and still was warm. A chunk of meat had been torn from the hindquarters, hardly a snack. Flies had not yet come. The big brown stag lay in a trampled circle on the grass. It was a noble beast, killed at the prime. Harry had once seen the killing of a sambar in the wild. It was a sight he sometimes dreamed again, just as he dreamed the stepping upon A.P. mines. He looked down at the sambar, whose last call he had heard from down there at the pool. He looked at this one ; he remembered the splendid and terrible taking of the other.

He went on to the foot of Bapu's tree. " It is a sambar stag," he whispered up. "What hast thou seen, Bapu ? "

" I have seen a swaying of the grass. It went slowly, slowly, sahib."

" Come down now and seek tracks. I will stand guard. Quickly, Bapu ! "

He went up the rise where the tiger had gone. It might come back. They generally came back if disturbed just after killing. This was the only covered way that it could come. The drizzle was lighter. A breeze shook a loud shower of raindrops from the trees. He was still warm. There was no grass here. He crouched for a view below bushes. What was the next thing for A. to do?

First, what about the opposition? The size of the sambar, and the fang marks—these made it a certain tiger kill. What tiger, he did not know. But no other tiger had been reported at Rimli for a month. And the quiet withdrawal, without protest—that seemed to fit the maneater. True, that first evening it had galloped; but then it had been cornered and twice disturbed. To-day, it had been mildly disturbed once. The grass was so tall and thick that it could not have seen either him or Bapu. Sure? Not quite sure.

The maneater fed on its human victims once; it rarely returned. This was an animal kill, and a natural one, and a couple of mouthfuls eaten. An ordinary tiger would certainly return. The maneater might, and with great caution; and if it was hungry. Five days? Yes, it might be very hungry. Or it might have been aroused from a well-fed sleep, and have killed for the sake of killing. They would do that, or anything, occasionally. It might have or it might not have. It might be or it might not be. This was the fascination and the rub.

He could see well beneath the bushes. Nothing doing. Bapu would know, if he found tracks. Bad ground for tracks—no sand, no mud. If not the maneater, go away. If any doubt, fetch *machan* and torch and all the paraphernalia, and sit up. Decision obvious.

Thunder muttered now again, and Bapu called him. They stood in the open glade.

" Is it the Bad One ? "

" There is one pug on rock, but the rain . . ." Bapu's throaty whisper, " Sahib, I do not know."

" I thought the way of its going was like the Bad One."

" I too, Sahib. But the air is strange, and the *Janwar* are strange to-day."

" Which tree ? " There was a young Bakli, with adequate leaf cover.

Harry waited again while Bapu cut grass to cover the sambar, and to open a line of sight. The latter might be suspicious, and was unavoidable ; the former was better than feasting vultures.

The vulture waited patiently. Bapu selected a piece of the ubiquitous bamboo, split the end, inserted a stone, cast wickedly and scored first shot. The vulture fell, a cartwheeling shambles of wings and neck, flopped and flapped, lay dead. It was a most useful member of the Indian bird creation, unregretted.

He put Bapu up the tree. He did not leave him the light rifle. He himself would shoot the maneater of Rimli.

Harry walked fast down-glade, past the pool where elephants bathed, across the *rao* and to the car. The drizzle had ceased, and the tops were clear. Black bastions of cloud were massing.

CHAPTER FOUR

BAPU GATHERED the grass and handed it to his acolytes, who were Cheddi Khan and a forest guard. They carried it away. Tattered Bapu was the high priest of this affair. It was amusing to see the tall Muslim and the dapper guard defer to him. He had a portentous, testy air, improbably reminiscent of Sir Thomas Beecham. He picked the last sheaves from the body of the sambar, thrust them into Cheddi's hand and turned to Harry. He looked up with a round, still face.

Harry nodded. *Go talking,* he meant.

Their voices rang about, and faded lower down the glade. He listened for the car. Safely away, and he was alone, never alone in jungle places.

The machan was a wooden framework, criss-crossed with string, roped from ring-bolts to the trees. He sat with his back against the trunk, his knees drawn up, the rifle resting on them. He had a clear view down to the kill, a leaf-chinked view to either side. The haversack hung from a branch. No loose objects. He was as comfortable as could reasonably be, although comfort would not last for long. He had tested the torch apparatus for alignment. It threw a beam even now in sombre afternoon. It was a clumsy contraption, clamped above the barrels.

Thunder grumbled outside the periphery of stillness. It was nearly half-past four. He had been away three hours or so. Nothing had come while Bapu held the fort. Then time frittered in trying the machan. The fretting and the frittering of time.

The storm was coming. He wished it would hurry up and come. He had been afraid of thunder as a boy. He did not exactly love it now when sitting up a tree. They said fear was what made you tick. Or they said it was the sexual urge. Everything they said was incomplete.

" KOKLI," it called. " I am the tree-pie." It landed on a tree

40

beside the sambar. It was rather a brazen bird, like any magpie anywhere, cocking an eye at the situation. It descended branch by branch, cautious and bold. It landed on the hindquarters, and flies rose. The tree-pie dipped in for a stringy sinew or such piece, tugged back. It flew to a branch, hopped higher, downed the morsel, down for more.

Thunder sounded from several directions. There was a segment of clear sky above the plains. But dusk was arriving early in this glade. Lightning played now on shadow patterns.

The tree-pie was down for the third time. It flew away, black and brown and long white tail, gone just like that.

A click? A touch of twig on twig? I wouldn't be surprised. Now is the time, before the storm, before night falls. Now is the nothing of not yet come. Now is the after of done and gone.

Harry began to turn his head, slowly to the right, slowly as the progress of a slug upon a cabbage. He saw the tiger's ruffed face, large and male.

He could shoot only straight in front. His heart made its lively tiger-pump. It still made that, and always would. He was a high-tensile performer.

Harry heard the wind a long way off. It sighed first, as in citified novels in the pine trees which are actually spruces. It came from the plains against the hills. It made a plaintive and peculiar sough. It marched up from Bondha where Christian Tanner lived. It rushed now at the lower fringes of the Rimli forest. He watched the tiger; the tiger had not moved. The wind grew and the jungle groaned.

It was coming; it was roaring; it was nearly here; it must be here. A frail thing am I in my spindly tree. The tiger's face had vanished. Harry made a first overt movement and clung to the tree trunk, and the wind did come. It arrived mightily, warmly thrashing and blasting the close, present world. It had arrived and it was gone, and the whipped trees rose again, but some were falling, and many boughs were crashing.

Is violence my true love? Is peace the aftermath and the aperitif?

How easy it would be. How difficult they always say, but
how easy to face the altar, saying after me : *I believe in God the
Father Almighty, Maker of Heaven and Earth: and in Jesus Christ, His
only Son Our Lord.* So easy to have the arrogance and comfort
of an immortal soul unlike the monkeys.

He watched the bushes where the tiger had been. Had it been ?
Certainly it had been. His machan, or elevated bedstead, was tilted
now. He wedged himself for safety but at the cost of comfort.
His stump throbbed under lateral pressure. He hoped that it would
go to sleep.

The plains wind had blown over the hills and far away. Now
another one came, but this was a cold mountain wind. It was not
a turnabout and hurry down to where you hurried from. There
were so many flashes that lightning rippled. How prettily it
rippled all about him, the rock, the swaying trees, the glade, the
polished antlers of the sambar. Ripple, ripple, cold and deathly.
He counted seconds from the brightest flashes. One, two, three,
four, five, six, seven, eight, nine, ripple of the thunder too, boom,
bang boom.

> Beat an empty barrel with the handle of a broom,
> Hard as they were able,
> Boom, boom, BOOM,
> With a silk umbrella and the handle of a broom,
> Boomlay, boomlay, boomlay, BOOM.

Now let's see. Nine seconds at eleven hundred feet a second
makes about what, two miles. Two miles to the Pass of Rimli.
Well, I suppose so. *You have a certain precocious facility with our
language, Black. That I unwillingly admit. But in matters mathematical
you are a moronic dunderhead. Do you know the word " moronic,"
Black ?—Yes, sir. But would that tend toward tautology, perhaps, sir,
like saying a pedantic pedagogue, sir ?—My witty friend, pray take this note
to the Head pedagogue.* Six on the bottom from the grunting Dean.

Brighter. One, two, three, four, five. The calico tearing and
the big bang crash, boomlay, boomlay, boomlay, BOOM. He
knew what this storm was doing. This storm was sneaking down
the horseshoe ridge, close to his defenceless head.

Rain joined the wind. There had been drizzle, and there had been dryness all the afternoon. Now the rain came, not the rains of Mr. Bromfield, not a sweaty, mould-erupting, fecund downpour of the monsoon. This was as heavy on a billion leaves. This lambasted all the thunder but the large explosions. This swallowed up the wind. This was rods of water in the violet flashes. But this was different. It was cold.

He crouched in his groundsheet, him and his rifle with the torch attachment. The wise and prudent laid down their guns when thunderstorms were raging. Trees drew lightning, and guns were apt to sizzle. Harry huddled on his swaying tree. He played treason with the notion of casting it away. He was cold and wet and tiny. Little Harry Black afraid of nothing but now again afraid of thunder. Be brave, he told himself. They often called him brave when he was fearless.

Now two seconds from flash to crash. Now flash, count one, crash. Now is the one, now ejaculatory. Come, please come, if come you must. Hiss and blind and deafen into the pinpoint of the core. Almagordo, Hiroshima, Nagasaki and Bikini. That will teach you, Peter Pan, dirty-minded little man.

Time was not a river, not an ever-rolling stream. Time went by fits and starts, by teeth chattering, by two stealthy swiggings from his flask, by ephemeral inward glow, by false departure of the storm, by true departure from the present me.

The storm flickered to extinction to a destination to the south. The wind died and trees dripped. The earth was loud with water in the middle of the night. The sky was lovely in the middle of the night, the famous jewelled velvet of my India, my love.

Things moved in the forest while Harry sat. It was dark but not black dark. The trees cut the sky ; the sambar was the dim bundle underneath. They had tied a rope from that tree to the sambar's neck. The kill must be anchored against the power of Tiger, who could remove six hundred pounds of property as easily as you could lift your suitcase.

But there were no tiger indications. Harry heard elephant behind him. Two males were in residence at Rimli at the present, a medium tusker and a big tuskless mukhna. There was a forestry elephant at his disposal, but it was female, and the attentions of the wild gentlemen had been a nuisance.

They were feeding now on bamboo. He heard the splintering and swishing a hundred yards or so away. Grown elephants had no enemies to fear, not even man if they minded their own business. But the men who moved in jungles were afraid of them. They feared elephants much more than ordinary tigers.

The wind, the light airs, puffed sporadically from him to them. He hoped they would not pick him up. His tree was stout enough to ride out a storm, not elephants.

The bamboo noises stopped. They had gone away, perhaps. Elephant moved with careless noise, or in uncanny quiet. The back of Harry's neck began to tingle. The stream was loud. He turned on his tilted perch. This was not easy. The blood ran painfully into numbness. He had heard aright. An elephant faced him at the corner of the glade, at the place where the tiger had moved *ahisti ahisti*, slowly, slowly, yesterday in Bapu's words, from grass across stream and into forest.

He could see the mukhna well enough by starlight. The ears moved. The trunk quested about but did not curl. If the black mood of *musth* was on it, things could be troublesome. People thought sitting up trees was a tame, picnicking form of sport. Go, bloody elephant, do go. I cannot go my several way in peace, but you go yours. I do not want to kill you.

The elephant skirted his tree, followed by the smaller tusker. Any sound they made was below the splashings of the stream. They had the ponderous lightness of some wonderful big ladies. They passed down the glade, and out of sight.

> Du temps que la Nature en sa verve puissante
> Concevait chaque jour des enfants monstrueux
> J'eusse aimé vivre auprès d'une jeune géante
> Comme aux pieds d'une reine un chat voluptueux.

The sensuality of Baudelaire to the libido of me. I once saw elephants loving in the moonlight. How human, I thought then

long ago, how touchingly like us, kissing purely, kissing in the
growth of passion. But they didn't do it. Think of God in an
elephant's image.

It was half-past four. He had been twelve hours up this tree,
the dirtiest of many nights up trees, and now it was a perfect
night with ninety minutes to the formal end of night. He was
cramped and cold and sleepless.

This was tiger time before the dawn. Harry watched and
listened and was not altogether here. He was up there in Mars,
and he was over there at Bondha. He was in other places too. But
he saw the tawny planet, and he heard a grinding of the crushing
of the cane, a factory murmuration, that was all. No tiger.

I must go over there to-night, whether I finish the job or not,
I really must.

Night wore a paler rim above the eastern hills. Jackals howled
before the dawn. " A-EE," they yelped. " *A-EE. Where is the
dead Hindu ? Where . . . where . . . where. . . . Over here. . . . Over
here . . . over here.*" An epidemic to and fro and round about,
demented ululation, stopped.

Small masticating noises on the other side, chop of jaws.
What ? Now what would that be ? Something scavenging the
vulture. It stopped too. The glade was changing quickly, harden-
ing to the many entities of day.

Slowly ! he adjured himself. Quietly now ! The tiger stood
broadside, head lowered to its kill. It was just light enough to see
the pattern of the stripes, not light enough for a sure positioning
of sights. It was the right tiger, from accounts.

He switched on his beam. The tiger's head whipped round.
The ivory bead was behind the great bulge of shoulder. He fired.
The recoil punched him off precarious balance, and he saved
himself. The tiger exploded through grass across the glade and
up the rocky slope. Silence. A slow heavy roll and tumble back.
The legs thrashed. It lay in the open. He knew that he had shot
it in the heart. He gave it the other barrel. A tame end to the
Rimli maneater.

Harry waited up his tree. He lit a cigarette. It tasted very good. He hung the rifle by the sling. He had been lucky not to fall out of the machan, which was tilted twenty degrees or thereabouts. Day was here, but the sun had not yet reached above the hill. He finished the cigarette and tried to beat out his cramps. They would have heard the shots. He could not get down alone. It was a time to despise his disability. Other people have sat up trees before in rain and thunder, through the vigilance, through all the deaths of darkness to a killing in the morning. That's patience, chum. That's a real achievement.

The Landrover came. They hailed him from below, from the Elephant's Pool, he would suppose. And there they were—Bapu in his hallowed jacket ; Cheddi Khan, that urbane rogue ; the Forest Guard, a dressy fellow.

Bapu went to the tiger and knelt and turned at once. " Oh, sahib," he called across to Harry Black. " This one is not the Bad One."

CHAPTER FIVE

HE ATE. His head drummed for sleep, and the chills had not left him. He measured the tiger. It was nine foot four between pegs, but very bulky. He did not want the skin, and he did not know what he would do with it.

"Bapu," he said, "if this one has come from another jungle near to Rimli, why might the Bad One not go to that jungle?"

Bapu grunted and went on skinning.

Harry climbed alone to the Pass of Rimli. The rock floor was still damp, and it gave categorical information. The maneater had not crossed since the storm. He thought now that it had gone back the first night, that night the Tanner family had come. He had covered the ground again and again. He did not think that it could hide itself for five days in so limited an area, in country so broken that all movement must be channelled eventually to trackable places. Tigers travelled to live.

Bapu had vague feelings or certainties that it was still at Rimli. If asked for explanations, he closed up at once. He could not explain, or he would not. Probably both. Primitive people did not tick by logic. They knew what they knew, instinct being strong, and reason weak. Bapu had the failings of his animal wisdom. He was infallible as a tracker, uncanny in understanding jungle evidence. But there was no jungle evidence. There were only Bapu hunches.

It seemed impossible that the tiger could still be here, subject only to the premise that all things are possible. Harry made up his mind.

Bapu was still at it. He worked slowly and very well. He laid down his knife. "News, sahib?" he asked, standing.

"The tiger has not gone in the night."

" I think the Bad One is still at Rimli," Bapu said.

" Why, Bapu ? "

" Sahib, I do not know. I am not sure." He turned slowly, with his head cocked, here below the banyan tree in shade, and the bright day outside. The tiger smell was nasty. Bapu seemed to search round the compass, like that radar aerial sweeping so knowingly on a ship. " Yesterday I knew, but to-day I do not know."

" I think the Bad One has gone. If there is no news by to-morrow morning early, we people will go to Ranipur, to the country below the mountains."

" *Ham log ?* " Bapu said. " We people ? " He rubbed his foot on the skin, grasping coarse fur delicately between toes. " But, sahib, I have been at Rimli for many seasons, and never have gone to other places."

" Oh brother, art thou too old for new things ? I need thee, Bapu."

" Wherever the master needs me, there I will go." He looked directly at Harry, which he rarely did. " Also, I fear now to stay here without protection."

" From the tiger ? "

" No, sahib, from men. This I have heard, that the hairy *bahnshut* plots against me." Bapu's hatred of Tara Singh was vilely explicit.

" Then we shall go together, and each night there will be two sups of whisky-wine."

Bapu grinned, raised magically from despond. He went back to the half-skinned body of the wrong tiger.

Harry spoke with Cheddi Khan, then went to bed. Sleep stayed away. Decisions made and plans to make. His mind ran vividly to this and that and here and there. I wonder if Cheddi can find anything out. These witch-makings can be singularly unfunny. There's only one way with the likes of Tara Singh. I shall have to scare the lights out of him. Well, off to-morrow morning. *Won't we ever meet again, never ever, Harry ?* That was what she said. Who cares about it ? Who cares about anything but sleep

that will not come. Sleep on a swaying elephant, a loud-leaved
tumult, *this one is not the Bad One, sahib.*

Sweep over, galaxy of sleep.

      *   *   *   *   ★

He stopped at the Range Office. It was a pleasant white-
washed building among trees. The forestry quarters were nearby,
and goats were grazing, and the grass seemed greener already after
rain. He could hear children's voices, but he saw no children now
in the afternoon. That was the only indication of the fear that
rode these people.

Two men crouched on the veranda, woodcutters from Garhwal.
One had a bleeding head, the other a swollen jaw. They did not
look up at Harry sitting in the Landrover. He wondered : *Tiger ?*
for a moment ; then he recognised that cuffed apathy of the
peasant malefactor. Same old dirty story.

Tara Singh appeared at the office door. " Good afternoon, Mr.
Black. I heard story of fine tiger but rotten luck." He was affable.
" I tell you one thing, sir, maneater has gone to Ranipur again.
That is my considered opinion."

" Who are these ? "

" Thieves. Contractor's fellows stealing bamboo to their own
pockets." He ran his pink tongue round the hair-rims of his lips.

" How much did they take ? "

" Each three long pieces. They will be punished."

" They look as if they have been punished." He was crabbed
with sleep and not enough sleep. He never could stomach the
callous inhumanities. " Three sticks isn't much when they risk
their lives to work. They're cutting your wood for you, Tara
Singh."

" Yes, Mr. Black, but you don't know fact. Fact is they take
advantage of tiger scare. We must make example."

" Did you catch them yourself ? " He knew that Tara Singh
had not been in the forest.

" My men nabbed them." He was an obtuse, complacent Sikh.
He had the cruelty, but lacked the guts. " With D.F.O. coming

on rounds soon and so much shoals of paper work, I have not had two seconds lately to get out about." Tara Singh smiled, a bland patriarch. He liked Harry as little as Harry liked him. He was not yet afraid of Harry Black.

"I came to tell you that if there is no news of the tiger by to-morrow morning, I shall be going round to Ranipur Division."

"That is wise decision, Mr. Black, very proposal I was making."

"Would you send them a message to expect me at the rest-house?" A forest telephone line went ten miles along the hills north-west. Thence there was a public telephone across the foot-hills and a forest line back to Ranipur. This three-stage relay worked sometimes in a garbled fashion.

"Gladly, sir, but our line is broken since storm, alas. My men are constantly tracing fault and as yet not finding. Communications will be fully established in no time doubtless." He talked like a comic-opera babu, but he was a corpulent unpleasantness.

"I should like to take Bapu with me, Ranger sahib," Harry said politely. He was a guest here, and formalities had to be observed.

Tara Singh came to the edge of the veranda, clasping hands upon his stomach. "But, Mr. Black, this is beyond possibility. The man Bapu is locally employed forest shikari of this division. Transfers cannot be permitted under regulations."

"I am not asking about transfers. I am saying that I want to take him with me temporarily. The Inspector General told me to use anyone I wanted anywhere I wanted. Perhaps you would like to see his letter again, or is that clear already?"

"Clear as a bell, Mr. Black, but there is added complication. There is question of man's personal safety, and D.F.O.'s last words to me: *Keep personal eye on Bapu*, said Divisional Forest Officer personally. *This is only sure protection*, D.F.O. said. Sir, you are off seeking tiger every day with peerless bravery. You do not have time for hearing dangerous common gossip. . . ." Tara Singh coughed.

Harry was watching the dejected bamboo-stealers along the

veranda. He had noticed their heads move at the name Bapu. He waited for Tara Singh. All the intriguers intrigue themselves into your hands, he thought.

" No educated person would believe rumours, of course. But these common people, they have much hate and fear of Bapu. They say one thing : *Bapu is in league with maneater, advising as to next victim*. They say one thing : *Bapu is maneater personally*. They say one thing : *Who is this Bapu, living many years at Rimli, but always a stranger alone among us ?* They say one thing : *Why is Bapu never seen by single human soul at time of killing ?* Merest tommy-rot, Mr. Black, by simple folk in dire terror seizing on chap's unsavoury reputation. But most perilous for Bapu. At Rimli Bapu is protected under my personal vigilance. But stories have flown to Ranipur also. What would surely happen at Ranipur ? *Here is maneater's alter ego*, they would say. *Here is living embodiment of wickedness. We kill him and we are safe at last from scourge*."

What did the little man say himself ? He said : *There is wickedness in this place*. . . . And he said : *The Bad One waits for me*. And he said : *The hairy Bahnshut plots against me*. I wonder, though. I just wonder if Bapu is holding out on me about something.

" I remember a strange thing in Bengal," Harry said. He was going to make this strange thing up slowly and with care to suit the case ; but it was an old Indian tale, and true in essence. " There was a district in the Dooars, near the Assam border, where they were plagued by a maneating tiger. It had killed over two hundred people in four years—two hundred and twenty-three I think the final number was when I got that tiger. It was a far worse case than this one—up to date, that is. Well, Sirdar-ji, you can imagine the reign of terror. You can imagine how every man, woman and child wondered who would be the next to die. You can imagine how desperately they sought and prayed for deliverance."

" Indeed yes, Mr. Black."

" It happened that there were two holy men in that area. One was a true guru who practised all the virtues, who had torn out all the roots of sin. The other was a false follower of Siva, a lecher with an odour of sanctity. He feared and hated the good guru. He saw a way of being rid of him. How do you think he did it, Tara Singh?"

"I am all ears, sir." There was a fixity of countenance.

"It was easy for the bad guru, and he did it cleverly. He only had to hint. He only had to say at the right time in a discussion: *Someone must help this monster. How else could it survive? Either it is the spirit of the last victim or it is the wicked spirit of one among us. Surely we people of these villages can find out whether any man or woman wanders abroad in the evenings when the tiger kills.*

"Now it is well known that the other guru did wander abroad at all hours, oblivious of danger. He was so saintly a man that life meant nothing to him.

"As I said, it was easy for the bad guru. It is always easy to sow a seed of wickedness in the minds of men." Harry paused. I'm doing well, he thought. Now, careful.

"These terrified people began to whisper. They whispered that the guru took on the form of the maneater, or that the maneater took on the form of the guru. *He has been communing with the tiger*, they whispered when he returned to his hut from a night-long vigil on a hill-top. Then: *A man was killed yesterday afternoon. Did you know that the guru's robe was soaked with blood when he came home at dusk?*

"The seed sprouted, Tara Singh. Soon they came to the wicked guru. *We know this and this and this*, they said. *What shall we do to the monster. Shall we kill him, holy one?*

"*No*, said the wicked guru. *Do not kill him without trial. That would be wickedness. Tie him to a stake outside his hut, and call to the tiger. If the tiger does not come, you will have certain proof.*

"So they took the saintly guru and tied him to a stake. He made no protest. They waited in the hut, calling loudly, sure that the maneater would not come. Was this guru not the maneater in human form?

"But the maneater came that night and killed him."

"This is terrible story, sir."

"Isn't it? Well, I haven't quite finished. Next day the elders of those villages met together, and they were ashamed. They said : *Undoubtedly that poor holy one was innocent. We made a grievous error.*

" Now, these were simple people who had sinned from fear. They were not wicked men, but only the tools of one wicked man who had been so cunning that no one could say : *His was the idea. It was the other guru who put us up to this.*

" The wicked guru had been clever, but he had made two mistakes. First, he had linked holy men and maneating tigers in the minds of peasants who were demented with terror. Second, he had not taken into account some unpleasant facets of human nature, as for example that if I do wrong, I may at first be sorry. But what tends to happen next ? I seek to justify myself, to prove that I was really right, to put the blame on anyone but me. In short, Tara Singh, crime begets double crime.

" So they realised their lamentable mistake and tied the wicked guru outside his ashram. This test took rather longer, two nights to be precise. By which time, of course, he was raving mad. The interesting thing about it was that I arrived on the scene the morning after he was killed. I followed the blood trail and sat over the remains of the body and shot the maneater. It was only later that I pieced the story together.

" I might have reported them to the police, but it seemed to me that justice of a sort had been done and that the only sufferer had been the wise guru, who was too saintly a character in any case to mind about death. So I appointed myself judge and jury and dismissed the case. You are the first person who has heard this story. Was I right, do you think, Tara Singh ? "

Silence here. Children's voices there behind closed doors. " Oh, indubitably, yes, Mr. Black."

" To come back to Bapu," he said gently, " I wonder if you put these ideas into the minds of these simple people ? "

" That would be unworthy most false accusation, sir."

" I wonder if you still object to my taking Bapu with me to Ranipur ? "

" Indeed not, Mr. Black. You must use *carte blanche*. But I was obeying D.F.O.'s personal instructions only. As for false gossip, I was recounting only. Sir, I assure you . . ."

Harry looked at Tara Singh. "You may or may not have started these stories about Bapu. That doesn't matter. The point is that I think you did. The other point is that I am a private individual, with influence of course, but no official power.

"The power I have is that I don't care about my skin ; hence I will stop at nothing. The weakness you have is that you care too much about your skin ; hence will do anything to save it. Two kinds of wicked gurus. All I want to say is that if harm came to Bapu, it would be most unfortunate for Tara Singh. I hope you understand me."

The Range Officer did not answer. He looked unhappy.

"Good afternoon." Harry drove away, and then he wished that he had included the wretched bamboo-stealers somehow or other in his threats. Tara Singh would take it out on them. Well, if it wasn't them, it would be someone else.

I wonder what sort of a chap this Tara Singh really is, he thought. *Really is.* There you go. Nobody really is. Am I, for instance ? Certainly capable of almost anything in my mood. *Harry*, Mother said. *There is a look in your face sometimes that makes me quite afraid. You must try to fight your temper, darling. Try every day.* Well, I did. I learned in the end to button my temper down. That was the thing I achieved in prison. I learned that, and I learned to believe in human goodness, not blindly, but essentially. And what has happened to my strength, my faith in myself and men ? It crumbled gradually like an earth bank, flop and little plop into the torpid river.

He was driving to Bondha. The forest road was muddy. There must have been two or three inches of rain to make the water-courses run in such lively fashion, each with a hub-deep torrent at the centre, at the side, at the lowest place in the inexorable law of flow. There was no dust this clean-washed day. Rain all gone. Soon the hot weather would be starting.

Yes, faith is the thing I lack. Belief, I mean. Belief that virtue is not self-interest. How can we believe anything ? Why should

we believe in the good hand of God ? How the hell can we now ?
The only God I see is God of the strong earth, God of the water
and the silk-cotton tree and the pretty little birdies and the killing.
But what about God of the atom bomb ?

He came to the forest gate, a draw-bar between posts. It was
open nowadays, there being little poaching in these woods. He
rode out between the tall sugar cane, half-cut, and bearded wheat
that was not half-grown. He ran across the sun to Bondha. He
had been pretending that he did not want to go. Nor he did. But
he also wanted very much to go.

> I saw Eternity the other night
> Like a great ring of pure and endless light.

No, I didn't. All I saw was the beautiful illusion that withers
away. Once cannot matter. I shall say good-bye, and I shall take
my Bapu and my Cheddi Khan and my old borrowed bitch and
my several adequate vain weapons and my bedding, and we will
all muck off to Ranipur together.

The manager's bungalow would be the big one at this side,
white with a red roof and a red-walled garden. *Bara Sahib ki Koti*,
big shot's joint with the best view, and others beyond, scaled
strictly down the hierarchy. What an extraordinary feudalism
pervades and permeates this exasperating sub-continent, even the
resthouses having senior suites and junior suites, and servants'
hovels by reflected rank.

Young Michael was riding a pony round the garden. " Da-da-
da-daah-da," Harry hooted on the old bitch's horn. Vick-Edward.
I have a message for you.

CHAPTER SIX

IT WAS not a child's pony but an arab of grace and quality, a chestnut gelding about fourteen hands. "Oh gosh," said Michael from his perch, "I thought you were never coming."

"That's a nice pony. What's his name?"

"Adonis. Daddy says it's a wrong name for an arab. I'm allowed to ride him in the garden. He has a lovely mouth until he really gallops, and then he takes a hold. Did you come about anything special or did you just come?"

Good question. "I came to tell you that I shot a tiger this morning early, but it was the wrong one. Hallo, Christian."

"A tiger! Gosh, tell me."

"Hallo, Harry." She was wearing a tweed coat and skirt. "You weren't out in that awful storm last night, were you?"

"Yes," he said. "I palpitated up a tree."

"There was the strangest gust of wind before. It blew over us like a scourge of whips. Look at my poor sweet peas. Darling, you've ridden enough now, haven't you?"

Harry helped the boy down, and watched him feed green lucerne to the pony. "Go home, Adonis," Michael said. "Adonis understands everything you tell him. He's a wizard pony and nice to everybody, even the cat with kittens in his stable always climbing over his feet, his hoofs I mean." The pony walked slowly round the bungalow, presumably to its stable. "Do you like Arabs, Harry? Could you tell me about the tiger, please?"

He smiled. "You and your mother share a habit of disjointed conversation."

"Let's sit in the garden, shall we, for a while? Desmond is still at that office. Yes, I must try to be better, rambling on and skipping about is so confusing, and boring too."

"I didn't mean boring," Harry said. He told Michael about last night, and about the puzzle of the maneater. "So I've decided to go to Ranipur."

"Doesn't it wear you out," she said, "never knowing what lurks behind your back and around the corner, and not enough sleep and so on?"

"Bapu is a great help. He's the only genuine jungle man I know. But it does tend to be an edgy performance."

"The snows are wonderfully near this evening. They invite you to come and they turn you down so coldly. I can't explain."

He looked over the toy hills of Rimli to the mountains. He wondered what she would have said about Kanchenjunga opposite his tea garden. Soon now the sunset would climb these lesser peaks, and the flush would grow and die. Soon now he would be off on his travels yet again.

"Here comes Mr. Hoopoe," Michael said. The bird flitted indecisively across the lawn and landed. The black-tipped crest flipped up and sank. It probed about the grass. "Mrs. Hoopoe stays in her nest in the garden wall. It's very stinky. Isn't it funny, such a nice mother bird with a bad smell, don't you think so, Harry?"

"Well," he said, "Mr. Hoopoe doesn't seem to mind."

Michael thought that vastly amusing. "Harry, why did the Barn Owl 'owl in the barn?"

He tried. "I give up," he said.

"Because the cuck-cuck-cuckoo drove 'er cuckoo. Now you ask me one."

"It's a mad family game Michael and I play. You don't have to, Harry."

"I'd like to," he said. He wanted to play their mad family game once. "I've forgotten them all except the razorbill and the sea urchin. But it's an ancient chestnut."

"That doesn't even count," said Michael ruthlessly. "Make one up, Harry."

A flock of migrant pastors flew overhead, which provided inspiration of a sort. "Why was the Rosy Pastor pink?"

"Because Miss Wagtail wagged 'er tail," Christian offered promptly.

"Ruder than mine, and not right."

"Give up."

"Because the Demoiselle Crane'd in church."

"I don't exactly see that," Michael said. "Well, how did the Bee-eater?"

"With one swallow. But darling, I think we've played this game enough."

"We never play games properly. We just stop."

"Ask Manoo Lall to put the drinks on the veranda, then please run over and tell Daddy Mr. Black is here."

"I won't say Mr. Black, I'll say Plain Harry like he said."

"I'm afraid he's rather spoilt. Do you think so, Harry?"

"I wouldn't know. He's very bright."

The pink snows were fading now. The half moon was high. The grinding of the sugar cane groaned up and down and on and on and night and day with juiced monotony. "Your flowers are good. Are you a gardener?"

"Yes," she said. "I love it. Shall we go in and have a drink? Every time I look at Rimli I think of a horrible tiger's face, and I worry about Michael. But Desmond says it's safe here with all that open land between us."

"It is," he said, providing the comfort and confirmation. They walked in the scent of sweet peas and syringa, and in the smell of after-rain. The air was patchily warm and cool, this a first envoy of a tyranny to come. The drink tray was on the veranda.

He knew how arrogant and foolish he had been even to imagine he might be too welcome here. He saw that the family house was built upon a rock at Bondha. He was glad that he had come. "I like that boy of yours," he said.

"It's astonishingly mutual. Did you have any children, Harry? Do you, I mean?"

"We had a son," he said. "Lived a month." He poured out his drink. He said No, if people ever asked. Now he had said Yes.

"Your poor wife."

My poor wife. But she's right. Everything she says is right.

"We lost our little girl two years ago. It makes it so hard to understand why God."

"I never understand why God," he said. "If any."

"I know," she said. "That's fairly obvious."

It was a long time since anyone had smote him coolly. People smote him in anger, or not at all. "I'm sorry about your child."

"It was worst for Desmond. He's been quiet since the war, shut off in himself, I mean, and sorrow is so hard for him. Do you think Desmond is all right, Harry?"

"He's the same good kind chap and always will be."

"You know," said Christian, looking from the lighted veranda to darkness to the moon-etched snows. "It was extraordinary the other evening how you two might never have been apart. I mean it's a queer feeling for a wife to have when a man steps out of the blue and she knows he knows her husband better than she knows him after however long it may be together."

"Yes," he said. "Ten years fly out of the window."

"Is it like that between ordinary men friends? I don't think it is for Desmond."

"Well," he said, "if you get to know a chap in dirty weather, you know him well enough for keeps."

"But people change, I think, don't you? I have, completely."

"As between prison pals, changes don't change much."

"Desmond has missed you," Christian said. "Have you missed him?"

"Yes," he said. But he had not missed Desmond these last years. All that he had missed was missing him, or anyone or anything he might have missed.

He had hoped to avoid a private conversation, and she had contrived a private conversation. He would give her a chance to say her say. "I wanted to see him after the war. But there was the skeleton of a complication . . ."

She smiled round at him in her lively charming way. "The skeleton of a complication dead and buried long ago, the kindest maddest complication that never happened, did it?"

" No," he said. " It never happened."

" Desmond and I are very happy, Harry."

" I know," he said. " It's good to see."

Now he thought it quite ironical that he should be the meeting point of one line from Desmond Tanner's corner and one line from Christian Tanner's corner, private dead and buried line from each, the skeleton triangle.

" What's Desmond up to? I drive miles to see the man, and he closets himself in a sugar factory."

" It's labour trouble. He was so disappointed you didn't come before, but I said you were hipped about the tiger."

" So I was," said Harry. " A single track mind is one of my many failings. And here I am at Bondha playing barn owl games, tiger all forgotten. But what's the labour trouble? "

" Something about the company losing money last year and so we're not paying a workers' bonus this time but *they* say the accounts are phony, and the Government is completely on our side, but they've given notice of a strike next week. You'll have to ask Desmond. I'm such a bum explainer."

He laughed. He was enjoying himself. " Graphic anyway," he said.

" These labour headaches never seem to end. I suppose if I understood it better, instead of living on ice beside a volcano, and picking up fag-ends. So many metaphors mixed-up. Desmond takes it all in his stride, but when I hear them shouting their wild slogans at the union meetings, I get scared that some day some fanatic will hurt him. Don't ever say I said so. I mean there have been cases. What is it like in tea? "

" Worse, I think. Tea is a much longer-established industry, and some of those old-fashioned planters used to rule with a big literal stick. Well, naturally enough, when exploited labour suddenly found its strength, labour was bloody-minded. But I think that get-your-own-back stage is over.

" The trouble in the Darjeeling gardens is that the labour force is Nepalese, and the Nepalese are far more mercurial than your plains people. All peaceful and friendly. Then one of

these red-hat agitators comes along, and before you know anything has started, the place explodes. That was what happened
to me."

"Go on."

"I had been up to the Club one day last autumn, and I came
back after rather too good a lunch to find all the hired help had
downed tools and were being harangued outside the factory by a
Communist. *Kill the red-faced plutocratic monkey!* he was screaming,
meaning me.

"That provoked me, because I had always got on well with my
people, and they looked at me now as if they would be glad to
carry out this demagogue's instructions. So I took the bull by the
horns, or the agitator by the scruff of the neck, and threw him
down the *khud*."

"Did you *kill* him?"

"No, some broken bones. The remarkable thing was that the
moment he disappeared over the edge, they were all right. Mobs
are very odd. I wonder if anyone has written a book about
humanity in the horrid mass."

"What repercussions?"

"The Deputy Commissioner, a Bengali and a tough man, was
delighted. But my dim managing director in Calcutta took a dim
view, and the Tea Association said how can we possibly achieve
good labour relations if planters take the law into their own hands,
and so on. It wasn't what they thought privately, but it was what
they had to say. The fact is that if I hadn't done just that at just
that moment, I would have been for it, and so might a lot of other
people later on. There hasn't been any serious trouble in the
district since."

"You believe in violence, don't you, Harry?"

"If you mean that it takes violence to deal with violence, yes."

"An eye for an eye," she said. "What a Biblical old fascist
you've become."

"Christ," he said, snap like that. "Don't call me a fascist.
Haven't I seen fascism?"

"I do wish you wouldn't say Christ that way. But fascist

wasn't what I meant. I'm sorry. It's only that you seem so drastic and disillusioned."

" May I have another drink ? "

He got it, and she said : " Was that incident why you gave up being a tea-planter ? "

" Ostensibly. They said that the next time trouble brewed, I would be a provocation and a dead duck. Which probably was true. But that was an excuse. The real reason the company eased me out on a year's terminal leave with pay was that I had been boozing my garden rapidly downhill. Also one or two other real reasons."

" You don't look like a shaky mottled booze-artist. You don't behave like a reformed one, either—I mean drinking a little and not on the wagon."

" There you go," he said. " What is my exact compartment ? Four-letter man ? Fascist ? Reformed booze-artist ? Violent misanthrope ? Get it right and make it simple for the girls."

Christian laughed. " *Touchée*. Women are such simplifying idiots."

" Daddy's just coming in a minute. He said : *Tell Plain Harry to stoke up*."

" I have."

" Could you please tell me about when you escaped from Germany and got your tin leg ? "

" It's a long story," he said. " I'll tell you sometime." There would not be a sometime to tell Michael that story.

" You'll stay for dinner, Harry, won't you ? "

" Many thanks. But I think I'd better be getting back."

" Desmond will be so disappointed if you go. Can't you forget about that animal for one evening ? "

" I can," he said. " I have, in fact. But I must make an early start to-morrow without a headache."

" Your tiger friend," said Christian. " Such a pity you couldn't teach it to drink whisky." She took Michael away to his bath.

He did not bother to consider meanings of that peculiar and tiresome remark. But he considered the inconsequent, sharp wits of Christian Tanner, serenely happy with a handsome, good and rather simple husband at a sugar factory in India, and a boy the apple of her eye. He was jealous, but he wished them well. He felt the good sad warmth of three reasonable drinks. He flew over the hills and far to the moon-cold mountains. It would be good to listen to Sibelius. I wish he had written a Himalayan symphony, not programme music I don't mean, but a high austerity of cold above a sexuality of heat, unendurable pain and pleasure ineffably transcended. I'm the male animal. I can't sit unstirred by the golden silken woman in her tweeds. And she knows it, and it pleases her, and she isn't having any. Which is the difference between man and woman. But what I have to feel and what I would do are perfectly distinct. Even if I were able, I would not play the cuckoo in this nest. I'm glad I came and found that out. What about another one ? But here is Desmond.

" I'm frightfully sorry, old boy. I've been trying to persuade these hopeless union people. Did Christian explain ? "

" She gave what she called a bum explanation, but I got the gist."

" . . . So the long and the short of it is a deadlock. I don't believe they will strike in the end. Not a leg to stand on."

" Much Anti-British feeling ? "

" Anti-management, not Anti-British in the least. Michael interrupted proceedings to announce the arrival of his hero, Plain Harry. You know, I wanted to ask you to be his godfather, but you hadn't answered my other letters, if you ever got them. So in the end I didn't."

" Desmond," he said. " I did get two." The hurt that must have caused had been in and out of his mind this past week. How ludicrous that he should be in a position to distribute favours writing letters to lucky Desmond. That was the fact, however. " I'm sorry I didn't write. I meant to every day for months, but things were slipping at that epoch, and I procrastinated and never did. You know how it is." The casuistry of half truth.

Desmond smiled at him. " Of course I do."

He listened to the cricket song, which was a song so high and never-ending that it went unheard. That and a hurrying blood-hum in his head. The cricket and the hum, the grinding of the cane, the voice of Michael beyond a door, the rubbery pad of servants in a well-ordered house. In the old days they made a different noise, barefooted.

Desmond looked round him, and he said quietly : " It was damned good of you to go and see Christian that time in Canada."

Damned good of me ! he thought. " I'd seen numerous P.O.W. wives in England," Harry said. " Why not Christian when I was over there ? "

" I don't mean that. I mean what you told her about my escape-fiasco."

He supposed it had to come. " You stumbled over the tripwire. That's what I remember happening."

" No it isn't, Harry. And you know it."

" Christ ! " he bit him. " Can't I remember what I remember ? "

" You're lying," Desmond said. " But what a wonderful bloody man you are. Let's have a drink."

He saw relief light Desmond's face, the thing spoken out at last, the cancer borne so long and cut away. How could you deny a divinity of aspiration ? I could have helped him years ago, a wonderful bloody friend indeed. Harry was ashamed. " One more drink then," he said to cover up. " One more, and just one, and so on. That's my trouble, except lately on this tiger job."

" Much ? "

" A bottle a day for a year or two. Steady, private, as opposed to secret, soaking."

" Wife trouble ? You told Christian you were divorced."

Husbands and wives, the private-detective teams comparing cosy notes. " That started it, perhaps. How do things start ? "

" I often think how lucky I am."

" You are," said Harry, " and so is Christian. *Schlanch!* "

" *Skol!* " It was their old toast, drinking hooch in prison when he got drunk but Desmond never did. Some of those days were the best days of his life, more real and sordidly simple and beauti-fully nightmarish than any days before or since. He drank to the

Tanners, to Bapu's Bad One, to Tara Singh that useless bugger and poltroon, to Himalayan mountains in the night, to a kaleidoscope of wire, tunnels, mud, putrefied latrine and cheerful men and hunched men. He drank to everything. This was positively his last.

They discussed the maneater situation up to date. Then Desmond said : " If you're determined to go to Ranipur to-morrow, I've got an idea. I know a wizard *jheel* about twenty miles along that road, and the duck are in. Why don't I bring the family along and we'll shoot it in the morning and have a picnic lunch ? Then you can go on to Ranipur. To-morrow's Sunday. Besides, I need a change from dear old Bondha. In fact I've absolutely had these labour squabbles. It's a red-hot shoot—pintail, mallard, teal. We can't make an early start very well, with Michael. Meet at the resthouse say at seven. All right ? " Mad keen.

Half a day would make no difference, and one more time to say good-bye would make no difference. Nothing much made any difference. " All right," he said. " Let's do that."

And here was Christian, changed for dinner. Desmond jumped up, clipped her round the waist and waltzed her down the veranda, back again. " Wife," he said. " You're on a picnic at dawn to-morrow. Get cracking about food."

She stared at him. " Darling ! What's got into you ? You haven't done a thing like that to me for years."

" I know," he said. " But I haven't seen old Harry Black for years."

Christian Tanner smiled at Harry. *Dear Harry Black*, she said but did not say. *Thank you for making him so happy.*

" Home for me," he said, and said good night to Michael in his bed, and went. He thought he had done well for once. The whisky died in him along the road to Rimli.

> Nur wer die Sehnsucht kennt,
> Weisz was ich leide !
> Allein und abgetrennt
> Von aller Freude.

There is no company for me.

c

CHAPTER SEVEN

HE SAT on the lip of the veranda, drinking tea. The sun was not yet above the Rimli hills ; the sky was a good clear blue ; the forest was a rain-washed green. It was the first Sunday in the month of February, and birds were singing. The bloody little birdies sang for joy or love or something. Dew made an infinity of spectrums in that open place below him. The grass tops swayed to a slow, eccentric passage. He supposed it would be a pig, rootle-rootle busy pig.

He would like to hear the bell of a small church where he might go alone. *Come, Harry, my son, and I will tell you of peace and understanding*.

But there was no such peal for him. Only his doom bells pealed this Sunday morning. *What is the point ?* they said to him. *Why another journey on the road to nowhere ?*

His first Sunday memories were of an Indian cantonment church, creaking and crammed with giant soldiers. His nose still carried that smell in retrospect—of musty church, male sweat unwashed, starched khaki drill and leather. His mother saying : *Compulsory church parades are barbarous. Quite lethal to Christianity*. Which was almost sedition in that day and age. *What balderdash you talk, m'dear*, said Father, who would have been colonel, no, second-in-command then.

The years as a boy, the years as a subaltern before the war, the years as a planter since. They made nearly half his life. He would not say that he loved the place, or that he ever could belong ; but India was better known to him than England. And there was an odd thing too—that this free India was his much more than the India of the ruling days had been his India. The men waited round there for baksheesh just as their forefathers had a hundred years ago. But in theory at any rate there was a difference—they were now his fellow-men. And it was more than theory. He could not tolerate the concept of a subject race. No farm in Africa for him. No *Herrenvolk*, no *Uebermenschen*. Which was why he had bitten when Christian called him a biblical old fascist.

She might be right about him, though, where a few years ago she would have been quite wrong. He saw nothing clearly now. He saw no purpose now. He saw a hypocrisy of his authoritarian way set against his theoretical ideal. He saw a parade of bottles leading to an exit.

"The baggage is loaded," said Cheddi Khan. "The men are waiting."

Harry stood up. His leg was giving him mild gyp. He had been doing too much. He went to the front of the bungalow, where they waited below the *neem*, a graceful and useful tree, killing moths and curing sundry ills.

He owed nothing to the chokidar and sweeper, the man who brought the wood, the carrier of water, the two forest guards, the boy who grazed his buffaloes by day. All his expenses here were paid. They knew this and waited. They were lean and hungry men in varying degree, and he was an anachronism in the land of the too fat rich and the too thin poor. It would be incomprehensible to them that he had once been hungry. This, however, made him a soft touch, even among the relics of the ruddy British. This and the fact that he liked to be liked by humble people.

He paid them well. The water-carrier asked for more, and was told fluently where he could go and what he could do and why. The others laughed. He wished he could deal with himself as well as he could deal with them.

There was un-sharpness in his head, but not a headache. Gloom lay upon his guts. He looked about the Rimli enclave, a jigsaw of watercourse and forest; at parakeets, lemon-green in the early sun, flying so freely, crying so shrilly, of all birds the ones he liked most to watch, physical grace without complication. He looked up to the red rocks of the heights of Rimli. He did not want to leave this place. Each place he left now was another filament broken in the thread. *Why not?* said the strong devil to him.

Why not give up this wild-goose tiger-chasing round to Ranipur, and stay near Bondha for a week or two ? They want to see you.

He stood on the gravel turnabout before the resthouse. The men were at one side. Cheddi Khan was at the car. They all watched him. He expected that. *I say to this man, Go, and he goeth ; and to another, Come, and he cometh.*

It was ten to seven. Desmond, Christian and the boy would soon arrive. He had been so wrapped in his useless self that he had not noticed Bapu's absence. " Where is Bapu ? "

" Until now," said Cheddi Khan. " Until now Bapu has not come."

He had told Bapu that they would leave at seven, an hour after the rising of the sun. It was not time yet.

He heard a sound. He swung instantly to listen. Could it be ? He ran dot-and-carry-one to the side of the resthouse where he had drunk his second mug of tea. The sound came from beyond that open place where dew was drying now upon the grass and where he thought a pig had rootled. It was a stridor, a frenetic clash of human voices, a high male jabber. " Rifles, Cheddi ! " he called back. But his true henchman, Cheddi Khan, had both rifle cases out of the car already.

He had heard that sound a good many times. Its tune was as unmistakable as " God Save the Queen." " Calamity " was its tune.

What lay over there ? A large *rao*, a lesser large one, a lopped herring-bone of small nullahs draining the plains-thrusting ridge. In the eye of his mind the setting was accurately mapped. He was less sure of the human cast. The grasscutter's hut well up the second *rao*, cutting *Bhabar* grass for rope—one family ? Too much to the left for this sound, he thought. The *Katha* concession ? That was more like it. The place where they axed tawny chips of *khair* wood, boiled them in pots, cooled the hellbrew or broth extraction for khaki dye and for the red mouth-staining stuff that Indians chewed with pan. He had watched the interminable chipping of the logs, the boiling, the cooling to a jellied glue. It was an interesting wasteless enterprise, since they used the enervated chips for fuel.

Several families lived there in shacks within a tiger palisade, a sort of zareba of pointed stakes, more like darkest Africa, not that he had been to darkest Africa. It showed practical resource, which was a thing that he admired. With the gate shut it was undoubtedly tiger-proof. The *Katha* people slept securely. But they had to go down to the *rao* for water. He knew also that they relieved themselves outside. He had observed the crouching men and women at all India's fashionable hour of dawn, and he had thought : Now if I was a maneating tiger, I would put this place on my superduper priority list. The Maginot line, the tiger palisade. He had spoken about it too. But the elder had replied : *Your Honour, we are too many people in this small place. And it is six weeks since the last killing.* Come what may. Better a risk than the defilement of a communal latrine.

" Glasses, Cheddi ! " He saw them now. He put up his binoculars. A good deductive guess—they were the *Katha* people, six men shouting as they ran.

Bapu ? Where the hell was Bapu ?

They were coming across the open place, not sensibly in single file, letting a leader break trail through grass, but all anyhow, hugger-mugger.

He distinguished a word in the torrent of words: *Mara.* Killed. He saw the pig break out. He had been right in thinking it was a pig. He was suspicious of being right too often. They straggled up the rise. They arrived and flung themselves in all but the literal sense upon him. Six men, including a well-built youth with a baby in his arms, a naked boy. The child howled ; the men gabbled ; this youth alone was silent, his heart fluttering the sleek skin of his chest. He wore a vacuous half-smile like the village idiot on a bus excursion. Six and an infant, making the lucky number seven.

" Be silent ! " he commanded. He pointed his finger at the man among them. " Speak, thou ! "

It was the wife and mother of the youth and baby. She had given him the child, and she had gone to the *rao* at break of day. Others had seen her move apart, to the first corner where the bank jutted. She was a modest woman. She was a modest, young,

obedient wife. The sahib might know the place ? Yes, he knew it.
She had not come back to feed her baby, and in a while her husband
called because it was time for him to start the chipping of the *khair*
wood. No answer.

So on from there. It was the perfect, inevitable story, the thing
that happens with a pattern so neat that you know afterwards it
was bound to happen. There was even this additional adornment :
that Harry had observed the modest woman. He had observed her
with a male eye the other day because she was the young and
comely wench. She watched him, and she bared her left breast
and held it in her left hand for the small seeking mouth. *I am
woman*, she had told him not modestly and not immodestly. *See
me, man, black or brown or white or yellow. I bring you forth and I
take you in.*

He remembered this now. He had an absurd trick of remembering things and linking them with Harry Black as Jonah. What
was one comely girl in a couple of hundred million females ? But
it pained him to know of youth cut off. The whole sordid maneating melodrama pained him. He was offended also by an atavistic
stirring. The Incas were not so long ago.

They had found the place, and they had found the beginnings
of the trail. Had they followed ? A chorus again, excluding the
young husband, who now began to weep. He wept, and his wife's
baby wailed. No, they had not followed. They had been afraid.
How could they, defenceless, save her ? It was already too late.
They had come running for the sahib.

He was thinking in a hurry. He let the vociferous tide roll on.
But, of a sudden, it had stopped. The electric hush was as positive
as the chatter had just been. Even the adult weeping ceased. Bapu
came running down the low ridge astride which the resthouse
stood.

" Oh, sahib," he panted, " the Bad One is still at Rimli. I
have found fresh tracks crossing from here to there." He made his
graceful waving gesture, north-west to south-east across the upper
forest.

They all stared at Bapu—these men, and the men Harry had

lately paid. There was a curious quality of fear and fascination in their faces, as the rabbit might stare at the dancing weasel. Bapu had again been absent at a killing time.

"Oh, brother," Harry said with evident affection. "There is sorrow. The Bad One has killed a woman of the *Katha* people." He turned to the others. "I blame myself for this. If I had heeded the words of Bapu that the Bad One was still at Rimli, I would have been out this morning early and I might have saved the woman." Nonsense, chances thousands to one against. "Is this not so, Cheddi Khan?"

Cheddi Khan inclined his head. He had immense dignity and presence. "It is so, Your Honour."

It was the best that Harry could do. They might be making a wicked shaitan out of Bapu, but he knew also that they made a fabulous figure out of Harry Black—the lame one, the hot one, the one who made them laugh, the one whose curses sang. He was under no falsely-modest illusions about that.

Yet now again he felt that there was something up Bapu's tattered sleeve.

"Sahib, we must make haste," said Bapu.

Which was well spoken, for this was the rare chance of being early on the scene. The girl had been killed since six, and it was now just seven.

"Which way would the Bad One go?" he asked him, taking rounds from Cheddi Khan and slipping them one by one into five stitched recesses in his shirt.

"The Bad One has not killed at the *Katha* place before. I do not know, sahib. But it will not have crossed the wide *rao* back to this side. If it has gone down, the chance is bad." By down, he meant in the plains direction. "If it has climbed below the ridge, the chance is better."

Which was what Harry himself was thinking. Pin the brute down, that was the problem. Corner it, the near impossibility. If it had carried its victim up left below the horseshoe ridge, there was a chance. If . . .

"Cheddi! Give me the Barking Dogs."

Cheddi smiled and brought the fireworks.

The forgotten Tanner family now arrived. They romped briskly up in their sugar-factory Landrover. " Sorry if we're slightly late," said Desmond. " You know what these women . . ." He took the situation in.

Harry thought instantly : I hope to God he hasn't brought his rifle. This was not a reflection on Desmond Tanner, but simply that there had been only two men in Harry's life whose partnership he welcomed on these particular occasions. They were perhaps not better men than many other men. They knew their stuff calmly from an immense experience. " I'm afraid you'll have to count me out of the ducks to-day," he said. " A woman has just been killed."

Young Michael's mouth fell open. Christian covered hers with her brown slim hand. Shock. Everybody hit by the horrible shock of a horrible expectancy come true. She was staring at him. There was more in her face than that. She looked as if she now, later in the proceedings, felt what he had felt from his waking this morning with something besides slight whiskyfied remorse. His Dostoievsky bells of doom ; the thing working out so pat ; the too perfect opening to the story. Pop ! Here were the Tanners too, and the pattern gathered, and the rest of the tale to be enacted.

But Desmond was speaking. He knew, of course, what Desmond said : " The ducks can count me out as well, old boy. I brought my double rifle. I'll come along."

" Oh, darling, please don't go."

" I'll do the job alone," said Harry. " I always do."

Desmond jumped out. He stood with his back to them in the car, looking down at Harry. He was a good deal taller. " Come on, Harry," he said. " I'd like to."

" I tell you what would be a great help. Could you go to the Pass of Rimli and cover that ? "

" The tiger would never cross by day. There's too much open ground up there."

" It did cross once by day."

" Yes, but a battalion drove it. That's so, Harry, isn't it ? "

" Probably," he admitted. True enough, it wouldn't.

" Look, Harry," said Desmond. " Let me come." He did not seem excited. He seemed cool and determined. But what he was saying was this : *Let me come, my friend. I must prove myself again to you.*

Harry's sensibility told him that, and his sensibility told him that here was a thing he could not deny to the man who was his friend. Vanity, vanity, but all is not vanity in the battle.

" All right," he said. " Have it your own way."

Desmond went for his rifle. Christian took his place. She put that blasted exquisite kind hand on Harry's hairy arm, and said : " Please, Harry, couldn't you stop him ? I've had the most awful hunchy feeling ever since I woke. I don't know what. Couldn't you, Harry, please ? "

His mind worked fast and true, as always in emergency. He could not stop Desmond, and he could not explain the trivial why to Desmond's wife, not the only one with hunchy feelings. " Look, Christian," he said. " I'm not old Desmond's keeper." Meaning it well, he said it roughly.

" No," she said, " you're not anybody's keeper. You use people, that's all, don't you, to suit your domineering self."

" Many thanks," he said. He turned his back on Christian Tanner.

The Landrover had been unloaded. Cheddi Khan was the rare one who thought essentials out and did them. The tent, the bedding rolls, the lamps, the tiger skin, the pots and pans and other junk were strewn about. Cheddi and Bapu sat in the back with rifles. He could do with one more if it was to be a large-scale party. " Come with us, brother," he said to the dapper one of the forest guards, " and give us loving comfort."

They laughed immoderately and incongruously at his tight little joke. He got in. Desmond sat beside him, long legs arranged, and the door slammed with a tinny aluminium clank.

" Good luck, Plain Harry," said Michael at his window. " And Daddy."

"Dear boy," he said.   He raised his hand to Christian, who stood away.   Her lips said something.

*   *   *   *   *

He might have used the elephant on this first level ground, for the blood trail advertised itself, and the *Kans* grass was uncomfortably tall.   Grass was the nightmare of this business.   But when he decided yesterday to move to Ranipur, he had sent her along the D.F.O.'s camp ten miles away.   No elephant.

They went in single file, Harry first, Bapu, Cheddi with the single rifle, Forest Guard, Desmond.   *I lead,* he had told them. *Or Bapu leads.   The front is mine.   Bapu's work is to track only.   Cheddi Khan will watch the left.   You, the right.   Tanner Sahib is to protect our backs.   Whichever of us sees urgent danger, says: Left, Right, Front, Behind.   We halt* ek dam, *immediately.   Is it understood ?   If suspicion only, touch the man in front, stop, do not speak.   Is it understood ?   Silence and stillness are our weapons also.   Is it understood ?*

It was understood.   The five of them moved as an unconventionally bunched army, whose strength lay in concert.   This was a tentative stage, when he could make use of men.   Later, given the right kind of later, he would work alone.

Their passage made a rustling swish.   There were indications that the tiger carried its victim by her waist.   It had not stopped to feed.

The grass was less high and less thick now.   The trail ran fairly straight for the horseshoe ridge, which rose a hundred yards ahead. There the tiger would stop, or it would turn left in the hills direction, or it would turn right in the plains direction.   There was need for greater caution.   Where it must stop or turn, it might also circle.

They had come a mile or so.   The day was warming up.   It would be every day a little bit warmer into the hot weather from now on.   So said the Coppersmith, the small green barbet bird, tonking metal up some tree.   Soon it would tonk monotonously all day.   Now it tonked for a while, and stopped, and was rather annoying not to tonk again.

Harry saw the woman's garment, a length of terracotta cotton.

It made a pretty splash of colour against green *Barsh* bushes with white flowers. He stopped. Bapu stepped up beside him. They were two highly expert pairs of eyes and ears, detecting nothing.

It was open this side of the *Barsh* bushes, no trees and no grass, a patch of rain-pitted sun-hard *muttee*. He went on. The rifle was getting heavy. His senses were sharp, not quite so sharp as they should have been.

The terracotta cloth had darker stains. The tiger had eaten a little here. Black hairs were about the place. It was a dirty, disgusting business that he hated. Yet he did it to assuage his demons, he supposed. He hated this degradation of humanity. Yet he was one who thought that man's failure was due to man setting himself apart from the animal creation. Christianity taught that, or formal Christianity at any rate. I must read what Christ Himself said, Harry thought, taking a breather beside the woman's garment. I'm confused in everything I think.

But he was not confused in what he thought about the job in hand. He saw that the tiger had gone left, the better way, where there was a possibility of forcing an encounter. He looked the others over now. Bapu was all right. Cheddi Khan was perfectly all right. The forest guard was not. You never could tell until you tried people out. The forest guard had given half a dozen jittery warnings. Desmond took a long swig from his water bottle, then handed it to Harry. He was thirsty too. He washed his mouth out and took one sip. Desmond looked fine, sweating a bit, but the atmosphere was sweaty.

"I think I remember this," he said in Harry's ear. "If the tiger follows along the bottom of the ridge, it comes to a dead end, doesn't it, where the hill and the nullah come together?"

Harry nodded. "Yes, but there are several places where it can break left, in fact anywhere between here and there. What about this bag of wind? I'd better get rid of him, don't you think?"

"I would." They were the old firm again from days before.

"Climb this tree and watch," he told the forest guard. "Make no sound unless you see the tiger. Do not move." Spared the man's self-respect for later on. He shinned up without regard for his well-pressed khaki suit.

"I will move fast on open ground," Harry told the others. He must reach the tiger before the tiger finished eating. Boldness and caution, these were the arms of a delicate balance.

*   *   *   *   *

Bapu nodded. He and Harry went back to the others. For a long way there had been no blood to follow. But there had been Bapu's uncanny skill, which was an endowment rather than a skill, questing about like a sober hound, no fear in his mind, nothing in his mind but this. "Sahib," he whispered now, "if the Bad One has not gone into the nullah, the Bad One must be there."

It might have dropped into the ravine, but Harry thought not.

Here it was. Here was the classic case of a maneater brought to bay. He had not liked the too perfect unfolding of this story; he was wary of things perfect. But he saw now that it was all right. He saw now that the perfect beginning was made for the perfect and inevitable climax.

The ridge swung forward on the right, a vertical barrier leading round and on and up to the Pass of Rimli a mile away and a thousand feet above. One impassable flank. The nullah or ravine curved in below them from the left. It was twenty feet wide and deep, and the walls were sheer. The ravine swung in to merge with the ridge itself a hundred yards ahead. The tracks of the Rimli maneater, and the occasional arm or leg scuffings of its burden, led into the convergence of ravine and ridge. This was a narrowing plateau, ridge to the right, nullah to the left, blunt-nosed at the very end or apex. It was mixed cover on there— bushes, rocks, grass, a few trees—adequate cover and sequestered. The tiger might have jumped down into the ravine and gone farther, for there was a widening to jungle up beyond the corner. But Harry did not think so. He thought the tiger was hungry for its meal. He thought it was probably now feeding in that scrub, which was not truly a cul-de-sac. He decided what to do.

"If you're going to use your whizzbangs, hadn't we better

make sure first that it hasn't gone on by the ravine ? If it has, and it hears those things, we'll never get a second chance."

True. Desmond was always sound, providing the checks if not the inspiration. Which was why they had been so strong a team. He did not think it had done that, but perhaps he should find out. A sandy bottom to the ravine—he could move in almost dead silence below the wall and muffled by it. Five minutes there and back.

He smiled at Desmond, pleased with him. "Okay, I'll go and see. Call if you see any movement. But whatever you do, don't shoot into that nullah. I don't want your bullets up my backside, Tanner."

Desmond guffawed without a sound, like his old self ten years older and a stronger-looking chap. "Let me go !"

He shook his head, went back to a gully, down into the ravine. Careful, vulnerable stalk along below the wall. Tracking was not a problem if it had jumped from that height. Any child could see the marks. None. But over and down to him came the uninhibited sounds of a tiger at its meal. They used to have crazes on words at school. Grisly was the fashionable adjective one year. Everything was absolutely grisly, my dear chap, too unutterably grizzle-grisly. Mission completed. He had been right and Desmond wrong, but no harm done.

Barking Dogs were things used not in the grisly days, but farther back than that. They were what you let loose in a crowd at your private school. They did not make the one glorious bang of a Thunder-Flash. They darted about the ground from lesser bang to bang, about ten in all, worrying people's ankles. They were wonderful erratic spreaders of confusion and alarm.

He had had adequate ersatz Barking Dogs made for him by fireworks people in Calcutta. He used them occasionally in situations such as this. He had shown Bapu how to light the fuse and throw them. Bapu had been entranced.

Bapu looked along the cliff face now. "Yes, sahib, I can go there. But a stone might fall."

"*Kuch fikr nahin.* It does not matter. Thou wilt not go till we are in position." He gave him three Barking Dogs and a box of matches. Bapu's hands did not shake at all. Thank God for wonderful old Bapu.

The plateau was not on one level, but on two. The upper shelf was flat against the cliff, and was divided from the lower by a drop of six feet or so. Thus, two terraces running to the broken scrub where Harry now positively knew the tiger lay. There was this difference of height, and also a difference of vegetation—for the upper terrace was bare and rocky, the lower patched with grass and bushes.

" I think one of two things will happen. Either it will break down into the ravine and go on that way, or it will break straight back this way on the lower level. I don't think it will come along the top. . . ."

" Why not ? "

" Because there's no cover, and because that flank is closed by the hill. They like freedom of action, choice of direction, same as you do. Now here's the plan." He changed into Hindustani, their *lingua franca*. He himself was fluent in half a dozen tongues of the hills and plains of north-east India, including Bapu's *jungli bhat*. " Tanner Sahib and I will go forward together. He will stand at that tall rock. He will be guard of the higher level. I will stand close above the ravine, and I will be guard of the lower level, and I will be guard of the ravine. Cheddi Khan, if he is not too fat a man, will climb this tree."

" Sahib, I can climb this or any tree, but I will come with you." Cheddi Khan was not amused.

" I have given the order."

" Sahib, it is my pride always to hold the small gun at your side."

Oh, damn the pride of all you people. But he gave way to Cheddi Khan. He might need the three-eighteen.

" Look, Desmond," in English again. " Don't fire too soon. It will be forty yards from you when it first breaks out. Wait. Above all, don't fire unless it's committed to the upper level, that is, unless it's going to stay on the upper level."

" You've just said it won't come on the upper level."

" It might. You never know what the sods will do." Nor you did, but he was putting Desmond in the most unlikely place in the lee of a rock. He was doing as well as he reasonably could by Desmond and by Desmond's wife.

One last thing : " Bapu, drop the Barking Dog close below thee at the bottom of the cliff. Do not throw. Is it understood ? " The higher the Barking Dog went bang, the lower the tiger would be driven.

He and Desmond and Cheddi Khan went forward. He put Desmond into place. He glanced at him. Old Desmond was all right, jaw muscles flexing as they used to, he remembered. He was glad that Desmond had come along.

He went down with Cheddi to his own place above the wall of the ravine. He put Cheddi into a cleft of rock beside him. Cheddi had nothing to do except change rifles in emergency, which he could do as calmly and slickly as any loader at a pheasant shoot in Norfolk. Cheddi was a stout chap with a brood of sons near Rawalpindi, a good rogue of a man's man and maker of small Cheddis.

Harry had thirty yards clear ahead. He had an excellent view left into the ravine and on. Desmond was behind and above him on the right. There was thick bush cover between him and the step to the upper level where Desmond waited at his tall rock, a thing like an obelisk or plinth. Clear to the left, clear in front, clear to the right. Blind spot half-right behind. As good as he could hope for. *A brilliant and intransigent officer*, they said in his Staff College report.

No movement and no sound in the dense cover at the head of the terraced plateau. Harry raised his hand.

He did not watch Bapu clamber up the rock face of the ridge. He looked straight ahead. If that animal saw Bapu, it might break before any persuasion of Barking Dogs. There was no unsharpness in him now. The fluid tension was all over and through him. You know, he thought, I never thought of it before. But this tiger is the last one I shall ever shoot.

The blackbird sings to him, " Brother, brother,
If this be the last song you shall sing,
Sing well, for you may not sing another ;
Brother, sing."

Now Bapu came into the field of his right eye. Bapu was goating it along a ledge. He was nearly there. He had stopped.

The air was so still that Harry heard the sizzle of the match. The toss of a hand, the feather of smoke over and down in parabola. But it had not reached the ground ; the smoke shivered up from the top of a bush. That was a pity. Barking Dogs could jump a longish airborne way. Their proper function was to chivy hocks and ankles.

The Barking Dog went off. It flew up and over, clear to the ravine side of the cover, reached ground this time, harried back— bang and petty bang and pester towards the cliff where Bapu stood.

Wrong, wrong, very bad. As the Barking Dog stopped barking, Harry's bells of doom pealed loudly now again.

Bapu called. He saw the tiger's head. It was making for him diagonally from the upper level. It was coming down, as he had said it would. It was breaking fast, not charging. Good, after all.

But Desmond fired. He saw the strike, a miss. Too long a shot—precisely what he told him not to do. The tiger switched direction into a full gallop, into a charge. The second shot crashed in this loud place, but the tiger did not falter as it moved out of sight.

He knew that Desmond could not reload.

" Round the rock ! " he shouted, and kept on shouting. Round the rock. Round and round the rugged rock . . .

Desmond ducked to this side.

Harry was shouting at the tiger. He saw the tiger for too small a fraction of a second to get in a shot. It spun at the rock. He had captured its attention. It saw him from up there down to here. Desmond had skipped to the other side.

The tiger's face and jaws were in a sanguinary mess, he noticed as it sprang down for him. He fired twice blindly into the heaving scrub, and the tiger came.

PRELUDE

CHAPTER EIGHT

In 1938

"I would like to have seen you wild and young and carefree."

HE SLUICED water over his hot head and down his neck. He got on to Abdul for the last chukker.

"You're not sticking close enough to Tickell," said the Colonel. "Ride him, Harry, ride him, understand me, boy?"

"Yessir." He had done nothing but try to ride Tickell since the game began.

Tickell was coming out now on the famous Jet, a black pony with a white sheepskin saddle, Tickell and Jet having a canter in a local tournament. Pray, Colonel, my revered C.O., tell me how the hell I can compete with Tickell with a handicap of seven on a damned great thoroughbred of fifteen-three. My handicap is nought, my Abdul fourteen-three. They have the legs of us, the skill of us, the height and weight of us, they do not even notice us.

"Come on, Abdul," Harry said to Abdul's ears, which flicked, one, the other; then both lay back. Abdul gave his preliminary buck and settled, hot up to the bit. They cantered to the centre.

Harry, One; Rabat, Two; Jumbo Cotter, Three; the Colonel, Back. They were a scratch side, all Regimental except Rabat, Indian Army doing his year's attachment. Rabat was a Rajput and a player. They had five goals start on handicap, but had not scored, still hanging on at five to four.

Harry was tired and sticky-sweaty in his saddle. There was a wonderful good-tempered fury in him, playing the game of games, even if he was only Number One : *Get off the ball, boy! Ride him, ride him, can't you hear me?*

The opposing One took it neatly at the throw-in, broke away, and Harry turned for Tickell, who played Back. But Tickell and

Jet were half-way down the ground—one smack, dribble-dribble, smack again, consummate arrogance and ease, a goal. Tickell tittupped up a little way amid applause. He patted Jet. They were having fun. Five-all. Change ends.

" Mark him, Harry ! How many more times do I have to tell you ? "

This time Harry connected from a clash of sticks, and was away along the sideline. " Go ! " from Rabat. " Leave it ! " yelled the Colonel. He left it. He saw Tickell lying back, Tickell and Jet waiting perfectly collected.

He and staunch Abdul came in hard. Tickell's left elbow happened at that moment to jut out. Harry met the elbow with his head. " Elbows ! "

" Watch your own," the lordly Tickell said.

Harry did his best to plague the man—head, shoulder, elbow, arm, knee and toe. Then he hooked Tickell's stick across the pony, not seen by umpires. " Don't foul me, damn you," Tickell grunted. He brushed Harry and Abdul off like irritating flies, and broke back to save the goal.

" That's more like it," cried the Colonel. " Ride him ! "

Oh, to be a Number Two, a glory boy, a scoring boy, not a wretched *ride him, boy*.

The ball moved diagonally left across the centre of the ground ; the opposing Two was on it. Would he tap it round the harder way, right-handed ? Would he try the other thing—draw the game over there, then a back-hander, a pass clear across to Tickell ?

Tickell broke from him again. Now was the chance—before Tickell's miraculous anticipation told him half a second early where to gallop. For a disinterested and knowledgeable party, it was a delight to see the man gather a pony and be gone—delightful because there was nothing much to see, no handle-pumping, no flogging heels. The back hunched a little more, the cream-silked buttocks thrust yet deeper in the plate, and that was all. The aids of hand and thigh and knee and lower leg and weight were not apparent. It was the fluid art of horsemanship, the lovely sailing ship of horse and man.

The number Two had not yet shown his purpose. He would swing right to the ball, or left—left for the back-hand pass to Tickell. But by the time Harry could see what he would do, Tickell and Jet would have departed with the familiar dry tattoo of hooves, the familiar offering of dust, the familiar backside view.

Tickell was looking over left. Harry came in from the other side. He came in with desperation at a quarter angle and a gallop. Here's a bump you won't forget.

Tickell and Jet—the best of all his ponies—were teetering on the brink of motion. Tickell did not appear to turn his head. It happened, however, somehow, at the last moment, that Tickell's shoulder dropped, that he and Jet passaged fast in this direction.

The bumper was well bumped, arsey-tarsey on to hard Indian ground, helmet bashed and a scraped shoulder, nothing much. The whistle blew. Harry got up. Poor Abdul stood again. He swayed and trembled. Harry, arms akimbo, glared at Tickell.

" You asked for that," the awful Tickell said. " Next time I'll hurt you."

"Don't stand there like a washerwoman," screamed the Colonel. " Abdul's winded. Get on Myrtle."

Now the Colonel's Myrtle was another story. She had been a racehorse in her youth, a winner as a two-year-old, an acceptance, so the legend had it, for the Thousand Guineas. But Myrtle had refused to start in her one and only classic race. Neither the fire hose nor any other stratagem had persuaded her to start again. The Colonel had bought her for next to nothing and had shipped her out. Now, aged eight, she was a perfect hack, as gentle as an Arab. She played slow chukkers beautifully. Myrtle hated racing, but she did love polo. She was controllable in fast chukkers for about a minute. There was an unwilling grandeur, after that, in being wafted across the open spaces by an ex-potential winner of the Thousand Guineas. She did not run away. She would circle as tightly as she could, and launch herself like a torpedo into a slow convoy.

A bare two minutes left. Harry's blood was high. He would, and could, ride Myrtle to the moon and back. His Colonel, who played games to win, was right in putting him on Myrtle. But through the blind all-daring polo heat, he felt a nuance of foreboding.

Myrtle started like a lamb. The Colonel struck the ball far up. " Take it, Harry ! "

Harry rode a ring round Jet. This was the life, ten thousand times the life. But he missed the goal. " Sorry," he said. " Sorry, Myrtle. Steady, girl." He sat back, closed his legs, played a light one-handed tune, and Myrtle gathered underneath him on her hocks. She always stopped the first time. She stopped so perfectly according to the book that the miracle must surely happen now at last this afternoon, and Myrtle play a model chukker out.

The score was five-all, a minute or so left to go. Tickell made to hit one of the head-high drives that were his unstoppable speciality ; instead, he flicked the ball to his Three who took it and was off, and the game streaked up the ground. Harry closed with Tickell.

The miracle had not occurred. Myrtle was taking charge. But she knew what to do and did it like a demon. Harry and Myrtle rode Tickell and Jet on less unequal terms. Crowd him, knee behind his, and pester him so that if Tickell broke, he must break in a full circle the wrong way round, thus losing distance.

Tickell did break now, with a deft and dirty whipstroke on Myrtle's quarters, and was gone.

" Take it, Harry ! "

Myrtle had seen the ball, saved and struck by Jumbo, the white ball rolling to a stop and sitting pretty now, well up the ground. Myrtle swung of her own wild will, and she was into her stride, her float away, fly away, *ventre à terre* and hardly touching.

But it was a race, for Tickell was ahead and coming in the other way. Both converging, neither of them had the line ; and one must yield. Tickell did not yield, least of all to a pipsqueak with a handicap of nought.

" Come on, girl ! " Harry murmured on Myrtle's neck. But neither encouragement nor dissuasion could influence Myrtle. She had the bit. They passed under the very nose of Jet, and

Tickell had yielded finally, enough to save himself and his ten thousand rupee pony. Harry connected on the near side ; the ball flew on ahead ; the angry shouts fell off behind. " Take time, Harry."

Harry struck again. Now he and Myrtle and the ball were lined directly for the goal. *Take time!* Here with the sun and the warm good wind and the Colonel's wonderful mad Myrtle and the goal before him, racing widely to him. " Steady, Myrtle."

His two-handed heavings were a waste of strength ; his *Steady, Myrtle*, was a waste of breath. Myrtle saw the ball bumping to a stop between the posts, five yards or so this side.

Harry did not try to hit it. He leaned over to tap underhand. He only had to touch the ball, and the goal was his, and the game as good as over.

Air shot. Complete, humiliating miss. He heard derisive laughter from the sidelines. Myrtle was starting a long left-handed circle back into the fray. He looked round to see Rabat score. The whistle blew. The bugle sounded. They had won the tournament.

But men and ponies were not walking slowly to their syces. They stood in the middle of the ground. Myrtle had no movement to break in upon. She stopped, blowing easily, just breaking to a sweat.

Tickell was giving the umpires hell. " A deliberate cross ! I've never been fouled as flagrantly as that ! "

" Nonsense ! " from the Colonel. " Black was on the line. His pony had the legs of yours. They got there first. What are you making a fuss about ? "

The umpires muttered to one another.

" That young fool's a public danger," Tickell growled. " I'll ride him down another time, by God I will." He turned and came away. He looked at Harry. His right eyelid drooped.

" Sorry," Harry said. " I was being carted."

" Game's over," the umpire said to Tickell. " Besides Black was nearer the line, if anything. But Colonel, that pony is a menace. I don't think you ought to play Myrtle in fast polo."

" All right," the Colonel said. Such a last-minute temptation would not occur again, for the Battalion was sailing homeward in a fortnight. The Colonel had used his wits to win his last tournament in India, which meant the last tournament of a long polo-playing life.

" Oh, Harry, you did so well," the exalted lady said, presenting him with his replica of the cup. " You stuck to Major Tickell like a limpet."

" Stick to me like a limpet," boomed Jumbo out of earshot. " I'm still the same friendly girl deep down inside."

There was the falling coolness of a January evening. There were rumours of the city of Calcutta ; but the ancient stench, the named and nameless hordes, the beggars and the bulls were far from here. Harry was thirsty, sweated clean and tired, and this afternoon was over, but to-night, to-morrow, all the promise of the world was golden. He drank fresh lime. He fed juggery, coarse sugar, to Abdul and his other pony. Abdul was all right again. He had had offers from reasonable people for them both. He walked along in the good smells of horse's sweat and saddle soap to speak to Myrtle.

" Are you selling Myrtle, sir ? " he asked. He thought he would probably forget all the ponies except Myrtle.

" I'm giving her to Angus Sherwood," said the Colonel.

" Oh, I'm glad."

The Colonel's face and neck were vivid as a monsoon sunset. His moustaches bristled out and up in affable ferocity, his olympian majesty the Colonel. " Dunno what yer father would have said about me puttin' you on Myrtle. Worked, though. I'm dining at the club. D'you want to come ? "

" That's very kind of you," said Harry. Dinner at the Bengal Club with this old bachelor and *bon viveur* meant good food, wine and entertainment. " But I'm afraid I'm going to Firpo's with the others—also Desmond Tanner, do you know him ? "

" The box wallah. Yes, a nice boy."

" You wouldn't like to come, sir, I suppose ? " For God's sake don't, he thought.

"Certainly not," the Colonel said. "I have no wish to wear lamb's clothing in your company, my boy." But he smiled tightly to indicate that he was pleased at being asked. "You have a celebrating air about you. Watch your step now. Understand me, Harry?"

"Yessir." It had been a troubled winter, off and on. "The four of us are dining quietly, no poodlefaking, Colonel."

"All the more chance of getting into mischief. But I'm glad to hear it. Tea-dances, good God Almighty! When I was a subaltern we didn't waste time messin' about with a lot of women at a tea-dance." Now he sounded Blimpish, which he was far from being.

"It wasn't a tea-dance, Colonel. It was drinks and dancing, more respectable, sir, don't you think?" The Colonel had a bee in his bonnet about one before-dinner dance sundry subalterns had once attended.

"Not a damned bit of difference. I never attended such a puking function in my life."

"You were different, though. You were tougher chaps in those days, weren't you, Colonel? I mean my father always says this generation is a namby-pamby pussyfootin' lot, don't you agree? My father says he in his young days and you in yours—he says nobody ever wasted time on women. Life had better things to offer. That was so, sir, was it not, in your experience?"

The Colonel turned away. "Get out!" he said.

Harry left his lady-loving and unfathomably-never-poodle-faking Colonel. His Colonel ruled the battalion with irascible benevolence, with tolerance for knaves but not for bores. He was a lazy man with brains and means and one ambition—to command —and that was satisfied.

*   *   *   *   *

The cabaret was juggling. They juggled knives and plates and multi-coloured hoops and billiard cues and curlicues. The man rode a monocycle to and fro about the dance floor, juggling again. His partner was a pleasing girl, considering. She rode the juggler's shoulders, and the juggler rode the cycle, and they juggled up and down to one another back and forwards on the move with Slavic cries, with pleasure and abandon. There were encores.

Dancing began again upstairs at Firpo's. It was crowded. Jumbo took the magnum from the bucket, filled his glass and passed it on. " Jugglers are such happy people," Jumbo said morosely. " I might have had a juggling girl to juggle with at all hours, but I never learned to juggle."

Desmond laughed and Harry laughed. Rabat laughed and frowned in pleased perplexity.

" What's happened, Jumbo ? Have the lovely jugglers made you sad ? "

" Just a bit," he said. " A tiny dagger of the *Might-have-been*. But there is a broadsword in my bleeding heart. It is the broadsword of the *Soon-must-lose*."

" The broadsword of the *Soon-must-lose* ? "

" Soon must lose my elephants," he said. He closed his eyes. A tear rolled down each cheek, two veritable tears. " God, how I love those beasts of mine."

" I know, Jumbo. I think I understand. But Rabat and Desmond haven't heard about your elephants. Could you bear to tell them ? "

Jumbo wiped his eyes. He was a large-boned officer, and fat. He overflowed his chair, like Castlerosse. He took champagne. " Common oafs," he said. " How would they have heard ? But yes, I will relate the sorrow of the *Soon-must-lose*. You are aware, of course, that I am not an ordinary mortal, that I have in recent history held the appointment of Aide-de-Camp to a Personage. Now, many are called to be A.D.C., but few give satisfaction. That I have given satisfaction is a tribute to innumerable qualities of mind, and to one great quality of body. I have appealed to my Personage from start to finish and from top to bottom. My Personage loves his little joke. I have been his not-so-little joke. The very first day at luncheon he quizzed me down the table with that witty, kindly, pro-Consul's eye, turned to the Military Secretary and said : *Jumbo will be my A.D.C. in charge of elephants. See to that, will you ?*

"The reverent hush that hangs upon my Personage's jokes was broken by the sycophantic transports that inevitably follow. *Your Excellency*, I ventured from my humble corner, *I will do my very best. I have always longed to work with other real big jumbos.*

"So, you see, I had made a splendid start. I was grateful. I was tactful. I was colossal. I was keen. Above all, I was the sort of decent-hearted simple-minded cluck who knows a good joke when he hears one at his own expense. I ate enormously. I became the fattest officer in this skinny land. I became the best joke-object my Personage has ever had. But now my term of office has expired. My Personage will mourn me, and I shall miss him dreadfully too. Just think, after all I've seen and done, just think of me back in the dreary regimental rut, Orderly Officer, a mere subaltern on Adjutant's parade, trying to butter up my Colonel who despises corpulence and fat-boy humour. He will bully me, I know he will. He will have me skin and bone. Oh, it will be an appalling let down. But I could lose myself in the trivialities of musketry and drill. I could endure the company of eager whipper-snappers like this Black. I could come through were it not for the broadsword of the *Soon-must-lose*. I fell in love. I am in love, not once, but time and time again quite hopelessly for ever." Jumbo wept again. "I love my elephants," he added simply.

"Passionately, Jumbo?"

"Body and soul, you wretched dolt."

"How many elephants have you got?"

"All the elephants in Hindustan are mine, I feel—not those brainless lop-eared Africans, of course. But under my care at present in this Calcutta season, I have only two. They are my very special Loved-ones."

"Where are they, Jumbo?"

"At the palace of the elephants. Where else, nincompoop?"

"If we stay here any longer, the jugglers will come on again to sadden you about the *Might-have-been*. Could we make a pilgrimage to the *Soon-must-lose*?"

Jumbo finished up the magnum. He frowned, alone with jumbo thoughts while the band played "Night and Day," the hackneyed tune and still the best, and there were many dancers, and some lovers dancing. "Why not?" said Jumbo. "Yes, indeed, by all means. Khidtmatgar, waiter, varlet, bring the bill."

They paid and went downstairs and on to Chowringhee to the cars. Desmond took Jumbo, and Harry, Rabat. The beggars came. Rabat routed them with harshness. He was Indian in that. He was an Indian, after all. Some of the Indians attached to British regiments were complete flops. Rabat, during his year, had become a sort of Regimental pet. Mr. Rabbit, the troops called him with affection, and would follow him.

Harry sang "Night and Day" for the benefit of Calcutta, for the benefit of late babus who looked with hostility at him and Rabat in the open car.

"This Jumbo," Rabat said. "He is new type of Englishman to me, and very funny. Does he really weep?"

"He turns a champagne tap on," Harry said. "Jumbo is unique."

"He is sad about his elephants, and I am sad about my British friends I soon must lose."

Harry laughed. Rabat spoke peculiarly, his skin was odd, and you forgot he was an Indian. Or you remembered, wishing Indians were like Rabat.

"Will you miss your India?" He said the "your" with a hint of a Hindu little edge now suddenly for the first time.

"Polo, shooting, Mr. Rabbit, this and that and so on. Yes, of course." But Harry did not think he would miss India very much. There were new things, places, people to enjoy, with the Regiment as family and home wherever it might be, and they had won the tournament this afternoon, and he had done well, he thought in private, competing with that fellow Tickell, and he did not feel like going to bed at all to-night, or not to sleep. Surely slap-happy *cooch-parwanee* Rabat was not a Congress Wallah.

"I tell you one thing, Harry," Rabat said. "This year with the Battalion has been strange for me. Into Saturday Club and Bengal Club I am not allowed, but with you people I have been a very special Wog belonging to the family."

" Woggy, wog ! " he said. " Come off it, Rabat. You've had too much champagne."

" Enough," said Rabat. " Not too much. No, Harry, it is just that you have all been good to me, and I am Woggy-wog, a human being, not a Wog, and I have seen the English as Indians do not see them, and now I am rather English too, so now what am I ? "

" I don't quite understand." He did, in fact.

" You are very intelligent, and you hardly ever think. Why not ? Because you are young, of course, but mostly because you are a pukka British sahib and sure of yourself and protected by the Regiment, and you do not have to think. I am intelligent and almost sure of myself with you people as a semi-English Mr. Rabbit, but I am not sure of myself really as Indian at heart, and so I must be thinking all the time beneath, not belonging to anybody quite, and not agreeing with my emancipated sister who hates all English guts."

" Does she ? Why ? Are we so awful ? "

Rabat rolled about the seat with laughter. " Awfully wonderful ! Particularly British Army people of crack regiments. India is what you call your oyster for fun and games, and you don't pretend like Indian Army and I.C.S. that you want us to be Indianized or have self-rule. You simply are not interested. It is of not the least importance. I like that very much."

" But surely they want you to have self-rule—eventually, I mean."

" That we do not believe. Now you are thinking : *What a bore old Rabat is.* Well, I am boring this once to you and not again because you are the one who took me under wing from the first day, and this year has been the best time of my life for which I am truly grateful, and I thank you sadly for appalling fate of almost understanding British point of view." Rabat laughed again. He laughed in hilarious waves, which was one of the numerous endearing things about him. " I love my mad English *Hathis*," Rabat said. " This is my broadsword of the *Soon-must-lose*."

They arrived at the Palace of the Elephants, or the elephant

lines in non-Jumboesque. " Reverent silence, I demand. Absolute
obedience. My Loved-ones may be sleeping."

He led the way into the presence of his Loved-ones, which
stood awake, but their mahouts slept beside them. " Mohammed !
Ali ! Stir your bones ! " he boomed in English. " I, Lord Mumbo-
Jumbo, King of all the Elephants, am here."

The mahouts were instantly awake. They made obeisance to
Jumbo, bulking darkly in his dinner jacket in a shadow of the
moon. The elephants stirred too ; their shackles clanked under
the high-roofed shelter ; and, at command, they saluted him
with trunks.

" Salaam, my noble Akbar. Salaam, my bonny Mumtaz."

" They seem to know him," Desmond whispered. " Listen ! "
Both elephants were rumbling in their bellies.

" Now I shall introduce you. Great Akbar is the stateliest of
state elephants. He bears the howdah of my Personage, and many
an inanity he hears. See the gleam of Akbar's mighty tusks. See
the dignity, the presence, see the wisdom of that brow.

" Little Mumtaz, on the other hand, she is the staunch angel
of the chase, she is my Personage's tiger-steed, a valiant poppet.
Akbar and Mumtaz, may I present, first, Desmond Tanner, a
commercial gent from dear old Cal. He is the lanky creature with
the black jacket and the snow-white pantaloons. Next I offer
Second-Lieutenant Rabat, a countryman of yours, not a bad
rapscallion, I would say. Lastly a worthless harum-scarum type,
whose name I dare not mention. Harry, how many times must I
tell you never to giggle in the presence of my Loved-ones ? Even
my Personage knows better than do that."

" Ali ! Mohammed ! Bring me sweetmeats."

Jumbo fed them balls of sugar wrapped in hay. He boomed
low endearments. His elephants quite evidently liked him too.
" You may pet Mumty, Mumtaz Mahal, the favourite of the
palace, and a friendly piece. But Akbar, the Emperor, he is a testy
tusker. He does not suffer fools."

" Do you speak Hindustani, Jumbo ? "

He shuddered. " Not a word."

"How do you get things done, then, in the Palace of the Elephants?"

"My Loved-ones understand me. My mahouts understand my Loved-ones. It is simple."

"Do you love them both the same?"

"What a slanderous suggestion. My Akbar is my hero, my Jonathan in a sense, although I was never quite sure about that friendship. Let us say, rather, that Akbar is my elder brother. He is fifty-eight. But Mumtaz, oh my darling Mumty, how I do adore thee! Look at her legs, I mean I ask you. Look at everything, so slim and perfect in the first full blush of feminine divinity. Mumty is a bare forty-five."

"Are they married?"

"No," said Jumbo crossly. "They may have had a fling for all I know." He turned. He was a moody chap. Jumbo's grandiloquent mood sank fast. "Salaam," he muttered. "Salaam, salaam, salaam with knobs on to the whole ghastly Orient."

"Just a minute, Jumbo."

"Well, what is it?"

"I've had an idea. The night is balmy and the moon is full; I simply wondered about a ride on one of your Loved-ones round the Maidan. A farewell by moonlight to the *Soon-must-lose*. You probably won't approve." The Colonel? Well, what about the Colonel?

Jumbo's mood returned full strength. "A capital notion, Harry, a last night together, a dignified farewell. Ah, yes! Ali, the howdah! No, cancel that. The lowly pad is better suited to this company. Quickly now!"

Ali looked dubious. He hovered before Jumbo with respect and deep humility.

"Tell him it is the order of my Personage that Mumtaz have night exercise in preparation for the Bengal jungles."

Rabat told Ali, the mahout.

They rode across flat open ground. To one side were river lights, the noises of the ships, the Fort; to the other, Chowringhee with its lamps, its lighted buildings, its late sporadic traffic ; here the cool glimmer of a January moon about the Maidan and the shadowed trees ; here the creaking of the pad, the grassy thud, the swaying gait of Mumtaz, and Ali in his turban on her neck ; here conviviality, but muted.

" I've never ridden an elephant before at night, have you, Harry ? "

" No, Desmond, I have not, nor ever shall again, I dare suppose." The florid speech of Jumbo's mood was vaguely catching. " And you, Rabat ? "

" No," he said. " It is jolly feeling."

Silence. " Only me you do not ask, and the answer negative. Only I, as always, dreaming of the *Might-have-been*, nothing ever perfect for poor Lord Mumbo-Jumbo, King of all the Elephants, my Personage's big buffoon. I wish you people weren't here. I wish the juggler's girl and I and Mumtaz and her faithful Ali were together quite alone. The juggler's girl would teach me a hundred tricks of jugglery, of hokery and pokery, of gladsome jokery. Oh, she would juggle like a dream."

" But wouldn't Mumtaz mind ? "

" Not a bit. She's awfully understanding, aren't you, Mumty dear ? "

A policeman stepped forward from the darkness of a tree. His sergeant's stripes were visible. He held his hand up, as to halt traffic.

" Greetings, Inspector," Jumbo said. " How are you ? "

The policeman walked round Mumtaz. His face was pale in the moon's pale light, dusky pits below his eyes. He was a watchful Anglo-Indian policeman with authority with tactful reservations as to whom he happened to be dealing with. " What is it you are doing ? " he began to Jumbo, adding as insurance, " Sir ? "

Jumbo waved his hand about the empty Maidan. " Night school for my elephant," he said. " What better place than this ? Mumty, say Salaam to the Inspector."

The man smiled. " Sergeant, sir," he said. " But it is against the . . . This is your own elephant, you say ? "

" You'd better tell him, Jumbo."

Jumbo told the Sergeant. " . . . And so you see, Inspector, my orders are that she must be perfectly attuned to every fancied tiger, leopard or policeman of the jungle night. I must be careful not to make an Absalom of My Excellency. That would be more than my job is worth. Although, of course, the man is bald, I now remember. Inspector, won't you join us ? We have room up here."

The sergeant laughed. " Now look, sir, you make one chukker round the trees and back you go, but please not on the streets, sir, or there will be trouble. I'm getting out of here before I see you." He saluted and rode his bicycle away.

" A charming fellow," Jumbo said, en route again. " They are unfailingly courteous, in my experience."

" Particularly those chaps with horses trained to bite the crowds."

" Harry, sometimes I fear that a social conscience stirs within you. Fight it down, my boy."

" We had to call in the police about misappropriations in my firm," said Desmond. " You should have seen them deal with the Indian clerks, talk about third degree. It made you feel quite ill."

" Let us not spoil this magic hour with the bestialities of man. Here we are now at the limits of the Maidan. One chukker round the trees and back, the nice policeman said. Home, I suppose, alas. Where did that policeman go ? "

" To Chowringhee. I watched him all the way across. Jumbo, what would you say to a fleeting call at One-Three-Eight ? "

" Not on the forbidden streets, but by the alleys and the little lanes and down the Lane of lanes to Numéro Cent-Trente-Huit. Harry, you have genius, boy. Just down the Lane and sip a harmless drink with sundry debutantes ; then up the Lane again and over the Maidan to the Palace of the Elephants. But is it fair on Mumtaz ? She isn't that kind of girl at all, you know. Would you mind, Mumty, just this once ? Oh, thank you so much, darling. No, of course, I never for a moment thought you were a prig. She says it's all part of her liberal education. I do so utterly agree. To honour the girls by courtesy of Mumtaz, that is a grandiose conception. Any objections, gentlemen, if I may so dignify you ? "

There were no objections. It was an excellent moon-mad idea. They rode circumspectly and in silence, meeting no policemen. " Safely at the threshold. Let us herald our coming with a song. I know : ' The Volga Boatmen.' The words elude me, but the words are not important. It is the melody that matters, so appropriate to the majesty of Mumtaz, so fitting to the struggles of our fallen sisters. Do you know ' The Volga Boatmen,' Rabat ? "

" I can sing anything like nightingale."

They sang sadly and loudly down the Lane. An audience appeared at doors and windows, and some began to sing, and soon the whole shady Lane was filled with song : " Da—daa—da, da —dada—doo-doo," that most melancholy air in time to the ponderous-footed Mumtaz. Jumbo was crying as they arrived at One-Three-Eight.

" What is it now, Jumbo ? "

" I weep for the chains of whoredom," Jumbo sobbed.

Mumtaz knelt. They slid off the pad. " Wait here, Ali," Jumbo ordered.

Cora, entrepreneuse and head prefect, met them under a dim warm light. " Hallo, boys," Cora said, jolly and hospitable. " We've never had an elephant before." But she looked at Rabat. " This is a European house. I am sorry."

" Don't be awkward, Cora."

" I am sorry," Cora said again with cordial equanimity and firmness. " It is our rule."

" I don't mind," said Rabat. " I'll stay outside."

" No, you won't. You're coming in with us."

" Quite right, Harry. A point of principle is what I say." Jumbo lurked behind. He was a born egger-onner. " Lead us, Black."

" Three jute-wallahs in the parlour," Cora whispered. " Let me suit them first. Then you can all come in. Please, Harry."

" Sorry, Cora. Come on, Rabat. Inside."

D

They were three gentlemen in their native cups.

" A wog," the first sahib said, outraged.

" A muckin' nigger," said the second.

" Put the bastard outa here," the third sahib said.

The ladies of the house were multi-hued, which made this colour question interesting, it occurred to Harry. " Just apologise," he said. " Say you're sorry for being rude."

Apologies were not forthcoming.

The girls piled in flimsy dresses into corners where they screamed. Harry and Desmond were engaged. Rabat hovered in embarrassment. Jumbo laughed himself to a vast jelly till it became evident that help was needed. Then he took one in each hand, bumped heads, twisted collars, cried : " This hurrts me far worrse than you, my braw wee laddies." Jumbo cast them out. The third capitulated. Cora's parlour was a shambles.

" Tidy up, girls," Cora said. She went to lock the door of One-Three-Eight. She came back. " You beat up customers. You break the place. You give us a bad name. And now you laugh. I am very cross."

" Love and honour," Jumbo said. " What is life without them ? But please forgive us, Cora. We shall reimburse you gladly, make good all losses of clientele and custom. However, an elephant awaits us, and it is my opinion that we may not wisely stand longer on the order of our going than one drink. We are full of grief to-night. First one broadsword of the *Soon-must-lose*, and now a second. Soon must lose Cora-Dora and the gels. Oh, dear, a nightcap for my bleeding heart. Quickly, Cora ! "

" Is it my imagination ? " Harry asked.

Desmond smiled at him. " No. You're going to have a beauty."

Almost all his friends were in the Regiment. He thought now that Desmond Tanner, *the Box-wallah, a nice boy*, the Colonel said. Oh, my God, the Colonel ! He thought Desmond was a wonderfully good, cheerful, undemanding chap.

" Come, Harry. We have bifstick. I will put it on."

He went with Cora.

" Lie down," she said, " and close your eyes."

He lay down. Kaleidoscopes of polo, deft jugglers, elephants, champagne, policemen, Jumbos, fights and so on danced about his painful head before his red-hot eye in Cora's boudoir. A spectre of his Colonel came and went amid the pageant of the others, and was there again. His Colonel had not been joking about keeping out of trouble. I'll say I got it in the game, he thought, a brilliant inspiration. But here was Cora, and the raw clamminess of beefsteak on his eye.

" Such a naughty boy you are," said Cora, a Hungarian and widely travelled. She was beside him, opulently warm and matey.

" Have a heart now, Cora. I'm severely wounded."

" You wreck my business. I should be angry with you, and I am, like this and this. I make you suffer, hothead that you are, nice wickedness, so clean and hard and young." Murmur, murmur, what a woman. " How is your eye now ? Is it better ? "

" Can't feel it. Can't feel bifstick even."

" Old-fashioned treatments, they are best."

Time was short in the consulting room of Doctor Cora. Harry yawned.

" Are you so tired ? " she asked him.

" Busy day," he said. It had been a long and busy day. " I must go."

" First you pay the doctor's bill."

He paid the bill. His eye was purple. It might have been purpler, he supposed, without Cora's old-fashioned treatment.

Shouts for Harry. He went through to the drawing-room of One-Three-Eight. " The police are outside," Jumbo hissed. " They are arresting Mumtaz for obstruction of this public lane. They threaten us with breaches of a dozen different kinds of peace. And whose fault is it ? Who suggested the Palace of Elephants ? Who enticed us out on Mumtaz ? Who seduced us down the Lane ? Who forced his way within these portals ? Who was the *éminence grise*, the architect of all our woes ? Who kept us waiting whilst he dilly-dallied vainly with a beefsteak under Dame Cora's tender care ? Who, but this innocent-faced stripling. . . ."

Some senior sort of policeman entered. "Names, please," he said unpleasantly.

*   *   *   *   *

Harry and Rabat got to bed at five. Physical training was at half-past six. He inspected his tight-lipped platoon. He took them for a two-mile run across the Maidan, scene of a recent elephant excursion. His skin was dry, but he was sweating by the end. Platoon dismissed.

Sergeant Johnson remained behind, graven at attention.

"How does it look?" asked Harry.

"A shocker, sir," said Sergeant Johnson. "How come, sir, if not a tactless question?"

"Polo is the official story," Harry said. "Strictly in confidence, however, not."

"Out with Mr. Rabbit, sir?"

"Among others, yes."

"That Mr. Rabbit, he's a real bad lot. You and him shouldn't ought to be allowed together after sunset. That's what I said last time, sir, I warned you. Trouble brewin', would you say, sir?"

"I fear so. Let's go as far afield as possible after breakfast."

They went as far afield as possible after breakfast. Still no summons when they had to return for an Adjutant's parade.

"Things look better, Sergeant Johnson. There is hope."

"Not too much, sir, if you look behind you."

It was the Adjutant's runner with a note: *You will report to the Orderly Room at once.* Signed Captain and Adjutant. No compliments; no please. Sergeant Johnson groaned. His platoon commander was a proper worry to him.

Harry reported. The Adjutant was icy. The Adjutant was rather a prudish, married chap.

The Colonel was not a prude. Icy or irate, the Colonel was a killer. Harry did not fear his father, but he feared the Colonel, five years his father's junior in the regiment.

He stared at the white-washed wall above his Colonel's head

while the storm beat him to bewilderment—Military Secretary himself telephoned. *What about poor Jumbo, what would they do to him?*—Leading an Indian officer into trouble—Battalion's reputation, final impression, red light district, disgraced the Regiment. *Oh God*—repeated warnings, irresponsible young hooligan—Thunder to a silence.

" My parade, sir ? " The Adjutant sounded vicariously shaken.

" I'll send Black out later."

The door closed. " Answer me ! "

" I'm sorry, sir. I didn't hear." He braced himself.

" Stop staring at the wall."

He looked down at his Colonel's blue eyes, bloodshot. Now on to the level of reason, which was worse.

" I asked you if you have considered what your father will feel when he hears about this ? Or do you find that funny ? "

Harry shook his head. The evening had been very funny ; it did not seem very funny. " No, sir," he said. Why always all the hell for him ?

" You wonder why I'm hard on you. First, because your father is a friend of mine. Second, because your family have served the Regiment for a hundred years or more, and have served us well. Third, because I believe you have great gifts as a soldier and a man. You work hard when you do work. You go hard when you play. You demand a lot from the troops and get it, and they like you. You are highly intelligent, and you arrive at the essence of problems with a ruthless dispatch and certainty which is very rare indeed." The Colonel paused.

These remarks were complimentary. The Colonel never paid compliments. It was ominous, and Harry waited.

" One of your troubles is that life is easy. You are too fearless, too popular with men and women, too natural a leader, too quick-witted. Nothing has ever been difficult for you in your life. You seem modest, but are in fact arrogant and self-centred. I haven't said any of this before, Harry, and I shan't again. But I know what I am talking about because you and I are much alike. You may find that impossible to believe ; it happens to be true, or it was true of my young days. I remember your father saying once when we were subalterns : *You would be a better chap if things came harder to you, if you failed occasionally.*

"Well, I had some money. I could afford to enjoy myself and look down my nose at the ambitious plodders ; and when the war came, I did well enough. But after the war I would probably have gone merrily to hell, except for one thing—you know what that was."

"The Regiment, you mean, sir ?"

"Yes. It's impossible to know who can fight and who can't, but I am virtually certain you can. When the next war comes, which it will, you will either be killed or you will do well. And if you do really well, you may become ambitious. But if you survive and don't get ambition, then I think you will go to pot. Why ? Because you are too arrogant to subordinate yourself, I mean to give yourself, to the Regiment or to any institution or belief. Also, of course, you have none of my snobbish weakness, which can make dull things worthwhile.

"Where you fail, my dear boy, is that you think the world is a pleasure-ground set aside for the particular selfish benefit of Harry Black. But when the pleasure palls, what then ?"

Harry said nothing. The Colonel seemed to be talking a lot of remote and high-falutin stuff. Well, if the old boy said it, he supposed . . .

"You had five days casual leave from to-morrow. What were you going to do ?"

Had. Were. "I was going after a tiger that's been giving trouble in the Sunderbunds, sir."

"Another hell-raiser. Well, you're not. You are orderly officer from now until the day we leave."

"Yes, sir. I'm sorry about last night."

"High spirits are one thing," said his Colonel. "Riding a State elephant to a fracas in a whorehouse is quite another. However, I suppose it will give them something to remember us by in this benighted city. You're too late now for Adjutant's parade. You had better tell me all about it."

CHAPTER NINE

In 1943

Sie kämmt es mit goldenem Kamme
Und singt ein Lied dabei ;
Das hat eine wundersame,
Gewaltige Melodei.

THEY WENT up the ladder and on to the bridge and over that and down through at the far end and out of the way. They were number Four team of ten men. The hut creaked and shook to a wood-thumped thunder, and wire twanged. Up, hold, cross, drop, metronomic, almost. Finished. They looked at him, individuals again, happy.

" Thirty-seven," said Desmond with the watch.

" Not bad, Jim. You were slow to the bridge. You're still not crowding the chap in front enough."

The record was thirty-three, made this evening. Two months ago the best time had been over a minute, unladen. Now all four teams could beat forty seconds with eyes shut, wearing packs. They were good. They were, in fact, phenomenally good. They rolled up and over and down more like a ten-bogied carriage devouring a switchback than anything readily imaginable. The passage was loud. This was the rarity among escape schemes, for in this job speed was the prime consideration.

" Pack up," he said.

Ladder down, bridge down, shelves in place, extra slats on, newspaper, music sheets. Four bricks per pack, forty bricks, double ten and double ten making supports for a third shelf. Once more the camp music room with a reasonable piano, with two music-draped wires stretched from beam to beam, ten feet high and eight feet apart, simulating the double fence of Oflag VIIY.

Harry was glad that the last packing-up of the last practice was safely over. But he did not heave sighs of relief. He had lived for three years now from climax to anti-climax, from real alarm to false, from patience to daring, from half-success to failure—all the stealthy wooing of his luck. Life was tension, and vice-versa.

"Well done, boys," he said to number Four team. They stuffed their home-stitched packs inside battledress blouses. They were tall and short, broad and narrow, lean and young and wonderful. "Night, Harry," they said, departing casually by ones and twos, masters of the wary art. A clever enemy might know them by their eyes, watching out, not in.

"Thank you, Dug," he said to the head of the Camp stooging system. It had been a good evening, only one German visit to the sing-song in the music room.

He went out with the four team leaders and with Desmond. He and Desmond were in number Two team. It was August, escaping weather. People walked the wire. People lay about. People threw those pointed footballs.

One chap was flying the model prototype of his kite. It sat up well in moderate airs. He had not yet evolved his man-strong cord, and he had not yet persuaded the escape authorities that he could land himself and kite without committing suicide. He never would. But he had a lovely time flying the model, thinking of himself up there and over the wire and far away, laughing at the Anti-Escape Committee who had failed to baulk him.

Then there was a man who folded his blanket and plucked grass to strew upon it, and sat cross-legged in a jock-strap in a yogi trance all day upon the grass upon his blanket. He was a courteous and charming fellow, quite ordinary in the things that mattered, such as minding one's own business.

There were men in all the walks of prison.

Harry and the others sat on bare-trodden ground baked from a spell of sun. The harvest was ripe beyond the wire. Sentries lolled against rails on their stilted platforms. People passed talking. See the people. Go to sleep and see the people. See the bodies in the room at dawn. See the Senior British Officer.

" I saw the S.B.O. He says he tried to pin the Commandant down to a date at their interview this morning. Nothing doing. *After two-three weeks*, was all the sod would say. But not sooner. He was quite definite about that. The Parcel Hatch have the same story ; so do all the Tame Goons."

" Where are we going this time, Harry ? "

" To Brunswick. To a camp with carpets and divans, and hot and cold in every room, and swimming in the lake."

" Christ Almighty, not that again. Women too ? "

" A virgin guard company. Displaced Ukrainians with shell-pink titties."

Good joke by Harry Black ; glorious prospect when I escape to paradise.

" What is wrong about this rumour is that it's too unanimous. He knows he can't keep a move secret. That being obvious, and he being a moderately cunning Goon, what does he do ? He gives out an approximate date fairly well ahead ; then he springs it on us without any warning."

" Sooner, you mean ? "

" Of course. Particularly if some lunatic has tipped them off about big escapes."

One of the friendly interpreters had said this, and it might be true. Some prisoner of war, mad perhaps, afraid perhaps, jealous perhaps, treasonous perhaps. Probably not treasonous by intent. There were peculiar people, and there were many timorous people after three years still safe at the mercy and the whim of men with guns. Mass escapes meant bullets flying. How could you find one man among two thousand men ? You could wait, and you might get him some day. Got or not got, he had had it.

The Germans had taken confirmatory action. They searched the camp with S.S. troops. Which was unpleasant, but did not much affect the chances of this scheme, for tunnels had been the main object of the search. What did affect the chances of this scheme were extra pickets posted now by night beyond the limits of the camp. But even that was better than it might have been. If X had said : *Massed wire escape*. But obviously he had not, because he had not known. This thing was vulnerable only at practice times. Tunnels were vulnerable to British eyes each day.

" If he ousts the camp suddenly one evening, we're absolutely bitched, as a four-ladder effort certainly."

" What do you want to do then, Harry ? "

" It isn't what I want, but I know it's what we've got to do— we must build the other ladders now."

" But that's a bloody awful risk. It's a miracle they haven't caught on long ago about the music room. With three more ladders and three more bridges scattered round the camps, quite apart from the risk of actual building. I mean, if they even see one, they'll guess the idea and double the wire guards or raise the fence, and we're well and truly mucked."

" And if we don't build them ? "

" I agree with Harry. There are forty of us in this job. We must cater for the lot. . . ."

" That's obvious. But . . ."

He let them talk it out. He already had the Committee's approval to build now, and he would impose his decision if he had to. But they would come round in a minute. They did.

" The next thing is : Do we hide them piecemeal or all together ? I believe it's a case of putting our eggs in one basket, in the false partition in the roof of J hut, to be precise. What do you think ? "

Agreed. There were many details to be settled while a slow summer evening hurried on to night. Time is not captive like the kite. Time is the enemy moon that rises early. Time is the friendly moon that rises late. Time craters the golden road to freedom.

" To-day week ? " he asked his four lieutenants and his Q man, Desmond. Harry was the youngest of the five. " First cloudy night from then ? It won't be perfect, or even nearly perfect, but it may be dark enough to have a go. Agreed ? "

They talked everything out to unanimous agreement. He valued their opinions more highly than his own, except only in assessing major risks. He was a better gambler. He might well value their opinions, for they were the cream of the veteran escapers. Desmond was as sound, if less experienced.

They made for home. The sunset was over. Perimeter lamps were on. A searchlight shone down the wire, swung in to prettify the sordid huts, to pick upon late people, swept out to harvest fields. From the four corners of this world the searchlights played at night. And how many nights would he have seen the searchlights play ? Eleven hundred plus. Eleven hundred minus, bearing in mind his nights at large. Two escapes, and third time lucky.

The full moon was up. The searchlights were superfluous under this next-to-harvest moon. It was twenty minutes to the curfew hour of ten o'clock. Somebody lurked in the shadow of the moon at J hut.

" Hallo, Willie."

" But Harry, so delightful ! And you, Desmond. How was the romp of the muscled army ? A *succès fou*, I trust."

Willie's languid contralto, light-boned face, knotted bandanna at the neck. In June Willie had cut through the wire alone and had walked a hundred and sixty miles to be caught on the Swiss frontier. He was lately returned from his cooler sentence, a trifle gaunt, more cynical and elegant than ever. Willie looked like a roaring pansy, which possibly he was. He was also the coolest fish in Christendom. Harry had chosen him to be the non-playing manager of this escape, a choice viewed at first with horror by the old brigade. They still disliked him, but had changed their minds.

J and K huts were at right angles to the wire on the south side of the camp. The length of this stretch was three hundred yards, a box sentry with machine-gun and searchlight at either end. The two sentries covered the wire by day, but at night three extra men patrolled—thus, five sentries. The space between J and K huts was the meeting point of the beats of the right or westerly ground sentries.

" Who's on to-night ? "

" Left is a nasty stranger. Right is Tossed Barmy in the tormented flesh."

The footsteps sounded up. They were of different quality— a shuffle from the right, Tossed Barmy ; a clipped tread from the left. Harry and the others eased out of sight. The sentries met and did not speak and moved apart. Harry watched Left Sentry go, hands in pockets, rifle slung, at ease and watchful soldier on the job, convalescing from the Ostfront more than likely. You could tell the graduates a mile off, the ones whose experience would tell them : *This is Diversion. Watch for the real assault.* Lord of the far-flung battle line, give us a couple of Tossed Barmies on the night.

"I don't like that one."

"I think he's simply horrid. I think all trained soldiery are simply horrid. Disciplined robots, that's what, Harry, even you."

Willie rambled on, watching the wire. He was an extraordinary chap. Voices and footsteps inside J hut, prisoners busying themselves for bed—the spectre-ridden—the hearties less hearty with the years—the old maids meticulously polishing their boots—the scruffy and the slugabeds—the disparate cohabitation. And now music, "Tales from the Vienna Woods."

"Dear Hoi-polloi," sighed Willie. "We shall have ' The Blue Danube ' next."

"I like old-fashioned waltzes," Desmond said.

"What a boringly precious snob you are, Willie."

"A snob certainly. Precious too. Boring perhaps. But my God, what I endure. I keep reminding myself that the common herd are a necessary evil. . . . Did you see that?"

"What?"

"A light, I thought, out in the Deep Field direction. There again?"

They saw it, the blink of a torch, the one glow of a firefly and no more, in the woods a quarter of a mile away beyond flat ground; prattling Willie, sharp-eyed Willie. This was the first sighting of the Deep Field, whose existence was known only by report. Or it might be a soldier and his girl. He had not addressed a woman for three years. He hoped the first one he addressed would be like this or that but not a bitch.

"What's the latest about them, Harry?"

"Some reports say ten men ; some say eight. But all the Tame Goons confirm that they exist. It's quite certain and quite a

nuisance." The unknown enemy, the risk you could not estimate.
" What's the best thing, Willie, do you think ? "

" You'll have to fan out by teams. Left team swing left and
so on. They won't want to do that. They think that if they're
eventually making for the west, they must start west at once.
Which is nonsense. So silly people are, as if it mattered. No, you
must spread out, and by teams, so that there isn't a criss-cross
shambles just outside. Then only a few unfortunates will buy it."

" A case for discipline, you mean ? "

" Harry, what a tease you are."

" Archie's tame Goon says the Deep Field are selected trigger-
happy types."

Desmond looks on the bleak side lately. Well, he's been
working far too hard. " I don't believe that," Harry said. " It
doesn't make sense, putting the bloody-minded out there in the
country, not when sixty per cent of the Guard Company are
dim-witted yokels or Tossed Barmies. Archie's Goon is talking
balls."

Now all the lights went out—the lamps in the huts ; the
sentinel lamps at close intervals atop the wire, guarding seven
furlongs of perimeter ; the searchlights from the boxes. All
extinguished by a master switch in a fuse-box in a guard room at
the east gate, such an easy thing to do. They simply pulled the
switch, hey presto. And what a moon, what a beautiful hostile
August moon to-night, what a machine-gun target running men
would make.

Still a few minutes to the lights-out curfew hour of ten, but the
lights were out. Germans screamed from all directions, a scream
of barbarous Goons. *Zurück! Nach Hause! Drinnen!* Back !
Go home ! Inside !

" I shall retire now," said the egregious Willie. " Rest well,
my dears."

They walked home by the inner path, the wire vicinity not
being healthy during air raids.

" I must check the detail for to-morrow. One thing forgotten
and we'll have a monumental nonsense. I'd better stay up late."

"There's no need, Desmond. You've worked it out to the last nail already. What you want is sleep." He was testy with him. Desmond was showing the pessimistic fussiness of strain. No wonder, at it twelve or fourteen hours a day. But who ever heard of the good Q man who could spare himself? It's my fault too, he thought. I drive him. "Any letters?" he asked as a change of subject.

"Not for three weeks. It's frightful, you know, Harry, but I've hardly had time to think about Christian lately."

He was a truly good-hearted chap, no vice at all. He was apt to be uxorious, but you could not blame him with such a winner of a wife, a driver in London in the Blitz, a humdinger of a looker of the highest order, the sort of amusing, kind inconsequential girl who might exist but you hadn't met her. Christian's photograph hung on the wall beside Desmond's bunk. He was the only married one among them, as it happened, and the four bachelor members of the mess felt that she was theirs through him in small degree. She had even visited Tommy's parents down in Dorset; who wrote: *Such a delightful unspoilt girl.* So Christian sat disembodied on a sentimental pedestal of Woman.

"That's what I'm telling you," Harry said. "Forget about this job, and go to bed and dote upon that wife."

Desmond laughed loudly like himself. "You randy old wizard."

And Harry thought: I didn't mean what he implies. But I suppose that's what the virtuous benedicts like Desmond do. Personally, I prefer to re-enact an *exhibition* in Lille, those shapely sluts, oh gracious.

Home to the hut without German interference, home to the smell which was a part of this existence, home to the annoying people who did not annoy him now in the flame of his escape, and it would fail like twenty others he was on, oh no, it wouldn't. Home to Tommy Treadwell, an excruciatingly amusing fellow. "You two get more pregnant every day. When do the little ones arrive?" But he valued his head and said it quietly.

"Mind your own bloody business," he said without heat to

Tommy. He undressed. The air raid sirens sounded from here and there and round about. The jackals, he thought of them, remembering India. But this was only a small three-howl alarm. It was early for a raid. It would be one of those new fleet Mosquitos, choosing a likely spot to prick. How well named was the Mosquito.

He climbed on to his upper bunk and under one blanket. He needed a change of mattress straw, but he would not bother. He let the prattle slide on past him.

Nothing to do but talk about the war, seek virtue washing dishes, draw Red Cross parcels, start learning German yet again and give it up and do accounting. But he had something he was going to do, given the time and given the luck, and forty people to be wise for. There was Desmond lighting his fat lamp underneath. A most conscientious, work-haunted chap was Desmond, unable to resist that notebook with the hieroglyphics.

Harry turned on his left side to see out across the quiet camp and the flat land and the wooded hills to a solitary alp far off, the Fröhlichberg, the merry mountain under moon and snow. Desmond and he would pass below the Fröhlichberg.

Perhaps he heard an aircraft down at the rim of distance. He did not know. The warning was on, and the lights were off. He wondered if it would work a second time? They had not been suspicious that night in May. They had not changed the wiring. The experts did not think they could have. Of course it was going to work. Now sleep.

He turned the other way and went to sleep.

*   *   *   *   *

The ladders were built next afternoon and stored at dusk. The second morning there was a search at the north side of the camp, a tunnel found and some escape kit. That was bad, although the tunnel was not nearly through. It meant Germans alert ; it meant the pre-move temperature a little warmer. Where next ?

" Look, boys. Four of our people lost stuff this morning. I

think we'll do the thing properly while we're about it, and store
the packs in J hut too."

" But my God, they'll probably search K to-morrow."

" They searched it last week," Harry said.

" That's what they do, though. Come again and catch you
with your pants down."

" They sometimes do. The odds are against it with thirty
huts."

" But Harry, if we lose our maps and clothes and food, we're
absolutely mucked."

" If we lose the ladders, we're absolutely mucked. The kits
are no good to us without an exit. The exit is an unhealthy joy-
ride without the kits. There's no other exit from this camp at this
moment, and you know it. We must gamble big. You can cut
off my head when the Goons find everything in J hut."

On the second evening they stored the packs, the civilian clothes,
the maps, the passes. That preliminary Rubicon was safely crossed.
It's not a good big gamble, Harry thought. It's a good big toss-up.
Well, if I'm wrong, I'm wrong.

On the third morning, old peasants, Russian prisoners and
deported women began to cut rye on the south flank of the camp,
out beyond the fifty yards or so of uncropped land. They did not
use a combine, but two ancient horse machines. The women
gathered sheaves into tall shocks or stooks. Half the camp turned
out to watch the women, to think about the harvest of another
year and about harvest fields of childhood, to watch the fluidity
of woman on the move. Some of them were beddable, according to users of home-made telescopes. *All of them are beddable*,
said a loutish man, or a man liking to be loutish. But half of
them were captive crones, which made the sight sadder and less
painful.

On the fourth evening, the moon did not rise till ten o'clock.
The moon was waning, still a potent moon. Harry and Desmond
watched the wire with Willie. They watched it every night. A
possible night was not far off. It was decidedly not here yet. You
could count rye-stooks into the distance to the south.

But clouds followed the rising of the moon. Was a change coming in the fickle sub-alpine weather ? Would a storm blow up ? Would the thunderheads be there to-morrow, those fabulous free mountains of the sky ? Forget about it. Forget and go to sleep. Sleep was never any trouble, least of all now at the needle-point of waiting. Why was that, he wondered ? Sleep.

*　　*　　*　　*　　*

The weather did change next day, but not to thunder. A wind blustered from the east, and cloud was low. Harry lay on his bunk all morning, reading *The Bridge of San Luis Rey* again, a convergent story that he much enjoyed. He supposed it was three months since he had read anything better than the German papers. He ate *The Bridge of San Luis Rey* at one lying. " Is it all off, then ? " asked the curious Tommy.—" No, we're ready."—" So you just take things easy on your bum. What a phenomenal cucumber you are."

The plans were complete at last. There were no new problems yet to mess about. There was nothing now to do but eat and sleep and read a book and walk a bit and placate the boys and watch by night and wait. Whatever he did, that was the thing he did. Which might be a weakness in the complexity of free life. It was his strength here in prison.

The wind held strong. Clouds hurried from the east. They walked the wire at five o'clock. You must have heat to enjoy cool weather ; you must inhabit a guarded dump to love the Fröhlich-berg too much, the black-tipped merry-breasted mountain, not visible this afternoon.

They went with the stream along the Lagerstrasse on the upper level. " I saw a letter for you, Harry."

" Yes," he said. " From my father, tenth of June. The monsoon had just broken. He sounded hotweatherish between the lines. But British Service caught in India, and just the wrong age for this war, and a desk general when all he ever wanted was command. It's hard on the old boy."

" You never say much about him."

" He used to be a fire-eater, mellowed now. Father is a good straight-thinking sort of chap." Father is also a bit of a bore to me, which I do not feel bound to say to Desmond.

" And your mother was all right ? "

Down the path and round the cinders round the football field. " Flourishing. *As many peculiar friends as ever*, so he said. By that he means Mahatma Gandhi and half the Congress movement. Father almost enjoys her inexplicable eccentricities, which is quite a nice thing. My mother is an intellectual and a rebel, and my father is a simple soldier, proud of it in fact."

" And you're the mixture."

" I don't know. I think offspring happen more or less. They don't work out by equally proportioned genes." He thought that he would like to have a bottle of port with Father, avoiding controversial topics. But with his mother he would like interminable disputations.

J hut on the dull afternoon. Everything peaceful, everything ready in that false partition.

" I wish the harvest had been a week later," Desmond said in the muted escaping-business voice. " That rye was wizard cover."

" It's easier running now. And the stooks are the height of men. We can jig about between them. No, I think it's better till they lead the harvest."

" I don't," Desmond said, " not with the darkness we can expect this month. When you remember the conditions we originally planned for—no Deep Field—machine-guns covered with tarpaulins—complete blackness in September—I mean I sometimes wonder if we aren't shaving the chances just a bit too close." He looked round at Harry and away.

" It's going to be all right," he said gently. " We won't do the job unless it is. Don't worry, chum."

He wondered whether Desmond might be right and he be wrong. Then he wondered something else. The moon rose last night at ten p.m., to-night at eleven minutes past, to-morrow at ten twenty-eight, the next night at ten fifty-three, and that was the first zero night. The mystery of figures that made fact. It was a sort of alchemy to him. His only clue was with imponderables such as people, risks and beauty ; such as thinking ahead to the unexpected. He would not say anything to Desmond. He did not want to bring things nearer to him than they had to be.

The east wind carried a latrine stink. Desmond held his fastidious nose. " I don't bind the sbell so buch," he said. " It's those creepy-crawlies. Have you seed theb ? "

Harry had seen them. They climbed from their breeding grounds in human ordure, legions of oily whitish caterpillar-worms, unimaginably loathsome creatures on the march. Primeval slime, they made you think. What new horrors might the earth throw up to herself some day ?

The air was clean again to windward. " I had a letter from Christian at long last. Three weeks from door to door, which isn't bad. There are four missing in between."

Really, such switches thought and conversation take, from moons to creepy-crawly worms to wives. But I might have asked him. " What's what ? " he asked.

" She's going back to Canada, I think, from various hints about seeing people."

" Oh, I'm glad," he said.

" Yes, except for those bloody U-boats."

" They're not bad now. How did she sound ? "

" In cracking form, as usual."

Indeed as usual. He had never heard of Desmond's wife in anything but cracking form. She wrote amusingly about nothing, and the excerpts Desmond occasionally read out were not in the least embarrassing, however much you feared they might be. Christian sounded terrific value. The thing which did not occur to the others but did occur to carping Harry was that she sounded almost too terrific value. Well, being a good girl, she might have said to herself : *I'll never be anything but cheerful in my letters.* " What did you say, Desmond ? "

" I said that she sent messages to the boys. Wait, I'll read it, just a sentence."

Oh dear, he's going to read it. You know, I ask myself fatuous questions about time and reality and such balls, when I might be thinking about friends. Look at us, poles apart in a dozen ways. If I knew about that, I might know something. Which goes to show you never can know nothin'.

"Here we are. 'Remember me to the people in the Mess, I feel I know them well by now, at least I know Tommy and Jack and Simon exactly what they're like but Harry the one you say most about and your real friend remains an enigma to this female like a paragon mixture of Al Capone and Good-time Charlie and Sir Galahad don't repeat this.'"

He laughed so loudly that people ahead in the procession turned to see it was only Good-time Charlie Harry Black. "My God," he said. "What have you been writing to the woman?"

"Nothing much. Just things occasionally you did and said."

They were on the upper level now again, reaching the end of their second lap. They must have walked nearly a thousand miles together in step at four miles an hour this summer to a lean teamed fitness they might never know again. The wind eased them along the surfaced Lagerstrasse.

What about that? he thought. What about that from the terrific female value to the paragon male mixture?

The fashionable way to walk the wire was anti-clockwise. The stream of ones and twos and threes, the haphazard crocodile, poured westwards down the Lagerstrasse. Now, at five-twenty or thereabouts of a wind-whipped afternoon in August, an unusual thing occurred: the crocodile wavered along there at the head. It stopped. Fast as the wind in the face of the wind the halting ripple ran up here: "CAMP MOVES TO-NIGHT." A scramble of details: "S.B.O. just seen the Commandant. Number One Battalion parades at eleven, others later. Pack at once. What we can carry. Rear party... Heavy stuff to follow ...." And so on. A giant of excitement, disembowelling routine. Laugh, curse, the mucking Goons.

Harry looked down south to J hut, to the rusty tangled barrier of wire, to harvest stooks on God's flat land, to woods where the

Deep Field lurked by night, to clouds hiding his Fröhlichberg.
" Desmond ! " he said.

" Yes ? "

" Find somebody in each team. I want you and the leaders and
Willie at the football field at once. Everyone else wait in huts. I'm
going to the S.B.O. Hurry ! "

He himself walked at an ordinary pace to see the Senior British
Officer. If he ran, so would the word run : *Harry's up to something.*
Old Busty called him *that citizen of Black repute.*

It was a short way farther. He was unfortunate enough to meet
Meierling, the Security Officer, a German he disliked profoundly.
Meierling was a bloody little Nazi Goon, of the *Gott-strafe-
England* mixed with the youandweshouldbefightingshoulderto-
shoulderagainsttheplutocraticJewryriddencommunisticapefolk persuasion. He had tried this on Harry during interrogation after the
March escape, and added some Rosenbergian mystical cockano-
clocks for good measure. Which was a little too much in the pit
of recapture. It was the last time Harry had lost his temper. He
took Hauptmann Meierling's theories apart in a cold rage in
German, which he spoke well enough by then to do justice to
the matter. It nearly cost him a bullet in the stomach. It cost him
fifteen extra days of cooler sentence. It cost him a scarlet top-
danger category *Deutsch-Feindlich*, German-hater, on his identity
card.

He could see now that Meierling made to stop him. God damn
and blast it, Harry thought. Is the little mucker going to round
me up ?

He was a picturebook squarehead Goon. " Herr Black ! " he
said genially. " *Der schwarze Judenfreund und Flüchtling! Wollen
Sie sich noch einmal aus dem Staube machen ?* Black, friend of Jews
and fugitive. Are you going to get off your marks again ? "

Harry stood to attention, hatless, and made a bow like that
courtiers nod to Royalties and Viceroys. He smiled ruefully at
the repulsive alien man. " No, Herr Hauptmann. You have made
escape quite and altogether an impossible waste of time. Since
three months, I have begun a new life, turned over a new leaf. I

have been reading Goethe's *Faust*. The first part is not difficult ;
the second is hard for me. But your Goethe is superb, greater than
our Shakespeare in my opinion."

Watch him bridle. Watch him lap that up. See the Wagnerian
organ swell. Unbelievable, but it worked.

Meierling saluted his admiring enemy, korrekt to the Teutonic
n'th degree, and moved on. That cost me a little pride, he thought.
Well, perhaps I can cost the little sod his job.

He entered the hut. The four battalion commanders waited
outside the S.B.O.'s door. " Sir," he said to the senior of them.
" I'm afraid I must go in." He knocked and went.

     ★   ★   ★   ★   ★

" So that's the situation," he said to the thirty-nine. " As you
know, there never is complete darkness in this latitude in August,
and we're still two days from a reasonably dead moon. The last
traces of daylight won't fade to-night before the first effects of the
moon are showing from under the horizon. On the other hand,
if the cloud cover is very thick, it may just be dark enough to have
a go. On yet another hand, the camp will be alive with Germans.
The goonery might stop us ; or I might cancel for light. I won't
commit myself."

And here was the tricky part : " The S.B.O. and the Committee
have agreed to the scheme." What they had actually said to-day
and many times before was : *This thing gives us the willies. We
don't believe in it, but we do respect your judgment, Harry.* " They
have agreed on a strictly voluntary basis. I want to say one thing
about that : It takes a lot more guts to back out than to go along.
The thing is a matter of opinion. You know the light conditions
as well as I do. Your guess is as good as mine, or better. Which
is why every individual is going to decide for himself. We'll take
five minutes now to discuss it."

He looked out. The cloud was still good. Rain? he wondered.

" One question, Harry."

" Yes ? "

" Are you on yourself ? "

" Yes," he said, " if we go at all." Stupid question.

" In which case why the bullshit ? I'm on too."

He looked down in the medley of voices. Then he looked at their faces one by one. He hoped he would do right for these people. He smiled. " Good," he said. " That's that, then."

He took his team leader, Bill, aside. Desmond and Harry had drawn numbers three and four on Two team. " Look, Bill," he said. " We'll have to change the order slightly. Move number five onwards up one and put me tenth. This thing is going to need watching to the last second. Leave Desmond where he is. We can rendezvous easily enough outside."

" But it will be decided by then and over to Willie. There's nothing you can do by waiting."

" Don't argue with me."

" What's this ? " asked Desmond.

Bill told him.

" In that case put me ninth." Desmond's face was brown, but fine-drawn. His jaw muscles flexed as they often did, faster now.

" No, Desmond. Stay in your proper place. I'll easily pick you up outside."

" Listen, Harry, we're partners in this thing. I'm going ninth." He was a selfless quixotic chap and not strong-willed, a stone wall of obstinacy on occasion.

In these conditions he had to go last. But why should Desmond's chance be spoilt ? He could not act the small dictator, though, not in their equal partnership. " Please stay third," he said. " I wish you would."

" No, Harry."

So many things to think of. Oh, to hell with it. " Have it your own way," Harry said.

*   *   *   *   *

He crossed from J to K and went in. He could just make them out, Three and Four teams sitting on benches. Their faces and hands were blackened. A mumble of quiet, trivial talk by preternaturally calm types or by types soothing themselves with talk, some of one

and some of the other, and a majority who did not talk.   Talk
stopped.   Packs creaked against the walls.   " All set, boys ? "

" All set, Harry."

" It's dark as Erebus," he said.   " Much better than I hoped
for.   May start raining ;   ladders slippy ;   watch for that.   And
remember—if Willie shouts *Stop*, get back out of it quick and no
damned nonsense.   Understand ? "

They understood.   " What's the goon situation ? "

" Somewhat confused, but so are the Goons.   Good luck then !
See you at the Bag of Nails."

Titters, some squeaky from dry throats.   " Good luck, Harry."
He went to the door.   " Did you hear that he's put himself last on
Two team ?   What a chap ! "

He was flattered by that.   He had to change his place, but
Desmond did not have to, and Desmond would get no credit.

Outside at nine forty-seven scheme time, twenty-one forty-
seven army fashion.   In this small army they did not need a twenty-
four hour clock.   Twenty-four minutes was roughly what they
needed and then the moon. . . .

He looked at the lamp-lit wire, blackness beyond, which was
contrast, not real darkness.   *Dark as Erebus*, but it wasn't.   Encourage
the troops and keep his own mind coldly undecided.   Now a
searchlight.   He shut his eyes against the dazzling treachery of that.
He saw a neat string of perimeter lamps above a criss-crossed tracery
of fence, wire convolutions—these on the memory screen of the
eye.   Brightness gone.   He opened them again.

" Diversions ready," Willie said behind K hut.   " Fusing ready.
Right sentry standing Red.   Left sentry Green moving Green."
Elegant Willie was quite terse.

" Goons in One, Two and Four Battalion areas," said Dug, the
head stooge.   " None here in Three now.   We're trying to keep
track of them, but there are so damned many. . . ."   Dug did not
sound entirely calm.   Dug was all right for the orthodox set piece
that they had planned for an ordinary night.   But to-night the
prisoners were chaotic, and the Goons were rife.   It was not easy
to be calm.

" Right sentry Red, moving Green—Left sentry Green, moving Red." Moving independently ; that was bad.

Sentry relief due at ten, or ten-five, or ten-ten or ten-fifteen, times of change deliberately varied—or at any hour or not at all on move night. Old sentries thinking of the stable, good. New sentries active, bad. These two old ones now, Left and Right, neither Tossed-Barmies nor Trigger-Happies, average unpredictable men.

" What do you think, Willie ? "

They turned in from the wire. There was one place they could measure darkness—in the dead angle of two huts nearby. They could measure it when no searchlights played out or in, or looped over from this or that, making a nonsense of natural darkness. Harry watched. Time nine forty-nine. He could see the man posted for visibility at twenty yards, or he could see a shape. He could not see the man at thirty. His eyes were getting night-accustomed, but still imperfectly.

Bloody searchlight now again, pretty searchlight sweeping a roof of cloud and down. All the boys waiting, thirty-nine like Buchan, and he the fortieth, Harry Black, M.C. for patrolling on the Saar, a fallible chap, and to this extent wise in his generation : he could think calmly, which he was doing ; he could forget himself, his pride to prove his own pet scheme, and carry this load only for the others ; he could weigh the evidence, and decide to go, and be absolutely right in his decision. But luck could make him wrong —the machine-guns might fire on their own men too—a strand might break, and a shambles of bodies in the coiled wire between the fences—the diversions might fail to hold—the lights might come on immediately again—these and many others, and no scope for offensive tactics as in battle : all they could do was run away.

The possibilities flipped into his cold mind and out ; but they did not matter ; they had been put in a balance long ago. What mattered now was light.

" It's a toss-up, Harry. I'm not sure." Willie's face was blackened too. A vestigal glow of searchlight made a girlish nigger minstrel out of Willie, smiling. Doubtful, but not weakly doubtful.

" It's all right," he said.   " We'll have a go if it holds like this."

They turned again to face the wire.   The wind had died.   A few spits of rain gleamed down.   The camp was a busy hive of people packing in the distance.   It was quieter near at hand, for these four huts had been evacuated except for small noise-parties. A lone gramophone played Brahms, he thought, but he did not know it.   Most of the camp were oblivious of what went on, he hoped.   He hoped that no bullets would find the peaceful packers.

" Left and Right stopped Red, talking."   Which meant that they had met between J and K huts, outside the fence of the tournament grounds.

Report to Dug :   " Two prowlers moving from Two to Three." The prowlers were sentries patrolling inside the camp.

" That's wrecked it.   What can we . . . ?   What . . . ?   Yes, Riot Squad ! "

" No ! " Harry said.   " Cancel that.   Johnny, go and play with them.   Lead the buggers under a hut or something, and don't get shot."

" Okay, Harry."   He was a boy of twenty-three, a good boy from school to war, grown up in this weird world of prison. Johnny went.

It was a time to be rough or get rid of Dug.   Harry went close to him.   " Calm down, Dug, damn you !   We can't waste the Riot Squad on two prowlers.   What the hell have *you* got to be excited about."   Shock treatment.   Might work, might not.

It did, surprisingly.   " Good point, Harry," said Dug.   " I'm sorry."   And he was calm.

Now the forty waited ;   and the hundred helpers waited ;   and the two thousand packers had heard a whisper, and they waited ; and the reluctant S.B.O., who was responsible for these madmen, wasn't he, after all, if officers were killed in a suicidal storming of the wire, and whatever he did was sure to be wrong, and he had weakened to that damned young fanatic, Black—the Senior British Officer waited.   Everyone waited while Left Sentry and Right Sentry still gossiped at nine fifty-seven.

The thing went through Harry's solitary head again, the thing about the loveliest virgin sitting on the peak above the Rhine, combing her golden hair, singing the sailors of the river to destruction.

> Sie kämmt es mit goldenem Kamme
> Und singt ein Lied dabei ;
> Das hat eine wundersame,
> Gewaltige Melodei.

That has a wonderful mighty tune. *Das hat eine wundersame, gewaltige Melodei.* The splendid German words came to him so often as the theme-song of this job. Heard them crossing the bridge in practice ; heard them as he enacted it in his lively mind ; heard them in bed at night. Never said them to anybody else. The perfect tune of the Lorelei for triumph, and the perfect call of the siren to destruction, bothering him, exalting him. Stay away now.

What did the sentries there discuss ? What things were they mumbling to one another ?

And now they moved at last. Right Sentry to the right, Left Sentry to the left, both still Red, both Red diverging to what in sixty yards would be a double Green. Time one minute past ten. Now the chance was coming, if ever a chance would come. He had not finally decided.

Harry kept his eyes open and put his hands over his eyes as a man puts his hands to pray if he puts them tightly to close away the tempting world.

" What's he doing ? " Shocked whisper. Seen chaps pray like that before. Harry's nerve cracked ?

" Don't be a silly goose," said weary Willie. " He's shutting out the light."

But Harry also prayed to the God he reserved for emergency. Oh God, he prayed. Give me strength to do this right.

" Left sentry Red, moving Green. Right sentry stopped Red."

He took his hands away to see the dead angle of the huts. He made the final decision if the chance should come while this darkness held.

" Meierling, underofficer, ten goons, just come in West gate.

Looks like business—moving along Lagerstrasse, making for One Battalion—No, changed direction, coming down to Three, marching."

" Riot Squad ! " said Dug, snap judgment, right.

Harry looked up the camp. He knew how Meierling and his posse must come—by a path running diagonally down the steep bank from the upper to the lower level ; thence directly here. How long ! Say two minutes at a walk, much less at the double. He saw the dip and gleam of an electric torch, which might be in the hand of Hauptmann Meierling himself. The small light moved diagonally downward now across the bank. The Riot Squad would go into action at any moment. They would hold Meierling with perilous ease, if Meierling did not smell a rat.

" My pack," he said, and somebody held it for him. Shoulder straps on, waistbelt tightened. The thirty pounds of food and clothes and this and that sagged into the hollow of his back. The pack and other loads were heavy to him.

" Left Sentry Green, moving Green. Right sentry stopped Red. Now Red moving Green."

" Sentry relief left Guardroom anti-clockwise." Four or five minutes round to here, drop new men off, pick old men up. No trouble for a while yet, but bad—extra men outside the wire. It was a steady, quiet drizzle now. It was four minutes past ten now. *Das hat eine wundersame, gewaltige Melodei*, in his head now.

" Left sentry Green, moving Green. Right sentry Green, moving Green."

He heard German screams at the Riot Squad. He could distinguish the odious banshee yells of Hauptmann Meierling.

" Fuse," he said. He covered his eyes again. His pack was heavy.

" Fuse," said Willie. The message went by light, by a small bulb in a long cylinder of cardboard, throwing a beam so narrowly secret that it had to be aimed like a rifle at the face of one watcher in one place. The letter F, dot-dot-dash-dot in morse code, and F, and again F, F, F.

" Acknowledge." Acknowledge from the experts in the

Cobbler's shop, the two magicians who had worked it out at his request and done it once and blacked out the place for fifteen minutes and proved their point for that time. It was a specialised riddle about the leads to the Cobbler's shop being taken from the main on the town side of the guardroom fuse box. Thus, if you shorted them, you blew the whole camp electrical caboodle and back into the town. It was a piece of prime German idiocy that made the experts chortle. It was the key to this escape. The key had turned once in practice. It should turn now in earnest if the lock had not somehow, inexplicably, been changed.

"Fuse." The warning went also by word of mouth to diversion parties right and left.

Now. Now surely, and he could not allow himself to look. His eyes must be sharply able to say No. Now surely the wizards were laying their iron bar across bared wires or whatever it was the wizards did with danger to themselves without reward. Does it go bang, he wondered? Does it sizzle? The wizard old wizards, as Desmond would say. He hoped Desmond would get over all right. Why so long? It must have failed.

He let in a chink between his fingers. Then the chink was not there. "Out," said Willie. Meierling's tantrum was thriving up the camp.

Harry moved to the open space between the huts. He could see a dim etching of the wire. He saw no harvest stooks. "Go," he said. He waited with Willie. He had always been waiting, standing away from himself a million miles or two, away from the uproar which was cleverly planned like every other thing about this job—a testy abuse of the scapegoat goons for having a mucking air raid while we pack, a sizeable hullabaloo, but not too much. I should be seeing my life unfold, he thought. But he did not see kaleidoscopes from his life. He saw himself from far away outside, like that feeling at night of minuteness in an enormity of space.

"Fused." The confirmation that it really had been done, that it was not a dirty coincidence of air raid warning.

His remote and fancy feelings stopped. He heard the diversions going in. He was grateful about all those people taking risks for nothing—mock ladders up ; grapnels in the wire, twanging rattles to right and left. The teams were coming out, a scuffle of ladders angled through the doors, a mild thump of rubbershod feet on wooden steps. Rubber would slip on wet ladders, but they could not get very wet in the time, in a timeless eternity of one minute.

Harry did not hear Meierling now. " Meierling ? " he asked. He could still stop this escape.

" Meierling held," said Dug.

And now a German voice was shouting at each diversion point : " Stand there, fool ! Guard the ladder ! Escape attempt ! Here Feldwebel Müller," on the left. " Do not move, damned dumb-head. Here Hauptmann Meierling," on the right. It was Hauptmann Meierling to the life. The man had practised him these last two months.

Now cries, now German expostulations, shocked goonery up and down the wire. Now a moderate hubbub of prisoners too. Now silence only here at the tournament ground beyond a moment of no return. Now a silent wonderful mighty tune as the four teams wheeled behind their ladders into line abreast. Four long shadows, four black ships going into the assault.

The front men crossed snare one, the tripwire, six feet this side of the main fence. It was the border of forbidden ground. *Beim überschritten, wird so fort geschossen.* At the stepping over, shoot at once. Someone had given the single strand a slap of white-wash, but white-wash was not luminous paint.

Nobody stumbled. Harry saw the four verticals go up. He saw these dark events more brightly than he had ever seen events. He heard the first touchings of the ladders—one, two, three, four light creaks nearly together. He heard the anchoring spikes kicked in. He saw the launchers push the bridges. He imagined well what he saw only in vague silhouette.

He saw the first men on the ladders, heard the sliding of the bridges, heard a ping and a drum of wood on wire, heard the locking sockets click bridge to ladder of number Three team, quickest now as in practice. Listened for the others—Yes, Two, Four, One.

It was working. Could it really be that it was working, this fantastic, fanciful assault ?

" Go on, Harry ! "

The diversions flourished to right and left. Shots. Don't let those chaps get killed. Up to now loud noises everywhere but here.

He and Willie were behind and between Two and Three teams. He saw Desmond's lankiness ahead of him and to the left. Time to go.

Then the sounds began. He had expected that it would be loud, but never so loud as this pounding, jangling pandemonium, like all the bitches in hell throwing enamel dishes, like all the angels in heaven lauding with cymbals. *Das hat eine wundersame, gewaltige Melodei.* The ten - bogied carriages were eating their several switchbacks up—all except One. Something wrong on One.

" Thanks, Willie. Over to you."

He ran forward. He could not hear the trivial diversions. He heard the sentries shout, running in, and he heard shots, and he saw the flashing shots, and the hump-backed shadows up and on and over. Half over now except on One team, a cock-up on One, bridge skew-eyed, broken away from ladder. The rest of One team coming back.

Six up, Seven at the bottom. Shots closing, crack in my left ear. Seven up, Eight at the bottom. It's getting very hot. My God, the racket. Ricochet—Whee-ee-ow-oh. No machine guns yet. Nobody hit yet, I don't think. Jabber jabber of frenzied goons.

Eight up. Desmond at the bottom. Shot. Shot. He's not going. " Go on, Desmond ! "

But Desmond turned and broke back and stumbled over the trip-wire by Harry. He picked himself up and ran clear as Willie shouted : " Stop ! "

Get back out of it quick, and no damned nonsense. Understand ? But this was his for himself and for nobody else. Harry broke the discipline that he had demanded. He went on. "STOP, HARRY!"

The uproar was lessening as he climbed number Two, seeing

a last man drop off Three and go. Now on the bridge alone, and the knee-sharp slats, and the nightmare barbed tangles below him, now behind him, coming to the end now, to the crossbar beyond the dropping space, and the sentry capering about. Harry saw the man's terrified face, and the rifle. He bellowed at him, animal wordless shout, reached for the bar that he knew would tip under his weight.

This is for me, he thought in the blinding and the deafening. But the shot was not for him.

The bridge did tip. He landed on top of the German sentry, broke his fall nicely, shambles on the ground, sentry had it, not even trying to hold him. " *Tut mir leid*," he grunted politely. " I'm sorry."

He got up and ran into adequate, imperfect darkness in the rain, and the other sentry fired wide, and here was a man, dodge. No, it was a first harvest stook.

Time ? he wondered on the crisp stubble. He was very tired. Forty seconds from the launching, I should think, he thought judiciously. How many got out ? Twenty-five, or thereabouts.

He heard cries of the Deep Field on ahead, a rumpus behind in prison. Pistol shots. He wondered if anybody had been hit. A quarter left was his direction, south-south-east through the Deep Field country, at an angle to the north-south lines of stooks, easy enough to the edge of the woods.

And he thought : That was the best thing in my life. If I lived a hundred lives, nothing could ever match it.

But he had no Desmond to share the thought with. Nor could Desmond have the thought. Desmond had given up his easy place, and then he had failed to make it.

Harry walked. His ears still sang. It was raining now a little. The moon must be rising at ten past ten. He thought that the darkness had weakened by one snippet. *Das hat eine wundersame, gewaltige Melodei.* So the melody had been. But the melody was over. The wonderful mighty tune was now three words niggling at tiresome variance with a lone man's pace, and the lone man's journey had just begun.

CHAPTER TEN

In 1944

Oh Timballo, how happy we are,
When we live in a sieve and a crockery jar.

HE STOOD at the back of the train on that open platform where a
warm wind blew engine fumes and a scent of woods, and he
watched the woods fall away behind empty. They were a dishevelment of stump and slash and second growth. He would have
liked to see them in the beginning, not in the birth of forests, but
in a virgin time before the plunder. Best of all he would have liked
to see young braves flitting about in the old woods. I bet even
Red Indians couldn't flit about with nary a rustle on dry leaves,
he thought. And he thought : I'm thinking a lot of damned
childish things to-day. Besides they don't say Red Indian. That's
goddam limey for an Indian.

Oh dear, he thought. Oh dear, like a maiden aunt, oh dear.
Half the time I think that if I have to enthuse even once again, I
shall go stark staring cuckoo ; and half the time I feel surprised
at myself all flattered and come over cosy-queer like a dour sister
people suddenly make love to.

I think it's wonderful. Boom, boom, I boom like old Big Ben.
I can say it now with the steely look that spells : *He's so sincere.*
I am too, in my shifty English way.

But lady, may I say first that I am no more a Lieutenant-Colonel
than you are a Contessa ; I am acting, unpaid, elevated for a month.
May I say second that I was taught to shy from the superlative as
a horse shies from a camel. May I say third that I am not Abou
Ben Adhem ; I like a few people very much, but the masses of the
lecture-happy middle-classes are in my opinion rather asses. May
I say fourth that when I see a crowd of people I see a crowded

crowd of prison people from whom I could not escape until I escaped to deliver lectures to new crowds of people. A couple of big slugs of gin gets me over it about the crowds. Well, I can get over it about the crowds. May I say last that your warmth and faith and love of life are better things than I have. But may I say, P.S., that I cannot see your lovely woods for all the crowds of lovely people.

The platform jostled. He liked to watch the narrowing backdrop of beyond. But it would be better from the engine, to see perhaps a deer, a moose, a bear, if anything lived in the empty woods. His stump started to nag again with the shaking and the standing, so he went inside the coach and sat down with his legs up to look at Invasion pictures in *Life* magazine. He shacked up behind *Life* magazine. There were a few passengers, but nobody came and talked to him until the conductor made his ticket round. The conductor was a large, deliberate man.

" First time down, Colonel ? " he asked as one speaks about the weather.

" Yes," Harry said. " I'm looking forward to it very much."

" Not a bad little place," the conductor said, punching, and went away.

He had lectured at army camps and air force stations, and to Canadian Clubs in some cities. He had been a prize escaped-poodle for a month from coast to coast and back by train and plane and car. They were proud of their cities and loathed their lonely camps. He had yet to encounter a not-bad-little-place.

He looked at *Life*'s monopoly of war. He wondered if big Uncle Sam would carry his little allies along to victory this summer. He thought Patton must be a good armoured commander, not in Rommel's class. He abandoned *Life* to see a lake that broke a monotony of woods. He wondered how Desmond was getting on beside the mythical lake in Brunswick. He wished that he could see old Desmond. He wished that he did not have to see old Desmond's wife and say the things he had said so many times to wives or relations of people he did not care about, and some of them he had not known from Adam.

My husband, Arthur Hopkins, he was in that camp with you. I wonder . . . ? Arthur Hopkins. I did know him. Now who the hell was he ? *I brought a photo of Arthur, just in case. Here, it's in my bag.* Got him, thank God. A dreary chap and a pretty wife. *Of course I know Arthur. He was working in the Parcel Hatch last summer, very well and cheerful.*

An easy one, but it was not easy for an unavuncular individual to be a universal uncle, knowing that wives who asked in that particular way were wives to whom his few words would be as diamonds. There were others who asked hastily what they did not want to know, did not listen to the answers, thanked him effusively and buzzed off to grasp a real live man.

And now Christian Tanner in Category One, letters exchanged, and hers were charming. I wonder if I'll know the woman at the station, he wondered. Of course I'll know her.

The train stopped yet again for no visible reason in the wilderness. " When do we get there ? " he asked the conductor.

" Twenty minutes, half an hour," the conductor said. The conductor was the boss of a Canadian train. Was the guard the boss of an English train ? Well, this conductor and his one-horse train seemed to have a leisurely understanding.

Harry was restless. He had done nothing but travel and talk and meet and eat and drink this past month after ten months of fretting in hospitals in Switzerland and England, and having his tin leg fitted, and practising with that, and seeing prisoners' people while the world champed at the bit of the invasion. Turned down for war, and peace not wanted or expected in a world of war. But what had happened to his freedom dream ?

The train started with uncouth joltings, and ran down the slaughtered woods again—the pine, the spruce, the canoe birches, and the less easy trees nobody seemed to know the names of. He had arrived at a conclusion, doubtless wrong, that the people of this land did not love the good earth of their land.

The train rambled out of woods to the sea on one side and woods still on the other. He went back to his platform. The smell of the sea was strong at low tide if you happened to like that order of smell, which he was not sure that he did, being an inland boy. But there was life in the rank tang, and death of course. God, he thought, it's a wonderful bloody vital country.

So with the clanging of engine-bell and the same hooting that had called wild and remote for him by night over woods and lakes, and across the prairies and through mountains and down to the farther ocean, this lackadaisical small train stopped at its destination in the afternoon.

" I'll take your bag," the conductor said, doing so.

Did conductors carry bags? He found fifty cents, which he hoped would not be beneath the episcopal dignity of the conductor.

The man waited at the door. " Not from that chest of medals, Colonel. Thanks just the same." He took down the suitcase. " Well now, Christian, how's my girl ? "

" Fine, Mr. Wolseley. Harry ! So you really came. Did you get to know one another on the way down ? Mr. Wolseley, this is Colonel Black who was in Germany with my husband."

" I guessed it would be, from the pictures in the papers. But I says to myself he must have had a bellyful of answering damn-foolish questions."

Harry shook hands with Mr. Wolseley, the conductor, whom he would remember. He and Desmond's wife walked over to the car. " I like that chap," he said.

" He's been our conductor ever since I was a child. Mr. Wolseley's sweet."

Harry smiled at the woman's word for a man, and he got into the car beside her, and she drove off. Nothing came to him immediately to say. He looked at pleasant white houses and ugly shops and unhurried people in the sun. He thought that war was in the planet Mars. He noticed her hands on the rim and a spoke of the steering wheel. " We live two miles outside the town," she said.

" It seems small for a town," he said.

" The summer people say village, and the town people say town."

" Aren't you a summer people ? "

" Yes," she said. " I happened to say town."

Harry laughed.

" It's uncanny to hear you laugh that way. I mean, knowing from Desmond how you explode."

" That's also why I laughed," he said.

They turned off a main road, and here were the woods again. " You must think them so disappointing and untidy. I noticed that when I came back last year."

" Yes," he said. " I would love to see the big old Indian woods."

" There are places with virgin forests still. But I suppose you never had a moment. You must be exhausted, are you, Harry ? How's your leg ? "

" It's been a bit of a nuisance lately, off and on. Neuroma, they call it, something to do with the nerve-ends. I'm going to have it fixed up when I get home." He wanted to talk about Desmond, not his leg, but he thought perhaps she would not at first like talking about Desmond. " It's nothing to speak of."

She smiled at him. " Oh, I'm sure not."

He changed his mind. " Any letters ? "

" The last I had was dated June the second. They take such ages, but I suppose it's the invasion."

" Yes," he said. " Mail was stopped before that ; and now communications get more chaotic every day. How did he sound ? "

" Cheerful, but piano sort of. He sent you messages by a code name. They wouldn't let ' Harry ' through, I guess."

" Anything special ? "

" No. Just wondering how you were. He was so pleased and proud of you about the escape. He misses you dreadfully, I think, and this last year I think it's been much harder for him without you to help him and make him laugh. I just sense it somehow ; he never says that kind of thing."

Poor Desmond who didn't make it. " I miss him too. Desmond and a few people. My pre-war pals are all right to connect with on a party ; but we don't speak quite the same language now-adays."

"I don't see how you could," she said, and turned into a drive. "Here we are. My father and mother are longing to meet you."

*   *   *   *   *

"Come along, dear. It's time for bed, and I know Christian has a thousand things to ask him."

Plump Mr. Foley and dowager Mrs. Foley went to bed.

"Are you tired, Harry?"

"Not a bit," he said. He was full of food and drink and amiable notions.

"Shall we sit out, then, for a while? Pour yourself a drink while I get a coat."

He got the drink and went outside. The moon was on the wane. The tide had turned, he thought, from damp glistenings on rock. He sat on one chair with his leg on another. Gulls lamented. The moon made a shimmer path from yonder on the bay. He heard voices in an upstairs room. He liked her parents. It seemed to him that everyone infallibly was kind, but they were kindly with reserve.

Christian arrived, and they watched the sea.

"Was the moon like this the night you did it?"

"Same size of moon," he said, "but a thick drizzly night, and darkish. It cleared later on." He hoped she would not ask about all that yet.

"One moon year ago. It must seem a century to you."

"Sometimes it does," he said. "Sometimes it seems much nearer than anything that's happened since."

"Your escape, you mean?"

"No," he said. "I mean the whole boring comic opera."

"Was it really funny? That's so hard to understand. I mean not just better laugh than cry?"

"That too. But we always had a genuine goonish villain to tease into his little tantrums. We became wonderfully good at that."

"Horrible Germans," she said. "I hate them, although I hardly dare to say it. Did Desmond hate them?"

"I think he despised them. He's too gentle a chap to cherish

hates. Anyway, some Germans were all right. But it was funny
at times, and very boring, and we had the Teuton as scapegoat
for all troubles. One good reason why it was more harmonious
than ordinary life."

"How fascinating. I hadn't thought of that."

"But the war's-nearly-over hopes and false alarms were
singularly unfunny. They used to drive me demented unless I
happened to be full steam on an escaping project at the moment,
when wars were of no interest whatsoever. But I'm an impatient
chap. Desmond has the most godlike patience."

"Yes," she said. "I remember."

He thought it sad to hear a wife remember the patience of her
husband of a month or two.

"What was the worst thing, Harry?"

"For everyone a ton of prisondom without end, I think, and
can't describe. Otherwise, different things for different people.
Some chaps whose wives took off for parts unknown, that might
be their worst thing. Some ambitious soldiers frustrated in the
bag, that might be worst for them. So many different things. I
think the crowding was my *bête noire*, no privacy I mean."

"So people were your worst thing."

"Worst," he said, "and best. Looking back, the tiresome
exasperating people were the best thing. Not that I really can
look back. I wear a different pair of spectacles outside."

"Good lenses, I would think," she said, and moved for the first
time. "You aren't wearing rosy ones on my account?"

"No," he said. "You see, we were lucky, comparatively
speaking. I'm sure there is a point in hunger or in fear beyond
which people, almost any people, become plain animal. That
happens in the concentration camps. We saw it happen in a
small Russian camp beside us. There were two hundred of them
in the autumn, and sixty left in March. The Germans starved them
systematically until the live ones ate the dead ones, or so the Goons
used to mention as proof about *Herrenvolk* and *Untermenschen*,
the Master race and the Sub-human. Christian, I shouldn't be
telling you this."

"I must hear it," she said. "Go on." She sat still again on her deck-chair with hands clasped in her lap. The tide was ebbing down to flats of mud. A breeze blew from the sea to this open place beside the shore, and the breeze spoke in the woods behind.

"They starved them to death, but they used to herd them round outside our wire and in the gate, and up to our delousing room because they were afraid the starvelings would spread typhus. I remember the chivied corpses stumbling along with mutual support, picking frozen grass to eat. And I remember forests of skeleton arms held out through the high windows of the delousing chamber—transom windows, I think you call them. We slipped the arms a fair amount of food.

"So we were lucky. We were hungry in the early days before parcels started, but not quite starving. We were just human beings in adversity and full of weakness, but I know that I saw nobility in human beings, a spark."

"Of God?"

"You could call it that."

"I remember the same in London in the Blitz. People were wonderfully unselfish and wonderfully brave."

He thought how much more this girl had seen and done than he had seen and done for his M.C. and his D.S.O. "That was adversity," he said.

"Are you disappointed in freedom, Harry, then?" She turned to look at him. She had a beautiful face, and the voluptuous substance of a woman, yet he wondered if she was quite substantial woman.

"I'm a fool," he said. "I thought I had life worked out, but free life isn't quite the simple sausage that I thought."

"It's a lovely thing to know that Desmond's friend came out believing more in human beings. You're the first prisoner I've ever talked to."

"Didn't you meet any of the repatriated people?"

"I suppose I could have, but I never did. Actually, I've been scared stiff of meeting you."

He laughed. "Same here," he said. His stump jabbed at him.

Go away, you, he told his stump. " It's good to find a bit of peace. The sea and the forest and the summer night. What do those moonstruck gulls keep carrying on about ? "

" They fly up with clams and drop them to break on rock. They're wonderfully good bombers in a moon. You must be so tired, Harry."

" No," he said. If he went to bed, he would not sleep. " I like sitting here."

" Could you tell me just a bit about the camp ? I mean the mundane things—what you and Desmond did and what you ate, and the amusing things, and the bad bits without a censor. I've never been able to imagine it ; perhaps I could see it if you talked."

It was odd how people said " the camp," when they meant camps generically. P.O.W.'s said " in prison," or " in the bag," or " in the shaft." Perhaps outsiders shied off that " prison " word. What was so terrible about prison ? What was prison compared with being shot at in a battle ? What a lot of sentimental soap had been talked in this war about the poor noble prisoner. To be taken wounded, or shot down on a raid, one thing—but was there nobility in putting up your hands ? Harry had made his glamorous escape. He was not a man who could puncture that balloon.

He tried to talk about the other life, which was more real to him than life before or since, than sitting here with Christian Tanner after midnight in the ebb of moon and tide three thousand miles away. It was a thing that he hated to recapture, and could not quite recapture, and could not quite believe that it still went on without him. He talked at random. He told her the cheerful nightmare rather well, he thought. He told her the truth, with a few reservations.

" I believe you miss it in a kind of way."

He knew that he missed people and things about it. " Life down to essentials, uncomplicated. Life with one purpose and a meaning. Yes, I do." He did not miss what he saw now, a faceless crowd of hunched men walking round the wire. The wire never got him down when he was inside it. Wire fences looked worse the other way.

"I've never said this. But the fear I have is that they might do something to them at the end."

"You needn't worry. I'm absolutely certain that won't happen. There are a hundred reasons why it never would." But he knew one reason why it might—that Adolf Hitler would try to take the Germans with him into an unscalable abyss of crime.

"You help me so much," Christian said. "Tell me, do you sometimes dream about it still?"

"Most nights, I think." On the nights I sleep, he said to himself. "Either I dream I'm being chased by monstrous dogs across Bavaria. Or I dream I'm digging tunnels, which is usually a pleasant dream, because tunnelling could be the best thing in the world. Or if I'm half awake, I wait for Desmond to get out of the lower bunk to go and shave. He's been an early riser since the early days." Damn, he thought. I shouldn't have told her that.

"Silly me," she said soon. "It's been rather a long time, Harry."

"Yes," he said. "It gives me the willies to think about the wives—having to see the rest of the world go on, and being young and human and all the rest." I suppose Christian is human, he thought. If she was really passionate and human, I wonder why she married my friend Desmond, who is a handsome chap and a good man for a man, but perhaps he hasn't got that physical bite in him that makes real live women collapse to die a pleasurable death. Dunno. Dunno anything. "Sorry, I didn't hear."

"I only said that it isn't hard to want to be and be a faithful wife. I just said : Sorry, chum, to the amorous beasts, and they soon caught on. Warriors are quite easy to compete with, really. Time is so precious to them in the realms of love."

Harry laughed. "You're very good value. Pray continue."

"Old-fashioned value, then, because I don't think I ever would have, even if I'd met someone devastatingly attractive. As for being hard, I guess it's easier for a woman who knows her husband is out of other women's clutches than it is for a woman who guesses her husband is hitting it up with every slut from Cairo to

Capri. Or perhaps not Capri, because that's the queer place, which would be another worse thing altogether."

He said to Willie once : *Willie, I think you shave your risks too close. The object of the exercise is to survive for something better.* And Willie had replied : *My dear Harry, I must take risks in order to survive to be an ageing pederast in Capri, which is what I undoubtedly would become.* " Would," he said, and Willie had not survived. He had been shot dead in a train escape before Harry got to Switzerland.

" What are you going to do about meeting Desmond ? "

" I joined the F.A.N.Y.'s in 1940. Do you know the socially okay Fannies ? "

" Alas," he said. " I do."

" Well, they were short of instructors over here last summer, and the C.W.A.C. asked me to transfer. So I said all right if they would guarantee me a priority flight back, and Daddy pulled innumerable strings, and that's the situation. I wish I was there now, actually. Buzz-bombs would lend some spice to a grass widow's life."

" Desmond would not agree."

" What should we do, Harry ? Should we rent a cottage in the country ? Should we go on terrific binges ? What ? "

" Take him away from people," Harry said. " Let him get as drunk as an owl, if he wants to. He won't want to, being Desmond. Pamper the man, and don't be sorry for him. Take steps to start a family. Advice ended."

" There's a rumour. Apparently some doctors say that prisoners may not be able . . ."

" I've heard that one. I'd like to string the doctors up. Never heard such b . . . such nonsense." He hoped that he had not started any families himself.

" Bang ! " she said. " You go off like a gun. I know about you and you know about me, bits of you and me. Did you discuss your wives and girls ? "

" Casually," he said. " No cozy talks. But if you live with a chap for long enough, you know what he reflects of his possessions. They even become yours mildly. I don't know."

"All I know," said Christian Tanner, "is that you're a comfort to one possession. I haven't felt so peaceful since he went to France."

And I, thought Harry Black. When was I comforted until to-night?

The tide had gone far out. The moon dipped to the wooded point, making shadows across a puddled sheen of mud. His leg was troublesome, and he was tired. The breeze had dropped. Mosquitoes whined about his head, and pricked the good ankle, which was one negative advantage he had learned in Canada. The time was nearly two o'clock. The gulls lamented less. The strong land and the strong land's sea were strong about him. "What was that unearthly sound?" he asked.

"That was a loon laughing in the bay."

"I've heard of loons," he said. "I've heard a lot about this country that I haven't seen."

"The natural world is what you really like."

"Yes," he said. "I learned about it when I lost it for a while."

"So they send you lecturing to crowds of loons in army camps and cities. Poor you."

"I've got nothing to complain about. Don't waste sympathy on me."

"Englishmen are so ridiculous," Christian said, "with their old school ties and their brushed up hair, terrified to let it down, I mean. Desmond is the same."

He smiled and said nothing and decided it was time for bed.

"Do you have to go on the Sunday evening train?"

"Ottawa on Monday, yes, I must. Could you and your parents endure me until then?"

"Endure you? This is the high spot of Daddy's war, having been in the other one himself. It's one of the nicest things to see an older man make a hero of a young man, like little boys the wrong way round. He hangs on every syllable that you emit. He may not bring himself to ask, but what he longs to hear about is your escape. Will you tell him?"

" Of course." He was not a simple enough character to relish glamourising Harry Black. He knew a lot of half-baked bums in prison who would lecture splendidly *ad grabem* on escapes they never made. He thought of that, and then it occurred to him that Christian seemed diffident on the subject of escape. It occurred to him also that she was the most restful woman he had ever met. She made Miriam and the others seem like jumping jennies.

" What would you like to do to-morrow ? Be sociable ? Or read a book all day ? Or drive around the country ? Or go sailing ? "

" Anything not too partyfied," he said. " Whatever Christian Tanner orders in the morning."

" The morning will be here so soon. Your leg is hurting, Harry."

" How do you know ? "

" Because you move it often on the chair. Does it keep you awake at night ? You don't look like a sound-sleeping man. How many good sleeps have you had this month ? "

She was standing. She was restful, but not particularly restful for a chap to look at, day or night or setting moon. He therefore looked out to sea. " Nothing spectacular," he said about the sleeping.

" I'll get you a pill then. We have some in the house."

" I don't hold with sleeping pills."

" I know," she said. " They're such a dreadful sign of weakness. But you're going to have one."

*　　　*　　　*　　　*　　　*

She was waiting in the car. " What did you see ? "

" Deer, porcupine, birch partridge, lesser birds, trees, and red flowers beside the river. Herewith one."

" A cardinal flower," she said. " How nice. I'll press it."

" We also saw moose tracks, but no moose."

" Sorry no moose," the other man said. " Scarce nowadays." He remained silent on the drive back to his house beside the highway. " 'Bye, then," he said to Harry. " Come again."

" *Come again* is rare warmth from the most taciturn man in Lower Canada," she said, en route.

He laughed. " I might have gone home bang-full of hustle-bustle good-guy bunkum about this country. So much for impressions."

" When I was young, I used to think first impressions were the right ones. Now I think impressions are the end."

" Now old and grey and full of sleep, you've changed your mind. But they do seem to be self-sufficient here. Individuals, I mean."

" You're hipped about individuals," she said. " Do you think that's what we lack ? "

He thought that freedom might flourish on the rebel and the man, and would founder on the conventional and the mass. Hobby horses were a bore. They ran into fog down near the coast. " Has Desmond decided what he's going to do ? He talked of Canada at one time."

" He seems to be keen on India again. His firm are holding the job for him, but he told me to write and ask if they could give him anything up-country. He said he wouldn't go back to Calcutta. That was this spring. Mackintosh and Garrett are the people. They wrote back and said Assistant Manager of a sugar factory in Bihar, with good prospects. What do you think about India after this war, Harry ? "

" I wouldn't know," he said. " They're going to have their independence, but they can't indianize their industry for ages. No, I should think it might be all right." He also thought that a sugar factory in Bihar might be a dim place to isolate yourself and a shining wife.

" Anywhere he wants to go," she said. " Only he sounded so keen on Canada before. I would love to see the East, but India as a place to live . . . You were born there, weren't you ? "

" Yes," he said. " We left when I was eight. And I went back after I joined the Regiment."

" I suppose you'll stay in the Army, will you ? "

" I'm going to the Staff College when I get back. I might stay in if they would pass me completely fit. I don't think they will. Can't take to my heels rapidly enough. There isn't much point in being a soldier if you can't command."

" Is command what matters ? "

" You can't get anywhere worth speaking of without it."

" To the very top, you mean ? "

" Yes," he said.

" All or nothing. Is that you ? "

He supposed that arrogance was him. He might have said that peacetime soldiering—command or not—would be a bore. He might have said that in his reasoning unreasonable essence he disdained ambition. He might have said a number of things that might or might not add up to what was him. They were nearly home on the second afternoon. He did not answer.

" And if you leave the Army ? "

" I may go back to India too. I heard from a chap the other day. He tried to get me to resign and go into tea with him before the war when he managed a garden near Darjeeling. Now he's a *bara sahib*, big noise, in Calcutta. I can think of worse things to do."

" Would your leg be troublesome in India ? "

" In the plains, it might, they say. But this is high and cool. If old Peg-legs can walk ten miles on none, I could damn' well learn to climb hills on what I've got."

" Thus gallop to the top in tea."

" Why do you needle me ? "

" I'm sorry," Christian said. " I meant the opposite. I meant there are so many things you could do without having to be a Field Marshal, and tea-planting might be a waste. Mind my own business."

He thought it would have been better if he had gone to-day. To-morrow he was going. " When is your leave up ? " he asked.

" Wednesday as ever is. Then back to teaching little girls to drive. Home in the murky mist," she said.

" I like a fog at the edge of the sea. It closes you off with rumours."

" I know," she said, and they went in.

" The wanderers return.   Where did you go ? "

" We drove around," she said.

" This leave has made a new girl out of Christian.   I wish young Desmond could see how well you look to-day."

Christian left the room.

" Poor child," said Mother Foley.   " You do say tactless things, dear, sometimes."

*   *   *   *   *

" . . . I had to put myself tenth on our team because conditions were so doubtful that the thing needed watching up to the last moment.   Desmond should have stayed third—third and fourth were the places we had drawn—and we could have rendezvoused easily enough outside.   But he wouldn't do that.   He stuck in his quixotic toes and insisted on going ninth. . . ."

She got up and went over to the window and shaded her eyes against the light.   " He would," she said.   " It's foggy still. Go on."

" . . . That tripwire was the snag.   We couldn't see it, and we were loaded down with packs, and we had to move so fast. Desmond stumbled over the bloody thing and fell flat on his face and that was that.   It was a most damnable bit of luck."

She still stood at the window.   " You couldn't help him up ? "

He had thought of that one too.   " Time was short," he said. " In fact Willie was shouting *Stop* when I was half-way over, but by then I was committed.   Actually, I landed on the sentry.   You see, speed was the essence of the thing, so we had to lay down that people must not wait for anything or anyone.   If I had stopped, we would both have been too late."

Well, he thought.   Have I told a convincing cock and bull ? Have I struck a balance between slightly justifying myself and being sure I did the right thing ?

" Did the sentry fire at you ? "

" Yes, he did."

" And if Desmond had stayed in third place and still had stumbled—would there have been a difference ? "

" Yes," he said. " He could have picked himself up in time. As it was, he damned nearly did."

She came to the fire, and he watched her looking down into the curl of a flame of birchbark. He thought that he had travelled far to be in this house by the shore in fog.

" Desmond will never think it was bad luck," she said. " And he will always know it wasn't on the cards for Harry to help him up. He will always think he let Harry down."

" That's nonsense."

" Oh no, it's not. That's what he means in his letters and doesn't say, and now I understand."

" You're wrong, Christian. He can't possibly mean that. I've told you what happened. I was lucky and Desmond was damned unlucky. Do you think I'm pleased about it ? "

She turned to him. " Of course not, Harry. But you don't seem to realise that to Desmond you're perfection. He failed to get over. Therefore he failed to measure up to the great Harry. Bad luck is not the point."

Has she guessed ? Or is this jealousy, or what ? I worked it out so carefully to get it right for Desmond, and she gives me hell. She does have fire. " If he ever imagines he let me down, tell him not to be a fool. I owe Desmond far more than he could ever owe to me."

" I know you feel that," Christian said. " But it's hard for a person as strong and unfaltering as you are to realise what you do to other people."

" I suppose I was strong enough in prison," Harry said. " Things never seemed to be much trouble. I'm a flop outside it."

" Why do you say that ? "

He was aware of her in the flicker of the fire, so he looked away. " Why not ? "

" Oh, Harry," she said. " Valiant-for-Truth. How dare you think that you're a flop. It isn't your fault you can't fight now."

" We had an expression for that: *Colonel Self-Pity*. Applicable?"

"It couldn't be less so about your leg. But I wonder..." She stared at him. He saw that passion and compassion were in Christian Tanner.

"Go on."

"I wonder if you aren't supremely good at making the world revolve round you, and rather bad and petulant about being revolved yourself. That's the genius-devil. The rest of us are much happier swanning along around the circle."

He laughed. "You're wonderful," he said. "You pat me on the head and give me a spanking and make me want to be a better boy."

"School-marm type," she said tartly. "A drink?"

"No, thank you." He watched her. He wondered what went on in the fair head of Desmond's wife. "Any plans for the morrow?"

"Would you like to sail before lunch if the fog clears?"

"Very much. But don't you usually go to church? Your mother said . . ."

"I'm going to early service by myself, hence now to bed. Sleep as late as you can, Harry. I'll leave a pill on the table outside your door in case you happen to decide of your own free will you want it. Good night." She smiled without enthusiasm, and went.

★　　★　　★　　★　　★

The fog burned off or went to sea or whatever the fog did, and they sailed at eleven. "Haven't you ever sailed?"

"I capsized my company commander's wife on a lake at Naini Tal in India."

"Was she a capsizable company commander's wife?"

"Eminently tippy. Word reached my colonel. He was the sort of idle colonel who knows everything. Anyway, he said sailing was too perilous a poodle-fakin' sort of sport for a subaltern of his; so he put me into another company on detachment and told me to devote my spare time to tigers. He was a good hard chap with a sense of humour."

"You must have had a high old time in those old days."

" Yes," he said. " My best time, I suppose, perhaps."

" When was better ? Prison ? "

" No," he said.

" I would like to have seen you wild and young and carefree."

And I would like to have seen you, Harry thought. He saw her now in those denim trousers they called blue-jeans, rolled nearly to the knee, and a pale blue workshirt, and they were sailing for an island in the bay. She had told him the island's name, but he forgot.

" How well did you know Desmond ? "

" For a year in Calcutta. We shot snipe together, and I took him after tiger once upcountry. We met at the Saturday Club, and parties and so on. We got to know one another pretty well."

" Did you go dancing ? "

" Certainly. We trotted round the fishing fleet, I mean the hopeful spinsters out from England for the cold weather." And hot B-class girls in the hot weather, not Desmond's form so much, he added to himself.

" Was he the same ? "

" Yes," he said. " More coltish but the same." He might have said that Desmond had been lighter-hearted then, but why say that to Desmond's grass widow of four years, five summers ?

" And Harry called the tune ? "

" Of course," he said. " If that's what you like to think."

" You're so quick," she said. " So quick to slap me down for making a carpy womanish remark I didn't really mean."

" I'm sorry. But you make me wonder if I'm human."

" Before I met you, I did wonder if you could be quite human."

Al Capone and Good-time Charlie and Sir Galahad, he remembered laughing at on the afternoon of the escape. " And the verdict now ? "

" So many Harrys," Christian Tanner said, " but they make one terribly human Harry." Her face was tilted up to watch the mainsail. " Soon we must come about."

"That's the difference between us," Harry said. "You're complete and only one."

"Shall we change our minds and sail right back and eat our picnic lunch at home?"

"My last day, and my only sail. Let me be human to this extent."

She laughed, and the moment had gone. She said: "That girl at home you mentioned the first day. Are you going to marry her?"

Who is Miriam? What is she? God forbid. "God knows," he said.

They sailed on the starboard tack on a bright sea to the island where there was one fisherman's house. The fisherman helped them to moor the boat to his running line.

"What's the weather going to do?" she asked the fisherman.

He looked south-east. He was a plain middle-aged man. "Hold up," he said. "But the fog will be in by half ebb." The fog lurked low and innocent along the rim of sea. "Make yourselves at home," the fisherman said, waving his hand about his island. "Plenty blueberries for the picking." He went to the door of his white house and turned to watch them.

"He has a good face," Harry said.

"Hard weather," Christian said. "Fathers and mothers and storms and trouble and a small bit of happiness. Let's pick blueberries, shall we, with a rule not to eat many till we have enough."

They picked blueberries and drank beer and ate their lunch. It would be a fine day all day while the fog held off.

"Have you never been here before?"

"No," she said. "Another island where nobody lives, that was our picnic island out there in the fog, if no fog and no trains to catch.

> "And all night long they sailed away
> And when the sun went down
> They whistled and warbled a moony song
> To the echoing sound of a coppery gong
> In the shade of the mountains brown. . . ."

"Can you go on?"

" O Timballo ! How happy we are,
　　When we live in a sieve and a crockery jar
　　And all night long in the moonlight pale
　　We sail away with a pea-green sail
　　In the shade of the mountains brown !

Twenty years, the Jumblies were away, and they sailed home safely
in their sieve. The fog is coming, Harry. Good-bye, island."

The fisherman hauled in the boat. " Come any time," he said.
" I like seeing young folks around the place."

" I'm afraid I'm leaving this afternoon. Do you live alone
here ? "

" My boy's wife and the two kids, but they're away right now.
My boy was in the Navy. You from the other side ? "

" Yes," he said.

" My boy was lost in English waters."

" Oh, I'm sorry," Christian said.

" You got any kids, you people ? "

She shook her head, and she put her left hand with the gold
ring on the finger on the gunwale of the sailing boat and went
aboard and held her other hand out to Harry. He was clumsy
getting into a boat.

" Good-bye," they said to the lonely fisherman. " Thank you
very much."

" Good luck," the fisherman said, and pushed them off. They
sailed before the light fog wind.

" Don't cry," he said to Desmond's wife. " Don't cry, my love."

" It would have been all right. It would have been all right.
It would have been quite all right except for that sad kind man
seeing we were happy. I wouldn't be crying, and you wouldn't
have said, would you, Harry ? "

" No," he said. " I would not have said."

" . . . I was learning Desmond again through you, and being
with him almost, and I knew you were tired out and your leg was
bad and you couldn't be bothered with people. But crowds and
crowds of people, that's what we should have done. It isn't your
fault, Harry, not one little bit. It's me."

" Of course it is my fault," he said.

" And last night when you insisted on telling me about that horrible wonderful escape, I knew then that it wasn't my dear good Desmond I wanted to learn about and know about, it was you, and I was hating myself and being so unkind, I just couldn't help it."

" It isn't a kind business," Harry said.   " As I discover."

" For the first time, Harry darling ?   Surely not after all your women."

" Yes," he said.   " Downfall of a cynic.   Eros only, I believed in.   Why say : *All my women* ? "

" It's obvious," she said, "as you well know.   Fifty must have told you."

" All I know," he said, " is that I have behaved in a peculiar fashion to my friend."

" . . . He came by the Pacific that time in 1939, and he had introductions to people in Toronto.   Anyway, we met, and I was twenty, and he was just that rare kind of good Englishman wanting to give people more than he gets and never looking down his nose, and pure in heart, which sounds so phony but absolutely isn't about Desmond, and so good-looking.   That was two weeks in June.   He went on to England, and then the war came, and of course being Desmond he didn't go back but wangled a transfer from the Light Horse into the Yeomanry, and he cabled and asked me to marry him.

" I went over and we were married and we were happy in those queer months till January when he went to France.   Not very physical, perhaps.   It happens to hundreds of people, and they never know unless the lightning hits them.   I'm old-fashioned, I suppose, but there's that rude saying about making your bed and lying on it. That's all.   I had to tell you this one and only time."

" There's nothing rude about it.   It makes sense.   Nor is there anything rude in me wanting you like hell."   He looked at her. She sat at the tiller, and he on the seat forward, so that he was looking at her and at the island of the fisherman.   " We could have laughed together in the night," he said.

" We have everything to remember because nothing at all, and nobody knows till they have been sad and happy in this unbelievable way, and we never will laugh together in the night. Is God angry with us, do you think ? "

" God knows we're only human."

She laughed. " Darling, do you believe in God ? "

" I do to-day," he said. " What God might frown on is that if I could live my life with you, I might always believe in God."

" And a better reason for believing, I suppose. We shall be home in half an hour. How comes the fog ? "

" No island now. We were just in time."

" Do you know what my mother said this morning ? She said : *Christian, my child, can't you see what is happening to you ?* "

" And you replied ? "

" I flounced. I'm not usually a flouncer."

" No," he said. " You're not a flouncer."

" Your leg has been hurting you all day. I can tell now when it does, from something in your face. My poor Harry."

" Don't you mind the idea of it ? Wouldn't a stump of a leg offend you ? "

" Offend me ? How idiotic can you be ? "

It was true about the leg. The pain was not steady. It thrust at him and went away and thrust again. It was a hellish little bitch of an intermittent pain.

" It makes a wonderfully complete nothing," Christian said. " Not even holding hands."

" I love your hands," he said.

" Could you take off the tin bit and lay your leg on the seat beside me ? "

" Yes," he said. He did that.

He watched her hand with Desmond's ring. He was sorry. He was happy. She did not ask him if her hand had banished pain.

CHAPTER ELEVEN

In 1952

"Your favourite frigid mistress."

THE RAIN was loud. It rained dawn and day and dusk and night except when it stopped raining. The rain came down the chimney to spit occasionally on the fire. It was rain-cool up here and rain-hot in the valleys and snow-cold in the imagined heights. He had not seen his unclimbed mountain for a month. He never was sure she could be there until she lay again, monstrously beautiful across the gulf. Kanchenjunga was her name.

He had been playing Beethoven's Hammerklavier sonata, but that was half an hour or so ago. The turntable still spun its laminated stack quietly in here within the loud rain and the loud cicadas in the trees outside.

He switched off the gramophone, stoked the fire and got a drink. Life was a great thing, and the great thing in life was proper order and decorum. Unto each day its bottle. Thus a reasonable ration and a reasonable target. He did not like that *target* word, being no Stakhanovite. He was not a Communist, a Tory, a Labourite or Fascist. As to what he was, well, did it matter? What mattered very much was going respectably to hell. The Gold Label did not dwindle in its own brown bottle. It was poured distastefully by Cheddi Khan at break of day into a Waterford decanter, and sipped from good cut glass.

He topped up and took the drink and walked a line of squares or oblongs on the big Bokhkara as straight as any plumb line to his chair. He was reading Yeats. He liked music and poetry late at night alone. The music or the poetry would shiver up the whiskied him and through his genial head.

> One had a lovely face,
> And two or three had charm,
> But charm and face were in vain
> Because the mountain grass
> Cannot but keep the form
> Where the mountain hare has lain.

It sounded well, and what did it mean? He read it again; probably it had no meaning. He read it numerous times until the meaning reached him. He was surprised at his tortoise wits, and delighted with the meaning. I must read that to my darling wife, he thought.

Here I am, he thought soberly and sadly. Here I am, the dilettante in dissolution. In short, old boy, I've had it.

The Indian night could be wisely, if roughly, divided into four quarters, like spring to nine, like summer to twelve, like autumn to three, like winter to six. The third quarter was half-way through on a Saturday night or Sunday morning in September, how confusing.

He went for the last of to-day's, or yesterday's, decanter, but he was called to the outside world to water his well-watered garden, which he did. The rain was balmy on his hotness. So rain came down and cloud came up and there was nothing but wetness, shrill cicadas of the wetness, fecund wetness, dripping wetness from the Sirus trees. Now the Sirus is a nanny tree, a nitrogen provider to the tea bush, may the Lord preserve us.

He heard Lalbahadur, his Gurkha chokidar, cough on the back veranda. He heard a car turn down from the Ghoom road. He listened. Years of listening had taught him much. Not only could he distinguish Jeep from Landrover from English tiddler, simple. He could distinguish drivers. The jeep whining down with low-gear caution was driven by Rex Wilbram, his wife's adorer.

A small earthquake rattled the bungalow. There were small earthquakes fairly often. Some year, soon or late, there would be another beauty of an earthquake to splinter the steep hills. And if it should strike after rain with landslides teetering, then what a Good-bye Darjeeling that would be.

Rex and Miriam, bless their little hearts, would not have felt this little tremor in the Jeep, and a good thing, too, for the peace of mind of Windy Rex, that admirable planter. To be fair to Miriam, and it was wrong to be unfair, she did have guts.

He went into the house, debating whether he would escape to bed before Rex had delivered Miriam safe and sound. He might achieve sleep at this late hour. But he decided that it was more important to finish the decanter, and she was flying home next week, so there would be few chances to welcome her politely. He knew that Rex would not come in.

The sound of the jeep swung nearer and farther across the hill until it ceased altogether, which meant that the next sound would be arrival. It arrived. The engine idled. Her door was opened by the perfect gentleman from Maida Vale. Her door was closed. The jeep drove off. Miriam came in.

Harry stood. "Good morning."

"Hallo." She lit a Player's Number Three. She seemed pretty sober for Sunday at 3 a.m.

"A drink?"

"I might as well."

He gave Miriam gin and soda, her invariable tipple. "Was the dance amusing?"

She had waterfalls of hair, chestnut at the moment. She was a touch blowsy from much gin. "There were inebriated gentlemen," she said in her ginny voice, which, to be fair, had been ginny in less ginny days. Miriam had a long drink of gin and soda, and put it down.

It's unreasonable of me, Harry thought, to be offended by gin and soda. I must be reasonable in all things. He knew she had something she wanted to say. That was a something you learned about a wife. He knew it about Miriam when she ran one hand down one side of the cascading frame of hair and fiddled with the curly in-sweep at the bottom of her shoulders, and repeated her caressing fiddle on the other side, and kept on doing it. "I would have speech," she said.

He used to be amused by her antiquated, if platitudinous, turn

of phrase, once upon a time. One fine day in the middle of the
night, he thought, two dead men got up to fight. He waited.

"How sober are you?" Miriam asked him. "Or vice versa."

"Tolerably," Harry said. He was intolerably sober in the
mornings; now he was tolerably sober-drunk.

"Will you hear my prattle out?"

"Gladly," he said. He knew what he was going to outhear,
aushören. He had an extraordinary intuitive knowledge of the most
expected things.

"Our relations," Miriam said, "have long been a conjugal
mockery or bad joke. Agreed?"

"Agreed," he said.

She drank gin and soda. Her hand was shaking more than
usual, he observed. He drank twice as much as she did, but his
hand was steady. Harry Black is a phenomenon, his friends would
say, if he had friends. He waited for Miriam. She was nervous.

"Go on," he said. He saw back through indifference to
squabbles, and through squabbles to the reconciling bed, from a
sweep of mountains to a crowded London restaurant *à deux* and
bed again. She was talking, but he did not listen very much.

". . . Will you!"

"Will I what?"

Miriam repaired her face with dabs and smears and peerings.
He wondered why she affected greasy eyelids. He had never told
her that he did not like them. Powder and lipstick were what she
applied now. "Must I start again?" she asked him.

"I'm so sorry," Harry said. He sat up straight to clear the
fuddle. The last thing he wanted was that she should start again.
"It's quite all right," he said. "I'll divorce you any time you like."

"Divorce *me*?"

"What else?"

"You did it to me," Miriam said.

He looked at the fire, which was nearly out. The roof dripped
rain, but he thought the rain had stopped. He was wicked, and
she an amiable troll. He waited for Miriam to enlarge upon his
misdemeanours, a thing that she had never done since the afore-

mentioned relations had become a conjugal mockery or bad joke.

"Item Number One : You never loved me."

He squirmed at Item Number One.

"You wanted me at first, of course. All the gentlemen have always wanted me at first. You had to have some pneumatic female to rebound with. I don't know who you were rebounding from."

This seemed to be a new idea of hers, and he began to grope about with it, but he forgot it, listening.

"Item Number Two : I was no tweedy milkmaid, but a London wench. The only place I'd ever known you was in London where we did have fun, you must admit."

"Yes," he said. "We did." They had had gouts of pleasure.

"Then you decided to be a planter, not because you had a yen to grow Flowery Orange Pekoe of the finest bouquet, but for the sake of doing something, or escaping, or taking it out on tigers, or spiting yourself or what I simply do not know. And you brought me as baggage to this god-forsaken wilderness."

"Well," he said mildly. "Wives have been known to accompany husbands as baggage to the wilderness."

"Yes," she said. "But they require a modicum of affection from the same person that they married. I could endure it for the year or so when you were learning and had to work like mad. And we did occasionally go out. Besides, I didn't want another man with what you gave me, I'm not denying that. I didn't mind a bit your passing the days with tea, although I did get lonely. I didn't even mind you filling the evenings with progressively more whisky, books, gramophones and sacred silence. I had made my bed and you did still lie on it at night, except when you were off being brave in jungles. Also you were kind to me in your own disgruntled way."

Miriam went for gin and soda. She flaunted a good enough body still for them that wanted it. He remembered something else about making beds and lying on them. He could not remember very well. He looked over to the uncurtained window as she came back. He saw a light across the valley on a higher hill. He knew what would be Item Number Three ; or he knew for a moment, and it slipped away like everything.

" Then the child happened, and you blamed me."

" I didn't blame you," Harry lied. The boy had lived a month. If he had been a sadistic chap, he might have said a word about the gin she lapped up all the time. But what was the use ?

" Perhaps you wanted not to blame me," Miriam said. " But could you bring yourself to help ? Have you ever been near me since ? Why not ? I know why not, because you blamed me.

" So I was down here at the end of this ghastly road, or up here on the brink of this ghastly perch, conspired against by Cheddi Khan and all the menials, repugnant to the master, beset by goblins of my own. Can you wonder I've become what I've become ? "

" You could have gone home," he said. " I suggested that."

" Yes," said Miriam. " But I cherished a small hope that you might change. You wouldn't believe that a trollop could happen to love a man. I did, and that's all over, and the word nauseates you, don't bother to tell me, and don't think I'm going to make a scene, because I'm not."

" Was going on the loose with every Tom, Dick, and Harry the best way to make me change ? "

Miriam giggled. For a second or two he remembered how much he had once liked tolerant, beddable Miriam, the party girl who giggled. " T., D. and H. are not nearly true," she giggled fruitily. " Certainly not about the Harry. So madly unlike you to exaggerate, and so madly like you not to understand that either I had to go on the loose or go off my head closeted here with a recluse who hated my body and despised my trivial intelligence and drank himself to seclusion. Besides, you knew I'd been friendly with lots of wartime gentlemen before we met. I told you. I never pretended to be anything but what I was. But I was faithful to you while you let me be."

" I know," he said. " Here, anyway."

" Oh, I don't deny that I might have weakened, let's say on a P. and O. boat in the Indian Ocean. I'm a friendly slut, that's all I am at bottom."

He laughed. The pious would call her immoral or a nympho, but they would be wrong. Honest Miriam was amoral, a friendly slut as she described herself. He thought about this.

"Harry," she said. "Couldn't we try again? Couldn't we stop drinking for a start? You could give up whisky if you really wanted to."

He thought he could give up with a struggle. That's negative, he thought, drunk and sober late at night. But boredom and distaste are not things to be given up, he wisely thought. "I'm awfully sorry," Harry said. "I don't believe it's on." He cared not at all, yet he did not like to hurt her feelings. "If you want to know," he said, "I think you're a damned good-hearted woman."

"How charming of you," Miriam said, "throwing titbits to the bitch."

She never lost her temper or she did not have one. Occasionally she could be provoked to bitterness. He did not think he had intended this time to provoke her. His own temper stirred now, so he got up from his chair and went over to the window. His head was clearing, and he did not want a drink, but he had to watch his equilibrium, which was phenomenal. He was a four-letter man with a marvellous capacity and sense of balance.

"If you're leaving on Wednesday," he said to the window, "I suppose we'd better decide about the stuff beforehand. I can have it shipped or anything you like. Please take all you want."

"Thank you," she said. "You were always open-handed. But I don't crave loot. What I crave is that you should suffer yourself to be divorced."

"Why? I haven't been unfaithful, have I?"

"You have been too faithfully wedded to the bottle." She turned to look straight at him. "It doesn't make any difference to you, Harry, not one teensome little bit."

"That's not the point," he said. "The point is that you can damn' well pay for what you do. Why should I indulge you?"

"Please don't be wrathful," Miriam said.

Wrathful ! What bloody silly words she uses, yet placating words. " Would you be kind enough to explain ? "

" Sarcasm makes it even harder," Miriam said. " I know you hate me and tea and yourself and the world, but couldn't you just help one teensome little bit ? " Teensome, teensome, now she sounded rather tight.

He turned round. He was surprised. " I've never hated you."

She mopped her eyes, gin-dewy. " You have found me tediously repulsive, which is worse. But I will explain. The divorce matters not one tittle to you or me ; it does matter to Rex, particularly now he's being promoted to his firm's London office."

" Good God ! " he said. He had not thought things out to this absurdly logical connection. " Are you going to marry that . . . ? "

" Don't wince when I say it, but Rex happens to love me very much. I know he isn't clever or intrepid or witty or well-born or blessed with filthy lucre of his own. In other words he has none of those attributes of which I have had such a plethora in my matrimonial bliss with you. But he is a kindly person, and he will look after me, and he won't constantly compare my failings with the perfections of some mysterious Venus he never knew, and I will try to look after him. How maudlin this must sound."

" Not maudlin," Harry said. " Not particularly romantic, either." What the hell did it matter ? " All right," he said, " you can have your divorce. Tell that niggling prig to tell me what to do. I don't know the enjoyable procedure."

" Poor Harry," Miriam said. " You can't even be chivalrous without twisting a knife in all concerned, including you."

That sounds rather good, he thought. The effect was spoiled because Miriam now got the hiccoughs. " Oh, damn ! " she said, and hiccoughed tearfully. " Damn me for an intoxicated bawd."

He went for water. " Here," he said. " Drink it the wrong way round."

She drank from the farther lip. Her bottom stuck out and her excellent untrammelled bosom peeped and her hair was a waterfall the wrong way round. They were obstinate hiccoughs, yielding in time. "You're so good. You always were so good about small practical fiascos like the hiccoughs, or if I was sick, or anything. I don't understand you. I never did. I didn't have to when I could make you laugh and make you amorous."

He turned away again. Darkness was thinning, and he could see the hills. "She might come out at last this morning. I think I'll go up to Watcher's Rock."

"To commune with Kanchenjunga," Miriam said. "Your favourite frigid mistress."

"Shut up !"

"Scream at me ! Throw things at me ! Beat me ! I wish to God you would. Then at least you might be kind about the bruises."

"Contusions is a more elegant word," he said. He went out with this elegant last word. Lalbahadur opened the doors. He backed the jeep from the garage. He drove fast. Daylight or dark, tipsy or sober, up or down, he drove with marvellous speed and skill. He knew the road, of course. He knew the probable land-slide places. He knew the probable boulder places. He knew what so many fools did not seem to know—that a hundred foot drop is as lethal as five thousand. But like common or garden, timorous mortals, he was faster uphill, having gravity to pit his power against.

There were two feet on the inside and the outside, more at the passing points and at the hairpins. He judged the first hairpin perfectly, making the turn in one long mounting gravelly scrabble ; and here was the orderly terraced tea again, with dark old foliage, and the bright green of the new flush, two and a bud, where they would start on Monday, on with the dreary dance, creeps on its petty pace from flush to flush. And here were some shacks of his own people, perched and stilted over the *khud*, here the cobbles, here one old man in a blanket hawking and spitting in the dawn. Speed again with the headlights paler. Speed to the next hairpin which no amount of skill could negotiate in one—up to the gullied bank, other lock and let her run, hold her neatly on one in three, and off we go.

" What a reasonable sod I am," he said, parking at six thousand four hundred feet. He got out and walked in the water loudness down and on to Watcher's Rock. Not being a fool, and not being quite so steady as all that, he stopped a distance back, sat, put his real leg and his imitation leg forward, and slid by arm-power to the brink.

The rock wetted his behind. The hill dropped below his shoes almost sheer but not quite sheer four thousand feet or thereabouts to the river. He could hear a rumble of the river. The lights of Kalimpong blinked weakly far away and lower to the East below the dawn, Kalimpong where Chi-chi fruits do grow. The sky was clear now this morning in the time of the monsoon. Green was the low colour in the dawn, green with a few red landslide scars, the disciplined green of tea, the rampant greens of riotous growth.

He looked fifty miles across a maze of valleys to the north. He could not see Kanchenjunga, but he saw the lower snows which, at this moment, were the colour of a fresh-run salmon.

He was sinking sober now, with a bleary weight of eye. He remembered snippets of a recent conversation. My God, he thought, why the hell should I let Miriam divorce me, whoring it up with all and sundry? Well, it was said, and no sooner said than done, and it was a noble thing, and he was an honourable cuckold. " I must admit, however," he said aloud to the mountains and the valleys, " that I am also what the troops would muckin' call a proper mucker of a muckin' bastard."

And, he continued in thought, I shall bear a splendid grudge because of being Sir Galahad. Oh, why does an old thing pursue me, the perfection of a mysterious Venus I never knew, aptly put by Miriam from her fount of intuition? Nonsense, poppy-cock and balderdash, as Father would have said, but not about that. Father had no doubts and troubles that I know of. Father was a man, and he begat, or is it begot, well he beget a beauty.

The clouds were higher on the mountain. The clouds had all

F

gone everywhere except from the flanks of Kanchenjunga. It was a supreme thing to see that roll of chiffon, tulle or other cloudy stuff rolling out of nothing in the depths or bowels of the mountain, up to hide the body and away to nothing, coming from nowhere, going nowhere. "Please come out," he said to his frigid mistress. "Please take those mucking clothes off."

He laughed loudly at his own bluff wit, and heard his laughter a dozen dwindling times. I must be courteous to Miriam, the old bag, he thought. I have Sunday, Monday, Tuesday to be nice, not nice enough to encourage second thoughts, but nice. *Take the enamel boxes, Miriam, the Jaipur ones on gold. I insist. Take this, take that, take any bloody thing you want.* No, that's the wrong tone of voice. *Take all the Tschaikovsky, I wish you would.* Cry *Cave* yet again, for in that lush slush we did not have a meeting of the minds. *Take Daphne du Maurier, oh do, but leave me Nancy Mitford.* Take absolutely everything I do not want. You know, he thought, even as between the likes of Miriam and me, there is a nasty little jab involved in sharing out the spoils.

I know what I'll do, he thought. I'll turn over a new leaf, come Wednesday, no Thursday. I shall reduce consumption drastically. I shall straighten up the books. I shall be genuinely infused with tea. I shall, by some scientific jiggery-pokery, increase hill production to the Dooars level, all in a week or two before the season ends. That done, I shall take well-earned little fishing jaunts. Then, in no time flat, I shall be fit as a fiddle, destroying maneaters in all the deep dark jungles, which is a thing I did do well. Thereafter, restored to virile health, who knows but what I might not cast my eagle eye about for some Jungfrau with a dusky alabaster apple-tinted skin and chummy concupiscent chuckles and Salaam Sahib night and morning.

He waited, very very sober, watching Kanchenjunga. He sat atop his trivial cliff, seeing the giants now, the bastions beyond his mind, cold and pure and black and white. The thing was happening with radiance on a monsoon morning. The tantalising chiffon ceased to tantalise, and there she was, his beautiful big mistress.

He watched snow feather from the highest inviolate peak. He was a small man in a small place. You know, he thought, I never believe she can be there until she is again, and I look for a minute ; then I feel uneasy. But the pleasure of the first moment of the seeing, that's one thing nobody can take away.

Somebody could, you know, he had a new terrible sharp thought, watching Kanchenjunga. Some blue-eyed well-trained church-attending, dedicated youth could fly along with a bigger and better more-megatonish H-bomb and take her down a peg or two. You say we can't move mountains. Why, of course we can. If not to-day, my dear sir, then certainly to-morrow.

The clouds rolled up. Kanchenjunga disappeared. He pulled himself back from the lip of Watcher's Rock. He drove home like the bats of hell to get a little sleep.

CHAPTER TWELVE

In the Year of the Story

Mon Dieu, mon Dieu, la vie est là,
Simple et tranquille.
Cette paisible rumeur-là
Vient de la ville.

HE WALKED along the lobby past the reading room, a crinkle of airmail paper, a bevy of neat ladies catching up on things at home. Poor old bitches, he thought kindly, the desiccated pathos, the absurdity. He went down steps to the portico where a male tourist in a pale blue suit and some yellow-leathered cameras was complaining to the doorman : " I give you five roopies to hold a goddam taxi, din' I ? " Lonely, resentful, bewildered by these crooked sons of bitches, and no wonder, five rupees to hold a goddam taxi.

Harry might have helped, but he did not like either himself or the little rich man very much. He turned out of the portico of the Continental before seven o'clock in his dinner jacket without an overcoat. The air was sharp, yet heavily inert with Delhi winter evening smells like dung smoke, flowers, flooded lawn, ammoniated stable.

Along the street, passing right and left across the framework of the gate, cycle rickshaws, pony tongas, motor tongas, every kind of overladen rickshaw-tonga raced and crowded ; while near at hand, beyond a wall, *dhobis* slapped the washing wetly.

A bearded soothsayer pounced upon him at the gate. He was short, for a Sikh, with testimonials. " Sir, you have lucky face. Master making trip to happy lady. I tell fortune Lady Villundon, Missis Ruzvel, all famous people."

" Oh, fair and comely one, with thy lucky face and thy long

journey and thy happy Missis Ruzvel, shall I tell thee some things thou mayest do ? "

The man guffawed. He was delighted. " Salaam, sahib," he said, but as to a fellow Old Etonian.

He walked a gravel path below trees beside the traffic, which included taxis, cars and common cycles. People, a convivial stridence, an altercation of my Aryan brother mounted or on foot, or pleading from the dusty gutter : " *Gareeb Admi!* " Poor man, poor woman with bambino, poor unhuman being.

And there a black, blatant C.D. Limousine. Most diplomats are having baths at seven. Pray, Mr. Ambassador, what time do you ablute ? Why, Mr. Black, why Harry, with a lucky face and a long trip by air on Thursday, and a happily-divorced Miriam now wed to Rex, what time do you ?

He had to cross Queensway at the roundabout. A taxi nearly ran him down, and he stumbled, fleeing. He shouted at the driver, who shouted back. Christ, he thought. I do fly off the handle. The temper ran out of him like emptying a bath, non-diplomatic. They were the politest of all peoples, possibly ; the rudest drivers in the world, perhaps. They were this and they were that, the callous, kind enigma.

He took other roads, narrowing to his destination. There was a light here, a light farther on, nobody in view. Traffic sounded— a dimming petulance of horns, a murmuration—elsewhere beyond trees and gardens, beyond alto voices of the people always lurking, always talking.

> Cette paisible rumeur-là
> Vient de la ville.

No, he thought. Not peaceable or peaceful here. Not in the city, in the village, in my late-lamented garden, in the jungle. But it was peaceful in the jungle once. Would it still be peaceful in the killing jungle ? Seek and ye shall find. Peace be to him that seeketh not.

He had flown from Calcutta in the afternoon. He was leaving India. He needed more assistance, which he would have now in a

minute with an old friend of his called Rabat. A friend? Well,
shall we say a friend of his friendly days, a man he liked enough
to say good-bye to.

He turned into number twenty-three. His leg twinged a bit
from different altitudes, climates and vibration. The bougainvillaea
was mauvely pretty in the lamplight. He went up steps. You
always went up steps in India. Did you go up steps in England?
Not invariably, he thought, or not so many. It was the kind of
important thing he had forgotten. I'm not to blame, he thought.
I mean, five years more are like an evening gone.

"Salaam," he said to the Muslim servant of the Hindu
Brigadier. "*Sahib hai?*"

The sahib came bounding. "Harry!" *Hari*, he said it, *Hurree*,
just like once upon a time. "Oh my God, I am so glad to see
you."

The room had black furniture and filigree, pink covers, a fire
in the fireplace, two tigers on the floor, the Midnight Steeplechase,
a good Amrita Sher-gil, a mezzotint of Garibaldi, a large live
Rabat with a large dead bison, a dreadful Rama and Sita sylvan
scene, Jorrocks, Hemingway and Rabindranath Tagore. A Red
Indian tomahawk would not have been especially surprising.

Harry drank, and felt the whisky again within him. He had
seen Rabat once or twice briefly since the war. Rabat was a lean
youth in his youth.

"I wish you would have stayed with me," said Rabat, a big
man now, a man who had gained in pounds and otherwise, and
certainly in self-assurance, and with vulnerable feelings like them
all. "But you are independent-minded, Harry, isn't it?" He
laughed.

"I only have two days," he said, "and a lot of dreary things
to do about the customs. I thought I'd better go to the hotel.
It was kind of you to ask me, Rabat."

"Kind?" said Rabat. "But my house is yours."

Harry smiled to show gratitude, to hide his mild perennial
embarrassment at that order of remark. "Anyway," he said, "I'm
glad to see you."

" A glimpse again, and then to England.   Are you sorry to be leaving India for keeps ? "

Harry considered this while finishing his drink. " Not particularly," he said.

Rabat laughed.   He gave himself complete to laughter as of old, but now with florid embonpoint. " In this at any rate you have not changed.   You never were too diplomatic.   You are ready for a drink ?   So, for God's sake help yourself, man."

He took his glass to the whisky, which was on an exquisite enormity of teak, ivory-inlaid with elephants capering heraldically, and one real elephant's foot as table-leg.   He sat down again. Rabat was watching him, but looked away.   A child cried somewhere in the house, a baby from the quality of howl, although he was not expert and not keen to know. " Yours ? " he asked.

" The new one," said Rabat with complacence. " I have three sons and one daughter now, and only five years married.   Is that not good work for an ageing man ?   Would you like to see my smallest son ? "

" You look male enough to father all creation," he said to skirt that obstacle. " An army of small Rabats.   Talking of armies, when will they make you a Major-General ? "

" Next year, perhaps.   It depends on if I curb my tongue and stay in favour."   Rabat stood up in his immaculate long black evening coat and creased white trousers, offset by jaeger carpet slippers.   His neck bulged at the high collar, but not apoplectically, it seemed.   He got his drink. " What are you going to do in England, Harry ? "

" I haven't the least idea."

" No plans at all ? "

" None," he said.

" What is Regimental news ? "

" I get the magazine," he said. " Otherwise I'm completely out of touch."

" And the Colonel.   What about the Colonel ? "

" He was living in Shropshire, the last I heard."

" That was a man," said Rabat.

" Yes. There was nothing wrong with him." Sometimes, even nowadays, he felt the Colonel's tetchy eye upon him, not that he cared about the Colonel's tetchy eye. " I think most of the people you knew have left. Or they were killed. Jumbo Cotter bought it in the desert. Do you remember Jumbo ? "

" Do I remember Jumbo ! "

Now I've hurt his feelings about something.

" Have you forgotten our ride on Jumbo's elephant ? "

The memory jumped at him whole, if hazy. " Of course not. I hadn't thought of that for ages."

" I think about it often, because of Jumbo and the mad funny night, and because of you fighting my way into brothel." Rabat shook briefly. " That is among reasons why my house is yours," he said in deadly Hindu earnest.

Harry felt quite good again, whiskied over the uneasy edge. The child had stopped crying. He did not think his battle in a brothel had been so noble, or for love of Rabat, actually. " What did you say, Rabat ? "

" I said there was another chap with us, a civilian, but I have forgotten him."

" Desmond Tanner," Harry said. " He and I were prisoners together. Desmond is here still, I believe, making sugar in Bihar. We became great friends in Germany, but I've never seen him since."

" You have avoided him, perhaps. You have avoided all your friends, perhaps."

He did not answer the implied question. He was thinking of something else, or of someone else he never had forgotten in the way of an idea, but the face of the idea had vanished long ago ; and India would have raddled Christian Tanner's face. He moved in his chair, dismissing the ancient sentiment of that idea, grasping for another. " My God, the Colonel gave me hell," he said. " He was the best giver of impartial hell I ever knew. But he gave me more than my impartial share on that occasion. I rather resented it."

" You should not have resented it. Some men are hardest on their favourite sons. Help yourself to drinks. Is your mind made up about England, then ? "

" About going now ? Yes, I told you."

" Think of the English winter for so choleric a man. Think of nothing to do but keeping cold out raising elbow in the Elephant and Castle." Rabat bubbled like a brewing vat, delighted with himself about the Elephant and whatnot. But he stopped his chuckling. " Harry, my friend," he said. " I tell you one thing." He paused. Rabat was a fighting soldier and a good one. He had commanded a battalion into Burma. But he was still a Hindu, treasuring your feelings like bone china. " I tell you one thing, are you all right, Harry ? "

" Asking me or telling me ? " He smiled to show old Rabat that his testiness was of affection, not offence.

" Your hair is still as dark as mine before I became hoary. You are a little thinner where I am become stout. Your face is lined, but it is the same face. And now that you are getting cross with me, your eyes have that nasty blue of when you punched the Scotsmen at One-three-eight. Oh yes, I remember the number even. Your eyes stare a little glassily with all this whisky, it is true. Your hand, how steady is it ? "

Harry held up the hand he was so proud of. " What do you take me for, a tremulous babu ? "

" Not strictly babu type," said Rabat. " So you are all right then, it seems ? "

" Oh yes," he said. " I'm simply wonderful. Thank you very much for asking."

Rabat leaned forward in the other chair. " That iciness," he hissed. " Do not waste it out on me because I am not having any. So you are the same, much, physically, if somewhat worn with use, and you are the same honest man of my acquaintance, and frightened of emotions worn like mine on shirtsleeves. But I am not as simple as you think."

He laughed. " Simple ! You devious old Hindu ! " And he thought now that he was very fond indeed, for the moment anyway again, of Rabat who had become strong in the sixteen years or thereabouts, and seemed upset by a weakening in him.

" But you are not the same," said Rabat. " You are sad. What has life done to you here ? " He put one outspread hand against the barrel of his chest. " And here ? " The other on his brow, and held the pose in serious drama.

Harry laughed again. He was a little tight, he felt. And he was quite silly. " You need more hands," he said. " Borrow one from Vishnu."

" That is vulgar blasphemy, and not nice. Now help yourself. Finish the bottle, there is plenty more, and everything I have is yours because I love you. I am afraid you do not love me quite so much."

" I love you madly," Harry said. " But I think I'll hang on for the moment."

" Love," said Rabat. He was thoughtful. " This romantic sexual love that persecutes you people and becomes an old sour cup of tea or coffee, but with us is managed so much better, like a nectar, like a feast. Is it love that makes you sad ? "

" Why all this poppycock about being sad ? You're boring me."

" My God, my God," cried Rabat, " the worst word in your vocabulary. *Ek dam* immediately stop being a bore. Tell me, Harry, have you been shooting ? "

" No," he said. " I haven't been near a jungle for eighteen months. Of course, I lost interest in ordinary tigers long ago, in shooting them, I mean."

" This is well known," Rabat said. " But the maneaters for which you became famous, what of them ? "

" The supply was limited. The leave was limited. The inclination became limited by my evening habits." He raised his glass, and it occurred to him to fill it, which he did. Six o'clock, five, four o'clock habits ; the reason given and the reasons not disclosed. What's the *real* reason? Fools asked about everything. He sat down.

" It is a pity," Rabat said. " Have you sold your rifles ? "

" No," he said. " Exporting them by air is why I have to mess about with customs. I can't imagine why I bother. What is a pity, though ? "

" That you are determined to leave India this very week. Because there is a bad new maneater where I have been on tour. Shall I tell you ? "

" Do," he said. He liked to hear about them in one way. He had two views about almost everything. He listened fairly closely with the usual skippings and excursions.

" . . . I sat up a night over the body, but it never came. Perhaps it had crossed the hills again."

" They hardly ever do come back," he said. " But that switch is interesting and unusual. Rimli, being so much smaller, is the place to try, I would imagine."

" You should try, Harry. You would be the best man in India to try, if you were sobered up."

" I've told you," he said. " I'm going home, unsobered up, in case it interests you." But now he had a warmly semi-drunken thought of being cool sober in the jungle in the morning.

" There is no sadness except this, that you live many years with us and you are perhaps glad about our freedom when it comes, but you are not sorry about quitting India rather drunk, my friend. You look down upon India and Indians, isn't it ? "

" If you say so, yes, of course. Why not ? "

" I am not offended," Rabat said. " You cannot offend me even trying hard. But I wish you would do this one thing—shoot this maneater. Then I would be very happy. Now I hear the car. We are four for dinner, do you mind ? My wife, of course, and my sister, Somola Pant, against whom you must protect me, do you mind ? " Rabat was pleased with himself again, perhaps at keeping this little secret to spring inimitably at the final moment.

He would have drunk less, had he been privy to the secret. However, he did not mind. He stood. He held the arms of the chair a moment and was steady.

" My wife," said Rabat. " And Somola. This is Harry."

He made the graceful greeting, palm to palm, obviating handshakes for himself and them.

Mrs. Rabat smiled, murmured, and sat down. She was a plump

and pretty little thing, withdrawn at once, a feminine demureness before men.

He knew, of course, of Rabat's widowed sister. Everyone knew of Somola Pant who wrote and radioed so brightly about Birth-control, Goa, Baby clinics, Village industry, Kashmir, Temperance and What not, a loud voice crying from the humble wilderness of Eve, *the Indian woman's point of view*, as conceived and prodded by Somola Pant. She was middle-aged and handsome, with the trim, prescriptive, vaguely military air of women of career, whether in plain dresses or in golden saris.

" I've heard so much about you," she said with virtually no lilt of India in a tuneful tone.

Harry smiled politely from a fuddle of less polite consideration. The humble celebrity, that sounded like.

" Whisky for you, Somola ? "

" You know I never drink."

" There, Harry. You see at once. Somola cannot say : *No, thank you*, in reasonable fashion. She must assert herself as prig and mouthpiece of official temperance campaign."

Mrs. Pant ignored her brother, and he shuffled out in carpet slippers. " I knew your mother well," she said, " and the General too, of course. It is sad to think that both are gone."

" Yes," he said. "They died within six months of each other in 1947." He heard his voice sound cold and anglified. He could not speak easily of that.

" They would have wished it so," she said, " after so much happiness together."

I don't know, he thought. And he thought : I think of my father and my mother so little nowadays, except as the strolling players of my childhood ; and I was not much with them after that. I shut my mind to the things I lose.

Rabat came in with a bottle of whisky.

" Lady Black was a good friend of India in the dark days."

" Dark days ! " Rabat cried. " What is this talk of dark days ? In and out of plushy prisons, do you mean ? Harry was in a not-plushy prison. Does he talk about his dark days ? "

"I don't know what he talks about," she said. "Rabat rushes like a bull," she said to Harry. "He did not hear what we were saying." She told her brother.

"Forgive my boorishness," he said, and put his hands together, finger to finger, and bowed his head, a large man, an exquisite grace of penitence.

"Harry is a friend of India," said Rabat in a while. "And he is leaving us. This is sad, as I was saying."

"He is English, not Indian," she said. "Why should Mr. Black not leave us?"

"There now she is free, but she must be still freer, like having ten baths every day until the British grime is washed off altogether, and we have taught the whole world to talk Hindi. How ridiculous! What common language do we have but English? Whence come our institutions? Who made our Army?"

"The Army is unimportant," said his sister.

"Unimportant! One day you shall see how unimportant."

"Do stop squabbling," Harry said.

They were enchanted, and Mrs. Rabat burst into tiny twitters, and they went to dinner, with him defender, protagonist or tipsy referee, but sobering up with chili-venomed curry, buttered richness, spice galore and syrup-loaded sweetmeats.

"The army people we remember with affection. But the I.C.S., what did they turn out to be but Muslim agents, what, I ask you?—Now look, Rabat.—They are barbarians, that is all, demanding allegiance for ten dollars. I prefer the Russians. They have the ballet and some heritage, at any rate. No, do not jeer at me, I mean it.—An American entomologist stayed with me last year. He was the most grown-up chap I've ever come across. You wouldn't even irritate him. He would simply smile at you in his slow way, and be sorry for the children.—And would he not be sorry for himself at home, being called a Communist, no doubt, and surely Egghead?—Oh, you are all the same. You seek out some dullest peasant in a field and you say: *Was it not better with the British?* So what does he reply to please you, that being his nature?—It is intolerable that there should be these foreign pockets, these Goas and Pondicherrys in our midst, plotting against our sovereignty, murdering our nationals. Our patience cannot last for ever—Look at the map, the wicked Davids and the poor Goliath. Do you really think the world can swallow that one ? What happened to Hitler's patience with the Poles ?—But we know that this is true.—You can persuade yourselves that anything is true. As for the moral lectures Pandit-ji subjects the world to— You do not like us, then ?—Of course I like you. Don't you know I like you ?—Yes, we know you like us. We are your children still in a sort of way to scold, and we do not mind so much. But, of course, you do not understand us. No Englishman has ever fathomed a Hindu."

" God forbid," he said, which pleased them. He enjoyed their company, the loving casuistry and innuendo, the violent amiable squalls, the posturings and gentleness. He did not understand them, but he spoke a language nearer to theirs than to the language of Milwaukee. They beguiled him, the plain-spoken man, into an intimate, improbable extravagance. It was great fun for a bit, and now and then.

" You have been teaming up on me," said Rabat after dinner. " But now, Somola, my notorious sister, I need help. I was starting to persuade Harry before you arrived that he should stay on a while in India for one thing—to shoot the Rimli maneater. You hear of everything from Kalka to Cape Cormorin. Have you heard of this ? "

" Oh yes," she said. " I have had letters from some poor village women. But Harry's plans are made. He has better things to do, no doubt, in England."

" Why should he waste priceless time on risking neck ? He could be shooting English pheasants, or Chinese are they not, but very English anyway by now, like our Oxford Ak-sents which annoy the Americans so much." Gargantuan guffaws.

" He could be killing something surely."

" Not pheasants," Harry said. " The season ends this week. At least, it always used to."

They considered that hilariously funny.

"Well, this is better," Rabat said. "At least no maneater pheasants to seduce him. Now will you excuse me, Harry, while I do some telephones? Look after him, Somola. Make him happy with huge drinks."

Rabat went out. Mrs. Rabat looked at her sandalled toes, smiling small, serene and secret smiles. Harry got his drink, a fair large snifter. Somola Pant behaved much like a western woman, except that she did not hold a man's eye directly. The orthodox wife, the emancipated sister; how peculiar it might seem, yet did not seem peculiar here. "And what thoughts will you take away of India?" she asked in his general direction.

What thoughts would he take away? Of nepotism and corruption creeping higher? Of invariable courtesy and kindness? Of brilliant plans and hopeless execution? Of love my child and let my neighbour's starve? Of caste abolished and going strong? Of Malthus waiting on a bad monsoon? "I don't know," he said. "It's too difficult for me, Somola."

Rabat's voice was filling the bungalow from another room. "*Tum Bluddi-ful,*" he screamed. "Have you not heard of Harry Black? Don't you understand King's English?" It sounded like a tantrum, but for the gusts of mirth. He came back, shuffle-shuffle in his carpet slippers. "Well," he said. "That is all right, tickety-boo, then, Harry. Rimli you said would be best chance. So then, Rimli resthouse is reserved for you *carte blanche*, servants, shikaris, everything in order waiting."

"Now, listen, Rabat," Harry said, "I have told you that I am not, N-O-T, going after your damned maneater. I am flying home on Thursday."

"So," said Mrs. Pant. "You wouldn't do this last damned thing for us that you do incomparably well? You would not save our villagers from death and terror? You will simply say: *Good-bye, India. I had my pleasure from you. Now you bore me.*"

"The population problem," Harry bit. "That's boring enough, God knows, but shouldn't we give nature's balances a chance?"

She stared directly at him. Somola Pant said nothing at all and looked away.

"I apologise," he said.

"You need not," said ruthless Rabat. "It is true and God knows am I not contributing? Well, you are not yourself, but a sarcastic Harry Black not meaning what you say. Now there is one difficulty still—a jeep or Landrover to take the wounded hero round about. Forestry cannot provide. I am even doubtful that we can wangle from the army unless . . ." He looked at his sister.

"I don't know why you pester me like this. Why should I change my mind?"

"Because you would make my husband happy," Mrs. Rabat said loudly and clearly, first comment of the evening. "He is your friend. It is duty to make him happy."

He knew this was a plot, one of those whimsical conspiracies so dear to them.

Somola came back. "That is quite all right. I did not say Harry Black. I said the son of Lady Black. *Of course, of course,* he was very testy with me. *Are we to be labelled ingrates for one piddling vehicle? Why do you bother me about such things?* But he likes me to bother him, of course."

"Is it not awe-inspiring," Rabat said, "to have a sister with this influence? But she will overstep. She will be our Ambassador to Luxembourg to get rid of her, so mark my words."

Now Harry saw the silk-cotton tree, the red-flowering *semul* in sombre forest, and a medley, a melody, a chatter of birds high in the silk-cotton tree. He heard the kharkar barking, and the cheetal's danger call. He thought of the scents of the first morning hour. "Well," he said, "it's been a wonderfully entertaining evening. I'm sorry to disappoint you, Rabat."

"No matter. It makes no difference. We shall have lunch together, shall we?"

"One o'clock at the hotel?"

"May I drop you now?" she said. "It is on my way."

He would have liked to walk, but it was a longish walk, and discretion questioned if he was in sound walking order. "Oh, would you? Many thanks."

Backslaps from the jovial Brigadier, smiles from Mrs. Rabat, and Good nights, and out.

It was a small car, and the night was cold, but he was chill-proofed. " My remark about the population," he said before he would forget. " Not a very pretty effort." He meant bad taste rather than bad thinking.

" But the apology was good," Somola said. " It might have been your father speaking, not that I ever heard the General apologise. He disapproved of us and did not trust us, I am sure, but he was always courteous in a rather baffled, hurt sort of way, and we could not help admiring him. He and your mother were so unlike and so devoted. Of course, your father was quite different, but there is a same kind of man about you too."

" My father did not indulge in caustic cheapnesses."

" But only a man could bark : *I apologise*, without excuse or explanation."

" Or someone who knew it was an effective manner of apology."

She was an execrable, chugging driver. She glanced round at him. " You suspect yourself too much," she said. " It is not late. Shall we go by Kingsway and the Secretariat, and so back? The lights for Independence Day may still be on."

" Yes," he said. " I would like to see them." He betted the fairy illuminations would be awful. " If it doesn't compromise you." To be driven about by a lone woman was unusual.

She laughed. " It couldn't matter less. Also, chivalry is a pleasant change from what a Hindu widow is accustomed to, even an ultra-modern public one like me."

He suspected the nice compliment, but he said : " It's true that I have taken a lot from India in my time, and given precisely nothing."

" The maneaters and rogue elephants that Rabat says you have risked your life to shoot in Bengal and Assam and so on, wasn't that giving ? "

" No," he said. " Not for anybody else's welfare, but for a bit of personal spice. My best times have been in the forests of this country. Do you like them ? "

"Gracious no. I am strictly a city woman, terrified of jungles. But that was not what Rabat meant. Oh, here is fog now. We shall have to crawl down Kingsway, seeing nothing. Well, never mind."

"What did Rabat mean, then?"

"India is a big country, and very small. Rabat had heard about your divorce and other things."

"He didn't mention my divorce."

"Naturally, he would not mention that. It would be indelicate. But he is attached to you because of the old days, and because of some special things you did for him that he has not forgotten and he will not tell me. I am a very inquisitive sleuth-hound of a woman, as you know. Perhaps you will tell me?"

How ridiculous, he thought. How absurdly typical that Rabat should owe me eternal allegiance because I once secured him a whisky and soda in a whorehouse not available to Wogs, that awful word of my youth and arrogance. What was her name? Nora, was it, Cora? Cora-Dora. "No," he said. "I won't tell you."

"Some man's wicked secret, it must be. So he knew all about you before even you wired that you were coming through. And then he shouted, thumping his chest, you know, like a gorilla: *I tell you one thing, Somola. I will not allow this. I will save this fellow from his going-to-pot. He has done things for me in old days. I will do things for him in new days. I will put him back in jungles to sober up with this Rimli tiger. But he is a strong-willed devil and by no means simple English chap we can make rings round with our wits. We must be very cunning.*" She copied her brother's extravagant English to perfection.

"So you had this planned and plotted in advance." It was irritating, and yet it also had the touch of kindness, he thought now. "That surprised interest all bogus?"

"Oh yes. Plots and plans are the breath of life to us. Well, we have failed with you. Which is why I am now driving you to see the invisible lights for Independence Day—because I have something else to say in private."

" Say on," he said.

" We are strangers really, and I am afraid of you, and perhaps I will offend you by my shocking taste, but I will say it quickly. You must have had sadness in your marriage. Well, in my work I hear of much dreadful sorrow of that kind, although different being Indian and from the woman's point of view. But it is strange that my faith in the love of men and women should be from two marriages. My own was a Hindu marriage of free choice, a rarity in those days. We were not blessed with children. I loved my husband, and I still do love him.

" The other marriage was not an Indian one at all. It was the love your own parents had for one another. That is a curious coincidence, Harry, isn't it, but true I promise you."

" Yes," he said. " It is a coincidence." He thought of his parents. He thought more clearly of the drink he was going to have when he got back to the hotel. " Darby and Joan," he said, " as I remember them together. Is that what you mean ? "

" Oh no, they were not like that. The impeccable, courtly, perhaps dull General ; and his vague and so amusing and haphazard wife. There was tranquillity, but there was always the feeling of man and woman joined together from before to afterwards. I can't explain it."

" They were happy," Harry said. " I suppose I took that as a matter of course when I was young. But yes, I think what you say is true, although I hadn't thought about it. How do my parents affect the issue ? "

" Didn't they wish well for you ? Are you not the child of their devotion ? "

It was an impertinence.

" I have angered you," she said. " I should not have stuck my foreign nose in. But your mother was my friend, and Rabat was yours, and with all our tiresomeness we are loyal friends, we Indians, that you will allow us."

" Indeed I do," he said. He wondered how much of this conversation he would remember in the morning ; he wondered also if he would stick to what he was just going to say : " I think I will have a go at that Rimli animal. Indian swansong, sobered up if I can make it. You know, with less conspiracy I might have jumped at the idea, and not for any noble motives, such as paying debts."

She laughed. "That is our trouble, we intrigue ourselves and other people inside out. But now I have a second thought, not being funny, that had not occurred to me before : You might be killed or something awful."

"That would be an irreparable loss," he said. "And all for love, to make it the more poignant."

"You speak so mockingly of many things. Have you never loved a woman, then, truly for comfort and not only infatuation ?"

How insidiously this Indian widow talked.

"Perhaps once, for a few days, I did think . . ." The memory still pained him, and he was offended at himself for weakening to speak of what he had never spoken.

"Please go on, Harry," said Somola Pant.

"She was the wife of my best friend. I had some rules then, and she was a girl with rules, and time was short. But looking back from now, I don't believe that then. It was different, though, and I haven't forgotten."

"Then you do believe in the not-cynical corner of you. For some lucky ones love is a short-cut to the tranquillity that we can also reach by faith or self-denial. Have you read the Gita ?"

"Negation is not my short-cut to truth," he said. He was thinking rather straight, considering, or because of. "I can't accept that we are created solely to deny the world."

"Oh no," she said. "We must never deny ourselves a thing." She was a damned clever sharp-tongued woman, a bit too clever. "Here we are in the great fogbound spaces underneath the Secretariat, and no lights to see. I must not deny the existence of the fountains, archways and other pitfalls that Mr. Lutyens and Mr. Baker, or I should say Sir Edwin and Sir Something, that they created to impede our freedom on a foggy night."

She negotiated these obstacles, and the ground mist petered out between buildings on the road again. She stopped at the Hotel Continental. "*Au revoir*, then. Or perhaps Adieu, because I am leaving for Travancore to-morrow."

"*Au revoir*," he said. "Thank you again."

"Good luck with tigers, Harry, in and out."

BOOK TWO

CHAPTER THIRTEEN

" Severe loss of blood. . . . Septicæmia. . . . Anti-biotics. . . . I am sorry if I hurt you."

He looked at the face with the arched nostrils, the pale pink lips, the woman's chin, the sad, suffering, brown eyes they have with whites so muddy too. " What's your name ? " he asked him.

" Doctor Roy Chowdhury, M.D.," the doctor sang. " At your service, Mr. Black. Now we must roll you with utmost care."

Roll him over gently. Roll him over slow. Roll over, clouds of the monsoon ; break, billows, break and billow on, the waves and clouds and rain, hot rain and sweat and purgatory asphalt-bubble on and on.

One time he was flying an old Gipsy Moth, was buzzing places in the plains of India, it must be, because of bullock carts and dust and women at the well, and he saw the wild blue eyes of water buffaloes struggling from a village tank and bright urchins whacking them with sticks, but people everywhere as far as the view extended from a biplane hopping mango trees and prison camps. *Look round*, he said into the mouthpiece to the black helmet in the seat in front. *I don't know who you are.* But that silent person never did look round. Well, it was a dummy, he supposed, and he saw a dust storm into which he flew, how daring into a solid turbulence of grit and out the other side, but no black helmet. Either that person was of my imagination, or I tipped that person out.

" Bluddifool ! What is this you have been doing ? "

" Rabat, how . . . ? "

" I flew up with these medicines for you."

" Thought I heard a . . ." Thought I heard.

" Others have failed totally. There is chloromycetin we may try as ultimate resort," sang Dr. Roy Chowdhury, M.D.

One time he was young again and fishing with a worm in

waters deep, in pastures green He leadeth me the quiet waters by.
But the trout were not taking. They were small ones till they
were big and boiled and grew and grew and jumped to fry him
in a pan to crispness for their supper when he had only offered them
a worm that he might cook one carefully in his secret furnace down
in Taylor's Wood, but Taylor's Wood was burning too.

Fire above and fire below, my ice-hot dwelling place, my igloo
is a lovesome place, God wot.

" Drink this, Harry."

It was nothing nasty. It was cool small pricks and sparks of
soda water in his mouth. Oh, it was a blessing. " Thank you very
much," he said.

" Go to sleep," she said to him.

Sleep well, my child. And now the icebergs drew away, and
now the flames ebbed down, and now he left the country of the
frost and fire to walk a desert with the compliments of Señor Dali,
and without the whims of Señor Dali. He saw no ending to the
clean perfection of his desert in the afternoon, and he was sorry
when it ended, and the pains were very bad.

" Hallo, Christian. Do you remember me ? "

" Yes," she said. " I rather think I do."

She smiled down at him with her lips compressed, as if he had
made a sort of joke ; but he was thinking of the desert and he
could not see it any more. " Too dark," he said.

He heard the noise of curtains, so he looked along between his
double-sighted nose and saw a veranda and a garden with a wall
beyond, and he heard the machinery that he was always hearing,
and who should come in but Cheddi Khan. He remembered quite
a lot of things while Cheddi salaamed with formal dignity with
both hands to his brow and inquired about Your Honour's state
of health.

" Very good, a kindness," Harry said. " All right," he said
then in English, because that was the reply Father used to smile at
when he was all wrong with typhoid, which reminded him about
the boy. " Where's Michael ? "

" Find Michael, could you, Cheddi Khan ? "

" What's the situation ? "

" You're getting better is the situation. Is your headache very bad ? "

He felt the cleanness and the coolness on his brow. That eau-de-Cologne or was it lavender water, he could not quite remember. " Wonderful," he said.

" Here's Michael now."

Michael was standing at the bottom of his bed.

" Michael, my son," he said.

Michael was there a little longer, but he put a hand up to his face and turned and ran, the loose-limbed child against the light.

" So muddled," he said. " I didn't mean to hurt his feelings."

" Michael's feelings aren't hurt. He's glad you're better."

" Desmond ? Bapu ? Help me, Christian."

" Everyone's all right. Sleep again now, Harry, till the doctor comes."

" You're good to me," he said. He hoped for his desert, and he found it. He was a lucky boy with Mother walking by his side across a desert of the tanny colour of a rich-tea biscuit.

" Chloromycetin has triumphed in grim battle," sang Dr. Roy Chowdhury, M.D. " I am very happy at this happy outcome." Concussion . . . fractured ribs. . . . Multiple lacerations due to mauling. " We feared internal injuries, thus did not move you one furlong to the cities. But all is well under my tender care. Are you most comfortable ? "

" Not *most*," he said. " Remind you I'm wrapped up like the late King Tutankhamen."

" Oh, this is funny, mummified, you see I recognise allusion, but there is difference of vital breath in you." Dr. Roy Chowdhury, M.D., giggled very gleefully. " You are my model patient. I am proud of you. Are you quite happy now ? "

" Yes," he said. " I'm happy," and he was.

There was a nurse, a Eurasian Miss Potterswell of middle age, a shadow woman at his service.

Christian, Desmond, Michael, Cheddi, Dr. Roy Chowdhury, M.D., and occasionally Bapu were the players with Miss Potterswell as lead although she was a self-effacing star and so unprimadonnaish that he sometimes almost wished she would be cross or even shout at him, the happy audience, but she never did. Miss Potterswell was more like a humble referee than like Tallulah Bankhead. He considered this, not forgetting Miss Potterswell's white cotton stockings dusky-tinted by her shanks, but what's the difference, only skin-deep after all, as people say. He would have laughed about Tallulah and Miss Potterswell. But, as it was, with ribs to hurt, he smiled at the anomaly and wondered if unkindness lay always at the root of schoolboy humour. He had so many blessings and he did not mean to be unkind.

" Salaam, Bapu." The little man was just the same in his relics of some ex-employer's grey tweed jacket. Almost everyone but Bapu had a Sunday suit.

" The Bad One has gone away," said Bapu. " Gone to the land below the mountains. This is the custom of the Bad One."

" Was the tiger wounded ? " Harry asked. The tiger was far off, and he was not concerned with tigers. He was concerned with the vivid, easier, awakening world he found each morning here at Bondha where the sugar-crush went on, and the hooter hooting at the eighth hour and the eighth hour marked the rhythm of his peaceful tune. But he knew that his Bad One loomed ever near to Bapu.

" The Bad One was wounded in the back," said Bapu. " But lightly, for there was again a killing yesterday at Ranipur below the mountains, and the *bara sahib bahadur*'s moon is not yet altogether dead."

" What dost thou mean, the great brave master's moon ? "

" Did the *bara sahib bahadur* not bow seven times with money tinklings of the pocket unto the infant moon on the evening of the Bad One's coming ? "

He knew he must have been a longish time at Bondha. *Nearly three weeks ?*

" The sahib has perhaps forgotten in his sickness, but that was the first day of two sups of whisky-wine," Bapu prodded delicately.

" I wonder if Cheddi Khan is on the back veranda ? " he called

to the curtained door behind which Miss Potterswell crinkled
at her *Statesman*. She did enjoy her *Statesman*, *dak* or mail edition
two days late.

" Give Bapu two pegs of our own whisky."

Cheddi Khan inclined his head an inch. He raised a lordly
hand, palm down, and flipped the fingers once to summon jungli
Bapu. Cheddi Khan did not approve.

Harry watched the lizards on the wall. The lizards were yellow
on the white-washed wall. They waited inanimate for ages, so
that you might wonder if they slept with eyes so beady ; but he
knew that the lizards were very much awake. Always in the end
they pounced like cold small dragons, seeming to get their bellies full
of insects, enough indeed to chip and chusp and chase one another
when in the mood for fun and games. He enjoyed the lizards.
Miss Potterswell did not enjoy them. Miss Potterswell was not
a bit afraid of mice, but she was terrified of lizards because of a
distaff superstition that if a lizard fell on you it killed you.

" Don't look round, Miss Potterswell," he would say when she
was working on his dressings. " But I think Clarence may be going
to pounce on you this very minute." Clarence was larger than
Clarissa, and presumed to be the husband lizard.

Miss Potterswell would give a muted squeal and rather love
his teasing, and say quaint things like : *Such a chaff, you are.* She
took time off in the afternoons from four to seven, so that she
could have her little walk when it was cooler in the garden. But
only in the garden, because Miss Potterswell had fearful stories of
the lusts of men. The odds were on Miss Potterswell, he thought.

So the evening was a good time, and the morning was a good
time between Potterswell attentions and his breakfast. Christian
would drop in to see him bareheaded in her jodhpurs back from
riding the arab pony named Adonis. There was always something
she had seen that she could tell him, like a tawny eagle, for example,
or a herd of blackbuck, or like saying that there was a breeze this
morning on the wheat which reminded her of Manitoba.

" I thought it was Toronto," Harry said.

" Yes, but Mother came from West of Winnipeg. We used

to go there occasionally in the summer time when I was young."

"You still look young," he said, not paying compliments, but all his thoughts were new, surprising and benevolent, and he admired the health of people, the strength that grew on him from them, he felt. Each day the pains were with him but pains on the way down and out, so he could be grateful for the lesser and the larger mercies. "What are you?"

"I'm thirty-five this June," she said, "and I must go now and feed the family."

"What's for breakfast?"

"Keventer's sausages and rumble-tumble," Christian said.

"Oh, yummy. Can I have lashions, please?"

"Harry Black and Michael Tanner, you're a pair." She went off to feed the family, including him, on sausages and scrambled eggs. He was her child at that time.

In late afternoon they moved his bed out to the veranda where he could watch the goings-on.

"Was that better, Harry?"

"Yes, but lean still further forward, elbows down, hands close in, and let the pony do it for you."

Michael trotted round the garden anti-clockwise on the outer circuit while Miss Potterswell walked the other way among the flowers. She did not wear her nurse's hat; she wore a solar topi with its oilskin jacket.

"Now to break to a canter with the near fore leading, sit down and. . . . That boy's a natural-born horseman."

"Yes," she said, "and so frustrating for him only riding in the garden, which is why I watch him like a hawk. I suppose we might afford a real child's pony so that I could take him out with me, but it seemed hardly worth it when we're flying home so soon, and Michael going to school in England this September, what a thought."

It was indeed a thought for mothers separated from their children. She seemed to like India, but he wondered.

He sat in bed with his binoculars to watch the wagtails on the flooded lawn, wet every night and browner every day. He watched

other birds as well, but he liked the wagtails best, dipping their tails
so busily about the place, the pied, the grey, the white, and even
the yellow-headed, he was almost sure. March had just arrived,
and migrants were flying north before the heat. He had seen that
in other years, but now life was on the move while he was still,
now life was his to discover and to cherish and be cherished.

The wagtails left ; and then, at the crowding in of night, flying
foxes went about their business, the giant fruit bats, not God's most
decorative creatures. But if he closed one eye to kill perspective
in the gloaming, he could think of them as pterodactyls possibly,
fusing the trivial immensities of time. Then, after flying foxes and
usually before the owlet, Desmond's lope would sound along the
gravel, and he would take the steps in two, and call : " How goes
it, Harry ?   Hang on a minute while I get myself a drink."

It amused him about hanging on a minute, because minutes
did not mean a thing to him ; but that was only Desmond's way
of talking. They had splendid casual gossips until the needs of the
stomach did give importance to the dinner hour. They reminisced
a little—about prison and the old days in Calcutta—but past and
future both were dim. The present world was Harry's oyster.

Desmond had told him bare details of the tiger episode—that it
had swiped him with a left hook, that he had fallen twenty feet
and hit his head. Thus far he remembered. But he had been saved
by falling, for the animal had left him then and made off up the
ravine to cover. *Oh, yes*, he said at the first calling, and shut his
eyes to shut the subject off.

But Desmond mentioned it again one evening after wagtails,
which was the evening of the March new moon. Harry's wish to
the sliver of the March new moon had been for this tranquillity.

" How are the aches and pains ? "

" My ribs are a bit precarious, head aches off and on, scratches
tickle hellish healthy—I'm nearly as good as new."

" It's incredible when you realise how nearly a dead duck you
were."

" Was I ? "   He supposed he must have been—he had risen high
from so far down.

" First, loss of blood. Transfusions settled that, although Chowdhury was afraid of a punctured lung. But all was well. Then the fun began with poisoning. He tried penicillin, aureomycin, sulpha, all that we could get. There didn't seem to be much hope left when Rabat flew up with chloromycetin. I must say Rabat has become a pretty terrific chap. He raised the roof with Chowdhury, took one look at our dispensary nurse and flew off to Dehra Dun for Potterswell, told the union leaders that if there was a peep of noise at any meeting he would hold them personally responsible, he, only a brigadier in the army. They lapped it up. If you ask me, this country could do with a little of the Rabat touch. Anyway, your temperature dropped from a hundred and five to normal in one day, thanks to the drug, not Rabat, although the general feeling in these parts is that Rabat did the trick unaided."

" I remember the fever coming down. I was in a desert in my dream. I still dream about that desert, so wonderfully peaceful."

" Have you seen those gashes in you ? "

" Yes," he said. " I've had a squint." They were rib-smashing beauties round the right wall of the chest. They were healing very nicely, thanks to Miss Potterswell and Dr. Roy Chowdhury, M.D., and to good food, and most of all to the kindness of the Tanners that made him feel like crying, but he was too old for crying.

" I've waited till now to speak about it, Harry. I'm damned sorry for letting you down again."

He might have given selfless Desmond an earlier chance to say his say, because he could read the runnings of Desmond's mind. " You missed twice," he said. " The point about tigers is that people miss them. What's the fuss about ? "

" No fuss," said Desmond. " But you told me to hold my fire, and not to shoot at all unless the tiger was committed to the upper level. What did I do ? I know what you did—you called the brute off me and down to you."

" You fired too soon on my account," said Harry. " So we're quits."

" I'm not sure I did. I may simply have lost my head."

" Now listen, Desmond," he cajoled him. " If I held post-

mortems into things I didn't do dead right according to the book,
I'd have been cuckoo long ago. As it is, regard me. Could there
be a happier clam ?"

Desmond sucked that immemorial tooth. " No," he said, " and
long may it continue. But guts, the lack of, never bothered you."

Which by and large was so, he realised, in the sense of physical
fears to face. And as to his old bothers far away and small, he could
not be bothered with dead things when life was parading for his
delectation.

" This last week," he said. " The best I ever had, I think. But
I'm sorry for being such a burden on the Tanners."

Desmond sucked in stress again. " I was saying last night to
Christian, and she agreed, what a comfort you are to have about
the place."

The spotted owlet perched on a wire to the garden lamp. It
was a sedate and talkative small owl; it muttered to itself and
stared him out. He stared back at the owl. He was touched at
being called a comfort.

And here came Michael Tanner in pyjamas. He was a boy of
spirit and good heart, lacking the physic of the company of other
boys. He would have that physic soon enough at school in
England.

" You and the owlet arrived together, which reminds me about
a wise old owl who sat in an oak. Know it ?"

" I know oak before ash we'll have a splash."

" That's only weather wisdom. This is particularly special
owlish wisdom :

> " A wise old owl sat in an oak ;
> The more he saw the less he spoke ;
> The less he spoke the more he heard :
> Why can't we be like that wise old bird ?"

Michael fixed him with a Michael gaze, unblinking and
inscrutable. Who said that children's thoughts lay on their faces ?
The days were hot now, and Michael's skin was pale. He looked
well enough.

" Why do you stare at me like a python hungry for its dinner ? "

" Because I was just thinking no stories if you were a wise old owl."

" He used to be a silent owl. Plain Harry has reformed."

" Perhaps he'll tell you one to-morrow," Christian said. " Go on now, darling."

Michael poohed, protested, dallied, shook hands and went with Desmond.

" Chowdhury says I can sit up in a chair to-morrow. I ought to be elated, but I'm not."

" Why should you be ? " she said. " It's such a lovely feeling getting well and learning the world from a quiet corner before the world comes nagging."

" Do you think the world must nag ? "

" No, Harry. But life has to be battles, doesn't it, to lose and win and start again each day."

" You know," he said. " I've never felt serene before, not quite like this."

" Look at all the battles you've been winning," Christian said. She knitted a blue sweater for Michael's English winter. They were steel needles with hard clicks, gleaming under the electric light. The fingers were so supple and so adept, thinking for themselves. The grinding of the sugar-cane continued night and day but it would soon be over.

" Easy battles being pampered in a bed."

" To suffer and never to complain, not once. I would call that bravery."

She said these nice things quietly for the first time now. He wondered why she said them. " Talking of serenity," he said, " I can't imagine life defeating you. My mother had the same thing in her different way. You're like a souped-up version of my mother, Mother Tanner, did you know ? "

Christian laughed. " You say such idiotic things." She looked down at her knitting once again. " I wonder if your mother felt as terrified as I do about Michael if she knitted sweaters for you to wear three weeks away in England at the age of eight, and it's

G

only overnight by air these days. No serenity in that jumble of confession."

" I know," he said. He had known that thought in Christian who was now his friend. He had seen it in the fingers flying faster ; and he had seen it in impatience with her only son. " You and Desmond, you're a good strong couple."

" It's a small thing," Christian said, " when God is here to help us."

He was tired. He closed his eyes, and now again he saw the colour of his desert of tranquillity. He was thinking, not about the desert, but about the beauty of the faith that spoke in Christian : *When God is here to help us.* He wondered how you came to that. He did not understand it and was not able to accept it, and did not need it here and now, replete with gratitude, contentment. He saw the rolling of his desert with the compliments of Señor Dali, with the colour of a rich-tea biscuit. He smiled, returning to the veranda of the bungalow at Bondha, umber floor, white-washed pillars, stars up there, scents of dampness in the dry March night, the brisk tattoo of knitting needles. Christian watched him, smiling too. Peace and trust were strong between them.

" If I could paint," she said, " I would paint you with your eyes closed smiling there like that. Resignation is perhaps the thing I mean. It wasn't in your face before."

She held the small sweater up to look at it. " Well, that's the body almost done," she said in her absent way. It was warmer every evening now, not hot enough to feel sweaty looking at a woollen sweater in the making. " I've been thinking, Harry," Christian said. " Do you like the sea—going on ships, I mean ? "

" So, so," he said. " Yes, I used to."

" I've been thinking," she went on more hurriedly than her wont, " that when you get really well and strong enough to travel, perhaps at the end of March, why don't you take a voyage slowly home by East or West ? "

" That's a good idea," Harry said. He had not considered plans. He had not considered anything beyond this here. He looked out past Christian to the darkness, thinking of her good idea of a voyage.

He shaded his eyes, and then it was not so dark outside, although
the moon had set. He saw the garden, the dim plain, a darker line
which was the frontier of the forest. He could not see the mountains,
but he saw the blackness of the heights of Rimli. The heights of
Rimli made a graceful sweep beside the sunrise or before the setting
of the sun or by a moon or even now below a quilt of stars. The
heights of Rimli were well known to him. He had lived in and
about them for two weeks, and he had watched them lately too,
and they were pleasing except at the hard hours of day.

They now rose of a sudden in their blackness. They menaced
him and challenged him grotesquely. " I will do that, I think," he
said. " But first I have a small account to settle." His pulse ran
up, and he was cold. He shut his eyes again.

*   *   *   *   *

" I suggested the sea voyage," said Christian to her husband
in their room at night, " and he agreed at once it was a good idea,
looking out, you know the way he does. And then I saw that
brute hit him suddenly again, and his face changed altogether. Oh
Desmond, what a fool I am."

" Not a fool, my love," said Desmond. " But the leopard
doesn't change his spots. If you knew Harry Black as well as I do,
you'd realise it was bound to happen. He'll be on the rampage
any day now, mark my words."

Change my spots and mark my words, she thought. Everyone
can't use original expressions, and the leopard is a deadly beast.

*   *   *   *   *

They were sitting with their backs against a tree. The jungle
was green and not a touch of brown. Harry did not have his leg
on. *He writes beautifully*, Christian said, *I know. But fighting is
really all he thinks about, and luck is like some old Jehovah to his valiant
heroes.*—*You're wrong,* said Harry. It was another of their lively
disputations.

But he saw Bapu's Bad One. He saw it past the spreading
banyan tree, past the bright green grasses, past the hillocks and the

hollows. It was watching them, he thought. *Christian*, he said, *I did a stupid thing. I left my tin leg in the car. Would you bring it for my peace of mind?*—*Of course*, she said, and ran off in her tartan shorts to do his bidding.

He could not see the tiger now. He thought the tiger might have gone away. He waited, alert as any deer, but nothing moved among the hillocks and the hollows, where he would be sure to spot it. And then he saw a weaving in the grass this side, a slow parting and a swaying and an after-stillness of the tops along this way. *Go home!* he thought of shouting; but it was wiser to be absolutely still alone with an immensity of jungle and the Bad One. Or could I hop now to the banyan tree? he wondered, and climb a flying root, and then I would be safe?

The swaying of the grass had stopped. He waited and he wondered and he watched. He knew that he was very well concealed. He was almost sure that it had gone away.

The tiger had not gone away. It stepped out of the tall grass to search deliberately right and left, the tawny orange and the black against the pretty greens. The eyes swept across his tree and round to thicker jungle on his right and back again and past the tree, not even seeing him, and steadied to the cover of the bushes on his left. That was to be the Bad One's way. It strolled across the open ground. It was a burly tiger of great size, the master of the jungle, the killer with a killer's rippling grace.

He saw the Bad One from the corner of his eye, but the Bad One had not noticed him. He had been so right to rely upon his stillness, blended with the jigsaw of the jungle greens. Now if he had lost his nerve, and hoppity-hop gone scurrying for that tree. . . .

But the dupe was Harry Black. The tiger came now from the left, silent, terrible, enormous. Now, now, now.

"What is it, Mr. Black?" Miss Potterswell in night attire and in a twitter, bending over him, that smell of cloves.

The house was a hubbub in the night. "Harry, old boy, are you all right? You let out the most god-awful piercing yell."

"Sorry," Harry said. "I didn't know. I'm quite all right." Had he shouted? What about?

Miss Potterswell retired next door. The veranda whispers went away. The chokidar hawked loudly in the garden. His ribs were hurting, but that got better and he slept, and in the morning he felt quite all right.

"Mrs. Johnson asked Mummy to go over, so she says : Could you start me on my Sunday lessons, Harry ?" Johnson was Cane Superintendent, English, with an Anglo-Indian wife. Desmond and Christian walked a tightrope of other people's feelings in this isolated place, and by their own good balance held a balance.

"I can have a try," said Harry. "Anything you say, chum. But it's not my usual line of business, so you'll have to help me."

"Here's Mummy's Bible, you take that, and I keep mine. You have to ask me the questions in the Catechism. We have a different one for every Sunday."

He took the printed leaflet with a child's picture of Christ and the Disciples and a multitude, and underneath : *If any man will come after me, let him deny himself, and take up his cross, and follow me.* "All right," said Harry Black. "Here goes. . . ."

Once he had known the Gospels fairly well. He enjoyed this lesson in the company of Michael, who questioned and accepted with a child's whole heart. How near the teaching unadorned, uncomplicated, unbedogmatised, lay to a child's whole heart.

"Only two or three more questions. First : Which is the great commandment ? "

"*Thou shalt love the Lord thy God with all thy heart, and with all thy soul, and with all thy strength and with all thy mind,*" said Michael rapidly and gravely.

"Full marks. What is the other great commandment ? "

"*Thou shalt love thy neighbour as thyself.*"

"What does *thy neighbour* mean ? "

"The person in the next house, like the Johnsons, doesn't it ? "

"Them and everybody else, the ones you know and ones you don't, the Eskimos and the Kikuyus, the whole bang shooting match, caboodle and palaver, I would guess."

Michael laughed with a whole heart too. "Oh gosh, you're funny."

" Order in the house. Absolutely final question : Which does it say is the most important one of those commandments ? "

" It says the first one, loving God. But I don't quite see that, Harry. Because if you have to love everyone the same, how can you love God any more ? "

He heard Christian's footsteps, and she came in, smiling at them. " We need assistance," Harry said.

" You have to love God best and first," she said. " Then you can love people better. Isn't that it, Harry ? "

He did not offer an opinion.

Michael frowned. He was a remorseless seeker after truth. " Well, then," he said. " That means if *you* had to choose God or your own family, like as if Daddy was sick, or me, then you just go to church or something."

" No, darling," she said. " I don't think it means quite that. But it means we ought to love God best of all. It's about the hardest thing to understand, like when Christ said : *Who is my mother ?* I can't remember where it comes. There's a Concordance, Harry, at the end."

He turned to the Concordance, where he saw a pressed flower, faded red. He looked at that. He found a reference in Mark. " *And the multitude sat about him, and they said unto him, Behold, thy mother and thy brethren without seek for thee. And he answered them, saying, Who is my mother or my brethren ? And he looked round about on them which sat about him, and said, Behold my mother and my brethren ! For whosoever shall do the will of God, the same is my brother, and my sister, and mother.*"

" You see, Michael, that was Christ speaking, and He was perfect, but we aren't a bit, so we just have to try, that's all, and not stop trying if we do get muddled. I think that's enough lessons for this Sunday, darling. Try to love everyone is all it really means, even if they don't love you."

Michael looked at Miss Potterswell's closed door. He leaned to Harry. " I don't love Gottasmell," he hissed. " She absolutely stinks."

Michael was rebuked. He muttered an apology and went.

"He's such a chameleon," she said. "An angel, then a fiend next minute. So much for Bible lessons." Christian lowered her voice. "But I must say Michael has a point about her, good nurse though I know she is. Her departure will not be mourned by me."

"Dim. And anti-Michael after beetles in the bed. She's not a bad old thing."

Christian shook her head. She seemed upset. She hardly ever seemed upset.

"What is it, Christian ? "

"Oh, nothing. She'll be gone to-morrow."

It was midday, time for his bottled tonic, as prescribed by Dr. Roy Chowdhury, M.D., as administered punctual to the minute by the paragon Miss Potterswell.

"Come in," he said.

"Oh, I did not mean to be a spoilsport. . . ." She often said quaint, silly things like that, coyly, but without the slithering sly edge of now.

He looked for some time at starched Miss Potterswell, so humble and so prim of lip. "Miss Potterswell," he said, "when I want you to be a spoilsport, I shall ring my bedside bell, tinkle tinkle, thank you very much. Now take that stuff away."

She scuttled for the door.

"Just a moment," Harry said. "Ask Cheddi Khan to come here, would you ? Then have my crutches ready, please. I'm getting up."

"But Doctor said . . ." Miss Potterswell thought better of what Doctor said. She was afraid of this new icy Mr. Black.

"So that was it."

"Yes," said Christian. "My ally, Mrs. Johnson, passed it on to me. Miss P. was over seeing them last evening—she murmured that you and I enjoyed our talks so much it seemed tactless to disturb us, various small innuendoes. So wicked, Harry, and so untrue, and so typical of my awful sex."

"It's not the sex," he said. "It's the frustrated virgins in it, having to leave their jealous mark behind them. Well, I'm not bothered with the turning of my other cheek.　I'll fix the old bitch up."

She smiled, but sadly.　" You were turning it," she said.

There had been no strain at all between them in this disembodied time.　The strain had now arrived, and not for him because of petty slanders by Miss Potterswell.　He was stepping from his cloister, and the world awaited him.

" Never mind," he said to Christian.　He was troubled at the truth of what had been untrue.

He watched her walk away across his room.　She was a slender woman.　He saw her as a woman now again, touchable, although he had not touched her, and he saw the touchings of her body on her dress, the roundness and the softness and the thrust.

" Christian ! "

" Yes ? "　She turned, a hand on the wall beside the door, an arm out straight and bare.　He had never held her ; he had never kissed her ; why should he deny himself his question ?　" That pressed red flower.　Would it be a cardinal flower ? "

Christian nodded slowly.　She shut the door behind her.

He sent Cheddi Khan to Rimli in the car for Bapu.　He rang his bedside bell to summon Miss Potterswell and crutches.　He was in a hurry now again.

CHAPTER FOURTEEN

" Until now there have been two killings Ranipur-side," Bapu said. " When a third man dies, the Bad One may return to Rimli, perhaps at the fullness of this moon, who knows ? "

Ten days to the March full moon.

" *Who knows ?* thou sayest, Bapu. But thou art wise, knowing many hidden things."

Bapu cackled briefly, squatting in the mango's shade in the Bondha garden. " Sahib, only I know that the Bad One waits for me."

" Is there a secret place where the tiger waits for thee ? " He watched Bapu.

" Is not every resting-place a secret to the tiger ? " Bapu drew his torn and tattered sleeve across his nose slowly, thoughtfully and quite gracefully from right shoulder all the way along to wrist, and sniffed. He was looking at the heights of Rimli, ugly in a dance of sun. " The tiger travels far to hunt by night and rests by day in secret places. But who am I to say such things to the Bara Sahib Bahadur, killer of many tigers ? "

" I am a killer of tigers," Harry said. " But thou art a man born to the secrets of the tiger. Listen now and keep this other secret : Cut two bamboo poles and smaller pieces, and with the strong jungle ropes well known to thee, fashion a chair wherein I may be carried to the Pass of Rimli. Is it understood ? "

" It is understood. But, Sahib, why a secret, the building of this chair ? "

" There are secrets within secrets," Harry said. " Wheels within wheels as we say in my own tongue. Therefore to-morrow morning make the chair and hide it. Now, at thy return give this letter to Tara Singh." It was a copy of his letter posted to-day to the D.F.O. and to the Conservator of Forests asking for immediate news by telephone of further human kills at Ranipur. A three-stage link—along between the foothills and the mountains, and across the foothills, and to Rimli—it might possibly give warning before night.

Bapu stood again. He seemed restless.

" How is it now for thee at Rimli ? Is there trouble ? "

" There will be no trouble till the Bad One kills again with us, for men fear the Sahib, who is my protector." Bapu bent swiftly, supple as soft rubber, and laid his brow against the point of Harry's slipper. " *Mera Bap*, my father," Bapu said. " At the first news I will come."

Harry watched him lope away. Bapu was always impatient for the comfort of his forest, not usually so impatient that he did not hover until he had planted a notion of two tots of whisky. Why the reverence and why the hurry ? What went on in Bapu's mind ?

He swung on to his crutches from the basket chair, steadied, and made back across the garden. It was only ninety in the shade, but the sun was hot on his weavy head. He should have worn a hat. The wind was dry on his lips and up his nose. The wind dried sweat coolly as it broke.

He concentrated on his landfall. " Sail on, O Ship of State ! " he grunted loudly, making a joke for himself of a hard voyage on a heaving sea. He rested in the portico beside Christian's potted plants. Now the steps, but they were troublesome. She must have been watching, for she came out with her fair hair flying, caught him and dumped him in a chair.

" You're crazy," she said with that crossness Michael evoked in her occasionally, when a submerged idiom and accent reappeared. " You're just plain crazy."

Things stopped going round. He was not plain crazy. He was getting ready as quickly as he could. There was no other way of getting ready. He was not a vegetable now. He had a purpose, and he nursed a grudge against an animal, and that was new and most exciting. Bapu's Bad One was no longer just a job. Getting strong, however, was a job to be efficiently accomplished without faintings, so perhaps Christian had a point. " Not plain crazy,"

Harry said. " Plain broken-hearted at Miss Potterswell's departure.
I tipped her, whereupon she wept, and Cheddi took her to the
station."

" You're so generous," she said. " You pay us far more than
it costs us for your board."

" I have nothing else to spend it on," he said. " Not even drink."

" And no desire for drink at all ? "

" No desire," he said, " for drink at all." He looked at bigger
dust-devils on the open plains, and smaller dust-devils here in the
Bondha garden, gathering and darting, those mysterious tornadoes ;
but they wreaked no havoc, and the dust-devils of the Bondha
garden died at the garden wall.

" I think that's wonderful," she said. She stood, watching the
dust-devils too. " Please hasten slowly," Christian said. " Please
don't go after that tiger till you're really well and strong. Promise
me, Harry ? "

He was not making promises to Christian. " *Festina lente* is the
motto," Harry said.

" Or would self-indulgence be the motto ? "

He did not see much self-indulgence in his staggering about on
crutches, and he wished she would not get at him ; but if he
annoyed her, she would go away. " Tell me," he said, " how do
you contrive to do your hair so well ? Have you a feminine
accomplice ? It has a plain elegance more like those slinky *Vogue*
girls than like a memsahib in the month of March." He said it
casually to divert her, but then he rather wished he had not said
it because the casual days were over.

" My brush is my accomplice," Christian said, " and you're a
flatterer, although I must say a compliment does something for a
woman in this climate." She touched her hair, and her face
coloured and went pale again. She put on rouge at night. She
wore those linen tartan shorts, long ones to the knee. Bermuda
shorts, she called them. Her legs were good enough to be even
more appealing with low heels. He thought she was going to
make off on her shapely legs. Well, if she went down the veranda,
he could watch her go. What was the dream last night that seemed

familiar and those shorts were in it ? He could not remember. I'd better check the rifles, Harry thought.

" You and Bapu hatching plots and plans," she said. " How to take Mohamet on his crutches to the mountain, I suppose."

Christian looked down at him and smiled. The wits of Christian Tanner more than matched his own, he realised. " Just a nattering of cronies," Harry said. " I like old Bapu."

" He's nice," she said, " but oh so goaty in the warmer weather. Well, if Michael and I are really flying on the thirtieth, I'd better go and sort his things."

" Three weeks and more," he said. " Talk about being on the hop."

" Is being on the hop another one of your prerogatives ? " she snapped at him, and went away.

That night he dreamed about the tiger, and he knew the dream. He remembered it next morning. He dreamed the horror every night.

His headaches stopped. His wounds were healed, and Dr. Roy Chowdhury, M.D., could strap him tight, and the ribs were hardly any bother.

He had three things now to do ; the first was to get strong ; the second was to find his balance ; the third thing was to harden up his stump, and that had shrunk, and his tin leg chafed him.

$$\ast \qquad \ast \qquad \ast \qquad \ast \qquad \ast$$

He and Desmond strolled the circuit of the garden, and the moon was all but full. He did well enough with one stick and with pauses in the wicker chair.

" . . . They said, Yes, they could find me a job of sorts in the London office, but I must understand that chaps like me are two a penny nowadays in England ; whereas people with practical experience of India are few and far between. . . ."

" That's true," said Harry. " How would the salary at home compare ? "

" Half what I'm getting now. Well, Christian has a little money of her own, and I think we might just swing it, including

Michael's prep. school. Or I could leave the company and look for something else, perhaps in Canada. That sounds all right until you try it at the age of forty-plus, and they say *What can you do?* and you say *I can make sugar in the plains of India*, and they say *Thank you very much.*

"So the company do us pretty well, and they have us in a cleft stick. But I may have stirred them up, because now to-day arrives this offer at twice my present salary, not half."

"They must think well of you," he said. It was not difficult to know why. Desmond was shrewd, sensible and moderate, a good man with his fellow men of any hue. He had not lost energy in this enervating land.

"I think they do," said Desmond without conceit. Vanity and conceit simply were not in him. "It's a pistol at my head, of course. You can accept our wizard offer now, or you can be a clerk in London, or you can stew in your own juice as manager at Bondha." He laughed. "Rather good, that—sugar juice. But a newly created job with fifteen factories to look after in Bihar and the U.P.—it means touring all the cold weather, and sweating it out in Lucknow all the hot weather, a pretty hellish lonely life for Christian, don't you think?"

What does it matter what I think? They had reached the far end of the garden. It was so light that he could see every reed or osier or whatever the stuff was, interlaced and slanting in the basket chair. He sat down for a breather and looked back at the bungalow and saw Christian walk along the veranda, and he heard her walking clipped and free. "What does she say?"

"She sighed first and said : *Are we to be nomads all our lives?* Then she said, of course I must take the job because it's such a splendid offer. But it's not only my life, Harry. It's hers and Michael's. I wish I knew what she really wanted."

"I expect she wants what you want," Harry said. "And you really want the job, so you'd better take it." That sounded uncompromising. Well, he could not help himself.

"It's a weakness of yours," Desmond said surprisingly, "that you see things simpler than they are. Right or wrong, sort of

absolute is what I mean. It's a strength too, compared with my
shilly-shallying. But I'm not keen on making twice the cash, less
whopping income tax, just for the sake of. I wish you'd sound
out Christian for me. You're great buddies, and she might spill
the beans to you, being a disinterested party, so to speak."

So to speak. "I might try," he said. He might not try. "In
any case you can't turn down the offer flat until you know the
details."

"No, and they said if I wanted to discuss it, I must fly down
to Calcutta the day after to-morrow. That means leaving by car
to-morrow evening. You see the point about a pistol at my head ? "

"Yes," he said. He also saw the wall of the moonlit Bondha
garden as a wall he had better scale right soon. "How long will
you be away ? "

"A week or so," said Desmond. "I must say it's a comfort
to know you'll be here to look after the others for me. I mean,
Johnson's not a bad chap, but he doesn't quite speak Christian's
language. Also, he's sugar happy at the moment."

Harry got up, and they walked again, and Desmond said : " Do
you ever think of the miles we used to walk together round and
round ? "

"Yes," he said. "I do." The prison life was always with him
in its own compartment. Asleep, he was a prisoner still. "If the
maneater comes across," he said carefully to his old friend Desmond,
"I'll have to go." He had not mentioned any such intention before
this ; indeed, it was his little secret from the Tanners, and from
Cheddi, who had joined the Tanners' league.

"Not this week, Harry ! You can't possibly go after that
animal for another fortnight. Good God, man, you can't even
walk a hundred yards without resting."

"I can drive the old bitch," he said. "I can ride an elephant.
I can sit still and shoot. What more do you want ? "

"What more I want," said Desmond, " is that you should
behave like a reasonable human being, not like a monkey on a
stick, with tigers on its little brain. You may not care what
happens, but we do."

He spoke with the round vehemence of a friend. Harry could not remember any other time that Desmond had rebuked him so forthrightly. He accepted the rebuke, which he might have heeded but for complications that had not occurred to blind old trusting Desmond. And he thought that *monkey on a stick with tigers on its little brain* sounded much more like a quoting of the Complication than it did like an original by Desmond, and the thought of their privacies grew more painful to him night by night.

" The best chance of all is in the Pass of Rimli when the tiger crosses," he explained. " I don't have to be mobile there." He saw the tiger now again. He certainly would not have heeded Desmond's counsel.

" What if you wound it ? "

" I won't wound it," Harry said. " Luck is all I need ; and if luck brings that charming animal, I shall kill it."

" I wish I had your confidence in myself," said Desmond, mild again. " Well, of course, you've earned that."

They neared the bungalow. The night was still. It was the first night without a humming and a hissing and a grinding, for now at last the sugar-crush was over.

" The Indian night is never quiet," Harry said. He had forgotten that in recent times, and in the boozy times he had not heard the quietness of nights. Drums beat out a complicated rhythm in some village of the plains. A jackal howled this side of Rimli, and the howl was taken up to east and west and south, a first jackal chorus of the night, and silence. " Listen," he said. " The Koel ! " That was a call of heat. " Ko-el, ko-el. . . ." Insistent, up and up the scale, climbing in excitement, scrambling to a summit, stop. The Koel was a cuckoo and a parasite, less fevered than its kinsman, the Brain-Fever bird.

" The hot weather," Desmond said. " Well, thank goodness they'll be out of it by April."

He called Christian, and she came to sit with them beside the unlit garden lamp. Harry watched the heights of Rimli, and thought he could see the far barriers of snow, but that might be imagination, for the sky was hazy now in March.

"Harry threatens to go after the maneater if it comes soon again, which I have a sort of hunch it will. I've been trying to talk sense into the man," Desmond said some time or other. "I wish you'd use your woman's wiles, my love."

"No," she said. "I won't."

He saw Desmond's head flick round to Christian. The Koel started up again, up and up and UP . . .

*   *   *   *   *

He took Michael with him the next afternoon. The part of the Rimli forest that he knew least well lay on the far side of the salient from Bondha, beyond the flat tongue of jungle jutting roughly south-west from the horseshoe, completing an oval, the upper half encased by cliffs, the lower bounded by the plains.

They followed the Rimli road almost to the forest edge, and the forest greens were dusty now. Harry swung left to skirt the salient, driving by rutted track, and across the sun-seamed land, over a bridged irrigation ditch, and on by bump and bund and dip of rock-hard muttee. The light was harsh. The wheat was ripening, and already the earth thirsted at the beginning of intolerable thirst. There was no wind to-day. Dust hung for each bullock cart, and rose for each man walking, and dust swirled in here to coat the metal floor, the seats, the wheel, the gear-lever knob, to sift about the stout Old Bitch, to make dusty millers out of Harry Black and Michael Tanner. The dust was clean. The heat of the day was not yet over, but the hot days had not come.

He drove slowly to spare his passenger and to spare his ribs. The strappings were unpleasantly confining. He let Michael change the gears. Wherever he looked, except to the forest to the right, men were working. Wherever a man might look in the plains of India, men and women would be toiling against hunger on the hungry land. But never, never in a lifetime would a stranger see the lustings of these people, so kindly to a stranger, so human in their kindness, so decorous in *moribus*, free to slave publicly by day, to breed privately by night. So it was in the beginning, and so it would be to an end. But the end and the ending lay beyond his sight. " Four hundred millions of them," Harry muttered.

" The people in India are very poor and hungry, aren't they, Harry ? "

" Yes," he said. " They are."

" Well, why does God make more and more people so that there are too many for the food ? "

" I don't know," he said. It was a mystery to him how anyone could see God and the milling masses of an Indian bazaar.

" I asked Mummy, and she said *we don't have to try and wonder why*. And Daddy said : *Don't worry*, and I thought perhaps you could tell me."

" Sorry, Michael," he said. " I can't."

" Besides," said Michael, whose deity was an intimate and baffling acquaintance. " If God makes everybody, who makes God ? "

" Now look, pardner," he said, " your Daddy and Mummy are good godly sort of people who might help about that knotty little puzzle. But I'm only an old sinner, and I can't."

" You're a jolly nice old sinner," Michael said. " I wish you always lived with us."

They swung round the bottom of the salient, and swung to see the hills again. They ran up a hardly perceptible slope between the Rimli forest on their right and the river Garda on their left. The river was low. It looked like bean soup. It was no physical barrier to a tiger, being wadable now, and swimmable at all times. But the crossing offered no appeal to tigers, for the country on the other side was open.

Michael did not seem to mind the dust or heat or glare or jostling. He was a tough-spirited small boy. Harry thought his mother had more steel than had his father, and he also thought that Desmond was too soft with Michael. He enjoyed Michael's companionship in talk or silence. The boy was dear to him as no boy had been before, and he was going to lose this boy as he had lost everything before.

They came to the wide watercourse which crossed from the forest to join the river Garda. It carried the floods of the Rimli watershed. It was bone dry at this season. They jolted over and climbed the far bank in low ratio low gear.

"Can we stop a minute?" Michael asked. "I've never been here before."

He stopped and switched the Old Bitch off, and they got out to see the river. An Indian boy grazed a flock of goats, but what they grazed on was a mystery. He was a child of about Michael's age, potbellied, with a lively look and a long Hindu topknot.

"What are these marks on the sandbank in the middle, Harry?"

"They look like a crocodile's tracks, where the old mugger waddled up to have his sunbathe."

"Oh gosh, I've never seen a crocodile. Could we wait for it to come out?"

"There isn't time now," Harry said. "Perhaps another day. But I'm not a crocodile authority. It might be a turtle for all I know. Ask that boy."

Michael went to ask the boy. He asked him in fluent Hindi. They faced one another, the dark child and the light child, wary puppies of two breeds. "*Itna, itna bara!*" Michael said with glee, returning. "He says it's a huge old mugger full of silver bracelets and dead ladies' bones."

Harry laughed, and they drove again. Ahead now was the meeting of the forest and the river, not quite a meeting, for they were separated by the steep ending of the horseshoe ridge. The river flowed hither from the north-west, taking the efflux of the foothills on its flank, making its bed along the utmost margin of the lands of silt; but the fault, which was the Rimli horseshoe, thrust into the silt lands and turned the river here a full right angle away down from the hills.

"Could you shoot the mugger for me, Harry? Then we could make a suitcase, couldn't we, pretty knobbly sort of suitcase?"

"Belly," Harry said. "Belly, him belly belly smooth good leather."

Michael laughed so hard that the dust streaked on his face, and he sobered up, then shook again at the birth of a witticism: "Him got belly-button?"

" Evelybody got belly-button," Harry said. " Mugger's belly-button belly smelly."

They went by the forest road on the edge of the fireline. They crossed the *raos*, and ran fast for Rimli, and at the Range Office, Harry's *bête noire*, that useless bugger and poltroon was waving his arms and prancing fatly, and what Harry had hoped and feared and wanted and not wanted had unquestionably happened, he knew before Tara Singh announced that a man had been killed to-day in Ranipur beyond the foothills and below the mountains.

" What time was the kill ? "

" Just now about one hour back, surely."

" Well done, Ranger Sahib," he said. " Get Bapu. Get four strong men. I shall be here within an hour." It was almost five o'clock.

He had his big rifle in the back, but he had Michael Tanner in the front. " Hold tight, Michael boy," he said. " We're going to belly-bounce like billy-oh." He put his left hand on Michael's shoulder, and held him down the five miles bouncing like billy-oh to Bondha.

CHAPTER FIFTEEN

HE STOPPED at the island in the main watercourse, where he and Bapu had separated to inspect tie-ups on the evening of his first encounter with the tiger. From the birth of one moon to the full growth of the next ; but it was a longer time than that.

Bapu and the four Garhwalis disembarked. They were chunky, thick-calved little men.

" Cheddi Khan," he said. " Wait here for the return of these people. Take them and Bapu down. Drive them to Bondha and bring our baggage, everything, to the Forest House. Is it understood ? "

" It is understood. But Sahib, the tiger may not come, and you are not yet well. . . ."

" The tiger may not come to-night," he said patiently enough, " but we must be at Rimli against the tiger's coming."

" The last words of Tanner Sahib to me . . ."

" These are my words, not the words of Tanner Sahib."

" Sahib, let me sit with you to-night. I have served Your Honour many years, and I ask this."

Harry had driven too far too long too fast. He was tired and in some pain. Cheddi Khan knew that the way to sit was to sit alone. But one of the reasons he was fond of Cheddi was that Cheddi did not fear him. He got out and turned his back on Cheddi's mutterings.

Bapu brought the chair, a craftsman's job, and he sat in it. " Quick ! " he said, for the day was nearly done.

They ran with a broken step, and the motion was quite pleasant, like a dinghy in a choppy sea, less troublesome to him than the hard-springed joltings of the Old Bitch. He closed his eyes, and he was Noah in the ark, whisked up steepening waters to ground upon Mount Ararat. He was almost anyone, being rather light of head. He might have been the Queen of Sheba in her palanquin, or Mrs. Hauksbee in her dandy. The panting hillmen, cheerful people, tough old goats, decanted him at the Pass of Rimli as the sun was setting. " *Shabash !* Well done," he said.

He wore a cardigan because there would be a chill up here before the morning. But it was hot now in the toasted cleft of rock, and no breeze changed the air. " Bapu," he boomed in the closed place. " When will the Bad One come ? "

" With a killing at afternoon, who knows ? The Bad One may not come. But if the Bad One comes in this night, then surely not early in the night, soon after feeding."

" I think you're right," he said to himself in English. He had a cushion. He was quite comfortable in his niche on the left side of the Pass of Rimli. " Go then, Bapu."

" I will go with these men to the motor-gharri. But I will stay to-night in a tree within hearing of the sahib." Bapu stated this ; he did not ask it. He spent half his nights up trees.

Harry nodded, and Bapu went.

He was in the middle of the pass, the horizontal cleft from one watershed to the other. He faced north-east to that opening of the cleft. He saw a pine tree close beyond the opening, and far away he saw the wall of the first big hills. He had the long torch with him, but not fitted to the rifle, for this was the night of the March full moon, and the moon would shine all through the night. He had a place to watch. It was simple. Indeed, this assignation with the last tiger of his life was the simplest in his whole experience, and he looked forward to it more keenly than to any previous assignation. It was his last tiger and the first tiger he had ever hated. But he knew that the kill had been too late. The tiger was more likely to cross to-morrow night. Or it might not cross this time at all. Or somebody might shoot it at Ranipur. . . . Now stop that, Cassandra, he enjoined himself.

Night had come, and the moon had risen. It was not yet shining on the smooth bare floor of the Pass of Rimli. This nook of his had a backrest and a roof. He would be in shadow the whole night. His rib-strappings itched perennially. His aches and pains were better. He had taken a wake-up pill of Dexedrine, provided by his ally, Dr. Roy Chowdhury, M.D. He felt all right and keen of eye. He had not lost the old skill of banishing his body. He watched the Ranipur gateway of the pass. He must never relax vigilance. But he could be too alert, seeing a tiger where there was no tiger, imagining the Bad One's bushy face loom low and stealthy at the gate.

He had a tried stratagem for that. He went wandering in his mind. He wandered with the noises of the night outside. Not many came in here. The rumours of the noises funnelled in behind his head from Rimli, and in before his head from Ranipur, and one sound grew and faded once above the pass. It was a gaggling of geese, a wild sound of the wild birds flying high to nest at high waters in the mountains—free travellers, and he the small earth-bound man.

She did not say *Good luck!* or that conventional sort of thing. *Kill it, Harry!* she said this afternoon, like meaning him to exorcise a devil. He wondered why she said that in that way, being a gentle person. He wondered many things about her, and knew none of them, and he supposed he never would.

What was that? Oh, it was nothing. It was a breeze stirring the long needles of the pine.

Desmond would have left by now. He could think Desmond's thoughts for him, driving in the coolness of the night to catch an aeroplane to-morrow morning. What's the *right* thing? Desmond would be worrying. What's the best for *them*? With humility and rectitude. Desmond might say: *You see things simpler than they are. Right or wrong, sort of absolute is what I mean.* But the truth? The truth: that Desmond had everything except the one absolute that mattered. He was not a windy chap in ordinary terms. All he lacked was an ultimate bite of spunk. He had failed to go in the escape. He had made a trivial balls-up with the tiger. He always would.

You either had it or you did not have it, and were subject to the law that governed every living thing. Or you should be subject to the law of taking what you were strong enough to take, and holding what you had guts enough to hold; and what was society but a conspiracy to hide that truth, to bolster up weak people? All the virtues were piddling without courage. *I wish I had your confidence in myself*, said kindly Desmond in the garden. *Well, of course, you've earned that.*

I have, he thought.

And now something stood in moonlight in the gateway of the Pass of Rimli. The jackal stood a longish time, although time was not seconds up to minutes and minutes up to hours. Time was the sweeping moon, and time was the jackal standing where nothing stood before. It raised and lowered its muzzle. It was satisfied. The jackal was coming through from Ranipur to Rimli. It walked on the shady side, and even there he could see it clearly, and it did not scavenge-skulk. It walked quite boldly, dog-like, fox-like on the prowl perhaps twenty yards this way along the pass until it saw him. The jackal fled brush-low and greyish in the moonlight back to Ranipur. I bet the little sod will go and tell the Bad One, Harry thought. His mind was fanciful.

And fancy took him on a voyage on their ship. *We aren't on the hop now, are we, Christian?—No, we're lazy easy quiet strong and slow. The phosphorescence, I do love it, Harry, that molten curl, running running shiver smash another wave is broken and another, and the phosphorescent sea is ours to love—The Lascar, did you hear him then, the look-out at the bow? Do you know what he was calling?— Tell me, Harry.—Hum dekte hain, he chants so slowly and so high. I am watching.—Tell me more things we can love.*

> *The moon regards them without shame. The wind*
> *Rises and twitters through the wreck of bone . . .*
> > *It is so hard to be alone*
> *Continually, watching the great stars march*
> *Their circular unending route . . .*

That is sad and we love it too, and we sail for ever to the Island of Socotra—But life has to be battles, doesn't it, to lose and win and start again each day? That was what you told me—No, my darling, no battles in our ship. Just sailing on and on for ever to the Island of Socotra. We love the flying fishes too, the way they splinter out, glisten skip and skim and dripping drops and gliding on for ever and away until they meet a wave. Happy out and happy in, the happy flying fish. Good-bye then, flying fish.

Something else was coming through. It was a small thing, tacking for passage on the moonlit floor, smoothness being relative, not absolute like guts. He looked down at the scorpion, hearing a minute scrabble, a tap of hard-shelled claws below him. He bore no grudge against the scorpion, a four-inch monster, but he thought its home might be in the rocky crevice where he sat. He had once been stung, which had not been funny. He thought of assaulting it with the coffee thermos Christian had made him bring on his moonlit picnic ; but he hesitated, not willing to break an impeccable stillness of half a night. It was a problem of the lesser and the greater evil. He who hesitates, he thought wittily, cannot put salt on a scorpion's tail. He listened for it in behind him. He decided to break the rules enough to have a look, so he turned his head and saw the scorpion's rear view half a dozen feet away, making a fair scorpion clip for the next bend in the cleft en route to Rimli.

That was a weight off his mind and a shiver off his neck, and no more one-way traffic came as yet from Ranipur. It was midnight, from the angle of the moon. Three would be a likely time, he thought, and the best time, for at that hour the moon would shine squarely from above him and behind him to the entrance of the pass. It was an eerie place, this cleft, a whimsy, freak or folly of the gods, a that-will-teach-you sort of gouge from times when the earth heaved and split to stand these hills in order, he supposed.

He liked the pass to-night, more macabre than ever in its wash of moon. He waited for the animal which had mauled him, and which had lately haunted him in the defenceless lands of sleep. The rational odds were against its coming, and he knew in his guts that sometime or other, soon or late, before this night was over, the maneater would suddenly be standing, suddenly from nowhere be filling the entrance of its only road to Rimli. He would put the first soft-nosed bullet from the four-six-five into the centre of the chest, or if the head was low, then smicky-smack between the eyes, and there might be some hullabaloo, no doubt, at closer quarters, but it would not get as far as here, and if the recoil stirred up his ribs and head, he would not begrudge that pain. The thing was in the bag, a slice of cake, or to use a rude prison term for things wrapped-up—it was a proper pot of piss.

He was uncomfortable in some places, and his head was aching. It was true about small pains tending to balance one another out. Get down, he told his tiresome body. Get down, you ! And it did.

You know, he thought of second things while never for an instant wandering from the cold true purpose of the first thing first. You know, I don't know even if she likes me. What I mean is that she liked me when I was a sort of chrysalis for conversation safely tucked away in bed. Oh, that was just the trouble, that getting to know the woman and to like the woman, talking to her, as you occasionally get to like a man, but always unexpected with a yield where we would keep on punching up the points, and with sweet lack of reason. She has the intellect without the intellectual qua intellectual type of woman oh my God the end. The only other one I ever knew, and this is very odd, the only other one I ever knew was my own mother. I suppose some gifted analyser would be sure to say that I was Oedipus to Christian. Well now, to continue, platonic friendship has never been my cup of tea. I have enjoyed putting the best ladies where they best belong, and let's forget the beauties of their thoughts.

So we are good friends without an edge of any kind, and then one morning I awake in full possession of my senses. And she, who liked me as an interesting invalid, dislikes my real self very much. She has not changed, but I have changed since a week-end, three sad and innocent and lovely days for which she pressed a flower. I was an honourable dolt. I should have taken her while picking blueberries on that island of the fisherman. It would have been treachery to Desmond, but Desmond did not make it, Desmond could not take it, Desmond had not earned it.

He heard two noises. First he heard the sawing of a leopard, thrust the blade forward, draw it back. He heard that once. It came up to him from Ranipur, from beyond the gateway, in the wakeful forest. That was a leopard on the prowl, and it could mean alarm, and the leopard feared the tiger. The night must be wearing through to three o'clock, for now the whole cleft from Harry to the gateway was shadowless before the moon, and now the rock had cooled, and now a puff of mountain wind passed through here and on to Rimli.

The second sound that Harry heard was a kharkar barking in the other wakeful forest. Perhaps the small brown deer in Rimli barked at the saw of the wicked leopard in Ranipur across the ridge. The kharkar was an alarmist, a barker at anything, including Bapu up a tree.

It was quiet at Ranipur, quiet at Rimli, quiet here at the receipt of custom, but quiet a relative, not absolute. Sand-flies were paying him some attention. How loudly they hummed in his listening ear.

Aggressive, she thinks me, tiger-vindictive, lusting to settle my account. She despises hate, so she said one day. Ruthless, she thinks me. Well, so I am. A courage fanatic. Well, so I am. An all or nothing. Well, so I am. A perfectionist for everyone but me. Yes, I'm afraid so. A humanist who dislikes humanity. I know, I know, I know. But I'm not a goody-goody wanting to be better.

He watched, and still the tiger did not come.

Let's pick blueberries, Harry, shall we, with a rule not to eat many till we have enough ?—No! We pick and eat and stain our mouths with blueberries.

He turned his head to a soft sound close behind him. The tiger stalked him on its belly in the Pass. Its fangs were bared and its coat had a patterned lustre below the moon.

He screamed. His right forefinger had lain along the trigger-guard these nine quiet hours. His finger snatched at the triggers, and the present world exploded twice. Harry screamed again while two bullets went on to Ranipur below the mountains, and one tiger went back to Rimli.

He screamed his terror to the jungles down ahead at Ranipur and down behind at Rimli. He screamed his terror in the March full moon.

CHAPTER SIXTEEN

"Sahib!" And again: "Sahib!"

Bapu. Who was Bapu? Would Bapu come baleful and enormous round this bend from Rimli? Harry huddled in his small retreat.

It was close now, that jungle voice, coming up and over and in here. "Sahib! Sahib?"

He shrank farther in, but he peered back while he heard himself cry: "No!" like some other little chap. He had not reloaded, and he could not.

"Are you hurt, sahib?" Now it boomed in a cracked way along the cleft.

"Who are you?" he asked.

"It is I, Bapu." And the man came padding larger than life and under the moon and along the Pass from Rimli.

Harry Black stared up at him. He felt tiny below this Bapu with the round face and the same old jacket. He feared the secret man who stood so still, looking down in here at him, then along the empty cleft to Ranipur. "Has the Bad One come?" he whispered like a conspirator against the Bad One.

"From Rimli."

Bapu snatched the torch from Harry's side without a by-your-leave or any comment, and he went back along the pass to Rimli, using the beam to augment the moon, and it shone brightly in darker places, for the moon was sliding down now to the right. I could shoot at him, thought Harry, while he puts on his searching act. But I wouldn't dare, and it would do no good, because he would just change to his other self, or he would go and call his Friend, and better the devil I know than that again, *that*, THAT.

Bapu came back without sound. "It is the Bad One. There is one scarred pug belonging to the Bad One. But how could the Bad One cross by day? Sahib, I do not understand this."

Harry shook his head, looking at Bapu's spatulate toes. He kept on shaking his head and swivelling eyes to watch Bapu's toes.

"I sat in the peepul beside the *rao*. I thought I heard a leopard call across the cliff in Ranipur, and then I heard a kharkar bark in Rimli. Except for these, I did not hear the *janwar* speak. I heard no other wild things in this part of the night."

Harry nodded for a change, and he put a palm against his chin to stop the chattering.

"The sahib is sick. The *bara sahib bahadur* was wrong to defy the weakness of his body."

Bapu whipped off his grey tweed jacket, which could not have been dry-cleaned for ages, and he put it like a cloak over the shoulders of the great brave master. He made sympathetic tutting noises. He took the four-six-five, a wonderful weapon by James Purdey. He freed it gently from the clutch of Harry's long-fingered hands with his own blunt-fingered hands, broke it neatly and firmly as a workman handles his familiar tool, and the brass cases flew away ping-ping against the rock, and Bapu leaned in to take two of the shells from two of the five stitched recesses on the right breast of Harry's bush-shirt. He always carried five, making the very lucky number, seven.

The shells slid home with a healthy *sonck*. The breech clicked shut. "Rest now, sahib. I will stand watch until the dawn."

Bapu went away. Good old Bapu, Harry thought with reverence for Bapu. He knew, of course, that it was all nonsense about Bapu. He did not sleep or rest for the remainder of the night, but gradually he came up from the piddling bottom essence of himself. He drank lukewarm coffee that Christian Tanner had made ready for him in a hurry. And he thought : What will Bapu say about me ? It was a new kind of thought for Harry Black.

The men arrived before the sun had topped the hills. There was gabbling outside, but he could not hear the conversation. Bapu came here for him.

"Sahib," said Bapu, "the Bad One did not kill *yesterday* in the afternoon. The Bad One killed the *day before yesterday* in the afternoon at a far corner of Ranipur below the moun-

tains. This true second message came in the night when we were
here. . . ."

How simply the inexplicable was explained. How much he
hated Tara Singh, about whom Bapu now expressed himself with
sibilant ferocity.

Harry went along. The Garhwalis stared at him, he knew, as
he stared over the Rimli forest in the morning. It was the pretty
time of a new day, and the air was cool, and junglecock crowed
the morning in the jungle.

But he saw the tiger in the jungle. He saw the tiger in the
crashings of a pig. He saw the tiger in the wavings of the pale
dead grass. He heard the tiger in a slither and a rattle in a bamboo
clump. He saw the tiger in the early shadows. He feared the tiger
everywhere as his carriers picked a running way along and round
and down the bouldered watercourse, widening to safety, but it
was not safe.

He was in his dream again, a version of his dream, and soon
now, any second now, surely now he would wake up to smell
cloves from kind Miss Potterswell, to hear Desmond's voice of
comfort : *Harry, old boy, are you all right ?*

It was still his dream with Cheddi Khan standing beside the
Old Bitch at the island. Cheddi and Bapu exchanged whispers.
They all stared at him. They gloated at him secretly.

" Sahib, you have a fever," Cheddi said with pity or contempt.

He took out his handkerchief. Perhaps he had a fever, but it
was a cold one. He felt safer and safer on the slow way down.
He did not mind that Cheddi drove atrociously, as always. He did
not mind the bumps, the dust or anything, and at last they reached
the Forest Rest House, where Chokidar and waterman waited to
salaam with smiles.

He went inside the room, a dingy ghost of all the Forest Rest
House rooms that he had known.

" The bed is ready," Cheddi said. " Breakfast, sahib ? "

" Bring tea," he said. He sat down in the long-armed Roorkee
chair. He closed his eyes, knowing now that this was not a dream
of his.

"Your Honour, you must eat and sleep," said Cheddi Khan with tea, "and I will drive to Bondha for the doctor."

"I do not need the doctor," Harry said. "You will in no wise go to Bondha, is it understood? Put the tea beside me. Go away."

He drank hot, sweet brown tea. He felt it do his body good. He was not afraid now behind doors and shutters in the room, darker than the Pass had been last night. But all the things that he had ever done were now undone by jellied panic in the Pass of Rimli.

He half-filled his mug again with tea. He went over to the cupboard. There were seven virgin bottles in the opened case. It was good to have a Muslim, and reliable about drink; and it was good about Cheddi being a methodical sort of chap, so once the cupboard always the cupboard in that house from then on unless the *bara sahib bahadur* should say some other place; and seven bottles was a lovely lucky lot of ammunition not to see the end of.

He laced the mug up to the brim, and drank it tepid, like Christian's coffee. Soon Cheddi came with inquiries about eggs for breakfast, with pious clucks and frowns of disapproval, and with pleadings.

"Oh, go to hell," said Harry Black.

Cheddi went.

He admired the first brown bottle, down a bit. "My friend," he said. He scuttled off to heaven with his friend.

*   *   *   *   *

Miriam! My friendly slut at bottom. I'm so gratified to see you, every big and little bit of you in satin tights with brilliants.—All the gentlemen are gratified to see me and to help me with the zippings of my satin tights, play bouncy-bouncy-bounce. No, Harry, muchas gracias, but I will not imbibe a gin and soda. Why? you will inquire. Because the witching hour has come for our escape from durance vile across the gulf to yonder edifice; hence this trapeze and hence my star-spangled tights. But Miriam, I see Hauptmann Meierling—He is the key to this evasion. I shall embrace him, thus covering your intrepid bunk.

Then Miriam launched herself with a powerful practised knifing thrust of loins, and she described a sparkling pendulum parabola down over floodlights and away and up to the arms of Hauptmann Meierling and bore the little Teuton to the ground, swallowed him in short order, you might say.

The trapeze came back. Harry did not hesitate one second. The first swing was very nice, a swoop hundreds of feet above the silly lights, but he did not make that building yonder quite, so back again to start again, but he did not make it back to durance vile. He described ever lessening parabolas with ever growing vertigos. *Hände hoch!* the odious Hauptmann shouted. *I can't get them higher*, Harry said. *Not really*. But the bullets started, and he felt most awfully sick, and so he dropped.

Creepy-crawly, Harry thought. No alternative to creepy-crawly. The oil lamp and the table and the charpoy and the walls were heaving, and the floor heaved most of all. He went creepy-crawly to the *ghusal-khana*, to the bathroom with a sort of picture of a cobra in his head, and he reached the thunder-box. He made that all right, and he was sick all right. He rested on the immemorial chasm, and then he closed the lid with proper decency and went creepy-crawly back to bed to finish up Friend Number Two. Friend Number Three was waiting, and so were Four, Five, Six and Seven. He had them with him. He did not trust that mucker, Cheddi Khan, one inch. His *sat bhai*, seven brothers, seven sisters, his *panch sath*, five or seven sisters.

Then light came through the shutters, hateful light but very little of it coinciding with the dying of his oil lamp, out of juice, poor thirsty *butti*. Some daylight escaped in, not enough to hurt, enough to see to do things, and enough to see a lizard in a corner of the ceiling.

It was not a nice lizard like whatstheirnames, like Clarence and Clarissa, the cheerful little yellow dragons having fun and games at Bondha. This lizard had no tail. It had a stump, a sort of bayonet boss, truncated knob, or ugly thing like that.

He was offended by the lizard's rude appearance. He disliked the way it swam about the ceiling, and the vulgar chirpings were unpleasant too. He shouted at the lizards, which pretended not to hear him. So he closed his eyes, quite angry ; then everything swam round, not only lizards, and when he opened them, the horrid coupled beasts were staring at him.

I really mustn't, Harry thought. I must stick to my noble principle of never killing anything unless it endangers sacred man, like scorpions and panthers and king cobras, that sort of thing ; or unless it provides sustenance to sacred man, like ducks and deer and oysters, that sort of thing. Actually, of course, you swallow oysters while they live and breathe, a ghastly thought however good, yet not so ghastly as what Charlie said about that famous Chinese statesman eating infant mice, dip them wriggling into golden syrup, schluck down the old red lane, suck his fingers, pop, velly velly tasty. But such ugly thoughts as this will make me ill. I must think of the divinity and dignity of man.

Lizards do not kill you, whatever Miss Potterswell may think. And roast undercut of lizard. Oh dear, but there I go again.

The tailless lizards squeaked at him. He could not stand such insolence a moment longer. The law of the jungle, after all. Manifest destiny says : Kill. I know Christian would disapprove. She disapproves of hurting anything. Well, here is a case for euthanasia. I mean, a lizard after he loses and before he grows a tail is as a man without his manhood, I dare say. I'm sorry, hateful lizards, but it has to be.

He held his automatic pistol in both hands. He closed an eye and took most careful aim. The lizard swam round and round. The muzzle of the point three-eight swam round and round. He was not in any hurry. He kept on aiming till they all swam round together. Then he fired. The lizard fell with flailing arms and legs. It was a damned good shot, as good a pistol shot as he had ever made ; but then, of course, he was a first-class shot with pistols too.

Rattlings of doors. They were bolted for the privacy that every self-respecting chap demands. " Sahib ! Sahib ! "

" Do let me have some peace," he called to that infernal pest. " I'm shooting lizards."

He felt sorry for the poor dead lizard, cruel brute he was. He
had another drink of number Three. Then he went off walking
once again. He walked alone between the corpses of some tailless
tigers in the lower jungle here at Rimli on a forest path. But there
was another one he had to find, another One. . . .

*   *   *   *   *

" Oh, hallo," he said. " How nice to see you." He saw her
dimly. There was the rather wonderful strange thing of knowing
it was her even in an Underground if all the lights went out, say
at Green Park Station.

But all the lights now suddenly went on, hard lights of torture
like them grilling you. " Shut it ! Please shut it ! " He put his
hands up, little monkey See-no-evil.

" No," she said, " not until this stink blows out. I'm sorry."
Not sorry, only saying it, the cruel woman, window open too.

His eyes were safe behind his hands. The hot wind was very
nasty. " What time is it ? " he asked.

" Noon," she said. Funny, saying noon the new-world way,
but a better word than midday, come to think of it.

" Awfully sorry," Harry said. " Elastic bandage stinks. Ribs
okay now. Take it off to-morrow."

" The bandage doesn't stink. The whisky does." Then she
relented and she closed the place again.

" Where's Michael ? "

" He's at home."

" Why you come ? "

" Because Desmond would have wanted me to come. Drink
this."

" What ? "

" Clear soup."

" No."

" Drink it, damn you," Christian said.

He drank some because he was afraid of her, but, poor fellow,
he was very sick. Poor me, poor little me, retching my remainders
in a basin.

H

" My fault," she said. " I should have had the basin handy."

He heard the scrubbing noise, and he looked over. She was on her hands and knees in a pair of shorts he did not know, and her back arched up in a lovely hollow heaving curve from thighs to shoulders at the scrubbing. The smell of creosol was bad, but not so bad as soup. " God, y'can't do that. Get sweeper."

" I would not insult the sweeper," Christian said.

She finished cleaning up his vomit. " Well, that's that," she said, and stood again and held the bucket.

" Have to tell you . . ." He was trying very hard. " Have to tell you. Only woman I ever liked in all my life."

She went over and stooped and came back and slapped the cold thing on his face. " Lizards," she said. " You like lizards." She dropped the lizard in the bucket.

" I know," he said. " I'm sorry."

" Now drink the rest of this."

" Can't," he said. " Kill me."

" All right, I'll kill you."

So he drank the soup, which swelled about him in his seething guts, then seemed to settle.

She wiped his face. She gave him something else to drink, bitter, like a drug he knew.

" Thank you," Harry said. " Please don't go. Please . . ." He looked at her. He was surprised to see tears rolling, slithering and slipping down her face that swayed beside him. " Please stay, Christian."

" Next room," she said. " Now sleep." Peculiar how she could cry so hard like that, and her voice be her own sweet sobless voice.

*   *   *   *   *

He woke up and he could not find it. Number Four, he thought, surely, wasn't it ? Four from seven leaves three precisely. But Four was not on his bedside table. Five, Six and Seven nowhere to be seen. He shouted for Cheddi Khan, who arrived intolerably later rather than sooner with a rude knock and a tea-tray. Cheddi closed the main-room door behind him quickly.

" Take that muck away," he said, or words to such effect. His mood was fairly lethal. " Bring the whisky."

" The memsahib waits in the other room," said Cheddi Khan. And he added pointedly and gravely : " The Lady Sahib."

Well, that meant Christian, for whom Cheddi Khan had an unprecedented, reverent devotion. He regarded memsahibs as the end, spoilt niggling creatures to be pandered to and flouted with disdainful courtesy, not least old Miriam. What the hell was Christian doing here ?

" The Lady Sahib has done sweeper's work to-day," said Cheddi Khan in Urdu. " You shave," he added in his tolerable English, which he had never used to his employer. He spoke English now as insult and rebuke.

Harry shaved in bed. He managed a water biscuit and a cup of tea. He put on his tin leg, sunproof trousers, a faded dark blue shirt, sambhar leather shoes—most respectable warm weather clothes—and his own particular stuff from London on his hair. Cheddi proffered crutches, but he declined them. The horror and the need, the weaving waves, the dread and the miasma.

He made it to the door, whence an arm-stretch took him to the table. " Sit down," she said.

He sat on the small chair, and she was sitting in the big chair in the corner by the fireplace with a book of poetry of his. The veranda door was open, and the sun was low, he noticed. The bottles were beside him. " I've got to have a drink," he said. " Sorry. Got to."

She came over and gathered the four bottles, the three and a half of whisky, to her bosom with her bare arms across, like hugging four midget babies, between, athwart and crowded on her breasts. The whisky was what he wanted. " No," said Christian. " Nothing doing."

" Just one. I must, Christian. Don't you understand ? "

She did not answer, did not even seem to bother, simply sat again and put the bottles on the floor between her knees as guardians, damn her.

Cheddi placed a second cup of tea beside him on the ugly

resthouse table. " For God's sake go away," he said to Cheddi
Khan, who waited for instructions from the Lady Sahib; then went.

" Why did you come ? "

" I told you," Christian said. " Because Desmond would have
wanted me to come."

How to get rid of her and get the drink, knotty problem,
cunning needed, and he feared her. He tried wheedling. She did
not answer. He was angered by these ill manners into ill-mannered-
ness himself. " I wish to Christ you'd mind your own damned
business," Harry said.

" I wish to Christ you'd let me," Christian said.

He was ashamed of himself for not being a gentleman when
drunk. " I apologise," he said. " I only meant . . ."

But he could not quite remember what he meant. He could
not remember anything at all except one thing vaguely. " What
happened, Christian ? "

" Nothing much," she said. " Nothing more noteworthy than
a jag."

" First jag," he said. " First one ever."

" My first one too.   Quite fascinating."

" Do you have to be so bitter ? "

" Poor Harry, should I say ? "

Her voice was cold and small and pitiless, not her warm open-
hearted voice. He had done something unmentionable, Harry
thought, because a thing he could remember was Christian weeping,
yet talking in her limpid sobless voice. " Did I make you cry ? "
he asked.

" No," she said. " You never did and never will."

" Once you did cry long ago," he said. " I was remembering
that perhaps.   Do you remember that ? "

" No," she said. " I do not remember that.   Now let's deal
with all your mucking bottles."

He could hardly believe such language from Christian, the fair,
gentle, terrifying woman.

" You love pistol practice at the lizards, and similar bravura.
Or would braggadocio be better ? To pour away your liquor

would be much too tame. Outside to the veranda, Harry. Go on out !"

She was hard on him, not even helping when he stumbled. She lined the bottles up, and then she brought his automatic pistol, which held eight, but one was gone already. "Shoot them !" she said. "Go right ahead and shoot your friends."

It seemed a bit ridiculous to him, but he went right ahead and shot them at about ten feet, three misses, last shot last bottle. Well, he had plenty of spare ammunition, and the bottles certainly disintegrated with amusing violence and splash and shard. But then, of course, the trouble was that he had lost his bottles.

She took away the pistol. She brought sunglasses for him and sat beside him on the other chair. "Oh dear," she said in her own soft voice again. "What a melodramatic bitch I am."

The plains wind blew this afternoon, loud in the graceful neem, and louder in the slender sal, loud in all the shade trees of a small eminence at Rimli, where foresters had stayed a hundred years or more, men to whom trees were life and children and companions. It was the start of the furnace winds. It was the finish of brief winter. The wind was falling now, so there was an end within the large beginning. A coppersmith tonked obscurely in the forest, a pleasant strike of metal and monotonous, and the sound moved with the turning of the barbet's head, the small ventriloquist, tonk and tonk and tonk from there and there.

Harry shut his eyes behind his glasses against the abominable world without. He opened them against the abominable world within.

"Tell me what happened, Harry."

"The tiger came the wrong way round," he said, shutting again to think to say it right. "I was facing Ranipur, and I was thinking, just at that moment, I can remember very well, I was thinking of you and the day we sailed, letting my mind wander but not really wander because I was sure it would suddenly appear from nowhere on its way to Rimli. And then I heard a noise, soft as a house-cat on a carpet, and I looked round, and the tiger was coming slowly for me on its belly. My finger pulled both triggers. The shots went off to Ranipur. All I did was scream my head off." He opened his eyes for a quick look round and over his shoulder.

" Bapu said you frightened the Bad One by roaring more fiercely than the Bad One. Cheddi Khan translated for me."

" Did he translate that I was paralysed with terror ? Did he translate that Bapu had to take the rifle out of my hands and guard the great brave master until morning ? Did he mention my behaviour coming down the hill ? "

" Poor Harry," Christian said. " Have you never been afraid before ? "

" Of course," he said, " but not panic-stricken to a jelly." He shivered, seeing it again now, for the easement of the alcohol was dead in him ; and why the hell should Christian Tanner take away his comfort ? " I can't," he said. " I can't."

" You can fail like anybody else," she said, less kindly. " It was high time that you did, and now you have."

So hard on him. " Only thing I hadn't failed in," Harry said. " Don't you understand ? "

" I might understand," she said. " But I can't sympathise. If you cared about a battle then you always won it. If you didn't care about it then you didn't let it be a battle, very easy, very arrogant and selfish. Now you're finding out the facts of life."

" I've even made you hate me," Harry said.

The wind had dropped to a dry stirring, to a flip and a flop of the great leaves of the teak, an exotic here, an experiment and ornament. The Brain-Fever bird was calling. *Brain-Fever*, quietly, wheezingly. *Brain-Fever*, louder and higher. *Brain-Fever*, querulous and mounting. *Brain-Fever*, up up up, insistent to its broken peak of desperation, to other muted starts interminably.

Pee-Kahan ?   Where is my love ?   Pee-Kahan ?   Pee-Kahan ?

You're going to die.   You're going to die.   You're going to die. Old words of men to the heat song of the year.

Tiger ! Tiger !—burning bright—In the forests—of the night,—What immortal—hand or eye,—Dare frame thy fearful—SYMMETRY ?

" I can't," said Harry Black. " I can't face it, Christian."

But when he turned, he saw that she was weeping in the way he thought that he had seen her weep before. He had been provided with a silk handkerchief by Cheddi Khan. He gave her that.

" You must," she said in her sobless voice. " You must, Harry." She dried them up. " Such an idiot," she said. " I'm going home."

" How did you get here ? "

" Cheddi Khan came over. But our driver got back this morning, so he brought me."

" I wish I could . . ." He knew that his body would not take him as escort in the Landrover, even if his spirit had been strong enough. " Cheddi and Bapu will follow you to the forest gate."

" I have three more of those sleeping powders in my bag inside," she said, " the ones you had when you were sick. Eat something, Harry, and take two, and go to sleep." She looked at him. It was a hard and level glance. " Can I trust you by yourself ? "

" I don't know," he said because he did not know himself, and now he had no drink to help himself.

" Promise me."

He did not promise.

" Promise me ! "

" All right," he said. " I promise." And there was a grievous thing : " Can't ask you to forgive me."

" I think we both might ask forgiveness," she said.

CHAPTER SEVENTEEN

THAT NIGHT a boy was taken from the taungya village in the lower forest. The boy slept in a high-walled pen among his goats. The people of the village heard a bleating, but men did not venture out by night for bleating goats, and in the morning eighteen goats were present and correct without the goatherd. No tracks were found. No blood was found. A child of ten—a tasty snack but not a meal—had vanished.

Meanwhile Harry slept.

" Why was I not told sooner ? " he said in the afternoon, petulant, thankful that he had not heard the news before.

" The Lady Sahib said that Your Honour must be left to sleep."

To sleep a jag off by command of Mrs. Tanner, damn her. He was purged of his digestive juices, dehydrated, stiff. The famous steady hand shook worse than Miriam's on Sunday morning. The ten-armed monster climbed his back. Hate me, hate you, poor me, vile me and you. He was getting better ; and what waited for him out there, getting better ? Pink elephants and purple pansies ? No.

" There is more to tell, sahib," Cheddi said. He waited courteously for permission to continue.

" Well ? "

" It concerns Bapu. There is danger now for Bapu. This morning as he went to track the tiger from the taungya village, men lay in wait for him and stoned him, and Bapu fled, firing a shot from his ancient gun, but over the heads of the villagers to halt them."

" Was Bapu hurt ? "

" He was struck by a stone and lightly bruised. There is this also about Bapu : Last evening, when we followed the Bondha motor to the forest gate, and were returning, Bapu said : *I hear the janwar speak. Leave me in the jungle.* I left Bapu in the lower

jungle, and it was before the time of the crying of the goats. I
have told this to no man. Sahib, I do not believe these jungli fears,
but there are strange things about Bapu."

" Are there not strange things about all men ? "

" That is true," said Cheddi Khan, adding carefully and coldly :
" About all men."

Strange things thought and dark things done. " From to-night
Bapu will sleep here in this house. Tell him my order."

" Very good, Your Honour."

" Go now to the Range Office and ask Tara Singh when the
elephant will come. Say also to Tara Singh—Say this from
me : *I have spoken once about the wicked guru and shall not speak
again.*

" Sahib, would you not write this in a letter ? "

" No. And do not let him come here."

He went to the bookshelf. He stared at them, his old companions. " What was this you said to me, that the memsahib did
sweeper's work ? "

No reply.

" Speak, Cheddi Khan."

Cheddi spoke.

" Jesus Christ," he said.

" Sahib," said Cheddi with compassion. " A strong man may
be weak."

He found a bit of paper and wrote on it : " I'm sorry, Christian,"
and put the paper in an envelope. " Take this to the memsahib."

" *Jawab hoga ?* Will there be an answer ? "

" No," he said.

It was dusk when Cheddi Khan returned.

" The elephant will come to-morrow morning. Sahib, Tara
Singh was much afraid at hearing the message of the guru. He
does not plot against Bapu now. I am sure of this."

" Did he not lie as to the killing Ranipur-side ? "

" There is hatred between Sikhs and Muslims. Yet I, a Muslim,
tell you that he is innocent of this also. The first message from
Ranipur was false. Sahib, you are a man of justice."

" All right, all right," he said in English.

" The Lady Sahib was waiting in the bungalow at Bondha, and after reading, smiled, said : *Thank the Sahib*, and went away."

" How did the health of the memsahib seem ? "

" The Lady Sahib was pale," said Cheddi Khan, " not light of heart, as is her wont."

The forest elephant did not come next morning. Harry had learned long ago to close his mind to the frustrations of what never happens in India to-morrow. But now frustration was conspiracy, and now he could not go on foot, and now he dared not go on foot.

" The Bad One is in the lower forest," Bapu said. They scoured the lower forest all that day, driving, stopping while Bapu searched for tracks. Bulbuls sang cheerfully at open places, and dappled cheetal fed below the trees where monkeys berried. Some jungle dwellers worked by day ; some slept against the coming of the night. But the tiger—Is the tiger here ? Is the tiger sleeping ? Is the tiger watching ? Is the tiger waiting for me in that withered grass above the bank above the track ? Hurry, Bapu, inscrutable small man, fearful of men, fearless of the tiger.

That evening they dragged a sack contraption behind the car. They dragged it on a track three miles along the fireline that divided the upper Rimli jungle bounded by the horseshoe ridges from the lower Rimli jungle bounded by the plains. It made a swathe of comparative smoothness in the ruts and dust. The dust was deep—fine as talcum, soft to the foot as powder snow. A panther crossed it in the night, a python, a sloth bear, and many of the hunters and the hunted. But no tiger crossed it.

The elephant had not arrived. This was Harry's third day, or it would be three days completed by whatever time the Lady Sahib had cut him off. He was eating largely now again. He had stripped the stinking plaster from his ribs. The scars were healthy, although tender still. They were a purplish pink, a neatly taloned testimony to what still waited where they came from.

" Sahib," said Bapu in the afternoon. " The motor-gharri does not serve to search the lower forest. Could Your Honour walk a small distance with Your Honour's hand upon my shoulder ?"

He had suspected this from confabulations between Cheddi Khan and Bapu, whispering below the banyan tree behind the resthouse. He had caught them at it. "Where ?"

"From the taungya path down the large *rao* by the salt lick and the waterhole and to the forest road. Four furlongs only. Would this, with many rests, be possible ?"

Four Bapu furlongs, meaning six or seven, but in a wide watercourse. It might have been much worse. They knew that he could do this. They would pin him down to do this. "We will try to do this," he said nobly. The hot wind cooled him at the thought of doing this.

"Go slowly, sahib," said Cheddi Khan. "I shall be waiting at the crossing of the *rao*." He was treating him as a kindly trainer treats a gunshy pup for which there may be hope.

They started down the *rao*, near-white and blinding in the sun. This was the watercourse into which all others flowed. It swung flatly down ahead, turned sharp right after a few hundred yards, thence meandered to the limits of the forest and across open ground to join the Garda. It was a violent river in the flash floods of the monsoon, the ghost of a river now. Beyond the right earth bank was forest. Just beyond the left bank was the thorn-brush hedge bordering the taungya, land cleared within the jungle. *Taungya* was a foreign word ; and indeed the fields seemed foreign here. He saw jungle babblers flit one by one from the left bank to that hedge, plain brown babblers, seven sisters squawking in a fuss. It was a wide watercourse and pretty safe ; but he could have used a nip, say a few fluid ounces from the residual bottles he had shot at the behest of Christian Tanner, damn the woman, prodding when he was afraid, stirring with him in his dreams at night. Life is hard, he thought, his hand on Bapu's shoulder. Life is far too mucking complicated for a little man who knows himself.

But Bapu's shoulder was no longer there. Bapu had vanished like the calibanish Ariel he was. The reason showed itself, a party of the taungya peasants. They were thin-shanked plainsmen armed with lathis. Loquacious people, silent now, panting in the heat of afternoon.

"What is it, my brothers?"

It was that they had heard the car. It was that one of them had lost his son. It was that their wheat was ripe and they dare not cut it near the forest. It was many deadly goblins. They were after Bapu, but they did not say his name or the name of his other self, the tiger.

Harry spoke gently to them. He took some time about it, soothing and cajoling. These were living creatures that he did not fear, and they were instruments he knew well how to play. When he judged them softened from their dangerous resolve, he made a licentious joke. They laughed. He then blistered them. He warned them viciously, made a second jest, and they went home. He thought it might be all right for Bapu till there was another human kill.

The voices dwindled. "Bapu!" he called softly.

Bapu emerged from a hiding place in tangled flotsam of the rainy season. Bapu made that embarrassing obeisance to him again. Bapu trusts me, Harry thought, and they went on down the middle of the *rao* with thirty yards of safety either side.

They passed the salt lick, turned the sharp bend in the *rao*, and here was the waterhole. It was not quite dry—a stagnant puddle, round the puddle a trodden greenish rim of mud, round the mud a fissured crust. It was below the outer bank, and there were no taungya here beyond the bank, but jungle, tired dusty jungle of high trees and low bush cover. Harry waited in the middle. He hoped that Bapu would not find the pugmarks of the tiger.

But Bapu had. "Sahib," he said in his sepulchral whisper, "the Bad One came down the *rao* last night and drank and went on yonder." He made his graceful sweep of hand over the lower reaches of the Rimli salient, two miles wide, two miles deep, a flat labyrinth of forest, shallow-ditched, with many tiger places.

"I am weary," Harry said, and was. "Let us rest a while."

They sat back to back on a sizeable hot boulder, a reservoir of heat. Nothing came yet to the waterhole, and nothing moved on land beyond. A hornbill dipped and flapped its clumsy way above the trees, a male hornbill possibly, a virtuous husband off to feed his wife plastered in her nesthole in a tree. Good husbands, Harry thought. He was thirsty, a genuine cold-tea-wanting thirst ; but the tea was in the car.

" Oh Bapu, I have had this thought : That we might close the Pass of Rimli with a great explosion, thus keeping the tiger for ourselves alone. To this end, Tanner Sahib will bring with him a box of the material called Dynamite."

He wondered how Bapu would react. He wondered when Desmond would come back. He thought : She and Michael leave a week to-day. And then ? What then ? I might have given up this tiger. But now I can't. I cannot face it and I cannot leave it. Or I could, you know. Why not ? Why play at being superman ? I've lost my nerve. Well, look at all the other chaps who lost their nerve.

Bapu was the stillest little sitter in the world, but Bapu moved against him. I could pretend here for a while, and then fly home, and then quite casually by mistake on purpose happen to be passing and drop in to see them at this cottage they have rented down in Dorset, down in Dorset, how conventional.

> Thou saidest : I am sick of love.
> Stay me with flagons, comfort me
> With apples for my pains thereof
> Till my hands gather in his tree
> That fruit wherein my lips would be.

Thou saidest : I am sick of fear. Bapu fidgets. He is horrified. I thought he would be.

" Oh sahib," said Bapu in cracked distress, " if the Bad One is denied its road to Ranipur below the mountains, then surely they will kill me. The Bad One waits for me, and yet I do not fear the Bad One. But, sahib, I fear the wickedness of men." Bapu trembled against Harry's back.

" I do not understand this, Bapu, that thou fearest men yet not

the tiger." Harry saw it stalking on its belly. He saw the bloody
jowls. He saw that forearm whip for the invisible left hook. He
trembled too.

"The sahib has the hard way of the soldier, knowing fear and
courage, and understanding all things if the sahib so wills."

A delicate prevarication. Such delicacy in this jungle man. How
delicately he imparts his little dig at me.

"Bapu," he said. He listened to the wind. He watched the
wind's caprice with leaf and dust and arid grass. "Bapu, hast thou
seen a tigress playing with her cubs?"

"Yes, sahib, I have seen this many times, for all my life I have
lived with the *janwar* in the jungle. It is a thing most sweet and
beautiful to see, the tigress and her little ones."

"Was thy Bad One born at Rimli, Bapu?"

Bapu's back was absolutely still. "Sahib, I think that this is so."

"Thou thinkest this is so. But Bapu, thou art a wise and clever
man, surpassing all the *janwar* in thy knowledge of the *janwar*.
Didst thou not watch the Bad One playing in his innocence?
Didst thou not see that thing most sweet and beautiful to see—
the Bad One's mother cuff the Bad One with a fierce mother's
pride and love, and then give suck?"

There was a silence of the two men here between the jungle
in the loudness of the wind, and now in another sound that came
above and through the loudness of the wind. Harry faced directly
to that sound, not a steady sound, a steady rushing as was the
rushing of the hot-weather wind. It was periodic—short blast and
short again, blast blast continued of the hooter at the sugar factory
at Bondha, three miles or so away. It was imperative and urgent
and alarming. It said *Alarm* as unequivocally as an air raid siren
wails Alarm. It stood the two men up. It hurried them two
furlongs down the watercourse, arm across shoulder, arm round
waist, the large man leaning on the small man.

Cheddi waited with the Old Bitch in the shade. The distant
blasting of the hooter still went on. "This is a fire alarm, sahib,
is it not?"

He did not know. He drove at fifty miles an hour along the

road, which served also as a lesser fireline, running the length of the Rimli salient. Half a mile to his right was the forest edge ; beyond that lay open ground and the sluggish river Garda.

He turned left, another fireline, this one cutting across the bottom of the salient. There were sunlit patches in the forest, but the sun was low, casting long shadows over to the left ahead. The wind was dying with the day, and wild things were on the move. A sambar hind stood bell-eared on the road, the big brown deer, and weaved and plunged, and she was gone.

Here was the junction with the Rimli-Bondha road. Here the jungle thinned, and he saw a gleam. Was that a fire ? No, it was the tall metal chimney of the factory at Bondha. Here was the forest gate, now open land, bare of its sugar cane, amber of its ripening wheat. No smoke, no fire. " Hang on," he said to dusty Cheddi Khan and Bapu.

Christian, Johnson, *babus*, servants, Dr. Roy Chowdhury, M.D., and the syce held the arab pony, which was in a muck-sweat.

" You've come," she said.

Michael had ridden at four o'clock. He had started his usual circuits inside the garden wall, trotting and cantering. Yes, the gardener was here, and the syce had watched a while, then gone back to the stable. Christian had been sleeping. Michael and Adonis were last seen trotting fast, and wide of the curving forest in the direction of the river Garda. Adonis was next seen coming at a gallop from the forest gate through which Harry had now passed. Babel, talk, confusion. Christian was quiet, watching Harry.

" I wonder if he could have gone to look for that big crocodile ? " She nodded. " Might," she said.

The bloody little fool, he thought. Can't blame him, just the sort of thing I used to do. Runaway horses take the short road home. This pony might have taken a short-cut from the crocodile place clean across the Rimli salient to Bondha. This pony pulls. This pony is not only blown. I think it has been badly frightened, Christ Almighty. " Bapu, hast thou seen the tracks of a shod-horse galloping ? Fresh tracks ? "

" Sahib, I saw this in the *rao* as we hurried from our sitting place to the motor-gharri. The *rao* is used as a wide safe road by men with horses. The headman of the taungya village has a horse of the size of this horse here, but it does not wear the iron shoes."

He looked at Christian. He thought that she could take the likely truth. He thought that she could take any truth she had to take. " I think he went round to look at that crocodile. I think the pony got out of control and made for home. Michael might have been dismounted. If so, he's walking back. If not, I think he either fell off near the river on the open ground, or I think he fell off in the jungle between the corner of the *rao* and the forest gate —we came along the *rao* ourselves, and would have seen him. Johnson, you go round to the river with Cheddi Khan." He explained in detail how and where to go. " Bapu and I will go in the factory Landrover, and then on foot." *On foot*, he thought, on foot in the dark in the bottom of the lower forest where the tiger moved last night. *Christ*, he thought.

" We need one more man to hold the torch." He gulped down his bottle of cold tea. *I can't*, he thought. Another thing he could not do was ask Christian Tanner for a drink.

" I will come," said that funny little doctor. " I personally will come with pleasure." Never set foot in jungles in his life, good for Dr. Roy Chowdhury, M.D., the only volunteer, it seemed.

" No, Doctor. You must be here in case Michael has been hurt," said Christian quietly. " I'm going."

" I said a man," he said.

" He is my son," she said, " and I am going." She wore her tartan shorts, unsuitable jungle garb. She was a phenomenally cool woman. Well, she was the only woman. " I'm damned well going," Christian said less coolly.

He drove the Bondha car, with Christian, Bapu and the driver. It was newer and healthier than his temporary Old Bitch. He had been at Bondha only a few minutes.

Johnson and Cheddi followed. He stopped at the parting of

their ways. He noticed that Johnson was in a stew. Thick jungle did not lie ahead of Johnson. He addressed himself to Cheddi. " If you find Michael, blow the horn again and again. If you do not find him, try to work along the *rao* to where you waited with the car before. Then listen. Is it understood ? "

" Sahib, it is understood." And Cheddi smiled.

Harry drove again. The sun was broadening to touch the earth. " I shouldn't have slept this afternoon," she said to herself or him, " I never do. But I was so tired out. And I should have guessed, because he kept on asking when you would come, and you had promised to take him to the mugger place, and so few days left, and I was cross with him at lunch to-day. Oh dear, is there anything I don't do wrong ? "

" You do nothing wrong," he said. He put his left hand on her right hand on her bare knee for a moment, the first time he had done such a thing, and this was to give comfort and to take it from her. Harry Black was much afraid. He took his hand away.

" Is the tiger down this end ? " she asked.

" It might be anywhere," he said. " It might be up at the top of Rimli. It may have gone back to Ranipur." He could smell that scent of hers, Schiaparelli, in the hardness of the dust.

If Michael had trotted all the way, how long would he have taken to reach the mugger place ? Say forty minutes, say five o'clock. The odd thing was that the pony, with or without Michael on its back, had gone up the *rao* from its confluence with the river Garda to its abrupt left turn beyond the waterhole— the pony must have galloped through just before either party, Cheddi at the crossing of the forest road, he and Bapu from above, had reached there. Well, it was odd, but was there anything that wasn't odd ? And the boy, the thought of that bright-hearted boy.

They were in the forest in the warm moment of the sunset. He stopped at the T junction. The Rimli road went right. The road across the bottom of the salient went straight ahead. He had travelled it the other way quite recently this evening. A jungle path bisected the angle of the roads. It ran a mile from here to the corner of the *rao* beside the waterhole. It was a narrow, jinking path. The thought of walking it in daytime would suffice to make him sweat.

Bapu found the tracks at once. " It is as we thought, sahib. By this path the Bondha horse has come."

Parakeets were screaming in to roost, the small parties and the big, the ones and tens and hundreds in their needled flight to perch, to rise again, to twist and wheel and stoop again with wild abandon, green birds at the end of day, the screaming, graceful parakeets. He did not admire the parakeets.

" Stay here," he told the Bondha driver. " Keep the headlights burning. Keep the engine running."

" Sahib, I fear to stay here in the jungle."

" Safely in a motor ? The memsahib does not fear to walk there into danger. What art thou, a man ? " And what am I ? he thought.

" Should we shout for Michael ? " Christian asked.

" Not yet. Bapu will read the tracks. He goes first with the small rifle. You go second. Your job is to give him light, and to shine the torch out where I tell you. But not in our eyes. Okay ? "

" Okay," she said. " Behind too ? "

" Where I tell you, don't you understand ? " Behind, he thought. Behind my back, the most likely place. Shivered. Could not help it. " Go quickly, Bapu."

The parakeets were settling now to sleep. Night hurried in. He followed Christian, the three of them in single file and close together. Cheddi and Johnson would soon be round there at the river. Would he hear the Old Bitch's horn ? Yes, in the quietness. Oh God, he pleaded. Please let them find him now before we reach deep jungle in the darkness. Was that ? He whipped round. Nothing. The lights still shone ; the engine ran ; the driver had not buggered off. He did not see the lights directly to be dazzled. They would lighten darkness just a little for some distance, like that movement light idea in the war.

Bapu went at a slow walk. It was sal forest on either side, leaf-carpeted and noisy. " Right." She swung the torch quickly round and slowly back, the grey-barked columns of the sal, centred on a pair of eyes. The beam was steady. " Civet," Harry said. He heard his voice crack up. " All right."

Her eyes flicked round to him, then on to business, lighting Bapu. What could have possessed him to let Christian come ? *I'm damned well going*, Christian said. She said things and she did them. She was frightened now.

The sal forest ended. Now a ditch. Halfway, he thought, and all the trouble is ahead, all the bushes, all the small ravines, all the close cover waiting for us, and Cheddi has not blown his horn. Harry stumbled. He fell against her, and she caught him. " Tired ? "

He was abominably tired and lame.

" Hand on my shoulder," Christian whispered, and the scent came close to him. He put his left hand on her shoulder. The right would have been better, but he had to keep his right side free. His left hand fitted on the roundness of her shoulder, firm. She touched his hand with hers ; the palm of her hand was wet. She took her hand away, and they went on.

Thou saidest : I am sick of love. Let me try to think of that to fight my fear. *Stay me with flagons, comfort me.*

Bapu stopped. He cast about. He went a few yards on, and then came back. " Sahib, the Bad One has come to here. The Bad One has chased the horse and then gone yonder." He waved, palm upwards, to the right.

It could catch any horse. Christian's shoulder trembled in the hollow of his hand. Her child, her only son, her prodigal, had ridden that horse this afternoon. He squeezed her shoulder. *With apples for my pains thereof.* But it was no good. He was terrified. He could not think.

Bapu moved again. He was the leader of this expedition, the jungle man named Bapu. The brightness of the torch in blackness, stars in the path-slit in the sky. Not a leaf stirred in the forest. Bapu breathed, hiss, ruminative hiss. Christian breathed, sigh, shallow sigh. *Till my hands gather in his tree.* Harry's heart ran on.

" Here the Bad One came on to the path at great speed from the left side, and here the horse came on to the path from the right

side. The Bad One's charge failed here. But, sahib, the horse
would not have come here straightly from the right side, for the
jungle is too thick beyond. The horse must have swung from the
path and swung back. There is a likely place where the path goes
round the banyan tree. There the Bad One may have lain in wait,
and there the horse may first have seen the Bad One, and there
the Baba may have been thrown down." *Baba*, he said. The baby.
Her ewe-lamb.

"The Bad One left the horse," continued Bapu, dispassionate
small genius, in much the unfinished tone he employed to hint
about sups of whisky-wine. Bapu's breath was bad.

"What does he say?"

"He says it may have happened just ahead."

"Can't we call?" She waved the torch round now, all round
the haphazard wall of jungle close about them, silent bush and
silent tree, still leaf and broken grass, illuminated, gone again, but
crowding closer in the blackness.

"Bapu, should we call the Baba now?"

"Sahib, if the Bad One is here, the Bad One knows that we
are here. Call, therefore!"

"Michael!" she called in her own voice in the night. "Michael,
darling!"

"Michael!" he called like a crow, it sounded. *That fruit
wherein my lips would be.* "Michael, boy! It's Harry."

Nothing.

"Quickly now, sahib!"

He was not able to go quickly. His good leg and his bad leg
did not serve him. But he went, leaning on Christian's shoulder.
The torch beam showed the banyan tree, a giant, fifty feet across
a base of trunk and bough and flying root, a strangler of the jungle,
noble and grotesque. The path detoured for the spreading banyan.
This was the place that Bapu meant.

Her shoulder heaved at Michael's voice. "Tiger's here,"
squeaked Michael's voice from somewhere in the banyan tree. Her
shoulder heaved to tremble in the hollow of his hand.

Harry's horrors left him when he heard the other sound.

" Right ! " he said.

The beam centred to that sound as he brought the rifle up, as the tiger turned away into a gallop broadside across a gap in undergrowth, jazzy amber, jazzy black. He fired. He saw the quarters slew. The tiger broke silence in the failing clamour of the shot. It roared, splintering the forest in the night. Many of the *janwar* called in witness to the fury of the tiger's passing.

" Hit him too far back and low," said Harry. " Well, I couldn't help it." He sat down. He was tired.

" The Bad One has gone far away," said Bapu. He took the torch from Christian, shone it at Michael up the tree, and went to the place where the tiger had been fired at.

She stood beside Harry. Her hand felt from his farther shoulder lightly to his face and to his brow. He rested his head against her. He was happy.

" Michael ! " she called. " Are you all right ? " Her fingers played in Harry's hair.

CHAPTER EIGHTEEN

" My hip's awfully sore. I fell on it." The boy was whimpering, light and lonely.

" Tell us, Michael," Harry said. Tell me and your mother in the dark, he thought.

" I just saw the tiger beyond the tree, and then Adonis did a sort of shy full speed. . . ."

" Don't start there," she said vaguely. Her body quivered against his head. " Won't you ever learn to start at the beginning ? "

" . . . We went very slowly up a deep place to the bank, and I peeked over, and he was there, Harry, an absolutely huge mugger on that sand. I watched him for ages, not ages really, and then I was going to shout to wake him up but suddenly Adonis backed down and sort of spun and knocked my cap off with his head and I saw some men on camels coming in a line. . . . We came galloping along this path and I was tired right out, and I seemed to see the tiger and be on the ground and be climbing a rope thing in the tree all at the same second but perhaps it wasn't," said Michael in a torrent and drew shuddering breath. " It's jolly lucky I can climb a rope."

" You never said a truer word, chum," Harry said. " Nor never will." He put his arm across and round the trembling curve to Christian's other hip. " It's all right now," he said to her. " It's quite all right."

" I hate it, oh I hate it." Thrust and press and draw. Her fingers played lightly and desperately in his hair.

" Bapu ! " he called yonder. " Make haste, Bapu ! " He was going to say to her : *Stop doing that, and help me up.* But he would wait, he would wait, he would wait for Bapu.

" Then the tiger came. I didn't see it for a long, long time. I heard it in different places round the tree, and once I saw it watching me, and then I heard the Bondha hooter and a car going very fast, and I remembered Plain Harry said tigers don't climb trees much, but I was sort of pretty well scared stiff. . . ."

" Tell us some other time."

" No. Go on, Michael ! " The tiger could have jumped that height, let alone have climbed to Michael up the staircase of a banyan tree. But this tiger had been fired upon from other trees, and time spent in reconnaissance is rarely wasted.

" Then it got dark, and I thought there was a light somewhere down the other way, and then I saw a moving light, and the tiger growled like a rumble very close, and I heard you call me, but I couldn't answer ; then I just managed to. Did you hear me ? "

" Yes, Michael," Harry said. Bapu was returning. " Help me up," he said to Christian.

But she did not help him up. She bent and found his lips to kiss them, and went away without helping him at all.

" Sahib ! " began Bapu on arrival, the inevitable Bapu prelude, introduction, day or night, in safety or in danger, *sahib !*

" Tell me later of the Bad One's wounding. Tell me this now only. Art thou sure the Bad One has gone far ? "

" Sahib, listen to the *janwar* speak along the way to Rimli."

It was beyond the range of Harry's ear.

" I hear a cheetal," Michael said. His voice was almost normal. He had talked the first of it away now for the present, even if all his life he might see a tiger at a banyan tree. " Can I come down, please ? "

Bapu helped him.

Harry cupped his hands. " Cheddi Khan ! " he called. " Cheddi Khan ! "

" *Huzoor !* " it came back, a full-throated Cheddi holler spanning the forest in the night, and Harry laughed.

" Forgotten you laughed like that," she said. She held the torch again, pointed to the ground, and the light reflected up to let him see her staring at him, but he did not think she saw anyone or anything much at the moment.

" Come on," he said abruptly. " Let's get cracking."

Bapu led to the waterhole, not far. Michael limped behind
him. Harry followed Christian. They reached the *rao* and saw
Cheddi's lights. " Tell me now about the Bad One," Harry said.
He was going short, but he could make it. He watched Christian,
shoulders still, a small undulance of hips against the lights.

" Sahib, I found a tuft of the pale inner hair. I found much
blood. I found no bone. I think the bullet struck high in the
right hind leg of the Bad One, not touching the other leg in passing
out. With the great soft bullet this is a severe wound, but it is a
wound from which the Bad One might recover and be lame.
Sahib, this is my poor opinion only."

Harry accepted the poor opinion as the best in Harley Street.
" With me there is no whisky-wine, but with the memsahib there
might be a bottle from which thou hast earned three mighty sups
of whisky-wine to-night."

Bapu cackled his discordant gusto, not at all a secret little man.

" What is it ? What's so terribly amusing back and forth about
the memsahib ? "

" I only told Bapu he had earned a whopping tot at your
discretion. Don't you think he has ? "

" Oh sure," she said. " Why certainly. Our modest cellar is
available for every dipsomaniac."

One more remark like that, he thought, he, the fool, behind the
graceful woman coming to the car. But then he had to give a
précis of events to Cheddi Khan and Johnson.

" Please, could we go and find my cap down near the river ?
I know exactly where it is."

" Sorry, Michael," Harry said. " Home now. We can get it
later on." Later on ? he wondered.

" You won't need it any more," his mother said. " You won't
be riding ever any more."

" My proper velvet hunting cap. It's a crash helmet too. If I
can't have that, I won't go home to England even."

" Now stop it, boy," he said. " Get in."

They went by the first fireline, then across the bottom of the
salient where he had seen a sambar hind that afternoon. He saw

no birds or beasts now in the forest. But against the pale dry jungle rolling to him in the lights, he saw a tapestry of his imagination.

"You'll stay for supper, won't you?" she said politely through the Old Bitch's whining from beyond Michael in the left-hand seat. "Cold prairie chicken and potato salad, would that do?"

"Cold prairie chicken? Here?"

"Oh," she said. "I wasn't thinking. I should have said cold tasteless scrawny garbage-eating bantam from our nice bazaar. Quite an amusing *lapsus linguae*, really what an unconscious humorist I am." Christian started laughing.

No one else laughed with her. Johnson said: "I say, now, Mrs. Tanner." Cheddi tutted anxiously. "Christian," he said, stopping beside the Bondha car. "Tell your driver to come along behind."

"You tell him. You tell everybody what to do. Oh dear, how funny!"

"Joke over," Harry said. "Now tell him."

Which Christian did, and sat quietly thereafter. They were part way across the open land to Bondha when the Old Bitch gave up the ghost. She did this occasionally, full speed, full stop. She was a stout Old Bitch, weak in her electrical intestines.

"Bapu will hold the light," said Cheddi, "and I will make repairs." He was an indifferent mechanic with boundless faith in his abilities, a born wrecker. "Sahib, you must go to Bondha and take food now for your strength. Also, the Lady Sahib is fevered in her mind and needs Your Honour's care."

My honour's care, he thought. I am not Uncle Cheddi to the goddess Lady Sahib. Yes, I will certainly go now to Bondha.

They dropped Johnson at his bungalow. The fresh peach Johnson married in the war was long lost in a dusky dumpling, poor old Johnson, decent chap and rather dim.

"My bruise is sore," said Michael, getting out, "but I'm not the least bit sleepy. I can stay up for supper, Mummy, can't I?"

"No," she said. "You can't stay up for supper."

"Michael," he said. "You're a good tough chap, but you've

been a silly little boy to-day. A spank and into bed's what you deserve."

"A beating not a spank. His father isn't man enough to beat him. Beat him, Harry, go on, beat him."

Michael looked at them and ran away. He limped at a run, small and forlorn across the veranda under the milling fan and into the bungalow at Bondha.

Harry went over to her. "You shut up!"

"I won't shut up. It's all your fault. We were happy till you came. We were. We were. Oh Harry, what have I said, I'm sorry. I am so sorry, Harry."

Dr. Roy Chowdhury, M.D., came bustling with his small brown bag, a brown one, an idiosyncrasy of this small brown doctor. He darted a glance at Christian. "Sit down, madam," he commanded, not humble in the least. "I will give mild sedative to calm your nerves, one prick, the merest nothing that is all."

"A sedative?" she said, shaking her fair hair which was dusty and had lost its sheen, but it suited her unruly too. "*A sedative?*" She stared at Harry, then at Dr. Roy Chowdhury, M.D. "No, thank you very much. I'm perfectly all right. But could you come and see Michael when I get him into bed?" Christian went away.

"I think she is all right," he said. "It seemed to happen just like that."

"Shock," said Dr. Roy Chowdhury, M.D. "What do we know of this? We know the chemistry, the physics of humanity, oh yes indeed, whole global poppycock and atom bombs we know. But the mystery of Mrs. Tanner snapping out of it by free will, now do we understand such things, tell me, Mr. Black, I ask you? The strong are strong and the weak are weak, we say. The good are good and the bad are bad, we say, all such sort of fiddlesticks. And when I, personally, look into beastliness of self with intentions nice and wicked totally mixed up and actions unforeseen, I know we are merest Doctor Babies in the Wood."

Harry laughed. Dr. Roy Chowdhury, M.D., giggled very gleefully, that quite enchanting man.

" But Mrs. Tanner, a brave Christian lady aptly named, although I am a staunch Hindu, of course—she is proof of human pudding. Everyone loves Mrs. Tanner."

It seemed that everyone loved Mrs. Tanner.

" Now, Mr. Black, what of your gallant self ? Let me examine you below the light. Disrobe."

" Not here," he said. Not here on the veranda.

" Upper clothing only, need I hardly say, to bare your manly torso, surely open secret. I would not have you mother naked."

He obeyed. He was clay in the hands of Dr. Roy Chowdhury, M.D., who much admired his scars, and inquired about ribs and head, all of which had ceased being troublesome. The new things were all right, and he was weak ; but the old stump had not filled out yet. Walking in dust and heat played hell with it.

" In this you are the doctor of experience, Mr. Black, not I, although the cure is obvious to both of us. But you are a man with mission to complete, and who am I, mere leech, to argue with your warrior pride ? What I must say is that you have taxed your system many times too much, hard-living and quick-healing, oh it is phenomenal, not one whit short, and I am proud of you. Your body is sound now but for this old pegleg, as you call it mockingly. Your spirit, Mr. Black ? "

He met the wise, sad, muddy eyes of Dr. Roy Chowdhury, M.D. " I'm troubled in my spirit," Harry said.

" Ready, Doctor," Christian called, and she came out. She laughed, her own gay laugh again. " What a place to choose ! " But she stared then at his chest, and her left hand rose from her side and dropped. Christian was left-handed. " Oh," she said. " My poor Harry."

Harry put his bush-shirt on.

" Drinks in the sitting-room," she said. " Will you have one ? "

" I don't know." A drink was vastly needed. " What would you advise ? " he asked Doctor Roy Chowdhury, M.D., who knew about jags and all the rest.

" I personally am teetotal through and through, but gluttony and other fleshly lusts abound in me. Do I deny them altogether ?

How can I be mundane G.P. in *mofussil* and holy man on mountain top ? No, I indulge moderately, seeking balance in my vices, toppling humpty-dumpty now and then to beastliness. Drink therefore, Mr. Black, and sparingly, is my advice. But if it must be alcoholic tubs, then take the pledge now, once for all. Mr. Black, you are my hero absolutely."

Harry went into the sitting-room. It reminded him of what his mother used to make with plain things and jazzy things to set the plain things off. Here, reproductions of Cézanne and Renoir, a Jimini Roy, and an Abani Sen, nice rugs of second quality, simple furniture of *sheesham*, tall flowers in low vases but the flowers drooped late in March, books and magazines about the place, a lived-in jumble of good taste adapted to the budget. It lacked the Tang horses and the good Bokharas and the jade. It lacked the cash. I could give her all those things, he thought, to give me back the pleasure that I saw them give to her. Can I give them to her ?

There was a gramophone, but they, she, never seemed to play it. He searched through *Oklahoma*, *Les Sylphides*, *Carmen* and *The Gondoliers*, rumbas, cariocas, Rudolph with his nose so Bright, all the things he did not need and some Mozart until he found a symphony of Sibelius, and put it on.

My hero absolutely got a drink and listened to Sibelius for a few minutes, perhaps ten, until the doctor left, and then he went to say good night, sleep tight, to Michael drowsy in his bed.

When he came back, there was a pink paper on the table. "Desmond's flying up to-morrow," Christian said. "Then driving overnight. I'll have to . . . I'll send the car early in the morning."

"Any word about the job ?"

"*Everything fine here*, he says," she said.

Christian had a drink while Sibelius went on. Harry wanted more and almost did and didn't.

"The third movement. Oh, listen to the pizzicato leading to the other tune."

A thoughtful plucking of the strings, the splash of melody,

splashing out of it full-born, a splashing witch of melody and pluck again. " It comes just once," she said. " It never quite comes back. Supper's ready, Harry. Don't you think we'd better eat ? " She stopped the fifth symphony of Sibelius.

" I didn't know you were a music person," Harry said.

" I used to be. It's a habit, isn't it, to be in and then get out of."

They ate cold chicken and potato salad without conversation. "They're good," he said about the bottled guavas. " I'm afraid the coffee's awful," Christian said outside again. " I never have found decent coffee in this country yet." The coffee was indifferent, not awful.

A mile away across the plain, Bapu still held the light presumably, while Cheddi made a mess of the distributor, no doubt.

" They must be starving."

" No. They both have food."

" If he doesn't mend it," Christian said, looking at the light which came and went and now was steady. " What then ? "

" I can't stay here," he said.

He looked at her and she looked at him. It was dark, but not too dark to see one another and to meet alone now on the veranda of the bungalow at Bondha.

" No," she said. " You can't stay here."

" That cap." He did not say *Michael's cap*, because he did not like to say it, and because of guile. " It must still be at the river unless someone pinched it. Shall we go and have a look ? "

She stared at him. " Is that what you want, Harry ? "

" Yes," he said. " That's what I want. What matters more is what you want."

" My wants ? " Her face crumpled to the smile, *gamine*, so unexpected always in her thoughtful face, so startling now. "Would they be influenced at all by yours ? "

He waited for her in the Bondha car. It was half-past nine. Some things had happened since night began three hours ago. Nothing much had happened. What was she doing ? Had she changed her mind ?

" Sorry," she said, sitting away in the other seat, and they started alone in the car together. " I couldn't hurry the ritual of what kind of eggs to-morrow morning, and I had to tell the driver too. The ancient *bandobast* takes time, and I know they'll do better without me when I go next week."

He drove fast to the light where Cheddi worked away at what he did not have a clue about. Harry was shy of Christian, not knowing what was in her mind with him, and the time for talk was past between them. " It's been a long time," Harry said.

" Yes," she said, " a long, long time."

" Sahib, after half an hour the olebits will be ready."

" Good," he said. " The memsahib and I, we go to seek the cap beside the river. Wait for me at Bondha."

Time ? What was time to Cheddi Khan and Bapu, half an hour or half a warm night through ?

He turned left to the main road before the forest. It was a worse surface than the other. He ran back with the lights of Bondha on his left ahead, then turned away across country to the river. No one else was abroad in the Indian night.

" You must be very tired," she said.

He was, and the throttle was in a bad place for his leg. " I am a bit."

" Let me drive then. Stay in, Harry, and I'll come round."

He stayed there, and she came round. " Well ? " he said.

" Can't you stop asking me ? "

He kissed her the first time for the blessing of their being together. Then they kissed one another. " Did you know you kissed me in the forest ? "

" I didn't mean to do it at the time. But when the doctor ordered sedatives, I remembered kissing you, and I thought : *I'm awfully sorry, everyone, it can't be helped*. But I'm not sorry. I'm not the least bit sorry."

" Chowdhury said that your snapping out of it was the mystery of free will."

" The mystery of more than I could bear. We tried. We tried so hard again."

"You did, anyway," he said. He moved over, and she drove.

"Too many things have happened to us—too many straws to the last one in the jungle when I knew you were afraid, and I was terrified, and you made yourself go on. I thought then : This isn't the disillusioned he-man who softens me against my will. And I thought : This isn't the man who couldn't take it when he failed. I just thought : This is my own brave Harry, and to hell with it, I don't care—Michael, Desmond, what I believe in. I'm sorry, God, I just don't care. That's why I cracked up, I suppose, and said those cruel things, like *we were happy till you came.* Please forgive me, darling."

"It's true," he said. "The sad thing is it's true."

"You did try not to. You tried as hard as I did. You never like credit for being good. You don't believe in virtue, do you, darling ? You look down on it."

"You made me go on this evening. You, not me. How can I look down on virtue ? Good-bye, virtue. Shall we stop again ? "

"Gracious no," she said. "There are limits to my powers of concentration."

"*Laugh together in the night.* Do you remember ? "

"You say the dumbest things sometimes for a clever man. If you remember, don't you know a woman would remember ? "

"I don't know much about you."

"You understand every single thing I ever mean. That same evening after you had caught the train, my mother came into my room. She said : *If you're going to be a true wife to Desmond, you must never see that man again.* Then she said : *Silly girl, you're not the only woman in the world this ever happened to.* My dowager old Mum, I've often wondered. And she said : *You know what is right, dear child. Besides, it's more beautiful to win against it.*"

"Go on," he said. "Talk to me, my darling."

"This once," she said.

He did not speak. He thought that what was said and done between them would be said and done for always.

"In her last letter Mummy wrote about you. We never open

one another's letters, not that it mattered. How can I talk like this as if he wasn't the kindest and best person and my husband ? I don't know. I don't know anything."

"And my friend," he said. But he thought that he and his worthy friend had fallen apart in many things. "What did your mother say ? "

"She said : *Dear Harry Black, I think of him so often. I hope he gets better quickly and can take a nice long voyage.* She said that, meaning : *Get him out of there before my prophecy comes true.*"

"Desmond. Did he guess ? " Would Desmond be surprised to know that I am taking his wife to the banks of the enchanted, soupy river Garda, and the moon is coming up ?

"Perhaps at the very last. I don't know, Harry. He trusts everyone, me most of all, oh dear. But he watched you drive off that last evening, and he said : *There goes Harry Black. He likes to think he goes alone.* And Desmond looked at me as if he knew quite well. If he was mean and selfish, it would be less bad, this running with the storm. You do like to think you go alone, though, darling."

"Go alone away from you ? God knows, I don't."

"For a confirmed atheist, you invoke the Deity a lot."

"Who said I was an atheist ? For God's sake don't start that again."

She sat back, with her bare arms straight to the steering wheel, and laughed at him until he laughed at himself with her. The waning moon rose now to dim the stars of the Indian night. They had left the wheat behind. They came to sands between the river and the forest, a tranquil desert of the moon where life and love might trespass at their peril.

"Do you remember . . . ? " Harry said. Do we remember the first time we held a boy's hand or a girl's hand, the tingle and the shock of seconds into hours, of moon and stars marching their circular unending route ? We are much older now, older and more wise and foolish past the sweets of innocence, of holding hands. And this is the miracle : That we are not.

"You drive all right one-handed," Harry said. He was learning the other one, finger by finger, line by line, the wrist into the palm, the fingers and the thumb, the soft strong instrument of hers for him to hold. " I can never close my eyes to see your face. But I can see your hands and think about them, beautiful and kind."

" You devil, darling," Christian said. " Let me have it back again." They crossed the *rao*. They had reached the place where the cap must be—hoof marks into a gully against the bank above the river. She searched back from there and to the *rao*. He watched her. The lights were on, and the engine ran. She stood in front in profile with the red handkerchief tied over her fair head, the white blouse at her breasts, the dark shorts at her thighs, the bare legs falling down away. " Are you sure this is the place ? "

He switched off the engine and the lights and went over to her. " Quite sure," he said. " I asked him again in bed. He said the pony backed out, and swung half-rearing on its quarters. It must have been just here. It stands to reason."

" Oh dear," she said. " One of those awful things again that stand to reason."

" Don't worry, my love. It can't be helped. We might still get the cap back if the camel people took it."

" We won't. I know we won't. And people will think we didn't even look. I know what people are thinking about us."

" They aren't thinking anything about us. What does it matter what people think about us ? "

" You don't care what people think about us. You don't care what anybody thinks. To hell with everyone is your motto, lone wolf having fun. But me ? What about me ? You don't care about me, do you ? "

" I do," he said. Her mouth was near below his mouth, not reaching down, not reaching up.

She had not come to him altogether. " We should go home. We should. Not even this once and say good-bye." But in a while now, standing above the river Garda, she came to him altogether. " We were wrong the first time, thinking that not even a kiss was a wonderfully complete nothing to end up with.

I

We're older now. So much has happened now for us to know."

His Enemy said to him : You know that nothing has happened to her for her to know. You know that she has known one man only, and you know she does not know. There is still time, Harry Black—Go away, he told his Enemy.

"You're strong," she said. "You're strong and hard against me. Darling, there's a rug inside that canvas bag thing in the car."

Fireflies glowed and went out across the river. Jackals howled in the moon-secret land. *Where is the dead Hindu ? Where, where, where ? Over there, over there, over there.*

Where is my Love aflame ? Where, where, where ? Here with me, here with me, here with me.

The fireflies and the jackals, the glowing and cacophony beyond, the wetness of bodies touching in the heat, the wounded tiger in the forest, where was he ?

"You make music with me. Such lovely tunes you play."

> "Ouvre ton âme et ton oreille au son
> De ma mandoline.
> Pour toi j'ai fait, pour toi, cette chanson,
> Cruelle et caline."

"In French now too. *Caline ?* I don't know that."

"Cruel and caressing." And he wondered : Cruel ?

"Not cruel," Christian answered for him. "Only cruel to remember music if you heard perfection once."

We sail now to the island of Socotra. We sail for ever to the island of Socotra. The phosphorescence curls now, molten running shiver smash, and another wave is broken in the rising sea, in the cradle of our sea, rolling us and pitching us, lazy easy strong and slow, up to Polaris riding off the Plough, down to Southern Cross athwart the sea. *Hum dekte hain*, the sailor chants there in the bow. *I am watching.* We are watching for the island of Socotra. We see it, the island where the aloes grow, the island of the battlements. Wait, island of Socotra. Wait, my landfall. Be cold, Socotra, far and small. Be tiny in the ocean. But the ocean rises. Let us choose our wave, climb this first wave, let it go. The second comes, the third, the fourth comber of the monsoon breaking, the fifth giant and its trough, and mount the sixth to see our seventh wave the sailors talk about. It gathers us. It takes us in the phosphorescence, in the molten curl, sailing sailing, and two flying fish are flying, glisten skip and skim, ever flying is the moment of the flying fish, ever sailing, ever flying, ever higher, ever ever to the breaking of our wave, the thunder of our drowning on the rocky island of Socotra, here.

"Peace, my darling. Storms and peace I never knew about. Peace and not alone."

"Not lonely and alone," he said, "the miracle with you." He kissed her on her left cheek and her right cheek, on her brow, and they were quiet. Time was not before. Time would not come after. Time was not with them, looking at the sky.

Not until the watchman called again. The watchman knocked at the door of Harry's head to say that it was midnight by the river Garda, and he drove her home.

"I've always been afraid of India," she said. "Liking things about it, helpless in it, hating it. I wonder if your mother was afraid?"

"I don't think so," Harry said. "I don't know. That's a thing brave women tell their lovers, not their sons."

"A lover, a lovely word I never heard before. I wish I'd known your mother, darling."

"Yes, and my father would have liked you. *Damn' fine girl, that,* I can hear him say it. I've been thinking lately what I missed about my father. We were too different, I suppose, and I was too arrogant to see. But my mother. My mother could laugh at me like you do."

"There's looking after you, and there's being your slave, to keep you in my heart for ever, even hurting me, it doesn't matter. Now I see why women live in shacks with husky drunks."

He laughed. "Not so husky at the moment, but a veritable drunk."

"No, darling, not a veritable drunk. You can beat that. I was watching you this evening. Was it nice, to be afraid at last and beat that too ? "

" It put me in my place," he said. " I'm still afraid, and now I know." He saw the wounded tiger waiting for him. " I've learned so much from you," he said, " about trust and other things I lost, my darling Christian."

" I don't know," she said. " I don't know any of the mysteries of sin and no repentance. Shall I repent this morning when I wake up to remember you with me ? Just once, I thought. Just once properly this time to say good-bye, and be a true wife always after to my husband. It wasn't your fault, darling. I wanted it as much as you. But I was wrong. Did you know that I was wrong, lover of women ? "

" Not any other woman," Harry said, and what he said was true. He was ashamed. He could not lie to Christian. " Yes," he said. " I'm afraid I thought I knew."

" *Cruelle et caline*," she said. " And never a whole life for you. A part of life, an episode, and off to hunt that animal to-morrow, and afterwards another tumble would be very nice."

" Please don't," he said. " That isn't true."

" It is, my love," said Christian close to him. " It's true about you that you never give yourself."

" My old Colonel said that to me once."

" Oh, that old Colonel, that sardonic sage, but he was right. You live for Harry Black, and I am what you want, and the tiger's what you want, and please God help you with the tiger and with me."

" I've always had a one-track mind," he said. " I've never had a two-track mind before. I find it most confusing." His heart was full and penitent about himself, and grateful. He kissed her as they bumped across the moonlit land of bund and ditch, cane harvested, wheat ripe now for the harvest. " The tiger is the episode," he said, " and when I've killed it, tiger's over."

" After that ? "

" Would I come down to Dorset ? "

" I don't know," she said. " I'm so ashamed and not ashamed.

I'm me with you and you. Don't ask, my love. Don't ask me now."

They reached the road, ran down with the few lights of Bondha on their right, turned back. They came soon to the Tanners' bungalow at Bondha, where Cheddi Khan and Bapu waited with the Old Bitch ticking over to display a cure.

" The Lady Sahib and I searched long and carefully and did not find the cap."

" Salaam, Cheddi Khan," she said. " Salaam, Bapu. Sleep well, Harry."   She went slowly up the steps.

" We will find the cap," said Cheddi Khan. " I will recover it this morning early from the camel *budmash* scoundrels. My-kell must wear this cap upon his head when flying in the air machine to Blighty. The Lady Sahib would wish it so."

They went back to Rimli. Harry Black slept well with love in the remaining hours of night.

CHAPTER NINETEEN

HE DROVE the fireline after dawn. His dust swathe was pocked by the cross-traffic of two nights. The season of lush grass and pools was over now at Rimli, and animals must travel far to eat and drink, to the lower forest flatly cradled by the plains, to the upper forest steeply cradled by the red rock ridges, back and forth and with carnivorous attendants.

Soon forest fires would start, and after this moon died there were still two moons to wax and wane through dust storms in the night, intolerable furnace winds by day, ever hotter to a core of heat.

The sky is plumbeous and pitiless. Clouds mass to-morrow to the south ; surely the rain will come to-morrow, or to-morrow ; but it does not come ; and then it comes.

These are the *chota barsat*, Small Rains, scouts probing for the enemy and beaten back ; and heat, the enemy, is stronger yet.

But now at last the veritable rains have come. Wild creatures stand below this blessing. Human creatures dance for joy below this blessing, this warm skin-splashing garment of delight. God has blessed the earth again ; and overnight the earth grows green.

He thought of the monsoon far away ; and he thought : Whatever I may do, or whatever may be done to me, I shall not see the Rains this year.

Bapu found tracks. The tiger had crossed the fireline at the east side, not far from the beginnings of the eastern ridge. It had moved on three legs, dragging the fourth, the off hind leg as Bapu had divined. There was no blood to make tracking easy. Bapu followed the trail for a hundred yards to muttee—baked mud, hard as stone—and there he lost it.

The tiger had entered the upper forest. Had it stayed, or had it climbed to the Pass of Rimli and crossed into Ranipur again ? Could it go six miles, and more beyond, with a useless leg ?

Certainly it could. Would it? Experience said No. But the criteria of experience did not hold. Harry thought, as well as felt, that this last maneater was more baleful, unpredictable and cunning than all or any of the others—tiger and panthers—that he had destroyed.

He thought : If I had not been lost elsewhere last night, I might have gone quickly to the Pass to wait, and then, oh Christ Almighty. . . . He saw the tiger coming from behind, from Ranipur, of course, on this occasion.

" Bapu," he said, driving home to breakfast. " Has the Bad One gone to Ranipur below the mountains ? "

Bapu grunts. He is a grunt-machine this morning. Does he grunt because the tiger may be in the upper forest, which seems to put him in a grunting state of mind ? Or does he grunt because I forgot the whisky ? Bapu likes his tipple even more than I do. Well, I can make that my excuse. I can go and borrow one from Christian, from my love.

The elephant, which had been positively due since four to-morrows, arrived now on the fifth ; not only better late than never, but on a morning it could be most useful.

They searched the Rimli horseshoe, anti-clockwise—up by the ravine where he had pinned the tiger and would have killed it but for Desmond's flustered *hagram-bagram*, balls-up. Then I would have gone away, he thought, and this would not have happened. Nonsense. This thing was ordained to happen.

Bapu slid off the pad again to search. Bapu's thoroughness and patience were phenomenal, not that it was patience. He came back, round-faced enigmatic little Bapu, put his bare prehensile toe into the proffered foothold at the tip of the elephant's prehensile trunk, and Begum swung him up to slip past the mahout to sit with Harry on the pad, and Begum lumbered on again. Bapu and Begum were old friends in close rapport.

They moved across the grain of hills and hummocks cut by the white ghost-torrents of the Rimli watershed, climbing to the apex of the horseshoe, the closed apex with the single opening in this red-rock barrier. Anomalous, he thought, a deviation from the

norm, an irregularity not to be expected. Tell me one thing that
was not. Oh go to hell, he told his troubled spirit.

They stopped at the last steepening below the Pass of Rimli.
Bapu slipped off again. His hand touched Begum's trunk in
passing, and the tip curled round to nuzzle him. Bapu climbed
bare-footed and in silence, anonymous and watchful, out of sight.

Harry waited. He was here, but he was by the river with his
love, with comfort, passion done, with peace.

" Sahib, the Bad One has not gone to Ranipur below the
mountains."

He looked over all the Rimli forest from up here. The vultures
looked down on it. Nine vultures, Harry counted, wheeling on
the watch, soaring in the depth of sky. No death this morning yet
to call a bird to close its pinioned wings to plummet with a rush
of wind with glory, summoning the others down to feast themselves to stupor, flightless and obscene. The vultures told him
nothing.

The elephant and the three men moved again, down below the
western ridge. The red cliffs shimmered. They were ugly, and
the sky was ugly, and the jungle here was ugly in the hardship
of the day.

Was there a change in Begum, a tenseness in the shamble of
her gait ? She would be bored with working in the heat. Bapu
was gruntish now again as they approached the bathing place
of elephants, where they had sat that murky morning before
he shot the other tiger. The Elephants' Pool had shrunk now to
a pot-hole. The wild elephants had left Rimli for the high cool lands.

Begum baulked below the bank. The mahout dug her with
the metal ankus, one vicious downstroke an inch into the head.
She hissed, and climbed. " There is a bad scent here," the mahout
said. " She is not happy."

Bapu searched about. " A panther," he grunted audibly.
Which might explain unhappiness.

Harry went round the pool on Begum. He could see well
enough from ten feet up. He saw the splayed pugs of an old male
panther.

Bapu came to stand below him. His face was blank of news. " Sahib," he said. " There are no pugmarks of the Bad One here."

" Mount then, Bapu," Harry said. And while Begum swung her old friend Bapu up, he looked at the red cliffs of the west ridge of the Rimli horseshoe. He screwed his eyes against the glare. He never wore dark glasses in the jungle. He saw the jagged, pitted but unbroken wall of rock, striated vertically here. He was getting hot, in a figurative sense as well, in the sense of Hunt the Thimble. *You're cold. You're warmer now. You're hot.*

He had just seen a fresh and good impression of the near fore-paw of the Rimli maneater, the rib of scar-gouge diagonal across the basal pad. He had seen it in the crusty ooze beside the pool. He had caught Bapu in a flagrant whopper.

" Oh Sahib," said Bapu, " the Bad One must lie yonder near another drinking place." He made his graceful sweep of stubby hand across the jungle between here and the eastern ridge three miles away. But with this gesture he embraced the whole jigsaw of the upper Rimli forest.

" Yes," said Harry. " We shall go there in the afternoon." And he thought : I must be careful about this. I am dealing with a very special sort of man. If I so much as hint that I am on to Mr. Bapu, then Mr. Bapu will take off, O-U-T spells out, and out of this game he will go, no more Bapu. We shall go in there this afternoon, and we shall happen to swing homeward by this *rao*, and Begum will *Baith*, Sit down, and Bapu and I will have a stroll alone, and I will say with Bapu pinned alone : *Tell me this now, Brother.*

They went back to the resthouse. " At half past three," he said. He drank fresh lime with wind-chilled water from an earthen pot. He had some food. He lay on the charpoy bed, a towel across his middle, in the twilight of closed glass and shutters. The stripling son of Mihtan pulled a rope on the veranda, and the punkah creaked overhead until the boy grew drowsy, and Harry called to wake him, and the dry wind cooled his sweat again. It was the ancient India.

I'll go this evening, Harry thought. Will she come out this evening ? With laughter into passion into peace and not alone. With laughter ? *We were happy till you came.*

*   *   *   *   *

He was awake before the aeroplane flew overhead. He tucked in his towel and hopped across the room and out to hold a pillar. The concrete was blister-hot, which made him keep on hopping like a hopping stork, and Mihtan's son, the punkah-puller, tittered shyly as the aircraft came in sight again. It was Rabat's high-winged monoplane, painted blue and silver. Harry had flown with him in Delhi.

Rabat buzzed the resthouse mildly, wagged his wings and flew south for Bondha, where they had a landing strip of sorts.

Harry hopped inside and into tepid water in the tub. He was pleased. He was elated at the thought of seeing Rabat, quite apart from his elation at the thought of where he had to go to see him. Someone he knew and liked outside this maelstrom. Someone also who might help him with the tiger, he now thought.

He leaned against the wall and dried himself, gingerly about the ribs, vigorously elsewhere. His body was a bit bashed up but it was a fair good body still but forty years were gone and how much longer ? He went back into the bathroom, dusted his stump with talcum powder, pulled on the sheath, strapped up the leg, and was dressed almost as quickly as a whole-limbed man. It was ten past three.

"Take Begum to the river where it turns away from Rimli. Let her bathe. If I do not come there by one hour before the sunset, then return."

"Sahib," said Bapu. "I go to seek the Bad One in the upper forest."

"*Kabardar*," he said. "Be careful, Bapu. The Bad One is thrice dangerous now wounded, and thou hast earned thy sups of whisky-wine to-night. Carry the small rifle, Bapu, for thy safety."

"I shall be careful," Bapu said. And for the third time now, he stooped to lay his forehead on the rubber toe of Harry's jungle boot. " My father, my protector," Bapu mumbled, took the rifle, and was gone with mystery.

" Sahib," said Cheddi Khan alone. " There is grave distress in Bapu's mind. I have been watching him."

Not only Bapu's mind is in distress. " I know this," Harry said. He told Cheddi Khan about the pugmark at the pool. Cheddi and he were allied aliens in this India, but that bond was incidental to his trust of Cheddi, an olympian confederate.

Cheddi shook his head. " These jungli people, they are not like us. Sahib, you are fond of Bapu, but you must beware of Bapu in distress."

Harry started the Old Bitch up. She was running well to-day.

" Shall I come to Bondha to say that the cap has not been found ? I would report this bad thing to the Lady Sahib."

Michael's cap was much on Cheddi's mind. Everyone had something on his mind, and some had more important things than caps. " I will tell the memsahib," Harry said.

He drove to Bondha. This was the first hundred degree day. There was a difference when it passed blood heat, a buffet and a nastiness, growing to the next difference at a hundred and ten about, which burned on lips and into lungs. Above that it was simply heat. To-day was a hundred, give or take, and less disagreeable than a prickly-heatish ninety in the mixed blessing of the Rains.

And he thought : The daffodils are out now down in Dorset, and the blackbird will be singing, and the young beech leaves may be breaking, and the cuckoo in another week or two. *The cuckoo then, on every tree, Mocks married men.* . . . Oh Christ, he thought, not piously but not profanely. What am I to do ?

Rabat's plane was parked in the shade of the mango at the garden wall. It was old, a three-seater he had bought from war-surplus stores. Michael was prowling round the aircraft. Rabat stood with Christian on the steps above the porch.

" Harry ! " Strong bull of Bashan. " Oh my God, I am so glad to see you." Standard greeting, but he seemed to be.

" So am I," said Harry, shaking hands.   " Hallo, Christian."

" Hallo, Harry," Christian said.   She wore dark glasses, not the very dark ones.   He could see her eyes.   She smiled at him, calm and unchanged from other days.

" The stormy petrel in a cloud of dust.   How else would we expect him to arrive ? "

" That's the way he comes," she said, " to smoulder quietly and leave again."

Harry took his glasses off.   " You look well," he said, " more prosperous and satrapish than ever."   Rabat wore his greenish uniform of drill, serviceable and immaculate, a soldier in the eyes of any soldier.   " How's the family ? "

" They flourish all along the line.   I am yet again to be a father. Is that not wonderful ?   Somola is still in Travancore, but she had heard about your accident and was inquiring in a letter.   Somola is employing sweet reason with the Communists."   Rabat bared his excellent white teeth.   " Sweet reason !   I would sweeten them with reason."

" Who's Somola ? " Christian asked.

" She is my mad sob-sister with whom I fight like cats and dogs, Somola Pant."

" Oh yes, I listen to her sometimes.   Shall we go inside ?   It's reasonably cool."

Harry watched her bring Rabat ice-clinking *nimbu pani* with two straws.   " You ? " she said to him.

" Please, Christian."   And he thought : Over-casual, under-casual, it can't quite be done.   " Rabat," he said.   " Thank you for rallying round when I was damaged."

" What did I do ?   Bring a few medicines.   Desmond and Mrs. Tanner were the guardian angels."

" I know," he said.   He knew that well.

" And from what Mrs. Tanner tells me, you have been paying back your guardian angels, rescuing Michael in the jungle in the dark, a terrible experience."

" How is Michael ? "   He clutched at the straw of Michael.

" The doctor gave him something, and he slept till noon.   Stiff and sore and more garrulous than usual, but all right. Really, children are amazing, casting off their horrors when their horrors are so real."

Yes, they really are, he thought. And which or what is real? Are we quite real here to Rabat with his Hindu sensibility?

"Besides," said Rabat, looking at his hands, one hairy mutton fist upon the other. "Besides," he said basso-profundissimo, "I involved you in this tiger pickle. I could not stand idly by to see you altogether pickled. That would not be nice of me. I would have reproached myself perhaps."

"I thought you loved me," Harry said.

Rabat guffawed largely. "Is he not a wicked fellow?"

Christian smiled. "Wicked?" she said. "I wouldn't know." Her eyes met Harry's again. Her eyes were dark blue and deep, unknown to him. He looked away.

"Whence, portly Brigadier, and whither?"

"I have been to Dehra. They let me use my rattle-trap for these inspections. Now I must fly on to Delhi, now in a few minutes. I came to inspect you too, my friend, and you are in fighting form, I see. Bony, and lamer than before, but the face has again the lively look I used to know. We were together, Mrs. Tanner, in some wild days getting one another into trouble."

"I know," she said. "He's told me all about you."

He, she says. He, not Harry. "Now you're here," he said, "I can make use of you to fly me over Rimli. Say fifteen minutes. What about it?"

"*Make use of me.* That is all these English do. You are Canadian, Mrs. Tanner, luckily not one of them, like me. Am I not right about this?"

Christian smiled, but did not speak. He wondered what she thought of Rabat. She wore a dress this afternoon, a print of green and white. She sat with her legs twined in that woman's way, one foot behind the other ankle. She is not the same, he thought. And I am not the same. There is the eternity of us together. Is it wrong that love is right for us? He looked at her, and she at him, and he felt Rabat watching. Why hide the beauty of this current flowing

to and fro between them in the room ?   We must, he thought.
But they were not.

"Well, let us go now for this fifteen minute flight.   It is very
bumpy, Harry, do you mind ? "

"I expect I'll lose my lunch," he said.   Which reminded him
so painfully of an atrocity of his he had been told about, that he
grunted like old Bapu.

Rabat took off and made a climbing turn to Rimli.   He was a
competent and cautious pilot.   Harry saw them in the Bondha
garden.   The boy was waving a white handkerchief, but Christian
did not wave.

"Where do you want to go ? "

He put his mouth to Rabat's ear.   "Up the line of the left-
hand ridge, above it on the inner side and as low as you can
manage."

"The bumps will be terrific."   Rabat put his finger on the map.
"Two thousand feet.   That is one thousand higher than the plains.
I must leave two hundred more at least for margin, and still be
climbing up the ridge."

The small plane lurched about.   It bounced in sympathy with
each change of land below—white *rao*, grey forest, and the taungya
patchwork ;   and there now was the main fireline that bisected
Rimli—beyond that, the resthouse on its flattened spur, the Range
Office over to the left, the upper forest laid out for inspection.   It
was no cooler at this height.   The glare was brassy.

"Belt tight ? "

Harry's belt was tight.   He leaned to his right-hand window,
and now the updraughts of the red-rock oven tossed the plane.   The
bumps were certainly terrific.

He saw the summit of the ridge two hundred feet below, the
cliffs dropping a thousand foreshortened feet to the glade where
he had sat out a thunderstorm in the first act of this melodrama.
He saw the small circle of the pool.   What was that ?   But it fell
behind.

He waved his hand to the right, and Rabat turned over relatively
calm airs within the horseshoe.

" Too high," he shouted. " Could you run it down the other way, close against the cliffs, about a hundred feet above the jungle ? "

" Do you want to kill us ? " Rabat circled left. The Pass of Rimli danced in a haze of heat above them. " Is this important, Harry ? "

" Yes. I must have just one look."

" The thermal currents. . . . Well, I will try it."

Rabat dropped the nose and throttled back, making a gliding turn to his line against the cliff. But his line was a gradual left curve.

" Closer ! " What Harry wanted to inspect was the rock-face this side of the Elephants' Pool. He shielded his eyes against the sun ahead. Rabat was at cruising revs and flying level now. He needed both airspeed and reserve power. " Closer ! "

Red rock. Vertical strata and striations. Jagged rock. Pitted rock. Polished rock. Rock unbroken. Then he saw it.

He placed it precisely in his mental map—a quarter of a mile, two furlongs, yes about—two furlongs upridge from the Pool. He saw something else as well, movement at the edge of a bamboo clump, a man running into shelter, a face staring up. Bapu's jungle lore did not include concealment from the sky.

The thermal struck them at Harry's first tiger glade. It whipped up the starboard wing, down the port. Full throttle, and full stick. Rabat straightened out.

Harry yawned and sweated. He held on to his lunch.

" You are a public danger." They laughed after that unpleasant topsy-turvy moment. " See anything ? "

Harry told him what he had seen, and briefly what he thought.

" Be careful," Rabat said, as Cheddi Khan had said. " These primitives are not funny with their bogeys."

He landed and taxied into the wind to Bondha. He closed the throttle ; the propeller idled. " Harry," he said quietly, " I have brought you much trouble with this tiger. I am afraid that I was wrong, perhaps, persuading you."

" Maneaters are always troublesome, this one rather more so. I'll get it now, I think."

Rabat looked round at him. He was embarrassed, not his

ebullient self. " That," he said. " But there is other trouble I am fearing, and if I am your friend I must say this to you knowing it is none of my damn' business and I may be wrong, but Desmond is a good chap and a closer friend to you than I am. I am sorry, Harry, if I offend you."

He fingered the handle of the cockpit door. He knew with what reluctance Rabat would mention such a thing. Harry was not offended, and he was not swayed. " I know," he said. " I know, Rabat."

" Then be strong of heart," said Rabat in stentorian tones again. " And good luck to you, *tum Bluddiful*."

" If and when, may I come and stay with you in Delhi ? "

" Have I not said my house is yours ? Must you insult me by this question ? Get out now, for I am late, thanks to turbulent Blacks and airs. My apologies to Mrs. Tanner for not thanking her in person. Remember me to Desmond."

Harry got out. He shielded his face against the dust of Rabat's turning. He watched him taxi down and swing and run her up again, a careful pilot who would take a risk. He waved to Rabat as the small plane bucked for the cooler and the calmer airs. *Remember me to Desmond.* He walked back to the bungalow at Bondha.

Michael was riding round the garden, hatless.

" That's fine. Now trot slowly, darling, for a while."

His face was tight. He trotted.

" I thought it was best, Harry, don't you think, bruise and all to make him ? "

" Yes," he said. " I do." And he thought : She is unselfish even in denying her own fears for her only child. " That boy has guts," he said. " Which is not surprising." He smiled at her, but she was watching Michael. He saw the shadow go across her face. He wished he had not said that as a compliment to her. Any remark was loaded except mundane remarks like : " You've taught him well. You ride very well yourself."

" I was a horse till I was seventeen," said Christian. " Shall we have a cup of tea ? "

" Rabat sent you his apologies and thanks."

" I'm sure he's a good man's sort of man, but I find him rather overpowering like a hearty bear. This Somola Pant, is she another one of yours ? "

" She's rising fifty," Harry said. " Come off it, honeybunch." Christian giggled. " Oh dear," she said.

" Talking of Rabat, I fear he was on to us in no time flat. A hearty bear, but astonishingly acute."

" He wouldn't have to be acute," she said. " Meeting a first time again, and looking at you and you at me. We can pretend now after this."

" There are limits to pretending," Harry said.

The tea came, and she poured it out for him and her. It was his own ex-best green tip tea that he had given them. " You've spoiled me for ordinary tea," she said, and bit her lip, and they watched Michael in the withered garden at a walk again.

" I was thinking," Harry said. " I was thinking the daffodils must be coming out at home. Haphazard, round about the grass, and under trees. Do you like them too ? "

" I like them best of all flowers," Christian said. " Carefree daffodils that die before the summer. You don't have to ask me what I like."

" I know, my love," he said. It was the saddest and the happiest thing he knew. *I know, Rabat. I know, Everyone.* " You've been with me all the time," he said, " ever since I left you, sleeping and awake."

She moved in her chair and did not speak. Another day was fading to another night. The Brain-Fever bird was calling : Question, Question, fevered question, no answer to the question, never finished asking ; start again and ask again, no answer to the question.

" I must go," he said. He should have gone before this to see Bapu. There were numerous things he should have done and hadn't, and had and shouldn't have. " Shall I come back later on ? "

" Take Adonis round now to the stable, Michael." She put the teacups on the tray. "No," she said. "You mustn't, darling."

"What are we going to do?"

"Was it true what you said to me that morning in your room at Rimli?"

Morning? He remembered bits about the afternoon. "I was drunk," he said. He did not look at her. "You'll have to tell me what it was I said."

"Wine mocks me," Christian said. "I can't tell you."

"When shall we meet? I've got to talk to you before you leave." But the tiger was between him and their meeting.

"Riding in the early morning is the only time."

"Not to-morrow," Harry said. "I'm on to this animal, I think. If so, it has to be to-morrow at the crack of dawn. But the next day?"

"To-morrow wouldn't do in any case," she said, "even if you gave me top priority. Had you forgotten my engagement for to-morrow morning?"

"No," he said. "What time will he arrive?"

"About six. It was six before, and I guess it will be six again. Dear Desmond, what have I done to him? What will I do again if you crook your finger? What kind of a shameless woman am I?"

She said these things quietly. There was nothing he could say to her.

Michael came through the house. "Harry, did they get my cap back from the oonty-wallahs?"

"No," he said. "I'm afraid they didn't, Michael. How would it be if I gave you a new one for a birthday present rather late? You could buy it in England, and let me know the price." Or I could buy it, Harry thought, in England.

"Gosh, that would be absolutely super. And Harry, I'm sorry for what I did yesterday. I'm supposed to say I'm very sorry. I mean I really am."

The three of them laughed. Laughing that time was good.

"Bapu didn't get his promised drink. Could you let me have a bottle, Christian?"

Our modest cellar is available for every dipsomaniac. If she had suspicions of his solicitude for Bapu, she did not show them. " Of course," she said. " I'll get one. Or Michael could. Darling, run to the cupboard for a whisky bottle, and don't forget to lock the door again and bring the keys." She took a key-ring from the pocket of her dress. " My badge of office, her worshipful bamboozlement, the memsahib."

" I'm going to buy it," Harry said. " How much ? "

" Twenty-nine rupees twelve annas, but you're not."

" Listen," he said. " I can't . . ." The hypocrisy of scruple in a lack of scruple.

" From me," she said. " I'll put the money in the brown purse, that's for household. My one and only present." But she added : " Up to now."

" Presents," Harry said. " I'd like to touch your elegance with barbaric jewellery from top to toe."

" That would make me rather knobbly," she said.

There was lightness then between them ; but he had another thing to say, and quickly, because he heard Michael coming with the least one of her many presents up to now : " Desmond is buying me that dynamite, which I think I'll need. Can you get him to send it with your driver first thing in the morning ? Not bring it up himself, is what I mean. The thought of . . ."

" I know," she said. " But the one thing he will want to do is take it up to you himself. What tactics would you advise me to adopt ? Shall I play Delilah in barbaric jewellery ? " She said that softly, blankly, and not bitterly, staring at him.

" Thank you so much, Michael," Harry said.

" You always seem to go just when I come."

" The tiger's wounded, darling," she said gently. " Harry has to go. Let's wish him luck."

" I'll say it in my prayers to-night," said Michael.

He went his way to Rimli. Dust was his companion. He thought of daffodils in the pleasant land, in England, in the island. He had seen the spring in England twice since he had learned beauty from a prisoner's book. His eye was strong for beauty now again,

stronger than ever it had been.   He saw the daffodils that die before
the summer.

> The lovers weep.   There is no rest or pity.
> There is no summer in that landlocked city.

Why   should   the   lovers   weep ?   Why   should   there   be   no
summer ?

*   *   *   *   *

" Oh Bapu, take one sup of whisky-wine ; then tell me of thy
doings ; then take two sups of whisky-wine."

Bapu produced his aluminium cup from the recesses of his grey
tweed jacket.   It had a hole one-third of the way up, which allowed
for a fair good tot.   No tilting to increase the measure was a rule
that caused much Bapu merriment.   " Level, brother," Harry said,
as always ; and as always, Bapu tilted from the hole.   But he did
not cackle merrily.   He swigged it down and looked slightly less
lugubrious.

" Sahib, I went by the Chilwa pool, by the five anthills, by the
great haldu . . ."   Bapu's description was of a half-mile circle
midway between the ridges, midway between the Pass of Rimli
and the resthouse.   " The Bad One has gone there, and the Bad
One rests there.   The peacock, the langoor, the karkhar and the
cheetal, they and many others of the *janwar* say this."

" Hast thou searched elsewhere this afternoon ? "

Bapu was squatting on his heels on the matting of the resthouse
floor, swaying back and forward slightly on the fulcrum of his
heels and toes.   The rhythm of his swaying broke and then went on.
" No, sahib.   For there I heard the *janwar* speak and there I circled
the speaking of the *janwar*."

" Oh brother, dost thou put thy trust in me ? "

" As in no man," Bapu said.   " The sahib has the hard way of
the soldier, knowing death and having understanding.   The sahib
is a true friend, true to me when wicked men have wished to
kill me."

A true friend, Harry thought.

" Also," continued Bapu pensively, remotely, swaying on his heels : " Also, the sahib walks with the wild things in his heart. Has the sahib not spoken of those days of hiding in the foreign jungles when the wild things did not fear him, when the small mouse and the large deer knew that he was one with them, and warned him of the coming of his enemies ? The great hunter has been hunted.

" Sahib, in my days of trouble when I left my people, I lived with the *janwar* in the jungle." Bapu waved his hand over his shoulder, general direction south-east, which was the run of the mountains' edge, and Bapu's people lived along the malarial *terai* below that edge. Blindfold Bapu in a darkened room, spin him round, ask him which way was home, and he would point.

" The high-born one, the humble one, the wild things have protected us. Sahib, I knew this from the first moment of our going in the forest, before the sahib had told me of his journey through the jungles of the enemy to the wounding and the freedom. There has been beauty in this thing for me, and comfort in new days of trouble."

" For me also, Bapu, and I am but a child before thy wisdom. For me also there is the beauty and the comfort of this thing that we have known that all men do not know." Harry stood up and closed the double doors behind the unrolled screen and sat again. " Oh Bapu, we are alone now in this house, and no man may hear us if we speak of secret things."

Bapu's eyes flickered to the outside door, the bedroom door, the third door. He had stopped swaying. He squatted, thighs flat against calves on his spade-ended heels. No, Bapu, Harry thought, watching Bapu's hands. You are not going to take off for parts unknown. " Bapu," he said slowly. " This secret of ours, is it as beautiful a thing as that thing most sweet and beautiful to see, the tigress cuffing her little ones with a fierce mother's pride and love, then giving suck ? "

Bapu sat still, looking at the floor. " Sahib," he muttered, " these secret things are beautiful like one another."

" Thou hast spoken of trust in me as in no man, Bapu. But

thou hast lied twice to me to-day. I saw the Bad One's pugmark at the pool. I saw thy face from the air machine, and thy face was not in that part of the jungle of the baby fishes and the anthills and the great haldu tree. Thine eyes looked up at the *hawai jahaz* from a place two furlongs from the Elephants' Pool. Oh Bapu, my brother whom I trust, why hast thou not told me long since of the secret place where the Bad One now lies wounded ? "

"Sahib," said Bapu. "This has been a grievous thing to me, because in all matters of the Bad One I have told my knowledge truly to the sahib, excepting only this." The little man began to weep. He sobbed croakingly without restraint. Harry sat easy in his chair, his pistol in his trouser pocket. Bapu would neither run amuck nor run away now that he was weeping.

"Tell me of this trouble in thy heart that we may share it."

Bapu told him. His people did not worship many images and idols, as did the Hindus, the top-knotted ones. His people did not worship human gods. His people built no temples, for the sky and land and water, the birds and beasts and men, the trees and flowers of the forest—these were the many temples of his people, and God dwelt equally in all of them.

They built no temples, but there were sacred places for the worshipping of god-in-all and all-in-god, and these places were most secret in the deepness of the forest, and the knowledge of the sacred places was the oath of manhood, secret and inviolable.

"Oh sahib," croaked Bapu with his tears, "I was an exile from my people, and always a stranger here at Rimli, and I sought my holy place to be secret from all other men. I found this place where the red rock wraps the rock, and the passage turns in secret to the open place within the rock. Sahib, no man but I has known this place where I have worshipped alone with God. Sahib, eight cold weathers back, I went one morning to my *pujah* place which was trodden neither by men nor by the *janwar*, and at the entrance to my *pujah* place I found the pugmarks of a tigress.

"Sahib, it is a blessed holiness with us, that the greatest of the *janwar* should bring forth her little ones in our most sacred place, and thus it happened, and my heart was full of joy.

" Sahib, the entry to my sacred place was now denied me, but there were holes and cracks for climbing on the inner wall where rock wraps rock, and I climbed the wall to look down upon that thing most sweet and beautiful to see, the fierce mother and her cubs, and this Bad One was the strongest and most playful of the three, the favourite of his mother.

" Sahib, they grew and went away, and the mother was shot in the Rimli forest, and one of the sisters was called to mating in the jungle next to Rimli, and the other sister was killed at Rimli. Only the Bad One stayed and grew to strength ; and the Bad One's cubs were born in my place also ; but in many of these seasons my sacred place was empty for my worship. In the April moon of the last heat, the Bad One was wounded in the leg, and only then, by accident and by the wickedness of cowardly men, did the Bad One become the Bad One.

" Sahib, in all other places do I hunt the Bad One and would kill him. But the Bad One has the safety of my holy place, and the Bad One waits for me. This I know. Also, in the telling of this secret, even in the telling of it to the *bara sahib bahadur*, my father and protector who has the *janwar* with him in his heart, have I betrayed my God. Does the Sahib now understand my grief ? "

" Brother, I understand this. Oh Bapu, do not the seasons grow and live and die as God ordains ? "

" Sahib, this is so, the seasons and all other things."

" Would thy god-in-all not say above us and around us and below us that the Bad One sins against the god-given habits of the tiger ? "

" Sahib, this may be true." Bapu no longer cried. His cheeks were salted. He stared at Harry.

" Would the god-in-all not say that the lesser wickedness would be the killing of the Bad One in thy holy place ? "

" Sahib, this may be true. The wisdom of God is hidden from us."

" This holy place of thine," said Harry carefully, oh carefully,

" would be a rocky place within the wrapping of the rock."

" A rocky place where nothing grows, most holy in the worship of all growing things in God, thrice holy by the birth and growth of the noblest of the *janwar*.   Sahib, is this understood ? "

" It is understood," he said.   It was vaguely apprehended.

" For the tiger a cold-weather place," said Bapu.   " Even the inner cave grows hot within the rock below the midday sun ; and the paw of the tiger is tender to the heat."

" Oh Bapu, wilt thou show me the outside of thy holy place ? Wilt thou take me there to-morrow in the morning early ? "

" That I will do, sahib," Bapu said.

" Is this a promise, Bapu ? "

" Sahib, this is a promise."

Harry stood.   He put his hand on the tatters of the shoulder of the grey tweed jacket, part cloth below his fingers, part brown skin.   Bapu in a closed and shuttered room was exceptionally goaty.

He took Christian's one and only present of the whisky, and poured some for himself.   " Tilt well, then, brother," Harry said. " Let these be two mighty sups."

Bapu tilted the cup well.

He raised his glass.   " *Sher Bahadur*," Harry said.   " Brave Tiger, I salute thee."

Bapu wept again, but now with smiles to catch his tears, and drank his third tot of whisky.   " Oh sahib, I am an exile from my people, and I have betrayed my holy place.   I know now why I long have known that the Bad One waits for me."

" The Bad One does not wait for thee.   I will protect thee from the Bad One."   But he saw the wounded tiger waiting in a cave for him as well as Bapu.

" Oh sahib, through these bad days there has been a thought of hope in me that I might go with my father and protector, that we might walk together in the jungles of the sahib's own land, and there I would serve the *bara sahib bahadur*.   But this is foolishness, I know."

Bapu in a Super-Constellation.   Bapu having lunch at White's.

Bapu stalking in the Highlands.   Bapu beating out a pheasant cover.
Bapu lurking in the daffodils.   Bapu in the jungles down in
Dorset.

Tears grew up to blur his eyes, the silly fellow.   " Oh Bapu,"
Harry said.   " Foolish men might hold thee foolish."

CHAPTER TWENTY

HE PUT out his arm to put it round her, round Christian Black. He felt the cotton webbing of the charpoy, flat, tight, interlaced.

The long hand was at twelve or so, and the short hand was at five. He heard the Primus boiling water for his morning tea. It was not particularly dark, but the glimmer through the shutters was the moon.

They said that hours of dreaming happened in a second, which was poppycock, as Father would have said. His dreams rolled on through hills and valleys, dales and fields ; and through a red-rock wilderness ; and through a desert with the compliments of Señor Dali ; and through the greenness of the island, through the daffodils; and through a strong dishevelment of forest to the river of the scarlet flowers, in Canada, her Canada. He walked with Christian's hand in his with Christian's hand on him, with comfort, not with passion. And lately now, still walking, he had given her a brooch made of a certain tiger's floating bone, the three-inch rudiment of clavicle, the curving bone, barbaric jewellery, and she was very pleased.

That was the reality, this godforsaken charpoy the illusion. There are limits, Harry thought. Dilly-dally, shilly-shally, not meeting things head-on. I'm a head-on meeter, aren't I ? Let me be one, then. I here and now dismiss my conscience with a hearty kick, wasting no more kicks against the pricks of what has been ordained to happen. Did my so-called conscience stop me from deliberately taking her ? What hypocrisy to talk about my conscience.

And he thought : You might think, from the way I have been going on, that this doesn't happen to a thousand people every day. It happened, for example, to one Harry Black. Now look, he told himself, you know quite well old Miriam was nothing but an amiable trollop, and you know quite well you drove her to it, and you know quite well Rex Wilbram was no friend of yours, but a nitwit you despised. Let's be honest if we must be honest.

The honest thing is that I can't do without her. The honest thing is that I can give myself to her to be a better chap because of her, although, no doubt, a bloody awful husband. The honest thing is that I am not ashamed of what I'm going to do to Desmond. Another honest thing is that I am sorry to cuckold, abominable word, to cuckold my old friend who has been most kind to me. And yet another honest thing is to admit that my old friend willy-nilly has become my enemy.

Desmond wouldn't take to drink. He wouldn't take a bullet to himself. I don't believe he would despair. He would go on being good, seeking the rewards of heaven. I pay you and you pay me. But we can pay love to one another. That's honest, isn't it? And is Michael going to suffer? No, he certainly is not.

Then Harry thought of his most humble, secret hope : that a child might come to bless them.

Knock, knock, who's there? Who but Cheddi with the roaring Petromax and with the morning tea, with *chota hazri*, small break-fast of one banana, two digestive biscuits.

He came back from his journey of decision to make the matutinal decision as to banana first, or biscuits first, and to decide banana ; and also to say formally : " Salaam, Cheddi Khan," in reply to Cheddi's dignified : " Salaam, sahib." He was back in Cheddi's good books he could tell from the nuance of expression in the morning greeting.

" Bapu has gone one hour ago, leaving this message for Your Honour : That he will await you at the Pool of Elephants at dawn, and in accordance with his promise."

" I told him to be here," he said in English.

" Sahib, it is not wise to place your trust in Bapu."

" Oh, nonsense," Harry said.

" This is my opinion." Cheddi Khan went out.

That animal came in. Was he never to be rid of it? Was that mucking animal ordained to wait for him, to haunt him *ad non-infinitum* till it killed him and the only true thing? Was that to be the ending of the melodrama ? But a melodrama ought to have a happy ending.

The banana went down easily enough. He sluiced one biscuit into him with tea. Gunfire, they used to call it in the Army, a bite to line the chasms of the stomach until breakfast. And when would he have breakfast this fine morning ?

The doom bells rang loudly now again for him, but with one difference : that below, behind and through their clangour Harry heard a tune, a splashing witch of melody to comfort him in danger with his doom bells ringing.

He shaved and dressed. He heard the Old Bitch ticking over. He went out. The sky was reddening above the eastern ridge, a shepherd's warning, and the smell of dew, the coolness of the earth refreshed.

Harry Black and Cheddi Khan drove down, across the rumbling bridge, right turn along the fireline, past the Range Office and the quarters of his corpulent *bête noire*, and on, and swinging on by watercourse and forest edge, not far, a mile or two, stop to engage low ratio, look back at the dust snake dwelling in the heavy air. Now slowly up the forest track, nearing a tryst with Bapu at the dawn.

" Keep the small rifle," Harry said within the loud Old Bitch. " Go back to the forest house and there await the Bondha driver with the dynamite that Tanner Sahib has bought for me. There will be the burning string, the fuse. There will be explosion-makers, detonators, also. The dynamite and fuse are safe. The detonators are most dangerous. Keep them separate from dynamite and fuse, and drive as if all thy many new-born sons lie sleeping not to be disturbed behind thee. Sound the horn on reaching here and wait."

Cheddi smiled at the tribute to his prowess as a boy-begetter, but he said : " Sahib, I am anxious in my mind about this Bapu. Let me come with you."

" No," he said. " Bapu has made a promise to me and will keep his promise. I, too, have made a promise. These are woman's fears." He said it lightly still, but felt his temper stir.

"Bapu took the ancient gun," said Cheddi, patient, riding his damned hobby horse.

Harry stopped. He turned the Old Bitch round. Day would soon be here.

"This also: If Tanner Sahib should come, do not tell Tanner Sahib where I have gone. Say that thou knowest not, and thank the sahib, and wait till he has left for Bondha. Then come thyself." And he thought, among other things: No more windy balls-ups thanks to Desmond Tanner, thank you very much. "Is this understood?"

"It is understood. But even I do not know where you plan to go. I know Bapu lied about a pugmark of the tiger. I know you talked long and secretly last night with Bapu. This is all I know. Your Honour, I must know where you will be this morning."

"Christ, man!" Harry gripped the wheel against his old black tantrum.

Cheddi Khan got out. He walked slowly round and opened Harry's door. "I am sad," he said, and Cheddi was not sad, but angry, "that after these many years you do not trust me. Therefore, Your Honour, I can no longer serve you."

"Don't be a fool," he said in English. But he got his temper back and wondered at himself. "Have I ever failed to trust you?"

"Never until now, sahib, and you are not yet strong, and there are troubles in your mind, I, even bluddiful, I know this. But I fear that harm may come to you from Bapu or the tiger. Therefore, you must tell me where you go this morning."

Cheddi's right, he thought. I needn't make a Bapu of myself. "I go to a place within the cliff, two furlongs from the pool." He pointed upwards to that section of the ridge, definable within a hundred yards, he thought, and he defined it. "To a cave where the wounded tiger lay yesterday. This was Bapu's secret that I swore not to divulge, but now I have told you, Cheddi Khan, and you will tell it to no other man. Is this a promise?"

"It is a promise. God be with you, sahib."

"And with you, my brother."

Cheddi ground the gears and went.

Daylight was here, subdued. The eyed train of the peacock was not iridescent, the wary peacock, running into cover. Spider filaments tickled tinily and damply, yielding to his face. He was mindful of Bapu and the ancient gun. He was almost sure that Bapu would not fail him. Yet he was aware that people who tell holy secrets may do unholy things to get those secrets back.

He looked up-*rao*. He saw sunlight touch the Pass of Rimli. He looked down-*rao*. He saw the old moon pale above the forest, pale beyond the forest, pale to her at Bondha if she saw the moon.

Shall I play Delilah in barbaric jewellery ? Desmond Tanner is a harmless chap. I am not a harmless chap, he thought. I have it in for Desmond Tanner, virtuous and nice as he may be. I want a piece of property of his he never should have had.

Harry crossed the *rao* and climbed the bank where Begum had baulked yesterday. He dismissed the more important thoughts and gave his attention to the importance of the first thing first. He was not waiting now, lulled by memory, by longings unfulfilled, by daydreams through a moonlit night to hear a sound, soft as a house cat on a carpet, to turn to see the tiger stalk him on its belly in below the moon, to scream. He was going seeking now, and they who seek alone, " *They know not well the subtle ways I keep, and pass, and turn again.*"

Bapu was his second and his better pair of eyes, and he had reached his rendezvous with Bapu at the semul tree beside the pool.

There was a whistle up the tree, soft and mellow, but it was not Bapu. It was a green pigeon, bird of the tree-tops, pretty bird so hard to see.

Harry did not try to see it. He looked round him. He was short of spittle, but he gathered some, put his index finger and his small finger in his mouth, made one abortive blast, then blew a whistle, anything but mellow. It echoed first from up the glade, and then it echoed loudly and less loudly and less loudly into nothing. No answer came. Green pigeons flew away.

The sun was breaking from the eastern ridge. There was beauty in the morning, and beauty is so brief a thing to grasp it while we may and lose it soon, and beauty dies but once for us and is not born each day.

He listened and he watched for Bapu. Bapu moved or waited like a wraith, but if he did not move or wait in secret, it was his habit to announce himself discreetly. *I am the jungle man. I cough. It's me.*

He has never failed me, Harry thought. He made a promise to me. And afterwards he spoke of going to the jungles of the sahib's own country. How touching that foolishness of Bapu's, that he would find his sylvan gods with me, and I am godless, and I feel sin in this way only : That I have made Christian sin against the God she loves. Yet I have seen a gleam of Something many times with her.

He went over to the pool. His mind was sharp with trepidation, and the world was near to him. In the crusted mud, greenish, seamed by a multitude of cracks, he saw pugmarks of the tiger. They were so fresh that moisture seeped into the indentations. An hour ? He did not know.

If he had come back from Bondha sooner. If he had not wasted hours with Bapu. If he had not been tired and in discomfort. If he had spent the night perched up this tree. If ifs and ans were pots and pans.

Still no Bapu. The situation now required a quick appreciation, old Army catchwords in his bones, and not a situation he appreciated much. Bapu might have taken off. He did not think so. Bapu might be up to mischief. This was the popular opinion which he did not share, but which he must respect. Bapu might be pinned by the tiger up a tree. This was a plain might-be or might-not-be. Lastly, *the Bad One waits for me*, to take him, or for him to give himself in expiation. Even this was possible.

Harry looked across the clearing to the open jungle, and through that to bamboo—ringal, dense and noisy. Beyond it was a small ravine running from ridge-face down across to *rao*. He knew that Bapu's secret place must be somewhere near the head of that ravine. He had been up the ravine before to thorn-scrub, stunted trees and tumbled rocks against the bottom of the ridge. *Sahib, this is not country pleasing to the janwar*, Bapu had remarked blandly with a sweep of hand on one of the early days at Rimli. The sandy nullah or ravine was an unhealthy avenue uphill. It was the only quiet one, the only quick and easy one for him.

What he had planned to do this morning was to go with Bapu as protector to locate the place ; and if the entrance where the *rock wraps rock* was as narrow as it sounded, then there was hope that he could lay a charge and tamp it tight enough and light a fuse and lock the bugger in. Thereafter, he might climb a bamboo ladder to Bapu's observation post, and with the encouragement of Barking Dogs, provoke the tiger from its inner cave and shoot it as safely as any potentate or Viceroy had ever shot a tiger. If not, let it starve. The pukkha sahibs might say : *I say, old boy, not very sporting, what ?* Well, this tiger was not absolutely pukkha, and he was not a pukkha sahib. He was a fearful man with an account to settle with his doom bells ringing and a splashing witch of melody that called him on through this.

So much for hopes and plans. But now his small genius had broken an appointment. Harry sweated. He could have downed three-quarters of a pint of tea, laced with one quarter of a pint of Christian's present.

Whatever the reason for Bapu's non-arrival, he knew this : That he must go quickly. And he thought : Those dreams rolled slowly with us through the night. But this perverse reality is crowded into minutes, and the sun is hardly warm, and I must hurry.

★   ★   ★   ★   ★

The nullah widened to a saucer of brown grass, a reservoir from which the nullah spilled. He had seen no pugmarks and no human footprints. He had heard no warnings. He did not expect warnings, whatever reception might await him.

Beyond the grass, the tumbled rocks ; beyond the rocks, the thorn scrub ; beyond the scrub, the red cliff-wall, and that was fifty yards away. It was not an even wall, for there were many dents and bulges. The faults ran up and down and not across the face.

He saw no perspective-depth to fit Bapu's *rock wraps rock* and *open place within* description. He should have made Bapu go into more detail, but he had been so careful not to push the little man too far.

He would make a rustle in this grass. He did. The small birds burst out from his feet to whir in all directions and to settle. *Tiri-tiri*, they soon would pipe to one another and would come together through their jungle alleys in the grass, a faithful family of bush-quail, so circumspect about re-union, such devastating little detonators at departure.

His heart beat down again. He did not think that either Bapu or the tiger had recently passed here. He reached the upper limit of the grass, and stopped with open ground behind his vulnerable back. In the nullah there had been no alternative to walking, fast as he was able, up, between, below the banks where bamboo creaked and rasped in the first stirrings of the daytime wind—but not from other stirrings, it appeared.

Now he had to go into those boulders, jagged throw-offs from the cliff-face, he supposed, haphazard, higher than a man. He did not know whether he could get through. He did not know whether he could make himself go through. What was the point? What *was* the point?

He heard that tearing, growing rush, like a jet plane at a certain angle. The vulture pulled out of its superb stoop. It stood on all its brakes of air, and levelled fifty feet or so above the bottom of the cliff and close against the cliff and a short way to the right, up-ridge, of where he stood. The vulture circled, neck low, eyes questing inwards, downwards to a point. It flew heavily away.

Harry saw the place. What had been a streak of darker rock was now a shadow cast by early sun. What had been flatness was now depth. It was like a puzzle picture, puzzle find the old man's face; and there it is, so obvious, how extraordinary not seeing that before. But this was not as easy as the puzzle picture, not a constancy of light and shade to be resolved. The sun cast no shadows into a broken cliff-face in the middle of the day; the sun shone down from almost overhead, and hot rock shimmered blankly.

K

That vulture stoop meant one thing only—food. The vulture had thought better of it. Why? Because something else was in possession of the food? Because vultures knew that helicopter take-offs were not possible for them, replete or hungry?

Both good reasons. Harry's doom bells sounded now again. They really did, the ringing of the changes on an English Sunday morning with the bass bells cracked, and his witch of melody splashed far and small. He heard his bloody doom bells ring for Bapu probably, if not for him.

He moved on, picking a way past this rock, and round that, a cul-de-sac, back again and try another passage through. He saw the last open space, the stunted scrub, the cliff. He saw Bapu's ancient gun, that fearsome weapon bound with wire, the breech-gaping piece that Bapu fired by pulling back the hammer with his thumb and letting go. Bapu's gun lay on the ground. There was a strip from Bapu's grey tweed jacket. There was blood. There were deep scufflings in the sand.

Harry stooped to break the gun. The cartridge case was empty. One of his own lethals bought from Manton. He put it to his nose. Fired recently.

Now, a shot fired in the centre of the upper forest might be muffled by the smaller hills and vales. But a shot fired anywhere against the sounding-board of cliffs would ring and echo to and fro and round about to every corner in the horseshoe. That set a time—the ten or fifteen minutes driving in the clamorous Old Bitch, a deaf man never hears you in a crowd. How long ago? He had a watch—thirty-five to fifty minutes.

Blood led him. *Where the red rock wraps the rock, and the passage turns in secret* described it admirably. A slit entrance sideways downwards in the cliff, not facing it, a U-turn within, a three-foot passage, tall and roofed, leading up inside an outer wall of cliff, and bending to the left to where the open place must be.

Harry stood within the U, just another lucky little horseshoe. He had entered by the right arm of the U. His rifle pointed up the left arm, which was flat, and the rock floor smooth and bloody. He was still not, perhaps, finally committed here. He might fire and scuttle out the other arm, perhaps. He listened. He heard the asthmatic thumpings of his body engine. He heard human moans.

He looked up. It was not a goatish climb, but quite an easy climb, twenty feet or thereabouts up a chimney of the inner wall to Bapu's observation point. The footholds were all adequate. He could lock the ankle so that the toe of his rubber boot would not yield to slip. It would have been an easy climb for him, but for adhesions in the right side of his chest that made any upward stretch, and any heaving . . . Well, he had not tried out any heaving. It was safe up there, though, wasn't it?

Harry listened now again. He locked the ankle joint. He slung the rifle on his left shoulder, and he climbed. He thought of poor old Bapu. He thought of him and poor old Bapu discussing T. S. Eliot in deck chairs on the boat deck all a slow voyage home. He thought of everything but this to beat this, and he could not beat it but he beat it with the tiger prodding him to safer heights.

He lay on his left side on the hedge. He felt better in a while, and was able to look crackwise down into Bapu's secret place where Bapu lay. Bapu's scalp was half torn off; his guts were hanging out, looped and grey and bloody; one of his buttocks was no longer there. Bapu moaned, still wearing a few relics of his grey tweed jacket.

It was a circular sort of place, circular in theme if not in detail, as circular in theme, but not in detail, as in the wall of death the motor cycle devils dare around, that sort of place, and in the middle of the open place within the rock, there was an elevation, a slab-topped chunk of rock. Below this and beside this Bapu lay. Upon this slab, or Bapu holy of the holies, were some objects— a pine cone from the Pass of Rimli, the golden feathers of a male golden oriole, a mound of pale brown earth, a clay vessel shaped much like a chamber pot, a few charred sticks—the living things of land and sky, the earth, the water and the fire, he thought absently, his doom bells ringing, and his melody.

Bapu moaned. The tiger was not visible.

" Oh, Bapu ! " Harry called.

" Sahib," he answered, yes, he did, and stirred and moaned.
" Shoot me," Bapu moaned. " Shoot me, sahib ! "

Once in the war a man wounded in the face had cried to
Harry : *Shoot me ! For Christ's sake shoot me !* But he had not
shot the man, and the man had recovered to be blind. Bapu
had had it, Harry thought—the blood alone. But who was he to
know ?

" Bapu, tell me this : Where is the inner cave ? Is it below
me here ? "

Bapu moaned and sighed and did not answer.

" Tell me ! " he boomed into Bapu's secret place, shouted
brutally : " Is it below me here ? "

" *Ha, sahib.*" Yes, master. " Shoot me, sahib."

He thought : The tiger cannot be dying if it dragged Bapu
thirty yards and into there, and ate from Bapu's backside. I could
drop a Barking Dog, of which there are four in my left breast
pocket. That might bring the cruel unmentionable out from the
inner cave below me, but it would certainly blame Bapu, and Bapu
is not dead, and how do I know what Dr. Roy Chowdhury, M.D.,
might not accomplish ?

" Bapu ! " he called again. " I come to save thee ! "

But when he had called that down to Bapu, weakness rose in
him and said : *I cannot. I cannot go down into that place.* Weakness
was clever too. It said : *The little man is in agony and dying. To
shoot Bapu isn't easy. It's harder and more merciful. Or I can wait
here till the tiger shows itself.* But Strength said this in him : *Bapu
gave his trust to me. Bapu moans down there, the tiger's mutilated mouse.
I might save him. For whosoever will save his life* . . .

Harry Black went down. He unlocked his ankle joint. The
bells of doom chimed loudly in the narrow place ; but the witch
of melody, the godly tune played too. This passage closed into a
tunnel, not open to the sky as was the inner place. I made some
tunnels in my time, he thought, not slap-up passages through solid
rock, but lowly burrows on my stomach short of oxygen, and
questions in my back. Desmond never liked it much. He never
liked the thought of falls. Who did ? But they were rare enough,

less tingling in the back than this idea : that the tiger may be outside after all. Harry had no room to turn the rifle. He looked round. Woman's fears, as he had said to Cheddi rudely, but with no intended rudeness to the female sex. He saw Christian. Her face was there just suddenly before him in the tunnel curving left to daylight. She looked at him with the look that he liked best, a clouded look she often had of having conversation in some quiet corner of herself, then smiling here again with him.

He was at the door of Bapu's secret place, circular in theme, a rough-hewn cylinder or pit, some thirty feet across, and in the centre of the circle was the squarish chunk of rock on which he had seen offerings to Bapu's gods. He could not see them now because the surface of that rock was higher than the level of his eyes. Bapu lay in against the bottom of that rock, quiet, breathing. The inner cave must be to Harry's left, and that was where the tiger would be waiting. He listened for the tiger, but he did not hear it. Bapu moaned again.

Harry gathered himself to do the gangster's trick, the one we all know from the films, the quick move to confront expected danger round the corner of the house. Two side-steps, bad leg leading, rifle ready as could be. The cave was dark. He saw blood on the rock floor at the entrance, dark against the pale red rock. The trail of Bapu led from here to where he lay. It was coagulating, blackening already. Bapu must have wounded the tiger with a lethal bullet from his ancient gun. A lethal bullet could be lethal in a lethal place. It lacked muzzle velocity—punch, impact shatter, stopping power, such as waited in two barrels here of his.

It had eaten a small amount. He did not believe that it was dead. The only other place might be beyond that central rock, big enough, perhaps, to hide a tiger. Behind the rock, or in the cave. He had seen everywhere else from Bapu's observation post. He could see everywhere else from here. Blood at the entrance to the cave. Only Bapu's blood trail on the floor. The tiger must be in the cave.

He moved sideways, back to the circle of the wall, back protected by the wall, round the circle of the wall. But the floor against the wall was broken. Harry stumbled once, recovered. Nothing moved in the domed entrance to the cave, yet another lucky horseshoe, God Almighty. He heard nothing except a light moan now from Bapu, and another. Was the tiger dead? Was it drowsy from a liver wound?

Harry had to leave the comfort of his wall. If he fell, and the tiger saw him fall, and there was any charge left in the tiger's battery, then Harry Black would certainly have had it. He could not manage the bumps and crevices of this unseen floor. He therefore crossed better ground to the protection of another wall below which Bapu lay, near the centre of old Bapu's holy place. When he got there, he would try to scramble up to sit among the feathers of the golden oriole, not a safe eminence, but at least a sort of castle to shoot down from.

He faced the cave. He had one yard still to go when the tiger broke silence with a short, deep, world-consuming cough, and came its fashionable way again from Harry's back, from in behind and round the corner of this rock. It came fairly slowly but quite fast. I really am a bloody fool, he thought, jumping for the lee, turning, firing the right barrel, or was it both, and the noise louder than the tiger's cough, and the stock of his rifle dug those same ribs of his, and he saw his prize Purdey rifle fly away yonder to snap in two against the wall. He saw the unspeakable Bad One go on past him to its cave. He saw with clarity, with an odd sort of deliberate observation, that the tiger trailed a useless off-hind leg, and weaved against a wounded off-fore leg. Yet life and hate burned strongly in the tiger yet, snarling out of sight. It had not touched Bapu in its passing. It had not touched him directly. There was the tiger stink and there was the stink of putrefaction.

He now sat with Bapu's offerings, his pine cone and his golden bird, his brown earth and his chamber pot, the charred sticks and ashes of a fire, made perhaps a week or two ago when Bapu's Bad One was away at Ranipur below the mountains.

Bapu lay below him. He tried to speak. Please keep quiet, Bapu.

" Sahib, my promise—the Bad One waited for me."

He looked down at Bapu. Bapu's guts were bad enough, and flies were at them, and at the concavity of Bapu's buttock, and at poor Bapu's scalp—the worst thing to look down upon. He faced the cave again. " Oh, brother," Harry said. " I know this. Rest well, brave Bapu."

Bapu coughed below. The tiger grumbled in the cave.

" Sahib ! " His voice was loud. He sounded like his own cracked self. " My father, my protector. Let my bones lie on this rock within my holy place."

Bapu died. The tiger was quiet in the cave. Harry Black was quiet on this rock.

His doom bells did not ring. He did not hear his pretty tune. He sat here on this rock, which was his now just as much as Bapu's, here on this rock within the open place within the cliff within the confines of the Rimli forest, in the U.P., in the Indian Republic, a sort of member of the British Commonwealth ; or think of it the other way, a sort of box within a box within a box within a box and so on to the very smallest one, and in the very smallest fissionable box, put one dead mouse and one live not-so-husky absolutely sober mouse, and one great huge big slightly punch-drunk pussy cat. Harry had that random kind of thought. He supposed that time was going dribble-drabble on, not a river but a pilferer who will not ask their pardon, was it breakfast time, was dead Bapu having breakfast somewhere ?

Time meant nothing much. He never had thought time meant much. Luck or fate or destiny or Kismet, call it what you will, my dear chap—fate was quite a different matter. Fate was an old bitch running on a railway, rolling you along the iron rails, slowing at the wayside stations, not allowed to disembark—station, scenery and station on the iron rails, slow and fast and helter skelter to the terminus. The child, the youth, the soldier and the prisoner, the faithless friend and lover, the lover all to no avail, no freedom for the prisoner ; well, extinction was a sort of freedom for the prisoner.

Harry Black was an impatient man, going after anything he ever wanted, just a puppet, yes of course, a wilful puppet riding headlong on his iron rails.   Now he sat quietly and tactfully and patiently and not afraid.

> The red rock wilderness
> Shall be my dwelling place ;
>
> Where the wind saws at the bluffs
>   And the pebble falls like thunder
> I shall watch the clawed sun
>   Tear the rocks asunder.

Bapu lay dead below him.   The boy who wrote the verse, the poet Sidney Keyes, was killed in Africa eleven years ago.   Harry heard the wind above his red rock wilderness.

The tiger growled now in the cave, and it had moved, and he could see the front parts of the tiger.   It watched him.   Then it licked its off-fore leg.   Then it watched him.   He had fired blind and just too soon, and the tiger had smacked the barrels of his rifle. He did not think his scars had opened up.   They ached a bit.

I was a bloody fool, he thought.   I've always been a bloody fool.   My good thing came to me at last.   And did I grasp my good thing, to cherish and to hold ?   No.   I had to satisfy my pride. I had to prove myself again, and kill old Bapu in the process. But that isn't fair, because old Bapu brought it on himself.   Well then, I could have shot him from above when he was dying.   Or I could have waited.   And if I had shot him or had waited, would I have lived well within myself ?   And even that, that most of all, is the irrational authentic tap of fate.

Fate knocks to say :   You and Christian are my playthings. You saw it, didn't you ?   Be thankful, then.   Die easy, Harry.

Yes, he thought.   I will die easier for seeing it.   But my Christian ? What pain will my loving and my dying bring to her ?

The tiger watched him.   It neither growled nor licked itself. He knew tigers, in so far as it was given to a fool to know them. He knew that the Bad One would be coming soon, and that one useless leg, one gammy leg, one leg a little weaker from an old healed wound, that these injuries would not prevent the Bad One reaching up to him and for him on his six-foot castle, dirty rascal.

He had a knife, which he would draw, but had not drawn as yet. He was alone, and not afraid now at his terminus. He thought of Christian, but he could not see her.

The bells of doom pealed now again. The splashing witch of melody played now again. He heard a sound.

Not from the cave where the tiger's face stared out at him ; nor from the cliffs and sky above this pit where the wind was louder with the day ; nor from Bapu's observation point ; nor from the forest world without. The sound came once and came again, a footfall, stealthy, pad and pad. It came from the tunnel entrance to this secret place, on Harry's left, half-left from the tiger's inner cave. Hope and fear returned to him.

How long since leaving Cheddi at the dawn ? One hour, two hours, three ? He did not know. He did not have a clue. The air was warmer. The sun did not reach in. He could not raise his head to see the strike of sun on cliffs above.

Time without hope was meaningless. Time with hope was very meaningful. Time now was every fearful second gained, tick-tock. The tiger stared at him, ruffed head low behind the legs, the paws, the claws. He stared the tiger out. He might hope to stare it out, *I stare you out*, until something changed the balance in that brain, that imponderable, smallish, feline brain.

Movement touched the outer corner of his eye. His linked eyes swivelled for perhaps one-half of one invaluable second, back again, no tiger in the frame of cave. **Is it coming at me ?** Is it here already ?

Fanciful and dreadful, but it had not come for him, no, really, pinch me tight, not so. The tiger had moved sideways or moved back. He saw blackness, empty in the wall.

Desmond Tanner had arrived, a lanky six foot two of Desmond Tanner ; lemon-yellow, rather, in the face ; carrying a rifle.

Harry did not swivel eyes again. He knew that the next quick movement, touching his left eye, was a replica of a move of his before—quickly round the corner of the house. It was easier for Desmond, with Harry sitting up and staring there, to tell him roughly what was where.

Desmond moved out of sight. He stayed with Harry in his mind, with hopes and fears in Harry's mind, with surprise in Harry's mind, with darkness in a labyrinth of Harry's mind. All thoughts are possible to men. All wickedness is possible in men. Truth, beauty, ugliness and falsehood—these are things men see alone.

He could not see the tiger. He heard Desmond coming. It would have been more sensible of Desmond, with two whole legs, able to negotiate rough ground unseen—to go on round the wall, his back protected, to come forward past this rock, one flank shielded and the tiger's cave still visible. Instead, he chose to do what Harry Black had done perforce—he crossed the open, some fifteen feet from where the tiger lay.

The tiger growled.

He heard Desmond breathing now. His breath hissed inwards round that famous sucking tooth, puffed out, hissed in.

Harry broke his yoga stillness. He held his left hand out to Desmond for the rifle, felt the barrels, gripped them somewhere near the point of balance. They were warm from Desmond's hand, and they were shaking somewhat from the shake of Desmond's hands.

He waited. Still nothing from the cave. " Get up," he said, and whipped the heavy rifle over to his right hand, to his shoulder, checked the safety catch, you never knew. A four-two-three, lighter than his late lamented, adequate.

Still nothing.

" Sure it's loaded ? "

" Yes," from behind him on the rock, croaked answer to a pretty bloody foolish sort of question.

" How's it shoot ? "

" Two inches high."

The tiger growled, but still it did not come. Barking Dogs, would they be needed ?

" Oh, Tiger ! " Harry called. " O, *Sher!* " Oh, never annoy the terrible beast by saying *Sher*, the beast's own name.

A cough, and into view, and cough again, thunder-thunder in

the circle of the birthplace of the tiger. He gave both barrels to the tiger. It thudded to the rock below him, thrashed about, lay twitching in the flow away of life. Bapu and his Bad One lay together.

Desmond was being sick.

Harry looked down at the Rimli tiger. He had hated it alive. He hated it now dead. He looked down at the corpse of Bapu. He had grown fond of Bapu in the two last moons of Bapu's life. He mourned poor Bapu. He looked up at the red rock walls of Bapu's dwelling place.

Harry sat, a wilful puppet, riding on his iron rails, helter skelter to some terminus or other, a prisoner as always.

CHAPTER TWENTY-ONE

THERE WERE things to do. He did not feel like doing anything, and Desmond said : " Sick as a dog, I'm sorry for that exhibition."

" I've seen worse exhibitions," Harry said, " than that." Desmond had dismounted from the rock and was staring down at Bapu. " Thanks, chum," Harry said.

Which brought him back to here and now with Desmond, who was not a windy chap in ordinary terms, just lacking an absolute in guts. Desmond yawned and gulped, sort of hypnotised, it seemed, by what he saw of Bapu. But thanks, chum, once is enough, is quite enough. " How the hell did you get here ? " asked Harry. The whys and wherefores were subsidiary to the fact. Still, everything must stand in order.

" Christian said you were in a hurry for the stuff, and she wanted me to send our driver, but the man is such a nincompoop, and in any case. . . . Well, anyway, I was handing it all over to Cheddi at the resthouse when a shot went off, and that put Cheddi in a tizzy. . . ."

It seemed that the people at the Range Office had stopped Cheddi Khan on his return, to ask about an earlier shot. But Cheddi had not heard that shot. " Bapu, it must have been," said Desmond.

" Yes," he said. " Came for a last look, I suppose, the bloody bloody poor old fool." I know, he thought. I know that rigmarole about death stands waiting for us all, and Bapu rests in peace, and if Desmond invokes the Deity, I shall scream louder than I screamed my valiant head off in the Pass of Rimli.

" So I extracted all he knew from Cheddi Khan, told him to follow with explosives, and I drove at supersonic speed. Then I worked along the bottom of the cliff, pretty hellish going through those rocks, and I never would have found the place except for the mess outside. But after I came on that, it was like following the blue light, I mean the red light, in the tube for Piccadilly." Desmond shuddered, squeamish about gore etcetera.

Harry ejected the empty cases, and they flew away ping-ping like in the Pass of Rimli, tinkle-tinkle like his bell to summon nice Miss Potterswell.

" A neat job, you made of it.   Look at those bullet holes."

Harry did not look at the bullet holes, smicky-smack between the eyes.   " Thanks to you," he said, and handed over Desmond's rifle, butt first, polite in action and in speech, a proper gentlemanly bastard.   Then he looked up at the sky, the million miles of dead-blue sky from down in here, although it wasn't blue, they said, but black the higher up you went, black empyrean, aether, he supposed, no substance, hence no colour, after all.

The vultures wheeled against the dusty blue, not high in vulture terms, not in the deep black yonder, a thousand feet or so, and close above the red rock cliffs above this double prospect.

" The barrels are all bashed to hell," boomed Desmond over there.   " And the stock is snapped clean off.   I dare say your rifle's mendable."

" Oh, muck my rifle," Harry said against his Adam's apple, watching the vultures in the dead-blue sky.   I've killed enough things in my time, was what he thought.   He heard Desmond come across to stand again beside him.

" You look like death warmed up," his old friend Desmond said without finesse.   " Cheddi will be there by now.   Why not go back with him ?   Just tell me what to do, and I can cope."

Harry stopped his dizzy gazing and came dizzily to earth. " Bapu made a parting plea about letting his bones lie on this rock."

" You mean he was still alive when you got here ? "

" Yes," he said.

" Oh, my God !   I say, old boy, let's go outside."

" All right," he said.   He climbed down from Bapu's offerings. A golden oriole—did Bapu shoot it with his ancient gun, or did he find a dead one ?   I say, old boy, the human animal is pretty queer.

The sun was high and hot outside.

" Do they cremate their dead, or what ? "

" They bury them," he said. " But Bapu was an outcast from his tribe, and there are none within a hundred miles of here, and no one else will want to touch him. We'd better do what Bapu asked."

" Leave him to the vultures ? "

" They can't fly out. If we close the door, they can't walk out. In which case they won't fly in. Vultures aren't bloody fools."

Harry's old friend Desmond smiled. " That sounds more authentic Harry Black," he said. " Just blow the entrance in, you mean ? "

" Yes," he said. " Now."

" Shouldn't we get witnesses ? Our word is not enough, and it would be fairer to old Bapu, wouldn't it, to scotch the rumours ? "

" That's a good idea," Harry said. He doubted if the way of Bapu's death would scotch the Bapu rumours.

" We'll need some chaps to carry the tiger to the car."

" No," he said.

" Are you going to skin it here, then ? "

" No," he said.

" Not even the floating . . ."

" NO."

" Keep your hair on." But then Desmond said in his kindly way : " Poor Bapu, I know exactly how you feel."

Which seemed unlikely. " You might send Cheddi up here with the dynamite," he said.

Desmond looked at him. " You're sure you'll be all right ? "

" Yes," he said mildly. " Quite all right."

He watched Desmond go to the tumbled rocks and seek a way and find it. Desmond's lanky lope was a familiar spectacle to him, a lope he was hardly likely to forget, a lankyness most welcome to him recently.

And he thought, sitting in scanty shade below a thorn bush, Harry thought : The fact that Desmond came and saved my bacon, to use a Desmondish expression—that fact changes nothing but my estimate of Desmond. It doesn't change the situation in the least. It only complicates it. Well, everything is always complicated. The world will say : *Talk about four-letter men. Chap saved him. Thanked chap by running off with chap's wife.* The world can go to hell. It was all settled before this.

Harry had tended to waver weakly for a while in there, watching the vultures in the sky. He was strong again. "I'm sorry," he said aloud. "But what is what is what, like Gertrude Stein."

Well, that was the complication settled. As the Colonel, *that sardonic sage*, she called him . . . Are you thinking of me, Christian ? Harry thought. I know you are, and that has been my help in trouble, and it always will be. As my Colonel once remarked : *You arrive at the essence of problems with a ruthless dispatch and certainty which is very rare indeed*. It's funny, isn't it, how that human, selfish and sardonic sage is with me after all these years, is with me very often nowadays, that testy old Jehovah. What would the Colonel say, if still extant ? Oh, damn the Colonel.

There were no signs of Cheddi Khan, so Harry got up carefully, that side of his body being sensitive. It would be a simple job, because all this rock-wraps-rock gaffuffle at the horseshoe entrance was caused by faults weathered down to slits and plinths that a sharp explosive punch or two would topple just the thing for ever and for ever, well, you know, for ages till an earthquake or an H-bomb or a Z-bomb makes anybody's private mausoleum rather academic in this pretty world where we must grasp at beauty while we may.

He would not have another chance alone, and so he went to say good-bye to Bapu. The sun came in there now. Bapu's secret place was loud with flies, tangy with new death in the sun, stinking with older putrefaction in the sun. The wind of day was strong above.

The agonies of Bapu had been grievous. But now the scalp was dry ; the guts were shrivelling ; the flesh changed in corruption. The sight of Bapu was not grievous, because this was not old Bapu.

Bapu of the graceful wave of hand, the throaty cackle and the grumpy grunts, the sups of whisky-wine so delicately hinted at, the calibanish Ariel, small genius of the forest with the wild things in his heart. Bapu had done his time and was no longer in this red rock wilderness. Bapu had gone away, leaving some things about himself that Harry did not understand.

All go unto one place ; all are of the dust, and all turn to dust again. Who knoweth the spirit of man that goeth upward, and the spirit of the beast that goeth downward to the earth ?

Harry looked at the dead tiger, his last one and his worst one. It was an exceptionally big and heavy tiger. Ten foot between pegs ? he wondered. He had neither shot nor seen a ten-foot tiger, and he would not measure this one. He thought old Bapu would have wished to have his Bad One lie with him below him in the cave which was its birthplace, because, you see, old Bapu had first seen the Bad One from that observation crack up there : *This Bad One was the strongest and most playful of the three, the favourite of his mother.* And Harry knew that Bapu had two pictures in his funny mind : The Monster ; the Endearing Innocent. No, it was right to leave them here together, rotting down to bone, turning to the dust again.

Everything was settled. " Good-bye, Bapu," Harry said alone. He picked up the pieces of his rifle and left old Bapu's secret place.

Cheddi Khan arrived with fifty pounds of dynamite on his shoulder in its well-made wooden box. He sweated and was out of breath. The carrying of loads was much beneath the dignity of Cheddi Khan, but he would do anything on occasion of emergency.

Cheddi puffed, mopped with the free end of his turban, hung his head, and finally looked straight at Harry. " Sahib . . ." he began his apologia.

Harry raised a hand like a policeman stopping traffic or like Adolf Hitler saying *Heil*. " Tanner Sahib came here and saved me. This thing is understood. Where are the detonators ? "

" Sahib, I go now for these noisome things."

" Step lightly, then, as the *chinkara*."

They were safe enough ; but detonators were as loathsome to Cheddi as the unclean beast since Harry had once banged one off to teach him caution. Also, the thought of Cheddi emulating a gazelle was not unfunny.

No purpose in recriminations. Recriminations rather silly, come to think of it. Harry's way was clear to him at last. He had no pricks to kick against. He was a fair to middling hand at demolition. He prepared one now.

*   *   *   *   *

Bapu lay with his pine cone and his golden bird, his brown earth and his chamber pot, his blackened sticks and ashes. The tiger lay near him in its cave.

Harry set caps to the two charges, linked them with instantaneous fuse, and that to the slow-burning, two minutes' worth. He lit the end and walked away. He had used the whole box of dynamite. He never did believe in doing things by halves.

It crumped. Commotion broke the sleep of noon. Some bits of rock flew up and fell. The hot wind carried off the dust. The jungle settled to the sleep of noon.

They went to look. " That's that door closed and bolted," Desmond said. " Trust you."

They walked down the nullah and along the *rao* and to the car. " Cheddi can bring the others," Desmond said. " I'll drop you off."

Desmond was stating things, he noticed. " What about your job ? " he asked when they had turned on to the forest road.

" I hummed and hawed, my usual form, but it was such a wizard offer that I took it in the end." Desmond yawned.

" You'd better get some sleep," he said. Peculiar, ordinary nothing about sleep. Peculiar, casual inquiry about job. Peculiar, still at ease with Desmond. Funny peculiar spanner he was going to throw. " Good about the job," he said. Still funnier peculiar.

" You'll come over this evening, won't you, Harry ? "

" May I let you know ? " he said. " I'm a trifle washed-out at the moment. Tired, that's all."

"I wouldn't wonder," Desmond said. "Come if you can, though."

"I thanked you, didn't I?" he said, going up the resthouse drive in dust and wind, a hateful day, not that a hateful day much mattered with the thought of England and the daffodils, and all decided.

Desmond stopped. "Twice," he said. "Hardly necessary. Have I thanked you for going after Michael the other night?"

What was Desmond getting at? "I didn't know you'd heard," he said. "But . . ."

"First item of news this morning. The only item I had time to hear. I suppose you were surprised at my contribution somewhat overdue, but that doesn't mean you have to thank me."

Harry Black got out. "I see the point," he said. He saw Desmond's point about friendship very well now it had been explained to him. Desmond's point struck him so sharply in the stomach that he opened his mouth to tell Desmond what kind of a friend Desmond had, and what Desmond's friend was going to do to Desmond. But he thought in time: I must see Christian first. Supposing Christian changed her mind?

"See you later, then, perhaps," he said. He watched dust devils swirl the leaves. *See you this evening, I certainly will not.* He remembered the evening when they first came here, when Desmond shone the torch, and the cold wind blustered, and dry leaves flew with it, and green leaves tumbled on lower branches, and the maneater was back in the Rimli forest.

"Don't worry, Harry boy," said Desmond. He smiled at him and went.

Don't worry, Harry boy, so kindly to the foolish boy, the wilful boy, the naughty boy. And did it mean: *I know?* Or did it mean: *I understand your sorrow about Bapu?* Or did it simply mean: *I am your friend?*

*   *   *   *   *

Deputations straggled up the resthouse drive. There were speeches. There were presents. It was quite a gala afternoon. He accepted milk, butter, this and that and goats. He kept the tokens and slipped back the goats, thus risking Cheddi Khan's displeasure, for Cheddi Khan was partial to a properly *halalled* young goat ; and what Cheddi could not eat, he would sell as Major-domo's perk, no questions asked ; or if asked, then one goat had been taken by a panther, lurid details ; one goat, the stupid one, had tried to eat a cobra ; one goat had been stolen in broad daylight, what an outrage. Cheddi Khan, that urbane rogue.

This terror of the Rimli people was now over. Their gratitude might seem effusive, but it was sincere, and must be met with patience. Harry Black had many faults ; he was a man of grace with simple people. He adjusted the facts of Bapu's death to make Bapu the martyr of the piece, the hero who had sacrificed himself for them—which was anything but true. He told the tale of Desmond's courage. He was a paragon this afternoon, even speaking civilly to Tara Singh. And that at last was that, and he was troubled in his spirit.

He went inside the main room of the resthouse, where Pandit Nehru and Mahatma Gandhi watched him from dim portraits from the walls. He took off the garland of the forest flowers. Pandit Nehru had a drastic way with garlands, Harry had observed on one or two occasions, watching Nehru : Suffer it five seconds, whip it off, thrust it at some understrapper. There were things about Pandit Nehur that Harry did not like but he admired that tetchy humanist, lover of mankind if not of men.

" Sahib, the elephant is waiting," Cheddi said.

" Go in the olebits to Bondha, Cheddi Khan, and give my salaams, and say that I am tired and cannot come this evening. Say that I am resting. Is it understood ? "

" It is understood."

" There is this also, Cheddi Khan : Seek speech with the Lady Sahib alone without letting it be known that you seek speech with the Lady Sahib alone. Do this, and say to the Lady Sahib alone that I shall wait to-morrow from the rising of the sun at that place within the forest gate where the Bondha car stayed on the night of Michael. It is the place where green parrots sleep."

He looked at Cheddi Khan, his go-between. He had a lingering annoyance with Cheddi for infallible I'm-rightness, and for this and that, and Harry did not wear virtue very well for very long. " Can I trust you in *this* matter ? "

" If Your Honour trusts me," Cheddi said, " I must be worthy of Your Honour's trust." He left the room.

Put me in my place again, he thought. He took his long khud-stick with the forked end you could use to pin a snake behind the ears, and he slung his binoculars on his neck. Begum and the mahout waited for him. The wind was loud in all the shade trees of a small eminence at Rimli, where foresters had stayed a hundred years or more, men to whom trees were life and children and companions.

The mahout helped him to the pad. He hung on while Begum rose. They went three miles by the big watercourse to the last steepening below the Pass of Rimli.

Begum knelt again. " Go back," he said. " I shall wait a while, then walk to the Forest House."

" Sahib, this is too far a walk for you. There is no bad tiger now. I will find tasty things that Begum may enjoy. We shall be happy here together."

He gave way. He was always giving way about the lesser things. He climbed slowly to the Pass of Rimli, stopping now and then. He had set his mind on getting there ; so he would get there ; and he did.

He went on through the cleft to look for just a minute into Ranipur beyond the foothills and below the mountains. They would have heard the news at Ranipur. There would be festivities to-night. He looked at the abrupt beginnings of the Himalaya, the neatly terraced spurs, the gashed ravines. These hills were browner in a brown season than the Darjeeling hills where Miriam and he had bickered. He saw one snow peak in the haze. The snows were the same untrodden snows, if less magnificent.

He came back from Ranipur to Rimli, past the nook where he had spent nine quiet hours on the night of this March full moon, and then had lost one absolute he thought was his.

He sat outside the Pass of Rimli. The sun was red beyond the red rock ridge where Bapu lay, red reflected to him from the chimney of the sugar factory at Bondha, red beyond the plains beyond this world. The day and the wind were nearly spent.

There is no bad tiger now, the mahout said. I fought that battle, Harry thought. I beat it, didn't I ? How sweet the prospect, not in this violent India, but in England, in the pleasant land with comfort and with peace, those things I have not learned about. But I can learn them now with her. Happiness, a silly word, I used to think before I saw that faith and trust are happiness, is peace and comfort and is passion.

He watched the parakeets, green against dusty green, green against brown and white, the long-tailed parakeets, the graceful birds at close of day, the purpose and the linked abandon, the tumble and the whim, the needled flight against the setting of the sun to roost where he would meet Christian in the early morning, and he would say to her : *My love, we tried our best. We're only human, after all. The thing that happened to us is a good thing, a thing so perfect that we must be strong about it. Say nothing now to Desmond. I will talk to him when you have gone. I'll say to him : Look, Desmond . . .*

The sun had settled tamely into haze, no question of that green flash everyone goes on about.

Look, Desmond, this has happened : And so on, say it out. . . . *And I will give myself.*

Desmond won't make a fuss. He won't complain. He'll say : *I know, Harry. I know you two were really made for one another.* Yes, he will say something chestnuttish like that, for sure. But his speculative look at me will mean : You aren't taking my wife from me to give yourself to her. You are taking my wife from me because you want her for yourself. You've never given anybody anything.

He listened to the jungle fowl, the crowing and the clucking like a farmyard there below him in the forest, cosy vespers of the jungle fowl, the ancestors.

It's true, he thought. All I have ever done is take. And what about those thoughts of mine of things ordained to happen? Wasn't it up to me whether I fought my fear? Wasn't it up to Desmond whether he came into that place to-day? Chance ordains that this or that will happen, that Bapu will be killed and I will not be. Chance ordained that I would come to Rimli, that they would be at Bondha, that I would be mauled by Bapu's Bad One; so on from there. But chance did not ordain what we would do about it. That was up to us. Or to be more specific, it was ultimately up to me. *My wants*, she said. *Would they be influenced at all by yours?*

So I deliberately put a seal upon her wants. I knew what I was doing, and I did it.

Such a charming way of saying thank you. Thank you for your kindness. Thank you for showing me some things I lost, and some other things I never knew. Thank you for showing me serenity and trust. Thank you for showing me a father and a mother and a son, a family within the world to grace the world. Thank you, in other words, for showing human dignity.

Down in the forest Begum squealed, one rather girlish elephantine sort of trumpet. Her wild admirers? *We shall be happy here together*, Begum's mahout said. Well, Begum might be happy if the wild gentlemen had come back, being a human sort of elephant; but it was doubtful if her mahout would be happy. Harry listened. It was dark. No elephants replied.

It does seem sad, he thought, that the things they taught me in my time at Bondha are the very things I'm going to destroy. It's what you'd call ironical, to say the least. *Thank you for my presents. Now turn your pockets out.*

I found my truth, he thought. But I have sinned against my truth. Can I have sin with truth confounded?

It's up to me. Oh yes, I know it's up to me. I'm not a monkey. I'm a man. It's up to me if I am strong enough. If I was strong enough, I would pack my bags—or to be accurate, get Cheddi Khan to pack them—I would pack my bags and bugger off for good and all, and never waken in the night to put my hand across to touch my true love sleeping.

But I am weak. I am not strong enough to go alone. *There goes Harry Black. He likes to think he goes alone.* He hates to think he goes alone. He cannot go alone.

There were lights beyond him in the Rimli forest—Lights at the Katha place beside the *rao* where a comely girl had died—Lights at the taungya village, where a small goatherd had been taken—Lights at the quarters of the Ranger and the forestry assistants—Lights of the Old Bitch coming through the jungle back from Bondha—Lights far away at Bondha where his true love thought of him. The drums were beating for deliverance. People sang and shouted, high and loud. The rhythm of the drums and the cacophony.

Harry sat alone. He had been reduced to size a few times lately, notably by Desmond Tanner for thanking his old friend for doing something for him that he did not think his old friend had the guts to do.

He sat now in a high place and alone. He watched the lights. He listened to the sounds. He smelled the warm March night, not a smell, a dry ruffle of the nose. He saw the stars, the famous jewelled velvet of my India, my love, my enemy, and my enigma.

If I had help, he thought. If only I had help against myself. If Gabriel would come to me as he came to doubting Joseph in the Christmas Oratorio :

> JOSEPH :   How then am I to know,
> Father, that you are just ?
> Give me one reason.
>
> GABRIEL : No.
>
> JOSEPH :   All I ask is one
> Important and elegant proof
> That what my love had done
> Was really at your will
> And that your will is love.
>
> GABRIEL : No, you must believe,
> Be silent, and sit still.

No, you must believe. Be silent and sit still. Harry was silent and sat still, the child, the youth, the soldier and the prisoner, the faithless friend and lover, the lover all to no avail, no freedom for the prisoner.

He sat alone at this gateway in the red rock wilderness. " All right," he said. " I'll try." He did not say that nicely. It was a thing he wanted very much to try about, and was suspicious of it, and resented it, and feared it.

You are not trying.

" I am," he said. " I really am."

No. You are arguing with yourself. Stop arguing, and try.

" I don't quite understand," he said.

Of course you do not understand. You cannot understand with pride.

" I want some help," he said.

Then help yourself. You are a man, the highest of the creatures, and the lowest.

" That's far too difficult for me," he said. " Too complicated, dammit."

It is difficult, not complicated. How can truth be complicated ?

" I don't know," he said. " I did see truth, though, didn't I ? "

You sinned against the truth you saw.

" All right," he said. " I don't know truth."

You know nothing till you give yourself. A jump to give yourself. Now jump.

He jumped. " I give myself," he said.

To win and lose and start again each day. Do not think it easy.

" I know," he said. " It's very hard. How wrong I was."

That is better. Now we can begin. Now listen !

" I'm listening," he said.

If any man will come after me, let him deny himself, and take up his cross, and follow me.

" I know," he said.

No miracles.

" I know," he said.

And no rewards paid out.

" I know," he said. " But that's a hell of a lot to ask."

Precisely. And you know that the choice is only yours ?

" I know," he said.

*And you know that I am in yourself alone with you. Or I am
not ?*

" I know," he said.

Then pray, My child.

He prayed.

The drums and songs of human celebration ; the dement of
jackals and the fever of the bird ; the alarums and excurions of the
jungle night. The sounds came up to him from Rimli. A rumour
of the sounds came through to him from Ranipur. Harry Black
was silent and sat still, and he was not alone.

*   *   *   *   *

" She called," the mahout said. " She was lonely for the wild
ones."

" I heard her," Harry said. " How long now hast thou been
with Begum ? "

" Since fourteen years ago when she was captured in the keddah
with her baby, and her wild baby died, as is the way. She mourns
the baby of her freedom."

They went down between the darkness of the forest. The
rejoicings of the Rimli people were now over. It was quiet, a slow
creak, a muffled measure on the sand, a thought of breath, a switch
of ear, home soon to a resthouse on the journey.

Begum stopped. Her ears went out. The mahout hissed. Harry
saw the dark something in the paleness of the *rao*. He put his
glasses up. The tiger stood, looking round at Begum, the tiger
and the elephant, respecters of each other's person. *I see you and
I hear you, elephant.—I scent you and I hear you, tiger.* The tiger
went its way, the hunting wraith, the phantom killer on the
prowl.

Begum also went her way. A cheetal called : *KYAA! Tiger,
boys and girls! Watch out!* A general alarm rang down the line.
Those that slept awoke, and those that fed stopped feeding. They
soon fed again alertly. Death is our companion, and so it will
go on.

" Sahib, you are late," said Cheddi Khan with kindness.

" Yes," he said.   " And we leave to-morrow in the morning early."

" The Lady Sahib said : *Tell the Sahib that I will come.*"

" Thank you, Cheddi Khan," he said.

He got himself a good strong drink and sat and thought while Cheddi started packing in the other room. He sat and thought and dozed in the remaining hours of night.

*   *   *   *   *

He stopped the car. The sun had not yet risen, but the dawn was here. Cheddi knelt to Mecca at his morning prayers, so Harry walked away from him, and from the parakeets awakening in the trees. He walked along the lesser fireline. He was stiff in body, and rather much alone in mind again this morning.

Oh God, he prayed. Give me the strength to do this right.

He had reached his decision as to what to do by careful thought, strictly a secular decision. He was faltering. He needed help in the hardness of the thing he had to do. But he was alone again, goddammit, and he was trying hard again to give himself, or was it an illusion, what he had known so sweetly and so quietly, no choir of angels and no clashing cymbals and no blinding lights ?

Oh God, he prayed anew. Let me give myself to have the strength to do it right.

And he thought : I must play this scene in character, not over-act it like some other cocky little chap, nor underact it so as not to overact it. I simply have to be the me she knows, the me I am, me come to my senses, free from the duel of struggle and desire, Harry Black who weakened her against her will, the selfish he-man with absolutes for everyone except himself.

Cruelle et caline, she said. *And never a whole life for you. A part of life, an episode, and off to hunt that animal to-morrow, and afterwards another tumble would be very nice.*

Which made him grunt like poor old Bapu.

The sun was up, and so he turned to meet the kindness of the morning sun, the dappled shadows and the shafts—and beauty is so brief a thing.

He waited at the forest gate. The mynas chattered and the bulbuls bubbled and the babblers fussed. The small doves dipped about, and flew with a fluster and a clap to feed again and *kroo* again demurely on the border grounds of field and tree. The birds were getting on with it.

He heard the squeak of bullock carts and saw the dust and saw the peasants harvesting the wheat, the crouching people with their sickles on the flat curved earth from here to Bondha and to anywhere you like to name, the ancient harvest of the wheat. The men were getting on with it.

He saw the dust before he saw the pony. Then he saw the pony. Then he saw the rider on the pony. Then he saw the golden woman cantering the pony. You know, he thought in the painful, quiet vision of his mood : Christian could ride a thousand miles alone in beauty through this India and she would never be molested.

" Good morning," they said to one another ; Salaams between Cheddi Khan and Christian. Uncle Cheddi to his goddess Lady Sahib, so unprecedented, so damnable, so touching.

" Shall we walk a bit ? " he said. He saw her glance at the Old Bitch loaded to the ears.

Cheddi held the pony, and they walked away from him along the fireline.

" Are you going ? " Christian asked.

" Yes," he said. " I think I'll go this morning." Then he told her. He told her very perfectly and well and in accordance with his character : that he was fond of her, most genuinely fond of her ; but in the troubles of his getting better and the hunting of the tiger, everything had somehow grown to be more real and desperate and important than it seemed now that the job was done at last and the obsession over ; and he had done some bad things in his life, and that was just the kind of chap he was, and fickleness a thing about him that he could not help. The theme, implied but not explicit : I must be cruel to be kind. It's really not my fault I'm so attractive. I pays my money and I takes my choice, and let's have no hard feelings, shall we ? He did it well, better even than his hopes and prayers, the nice philanderer, Casanova with regrets.

four-letter-man, I know, but suitably ashamed, and with the delicacy of a gentleman, not saying to a lady that he knows she lost her foolish heart to him.

" Have you finished ? " Christian asked him, walking side by side, like a man and woman strolling out together, even through the daffodils, perhaps, in springtime, in the pleasant land.

" Yes," he said. He had said his say to plant the seed to grow the flower of contempt for him.

" Tell me something : Is this good-bye to me, good-bye to all the Tanners and away ? "

He wondered at the question, and he looked at her, and saw that she was weeping. The tears were slithering and slipping down her cheeks. Her voice was her own soft sobless voice.

" Well actually, yes," he said. " You know what I'm like about good-byes." He looked at the brown grass and the dust before him.

" You want to do a good job, don't you ? "

He did not answer, neither knowing what she meant, nor well able to endure her tears.

" Harry darling, there are three of us at Bondha, and love is many things."

" I did my best," he said. " I thought it would be easier for you."

" Dear love," she said.

She dried her tears. They had walked, perhaps, a quarter of a mile, one Bapu furlong. They turned to walk it back.

" How do I look ? " she asked him.

" Well," he said, " a trifle blotched, but quite all right to me."

They laughed at that. They might laugh at anything together.

" What are you going to do ? " she asked him.

" I'm going to Delhi," Harry said, " to stay with Rabat. Then to Bombay to catch a boat and sail the seas a while. Then there are things in the world to do."

" I'll pray for you," she said.

" I'll pray for you," he said.

" Pray to God for me ? "

" Yes," he said. " A family called Tanner taught me."

She smiled at him. " Now I can bear it," Christian said.

And back to Cheddi Khan who held the arab pony named Adonis.

" Give us half an hour. It was fried eggs this morning, but we'll change to scrambled in your honour."

He watched her ride away. She had a good seat on a horse. *I was a horse till I was seventeen*, a Christianesque remark.

And then he said :

" Sweetest love, I do not goe, for weariness of·thee,
    Nor in hope the world can show a fitter love for mee."

" What are these words, sahib, in the English tongue ? "

" The poet spoke of love," he said. He wished that he had thought of them before, but now he could not say the words to Christian.

" Oh sahib," said Cheddi in a monotone of pain. " Is it farewell that you are saying to the gentle Lady Sahib ? "

" Yes," he said. " And farewell to you soon, Cheddi Khan, my friend."

" Will you not come to Pakistan to stay in my house beside the Jhelum road ? "

" Who knows ? " he said. " Some day I may come to see you and your sons and grandsons."

" Sahib, I will speak to my sons of you, of a man true unto himself."

" If you speak well of me, speak ill of my sins and anger, Cheddi Khan."

" This I shall also do, for my sons should know that a man comes to his strength through weakness and through sorrow and through ill. Sahib, is this not so ? "

" Don't ask me," he said in English. The way to grace was long and hard.

He drove after the half-hour. Brown monkeys loped across the road. One child found a dried-up shoot of sugar cane, a dusty relic of that season. The monkey held it in its hands and nibbled thoughtfully before the car.

He stopped. He could not see the monkey very well. " Silly little monkey," Harry said. " Buzz off."

" Sahib, let me drive the olebits this short way."

" No," he said. " You're such a bloody awful driver."

Cheddi muttered to himself. " *Bluddi-ful*," he muttered. " *Bluddi-offle*. It is always thus."

Harry Black had scrambled eggs for breakfast with the Tanner family at Bondha. He parted from his old friend, from his young friend, from his true love.

THE END